"I feel foolish," Lydia said,

flinching when Jakob dabbed the cool, sticky salve on her bites.

"Nothing to feel foolish about." He lifted her tangled hair. Loose tendrils clung to her slender neck. He wanted to lay his lips on the soft skin.

She turned to him, an innocent expression in her gold-flecked eyes, and he knew his own expression was as guilty as...sin. Her dark gaze was luminous and questioning. "Jakob?"

His name on her lips was more than a question. It was an invitation. He dragged his gaze from her eyes to her full lips, slightly parted, then to her hands, clenched on the white cotton over her breasts. With deliberate movements, he pulled the garment away from her. At first she resisted; then her arms slackened. The material peeled and fell. He turned her shoulders and looked at her body for the first time....

Dear Reader,

Our featured big book this month, *The Honor Price*, by Erin Yorke, is a stirring tale of adventure and forbidden passion. One of Harlequin Historical's most popular authors, Yorke brings readers the story of Alanna O'Donnell, a young Irishwoman whose flight from her uncle's treachery brings her into an uneasy alliance with Spanish nobleman Lucas del Fuentes— a man she should by all rights hate.

Cheryl St.John's first book, *Rain Shadow*, was part of our March Madness 1993 promotion. Don't miss *Heaven Can Wait*, the gripping prequel to *Rain Shadow*. Heartland Critiques gave both books a GOLD ★★★★★ rating!

Aisley de Laci is wed to a knight rumored to be in league with the devil in *The Devil's Lady*, a remarkable medieval by Deborah Simmons. And finally, Laurel Pace's *Winds of Destiny* is the long-awaited sequel to *Destiny's Promise*.

We hope you enjoy all of these titles. And next month, be sure to look for the new Theresa Michaels, *Fire and Sword*.

Sincerely,

Tracy Farrell
Senior Editor
Harlequin Historicals

Please address questions and book requests to:
Harlequin Reader Service
U.S.: 3010 Walden Ave., P.O. Box 1325, Buffalo, NY 14269
Canadian: P.O. Box 609, Fort Erie, Ont. L2A 5X3

CHERYL ST.JOHN

HEAVEN CAN WAIT

Harlequin Books

TORONTO • NEW YORK • LONDON
AMSTERDAM • PARIS • SYDNEY • HAMBURG
STOCKHOLM • ATHENS • TOKYO • MILAN
MADRID • WARSAW • BUDAPEST • AUCKLAND

ISBN 0-373-28840-9

HEAVEN CAN WAIT

Printed in U.S.A.

Books by Cheryl St.John

Harlequin Historicals

Rain Shadow #212
Heaven Can Wait #240

CHERYL ST.JOHN

remembers writing and illustrating her own books as a child. She received her first rejection at age fourteen, and at fifteen wrote her first romance.

She has been program chairman and vice-president of her Heartland Romance Writers of America chapter, and is currently proud to serve as president.

Married mother of four, grandmother of three, Cheryl enjoys her family. In her "spare" time, she corresponds with dozens of writer friends from Canada to Texas, and treasures their letters. She would love to hear from you.

SASE for newsletter and bookmark:

Cheryl St.John
P.O. Box 12142
Florence Station
Omaha, NE 68112-0142

As always, for Jay.

For Margaret.

For Diane Wicker Davis,
who recognized the potential
and pointed the way.

And for all my St.John cousins near
and far who remember the cat clock,
Chipper, Amasandra, crisp line-dried sheets,
the rollaway bed, the claw-leg table,
choir robe costumes,
ice cream and Oreos at 9 p.m.

'Love and prayers,'
This one's for you.

Chapter One

April 1888

The Outsider was the most beautiful woman Lydia Beker had ever seen. Wearing a dress the vibrant blue of a spring sky on a frosty morning, her eyes glittered the luxuriant green of the goose meadow after a generous rain. Thick, shiny hair cascaded from the back of her head in long spun-gold coils.

Lydia smoothed the crisp white apron covering her drab gray day dress and imagined the silky, cool texture of satin. She tucked in wayward tendrils of mahogany hair escaping the confines of her white Norman cap. From the kitchen doorway, she observed the Outsiders eating pie at the only occupied table in the bakefront. Fascinated by their unique dialect and by their conversation, she lingered as she polished the silver.

"Well, this is all pretty appealing," said one of the two young men, who were obviously brothers. "Everything's simple, basic. These colonists are agricultural and economic geniuses! They even have a steam engine in their cotton mill." His praise of her home and the pleasant sound of his voice stabbed Lydia with a wicked glimmer of pride.

The pretty woman placed her hand on his arm. "Jakob, these people eat sheep."

The other brother snorted. "Don't worry, Peine, Jakob wouldn't last a week without a cup of coffee. And his fancy boots aren't the accepted footwear around here."

The boots in question were gray snakeskin. The woman's feet were encased in exquisite leather high-top shoes. Lydia's own sturdily made black shoes had to weigh ten times as much. Guiltily she imagined slipping her feet into dainty shoes, sitting beside the young man called Jakob and boldly resting her fingers on his arm.

"Nikolaus is getting tired."

The woman hugged a baby to her breast and kissed the top of his head. Lydia guessed that he was about a year old. He patted his mother's cheek with a chubby hand. A familiar longing threaded through Lydia with a haunting intensity.

Caring for her younger brothers and sisters had only intensified her yearning. As soon as they grew out of babyhood, she'd been forbidden to caress and cuddle them. In the privacy of her own home, she'd love and touch her child to her heart's content—if she ever had a child.

The woman snuggled the baby. Lydia swallowed her envy. What a fortunate young woman! The pretty Outsider didn't know how blessed she was!

Lydia continually fought her vibrant spirit, striving to discipline her will according to rigid Rappite doctrine. In Accord, every believer was the same. Every structure, every walkway, the same. Every day was the same.

But Lydia was not the same.

Again she wondered why the comfort and solitude of the Harmony Society left her incomplete. Why did she crave an elusive something to fill the secret void in her cold life? She longed to see a city, with its variety of businesses and homes and its bustling inhabitants dressed in colorful clothing and hats, and to hear children's laughter, to see horses and buggies—

"Oh, Nikolaus!" the woman exclaimed. The child had accidentally kicked a tin cup from the table's edge, and Lydia scurried to mop up milk with a towel.

She smiled hesitantly into the baby's wide blue eyes. He pointed a finger at her and laughed. Her heart warmed.

"Thanks, ma'am." The older man, dressed in faded dungarees and a plaid work shirt, smiled. Cracks formed at the corners of his eyes, making them look like a parched streambed.

"*Bitte.* More pie would you like?"

He raised a huge hand in refusal, but his sons nodded.

"May I try the apple this time?" Jakob asked, and presented his empty plate. His voice awakened vulnerable longings Lydia had worked hard to bury. He held on to the plate a second longer than necessary, and her gaze flew to his bright blue eyes. Alive with warmth, they smiled at her. His full lips turned up and tiny lines appeared at the corners of his eyes, as though he smiled often. How different from the somber men of Accord he was!

A tiny hope sparked to life. How wonderful it would be to know a man who smiled!

Warmth crept from Lydia's plain gray collar up her neck and suffused her cheeks. Rarely in her twenty years had she spoken to anyone outside the colony. This stranger was not only an Outsider, but a man, and she couldn't disguise her discomfort. She nodded, quickly carrying their plates away.

"It's shameless to encourage that girl, Jakob," Peine scolded, her voice carrying across the barren room. "She's probably never had a man make cow eyes at her before. Can you believe that awful dress?"

Lydia's step faltered. She forced herself into the kitchen and placed the dishes near the sink. She raised both palms to her burning cheeks. She'd never experienced the confusing humiliation that washed through her now. Was that really how others saw her?

Back at the table, Jakob's glance raised to the kitchen doorway. "Dresses don't matter. The widow Parkhurst wore one from Paris, France, and she's still a pruneface." He leaned toward his father. "Pretty, isn't she?"

Johann Neubauer's faded blue eyes lit with amusement. "Yep. Be nice to have fresh desserts again."

Jakob grinned. "Courtin' her wouldn't be for her pie."

Peine bristled. He couldn't! Jakob couldn't mean to court that church mouse! Why, the girl was as plain and ordinary as a lump of coal! Jakob was hers for the taking, but she needed more time. Possessively she curled her fingers around his wrist. "Jakob," she purred, "you're not really interested..."

Peine's husband, Anton, propped his fork on the edge of his plate. "A woman who can bake like this would be mighty welcome, from where I'm sittin'."

"But she's obviously . . . noticeably . . . different."

Anton snorted. "You're a snob."

Peine glared at him, her palms itching to slap him hard. She needed to vent her anger and frustration. If only she'd waited! If only she'd met Jakob first! Now she was trapped with Anton. "You're an insufferable bore."

Her Jakob was too good for that backwater toad. She placed the sleeping child in Anton's arms and flounced to the kitchen doorway.

The girl looked up, her surprise obvious.

Now that they were face-to-face, a nagging sense of familiarity annoyed Peine. Impossible! "What's your name?"

"Lydia Beker."

"Peine Neubauer." She gripped her clutch purse. "Pleased I am to make your acquaintance."

"The gentlemen are impressed with the pies." Peine's gaze flickered over Lydia with thinly veiled disdain. "Perhaps you'd be kind enough to share the recipe."

"My pleasure. I will write the ingredients down for you. I have paper and ink in here." Lydia scampered into the kitchen.

"I'll just look around," Peine said, following. She strolled the length of the long, narrow worktable running down the center of the room. Risen mounds of dough lined rows of trays. An older woman, the image of Lydia, stirred an enormous kettle.

"What's back there?" Peine pointed past the wall of red-brick ovens.

"The storeroom."

"Oh. I could certainly use some tips on service space. Mind if I take a peek while you're writing?" Without waiting for an answer, she bustled by. Staring at neatly stacked barrels of flour and dried fruit, she saw only the serene face of the Harmonist girl. Peine would remove the temptation before the girl blinded Jakob to what he really wanted, what was best for him, for all of them.

Peine opened her reticule and flicked a tiny flat tin open with her thumbnail. With steady fingers, she selected a match and scratched the head across the striker inside the lid. A newborn flame hissed and wavered...a friendly blue...a spirited problem-solver. The solution had worked in Pittsburgh. It would work now. She'd rid the world of one religious fanatic...now she'd make it two.

Peine lowered the match from her gaze and held the tiny flame to the hem of a flour-sack curtain. An arc the size of a half-dollar disappeared immediately. The burning edge of the fabric crinkled and retreated rapidly as the flame changed colors and leapt upward.

Peine hastily returned to the kitchen and found the girl waiting for her.

"The men are ready to leave," Peine said. "I must go."

"The recipe."

Peine accepted the paper, stuffed it in her bag and hurried toward the bakefront.

The men waited, their broad shoulders filling the doorway. The sleeping child lay draped over his father's shoulder.

"Much obliged, ma'am." Jakob worked his hat in a circle, long fingers curling the brim absently. "I'm partial to the apple."

At the sight of his hands—strong hands, browned by the sun—a curious, unsettling flutter sprang to life in Lydia's stomach. He smiled without pretense, and she studied his face. It was tanned and lean-cheeked, with a broad forehead under a shock of hay-colored hair. His nose was long, but not dominant and his lips were full and mobile. Bright blue eyes studied her in return with unblinking interest.

Peine tugged at Jakob's blue shirtsleeve with a pampered, well-manicured hand. "Let's go," she said in a wheedling tone. "I'm tired, and you promised to—"

From the kitchen came a piercing cry Lydia recognized as her mother's. "*Feuer!* Fire! In the storeroom!"

Lydia ran to meet her. Her mother's pupils were dilated with fear. "Go for help, *Mutter*," Lydia directed. "I will get water from the kitchen pump. Hurry!"

Lydia spun around and raced into the kitchen. Black smoke belched from the storeroom. Lifting two enormous kettles from a shelf, she pumped water. She'd never noticed how long it took to draw the first splatter. Barely an inch in the bottom of the metal container! With both hands, she again raised the metal lever and pumped.

Water gushed into the kettle at the same instant an explosion rattled the floorboards, temporarily sucking the air from the building. Lydia caught her breath and whirled.

Flames licked across the floor, nipping at her hem. She wet a towel and batted at her skirt until the fire was out. Pulling her apron over her nose and mouth, she stared into the flapping flames, which were growing taller and closer in irregular bursts. She jumped at another cracking noise. The ceiling over the back door caved in.

Lydia dragged her gaze to the flames licking across the wooden casing of the door that led back into the bakefront.

Both routes of escape were blocked.

Billowing, dense smoke churned from the storeroom, blinding her. Instinctively she dropped to her hands and knees and crouched under the long table. She coughed into a fistful of her apron. Her eyes stung. Her lungs felt as if they were packed with dirty wool.

Saying a brief prayer, she asked God for a quick death. She'd die with a prayer on her lips and regret in her heart. She'd never see the outside world or feel a silky blue dress against her skin...never ride in a buggy...never have a baby...never love a man with smiling blue eyes....

Every breath was sheer agony. Tears streamed from her eyes and she choked on the searing air. *Sie Gott*...

Something damp and smothering dropped over her head. Strong fingers pried her grip from the table leg.

Through her tears and the thick, black smoke, Lydia recognized the Outsider bent over her. "Watch your head! Put your arms around my neck."

Responding instinctively to his gruff command, Lydia crawled from under the table and groped for his neck. Her fingertips found his shirt and followed solid, muscular shoulders to his throat. She threaded her hands behind his neck, and Jakob lifted her effortlessly. Lydia found herself cradled against the stranger's massive chest. It was the closest she'd been to another person since infancy.

"Hold on," he ordered. Lydia clung to his strength, and he shielded her face and head with the soggy fabric.

The Outsider ran as if the hosts of hell were on his heels. Searing heat nipped Lydia's legs and feet. Acrid smoke stole her breath, replacing it with a red-gray haze of panic. She gritted her teeth against a sharp pain in her chest. Why had he taken this risk?

The red haze deepened. Dazed, Lydia struggled for consciousness. A deep-timbred voice resonated against her flattened breast. A magnificent voice. Jakob's. His arms, like bands of steel under her knees and around her back, bound her against his chest, warm and decidedly solid beneath his shirt. A lovely way to die.

They raced into the sunlight. He gulped in great, heaving gasps of air. Lydia rose and fell against his broad chest with each convulsive breath.

Jakob's knees buckled, but he held her tight, breaking her fall. He twisted to lie faceup, and she sprawled on top of him.

His heart raced against her open palms. His chest was broad and hard and...and...oh! She could feel him! She hadn't died! A coughing spasm racked his body beneath her, and a helpful colonist assisted Lydia to the grass. Dazed, she sat up. Billowing banks of smoke uncurled into the innocent sky over Main Street.

She coughed repeatedly, each expiration sheer agony. Lydia fought to shrug off the dreamlike quality of her vision. *Mutter* assisted her to a sitting position and raised tear-filled eyes heavenward in thanks, then stared in awe at the two Outsiders.

"You all right, son?" the father asked.

Here and there, under soot and ash, a frazzled patch of Jakob's hay-colored hair shone in the sunlight. His eyes appeared sharp and blue and his teeth were startlingly white. He raised a large, reassuring hand and placed it on his father's shoulder. At his feet lay the limp, blackened tablecloth he'd placed over her head.

"I never knew breathin' could feel so good and so miserable at the same time." His palm flattened against his shirtfront, and his voice rasped from deep in his chest. He grimaced, and his teeth stood out in his charred face in a parody of a smile.

"Looks like they're handling the fire." His father batted affectionately at the soot on Jakob's clothing with his rumpled hat. "Think you're up to the ride home? Annie'll skin us alive if we're late for dinner."

Jakob couldn't leave, Lydia thought. He must know how much his actions meant to her. She'd been prepared to die, and he'd given her a new chance at life!

"Nein!" Lydia choked painfully on the single word. The older man turned toward her immediately; Jakob looked first to his father, then to Lydia. "Wait," she insisted, her lungs on fire. "I must thank you."

Jakob squinted against the sunlight for a long, motionless moment. She blushed wildly under his stare. "I'd be willing to call it even for a drink of water."

Lydia nodded to a freckle-faced girl standing nearby, and she ran to do his bidding.

Lydia stumbled to her feet and faced the man who had risked his life for her. Words were inadequate. She knew nothing of him, save that he favored apple pie. She didn't know where he came from or where he was going, yet a tenuous bond had formed between them. A link that somehow surpassed familiarity.

And she was afraid.

Afraid she wouldn't see him again. Afraid she'd been given a second chance at life, only to have it continue as it had. "How can I repay you?"

Jakob managed a lopsided grin. Pulling a kerchief from his rear pocket, he swiped ineffectually at his face. "How about a pie for my pa next time we're through?"

Hope kindled within her. She lifted her hand for the kerchief. He followed her to the trough near the street's edge, and, after soaking the red cloth, she wrung the water out on the grass and held it toward him. "Allow me, please?"

The moment stretched between them, the sunny day evaporating into a hushed blur. There was no sound except the thumming of her heart in her ears; no sight but that of his merry blue eyes gauging her; no feelings but those of wonder that he didn't take the kerchief, then dismay at the realization that he was daring her to touch the cloth to his face. She imagined doing so, and her breath stuck in her chest. She pictured wiping the cool cloth over the heated skin of his lean cheeks, the curve of his brow, across his shapely lips.... He was looking at her as though he wanted her to—

The freckled girl returned with water, interrupting their silent reverie. The tall Outsider took the mug and drank thirstily, his Adam's apple bobbing in his tanned throat. Lydia had never seen such an enchanting sight.

He handed her the empty mug, accepted the damp kerchief and ran it across his face and throat. Lydia regretted not having had the courage to enjoy the task herself.

A springboard loaded with seed bags and supplies pulled alongside. A large, well-fed pair of horses, their maize-colored coats lustrous from many brushings, bobbed their heads.

"Wie bald Ruckkehr Sie?" Lydia said softly before he could move away. Jakob looked at her without comprehension. "Your return will be soon?" she translated.

"I'll be back soon," he replied. He leapt up onto the wooden seat beside his father and touched the brim of his hat politely. The horses pulled them away.

Lydia had always believed that those of the outside world were self-indulgent, proud, haughty, concerned only with their own profit. But there was nothing self-seeking about the Neubauer son who had risked his life to rescue her from a certain death. Outsiders were vain and untrustworthy hypocrites— *weren't they?*

Was Jakob the exception? Or was he the rule? It would be unfair to condemn Outsiders without firsthand knowledge. Her comfortable cloak of assumptions had holes the size of Pennsylvania shot through it!

She turned and watched her father direct the cleanup. Hatless and dressed in shirtsleeves, he looked odd without proper attire. His voice rose authoritatively.

According to her father, it was sinful to waste time on inconsequential matters. Most of the time she disciplined herself to say and think and feel all the proper things.

But Jakob Neubauer was not inconsequential—not to her. Through him, God had given her a new life. She didn't believe in coincidence. She must make the most of this blessing, and not allow the opportunity to crumble into ashes, like the inside of the bakery.

He would be back.

Chapter Two

A sky blue parasol shading her, Peine let her gaze drift from the acres of monotonous windrows to Jakob's broad back. Perched on the wagon seat above her, he swayed with the motion of the springboard.

Jakob had risked his life for the girl.

Peine disliked Lydia Beker immensely. She knew her type. A religious fanatic who considered herself a cut above the rest of mankind. Peine had experienced persecution from Lydia's sort plenty of times while growing up in Savannah Stockwell's establishment in Pittsburgh.

As a child, Peine had never comprehended exactly what her mother did that incited the respectable women of the city to peer down their noses and hold their skirts aside as she passed. Peine only understood she was different. *Wicked child. Spawn of an unholy alliance. Bastard.* The list was long and ugly.

As an adult, she'd come to know her mother's vocation: whore. Peine had vowed to do whatever it took to get herself far from that place, to live a life completely different. And she had.

Nobody here knew about her mother or where Peine had been raised. She'd fabricated a convincing story of a well-to-do, doting father who had been unjustly accused of embezzling funds from the bank of which he was vice president and was now imprisoned. The tale included a mother so humiliated that she'd been placed in a hospital.

Poor Peine, devastated herself, had needed to get away from the city and its ever-present reminders. That was when she'd seen the ad in the Pittsburgh *Gazette.* Envisioning the marital offer as her ticket out of the city she so desperately wanted to escape, Peine had written immediately.

Two weeks and two letters later, she'd boarded a train bound for Butler as Mrs. Anton Neubauer. Anton was good-looking, clean and nice. Most importantly, he'd married her before initiating her in the physical act she'd sworn would never be her desire to perform. She was respectable. After a one-night honeymoon on the rails, Anton had taken her home. And then she'd realized her mistake.

She'd married the wrong brother.

Jakob's hoarse cough dragged her attention back to the present. Johann pounded him on the back. "Y'all right?"

The wagon lurched in and out of a rut, and Peine's shoulder bounced against her husband's. Straightening, she met his eyes, which were a darker blue than Jakob's. Anton didn't smile as often as his brother, and his laugh was more reserved.

She'd been drawn to Jakob immediately. His deep voice haunted her days and nights. His hearty smile triggered a warm response for which she was never prepared.

Jakob was perfection. To look at. To listen to. To love.

She didn't love Anton. Submitting to his lovemaking was almost like prostituting herself. Wasn't a mail-order bride the same as a whore? Whores received cash; she'd collected a place to live and a mask of esteem.

Idly leaning against a stack of seed bags, Anton caressed Nikolaus's hair. Peine imagined Jakob's hands touching her just so. Anton's gaze, deep-set and unfathomable, met hers.

He wasn't a terrible husband. She had no reason to leave him. He simply wasn't the man she desired. She'd have to discourage Jakob from courting the Rappite girl. Then she could have him for herself. But how?

There was a way, and she'd find it. Just as she'd found a way out of Pittsburgh.

"It pleases me you are allowed to work outside the kitchens, Lydia. You must feel as stifled as I did all those years," Rose Beker said.

Since the fire, Lydia secretly enjoyed the opportunity to work in the gardens and nursery with her brother Nathan, who was scarcely a year younger than she. "Grandmother, it's not our lot to wish for pleasures and desirable positions. Father says we must be of one mind and one accord." She stopped and perused her grandmother's beloved face. "I'm not certain what I think and feel anymore."

Wizened eyes flashed a smile. "Your grandfather used to say young people's sap flows in the spring. I recognize that in you."

Lydia cleared their lunch dishes. She dared to share her thoughts only with her grandmother. She could fool everyone else, and once in a while herself, but she never fooled Rose Beker. "I shouldn't have said what I did."

"Nonsense." The old woman patted the air in a silencing gesture. "Things were different when your grandfather was alive."

Lydia nodded. Her grandparents had been among the original settlers of Accord when the town's founder, "Father" George Rapp, relocated twenty years before. Matthäus had become discouraged by the harsh self-denial Rapp taught, unconvinced that celibacy was the only road to heaven. "I know you miss him."

Her grandmother shook her head sadly. "When we moved here from New Harmony, we had plenty of lean years. With all you have, Lydia, you can't imagine. Endless days of work, meager meals . . ."

Lydia detected a note of wistfulness in her grandmother's voice.

"I was twenty," Rose continued. "Same age as you."

"Sometimes I wonder how you left your family and everything familiar to come here."

"Walk me to my room for my nap and sit."

In the bedroom, the elderly woman lay on her narrow cot. Bending, Lydia pressed her cheek against her grandmother's soft, dry one, and experienced a familiar pang of guilt. Such displays of affection brought harsh reprimands. How could something so natural, something that felt so good, be so sinful? Grandmother was her precious friend. Her only friend.

Grandmother gave her the only acceptance and love she'd ever known. In the past several years, Lydia had realized how lonely and deprived her life was. She entertained thoughts that were out of place in her world. It had been her burden to bear to see herself as inconsistent with the mold she'd been made from.

She was missing out on so much! She read every book she could find, and stayed abreast of current local and national events. *Vater* Beker encouraged awareness, but not participation. Longings such as hers were strictly prohibited.

A child, perhaps a home of her own, would help fill the distressing void, but she dreaded marrying a cousin or a young colonist. In Accord, no one was special. *Shouldn't a husband be special?* Shouldn't children be special?

Of late, her father had been pushing her to promise herself to a colonist. She must marry soon or move to the singles dormitory. She was well past school age, and it was unacceptable for her to continue living with her parents.

"I must go. I have flour to blend this afternoon." Smoothing Rose's quilt, Lydia enjoyed the familiar feel of the stitches. One day this wedding quilt would belong to her. Not long after, she'd hold a baby of her own. As always, the dream comforted her.

Jakob pushed his hat to the back of his head and squinted. Behind him, acre after acre of hayfield lay plowed in geometric windrows. He was pleased with his morning's accomplishment. As always, he experienced a deep satisfaction from his work with the land. Land that his father and grandfather had worked. Land that would one day be worked by his sons.

Off to his left, a parade of holsteins plodded through the morning mist from barn to pasture. From the sloping hill east of the barn, he watched his calico-wrapped sister-in-law, Franz's wife. With sheer grace, Annette raised one arm and pulled the perfectly balanced sweep, letting a bucket down into the cool depths of the well.

A wife of his own would do the same chores, would hold dinner for him while he washed at the pump. He conjured up the picture often. Often enough to stir his blood. Since the fire, the vision had a face—tranquil and fine-boned, with ivory skin—and a name.

Lydia.

He remembered the lingering feel of her clasped against his body as he'd run through the smoke and licking flames. Delicate. Desirable. Strange—he couldn't recall the heat or the choking, blinding smoke as vividly as Lydia Beker's softness and her gentle, womanly scent.

Why had he done it? Would he have felt the same urgency, the same panic, if just any stranger had been trapped in that burning kitchen? No. He was a first-class fool, but he felt something for the young woman. He had felt something since he first laid eyes on her. She was different, unlike any girl he'd ever known.

Even in drab gray, with her hair bound and barely restrained under her white cap, she was lovely. Her wholesome candor added to Jakob's attraction. A full unpainted mouth complemented her fine-featured face, with its high cheekbones and somber expression.

He smiled in self-derision. He'd first seen her several weeks ago, when he and his father had happened into the bakery. Though he'd tried to catch her attention, she'd never looked his way.

The day she appeared at their table, his heart had bobbed into his throat. She'd looked at him as though he fascinated and frightened her at the same time. He'd eat pie until it came out his ears if she served each slice with the same look in those guileless dark eyes. "Pa?"

Johann didn't glance up from where he crouched, changing the feed on the manure spreader. "Yup."

"I've been thinking."

"Figured."

"About the woman in Accord."

"Mm-hmm…" Johann straightened and brushed his palms on his dungarees. "Purty thing."

"What if I court her?"

His father squinted at Annette, who was pouring water down a row of the vegetable garden. "She's a lot different from us."

"That's part of it." Annette wasn't vain, but he'd seen enough of Peine's primping and fussing to know he didn't want a woman more concerned with her hair and her lip rouge than she was with him. While Annette did the work of two women,

Peine disappeared or complained of a headache every time a meal was prepared. He wanted a wife who could carry her share of the work load. He wanted a wife to share farm life—the days, the evenings . . . and the nights. He wanted a home of his own. A family.

"She's so pretty," Jakob commented wistfully. "And the way she looks at me and listens when I say somethin' . . ."

"Like Sylvie did?"

Jakob jerked his gaze to his father in surprise. He hadn't thought of Sylvie for—well, for a long time. Sylvie. Her name didn't hurt anymore. Not the way it had at first. "Does Lydia remind you of Sylvie?"

"You trying to replace Sylvie?" his father asked.

Sylvie had been different, too. Painfully shy and self-conscious. A childhood stutter had prevented her from making friends. Jakob had drawn her out, encouraged her to join in activities and dared anyone to think less of her.

Jakob shook his head. It was pointless to wonder if she'd still be alive had he not coaxed quite so much. But Lydia was no Sylvie.

"Her pa might not take to you sniffin' around his daughter," Johann went on.

"I figured I could go to some of their meetings. Get them used to the idea of seeing me."

"Thought it all out, have ya?"

"Pretty much."

"You're sure?"

"No, but I'm willing to give it a whirl."

The wind that had carried the stench of manure away from them changed, and Johann pulled his kerchief up over his nose. "Then good luck, son."

"Lydia! Come quickly!" Christine Beker exclaimed, with an eagerness Lydia seldom heard in her voice. "The Neubauers!"

He was here! Even sooner than she'd expected!

In the bakefront, her mother smiled. "Take our guests pie." The older woman hurried toward the new storeroom. "Pack one for them I will."

Fingers trembling, Lydia sliced pie and carried it to Jakob and his father. Johann thanked her. Jakob studied her.

Self-consciously she tucked stray tendrils of hair under her cap. She must look a fright! She touched the back of her hand to her cheek and lifted her gaze to his face. Surely embarrassment glowed from every flour-dusted pore on her face.

She struggled to compose herself. Socializing was unheard-of in Accord, and she lacked the experience for cordiality.

"You seem sound. A lot better than the last time I saw you." Jakob's voice was deep, its tone unhurried; there was no trace of the hoarseness of his utterances after the fire.

"Hale and hearty I am, Herr Neubauer. *Herr Doktor* said I would have died had you not reached me when you did."

Lydia tried not to study his strong jaw and healthy skin as he ate. She'd never learned to use words such as *handsome* or *good-looking* in regard to appearance, so she didn't set his looks apart from what little she knew of his character. He was a strong man of great courage and selflessness.

"Fräulein Beker," he said in that emollient, deep-strung tone. "Would I be welcome at one of your meetings? I'd—" he smiled disarmingly "—like to learn more about your colony."

Perhaps he was interested in her! Her mother returned, carrying a flat carton. Lydia's gaze again collided with Jakob's.

"To hear the gospel we welcome everyone. There is service each evening at seventh bell. Men enter from the west door and sit on that side of the assembly hall."

Jakob nodded and finished the last bite.

The older Neubauer retrieved his dun-colored hat and walked to the door. Jakob rose to his feet. Lydia stood awkwardly in front of him, her eyes level with his brawny chest.

He wore a blue flannel shirt with the first few buttons open. Her glance skittered from his tanned throat to his blue eyes and down to the flour-dusted toes of her shoes. Heat crept up her neck, warming her cheeks. Her pulse roared in her ears.

"Thanks for the pie."

She forced herself to meet his sparkling eyes. "The gratitude is ours."

Bending from the waist, he leaned across the table to pick up his hat. "Will you be there? At the meetin'?"

He might as well have asked her something indecent, the way her insides quivered. She managed a nod. What would she have answered *had* he asked her something indecent?

"I'll be there tonight."

Something forbidden rippled through Lydia. Something expectant and trembly. Something warm and delicious and too good to stifle. Every dormant cell in her body awakened and bubbled with life. She would see him tonight!

He stroked one long finger across her chin and rubbed his thumb and forefinger together. "Flour, hmm?"

Her skin burned where his finger had touched. Lydia's eyes widened, and she took a step back. No one in the colony touched another person in public!

Bold as brass, Jakob only smiled and adjusted his hat upon his shock of hair. "G'day, *fraülein.*"

Long strides carried him across the room, and Lydia's wide-eyed stare followed his massive form. He filled the doorway briefly, then disappeared.

Chapter Three

From his seat at the table in front of the congregation, Etham Beker exhorted the colonists to remember their heritage and to keep their eyes on the glorious future and on Christ's coming.

Jakob glanced down at the hymnal courteously placed in his hands by the young man next to him. Even though it was open to the correct page, all he could do was listen to the strong male voices around him. The songbook was printed in German. His father could read and write the language of their ancestors, but until now Jakob had never had the inclination to learn.

Stealing another irresistible glance across the room, he found it impossible to distinguish Lydia from the field of gray dresses and white bonnets. How would he locate her after the meeting?

The song ended. Every head disappeared as the colonists leaned forward to pray, their noses nearly touching their laps. It was the oddest thing Jakob had ever seen.

When the meeting ended, the colonists gathered around him, introducing themselves and shaking his hand. Over their shoulders, he sought and found Lydia. Jakob gently excused himself and shouldered his way to the door.

Outside, soft female voices blended into one another in the night. He loped ahead and located her on the footpath. "Miss Beker."

Lydia grasped her young sister's hand and swung to face him. "Herr Neubauer!"

"Herr Neubauer? To our home will you come?" her lanky young brother offered in eager invitation. "Our grandmother has *Kekse.*"

Jakob understood. "What kind of cookies?"

"Oatmeal and raisin," he answered quickly. "I am Nathan."

Jakob extended his hand. Hesitantly the youth shook his hand. Jakob knew nothing of their custom. "Will it be...all right?" he asked Lydia.

Lydia glanced at her younger siblings' eager faces. "*Ja.* Do join us."

The Bekers' kitchen was meticulously clean and startlingly devoid of any ornamentation, save cut flowers next to the few work surfaces and on the table.

Lydia filled a teakettle and placed it on the narrow stove. One of Lydia's sisters positioned small plates around a table. The smaller children sat at the table awaiting their treat.

"Nathan, ask grandmother to join us, *bitte.* Be seated, Herr Neubauer."

He took the chair she indicated.

Nathan returned with a small elderly woman. An intricately stitched shawl draped her emaciated shoulders. Her ancient eyes, dark and curious, with deep golden sparks visible in the gaslight, inspected him.

"Ah, the hero." With a mischievous twinkle in her eyes, she seated herself at the corner of the table. "Just like the angels in the fiery furnace, huh?"

Jakob shifted in embarrassment.

"Grandmother." Lydia scolded her softly in German and bent to pour her tea. She served Jakob and herself, then took the last remaining chair—at the opposite end of the table.

Jakob covered his disappointment with conversation. "Where are your parents?"

"Mother is tending a sister who is ill," Lydia answered. "She will be home afterward. Meeting with the *Diakon* is my father." She passed the plate of cookies.

"Where are you from Herr Neubauer?" Grandmother asked, and selected a cookie.

"I farm over to the north, with my pa and brothers."

"You are German?"

"Yes, ma'am. My grandparents worked as bond servants to pay their passage over. Grandpa took up his watchmaking till he staked the farm."

"Quite a legacy," she said with admiration. "I was just a child when my parents came to this country, but I remember the hard years...."

The old woman stared at Jakob for a long moment. He could remember his own grandmother with that same reflective expression on her face. He smiled.

"*Ach*, well..." She shrugged her bony shoulders. "If something comes too easy, it is probably not worth having."

One of the children tapped Jakob's sleeve and pointed to a silver ornament cinching his black string tie up against his stiff white collar. "What is that?"

"A dollar."

Inquisitive faces turned to Lydia.

"*Münze*," she explained. "*Sein Geld*."

Several pairs of eyes widened and stared.

Jakob's last bite of cookie stuck in his throat. He fought the urge to swallow and send the object of their undivided attention bobbing.

Grandmother came to his aid. "Prepare for bed, children. Rachael, tend to the dishes, please. *Guten Abend, Meier Neubauer. Sehr erfreut*," she said, wishing him a good evening.

He called upon the meager German he'd learned from his grandmother. "*Danke, Frau Beker. Auf Wiedersehen*."

Rose smiled indulgently at his accent.

Lydia showed him to the door, but he didn't want the evening to end. He needed more time with her. "My horse is stabled on the other side of the common. Want to walk partway with me?"

Nathan gave Lydia an almost imperceptible nod.

"To the common I will walk," Lydia replied softly.

The town was silent. No dogs barked. No cats yowled. Even the crickets, their chirping muted and distant, seemed to respect the hush blanketing the settlement. No off-key piano tinkled raucously on Main Street. The inhabitants of Accord were all tucked peacefully away in their homes after a tiring day of work.

"I learned a lot tonight. I take it there's another colony like this in Economy?"

"Yes. Father Rapp's granddaughter, Gertrude, lives there with the last of the original Rappites."

"You say 'the last' as if there won't be any more." They had reached the common, where fragrant flowers planted in precise rows and borders edged the footpaths. They stopped beneath the light of a gas lamp, and he faced her.

"Die out they will, if Christ comes not in their lifetime."

"Why?"

She gestured for him to sit on a stone bench. "Father Rapp believed family interests should not be put ahead of the community, that the people shouldn't be distracted from their work and the burden of the community would be less with no children." She regarded him cautiously, as if awaiting his reaction. "No marriage is there between risen saints, the Bible says," she hurried to explain. "Children were unnecessary, since Christ was due any second."

She faced the flower bed opposite them. Jakob studied her fetching profile. He absorbed the information, first rearranging her peculiar sentence structures in his mind. Lydia's parents and grandparents were married, and she was one of *six* children. "I take it you folks don't see, uh...marriage...the way Father Rapp did."

"That difference drew my grandfather away. He and Grandmother started a new colony of married believers."

Seeing her silhouetted against the night sky, he marveled at her unaffected beauty. She probably didn't know how pretty she was, or how her graceful gestures and chaste manners pressed lasting pictures into his memory—pictures that he would review again and again until the next time he saw her.

Wanting to touch her, wanting to pull her against him and smell her soft, feminine fragrance, he rubbed his damp palms on the thighs of his trousers. He balled his hands into fists and resisted the growing desire to reach for her.

Her gaze turned to him. "I must return. It is time for the last bell."

Jakob stood with her. His wants churned his belly into an aching sack of gravel. *Don't scare her off, Neubauer.* He stuffed his thumbs in the pockets of his trousers and rolled back on his heels. "I like your family."

She smiled. *"Gute Nacht,* Herr Neubauer."

"Jakob." Her velvet-soft eyes met his, and he wished more than ever that the darkness didn't hide the golden flecks he'd seen earlier.

"Good night." Her voice floated soft and warm on the night breeze, and she disappeared, leaving him aching. He'd have to tread lightly and patiently until she learned he was no threat. Did he have the patience?

He wanted her more every time he saw her, every time he allowed himself the indulgence of picturing her as his wife.

Somehow he would find the patience.

At home in his upstairs room, Jakob lit the oil lamp on the chiffonier and surveyed his reflection in the mirror. Did it matter to her that he needed a haircut? Did she notice that his nose was too thin and his jaw too square?

He flopped back on his bed. Franz and Annette whispered and giggled, tiptoeing to their room. An aggressive heat radiated throughout Jakob's body. He closed his eyes and tortured himself with thoughts of them undressing and snuggling in their bed. Lord, but he needed a woman!

He loved his family, the farm and the work that pushed him to his limits. He'd been happy here, but he was twenty-eight years old, and he needed a wife.

Watching his brothers with their wives and listening to the sounds from their rooms had become an abrasion he could barely endure. Years of waiting pressed in on him until he wanted to burst. He needed a woman's touch, not just a presence or a memory.

His mother had died eighteen years ago, his grandmother a few years later. Annette was warmhearted and ambitious, and she unquestionably loved his brother. She and Franz had been childhood sweethearts. Jakob couldn't remember a time when Annette hadn't been in their lives.

Peine, on the other hand, was aloof and disdainful, hovering on the fringe of activities, watching, listening—never participating. The couple fought often and bitterly. Her caustic tongue had caused many hard feelings among the family members, yet Jakob had never been berated. Anton, obviously disappointed in his wife, had withdrawn the affections he'd no doubt hoped to lavish on her, spending them, instead, on Nikolaus.

Sylvie Schelling, only daughter of Butler's Methodist Episcopal preacher, had been Jakob's girl. They'd planned to marry, but at the tender age of seventeen, she'd died.

Jakob no longer had a childhood sweetheart, and he'd always balked at the idea of advertising for a mate. But since he'd met the young woman in Accord, the thought of a wife had taken on a more pleasant aspect. Lydia Beker had ignited something volatile…a longing that smoldered and spread and seared his formerly contained yearning into a blazing, all-consuming need.

He knew what he wanted. He knew *who* he wanted.

The ways and means of surmounting obstacles in his path didn't daunt him, especially after the old woman's encouraging words that evening: *If something comes too easy, it is probably not worth having.*

Lydia looked forward to Jakob's visits. It rained mercilessly, which afforded the young farmer time to travel into town for baked goods. At least twice a week he attended a Society meeting and walked her to the common afterward. Her family was aware of the attention he paid her, and Etham invited Jakob to the *Diakon* meeting, where the Society leaders introduced themselves and enlightened him on the Scriptures.

It was only a mild shock to Lydia when Jakob touched upon the subject of marriage one evening as they sat, a proper distance apart, on a rough-hewn bench in the town common.

"Do you have suitors, Lydia?"

"Suitors?" she repeated without comprehension.

"You know, men callin' on you? A beau?"

"It is not the custom."

"What is the custom?"

"If a man finds a woman suitable, he requests of her father a union. If her father approves, they are married."

Jakob absently ran a thumbnail along the crease of his trousers. "How do they know if they're suitable?"

Lydia watched his hand and remembered him drawing his finger across her chin. The thought of him touching her supplied enough jitters that she was hard-pressed to keep her own hands still in her lap.

"In Accord we are familiar with one another. Most of the young men are my second or third cousins. The older men are mostly widowers."

Jakob mauled his hat, curling the brim in a thoughtless gesture that revealed a worn leather band.

"Would you marry me if your father approved?"

Lydia's heart pounded erratically. She hadn't allowed the possibility to take shape in her mind. It was preposterous to think of marrying a man she'd known for only a short number of weeks . . . it was against the Society's nature!

But there was no one else she would *rather* marry! She couldn't visualize marriage to a colonist, especially not after meeting Jakob.

Her eyes flickered over his earnest face, then to her lap. He was like no one else she knew or could ever hope to know. He was from an exciting world she'd never seen, and he'd a wealth of experiences she knew nothing of. She conjured up a vision of Jakob joining the colony and becoming her husband. A giddy bubble inflated her chest, and she fought to keep from laughing out loud, lest he think her insane.

"*Ja.* I would marry you if my father approved."

They gazed at one another openly, exchanging mutual looks of surprise and uncertain hope.

"And if he doesn't?"

"Why would he not? You are a fellow German. To the *Diakon* he welcomed you." Excitement knotted her stomach. "Will you ask him?"

"Tomorrow." He noticed the beating his hat had taken, and attempted to straighten it. "I'll talk to him. I'd be a good, faithful husband. I can provide for you. I'd do everything in my power to see you were never sorry."

"I believe you would." She turned her gaze up to his face and heard him catch his breath.

His firm hand took hers from her lap and urged her to stand. His broad form blocked the moon. The vivid memory of clinging to his strong arms and shoulders assailed her. Lydia's fingers trembled in his callused palm.

"Tomorrow I'll ask him." He lifted her fingers to his mouth and pressed his lips against her knuckles. Heart racing, she allowed the intimacy.

"Tomorrow," she whispered.

Peine perched girlishly on the porch rail. Jakob scraped mud from his boots. He knelt below her in the dooryard, grass poking through his bare toes. "You went to Accord again last night, Jakob?"

"Yup."

"What *is* so interesting there?"

He glanced up at her, pausing to thumb his hat back on his head. "Oh…" He returned his attention to his boots. "They're fascinating people."

"If backward is fascinating," she said scornfully.

"They're not all backward." He flipped his buck knife closed and straightened. "I talked with some of the men, and I plan to use their ideas when I build my house. Stone footings, cellars with a tunnel for cooling…"

Peine tapped her fingers on the rail distractedly. "My, my…"

"They insulate with slabs of wood wrapped in straw and mud. They call 'em 'Dutch biscuits.' "

"Jakob, you're not thinking about bringing that girl here?"

Jakob stood taller, glanced at the knife in his hand, then back to her. "I am."

"She's too different!"

"That doesn't matter to me."

"You can't know each other. I'll bet you've never been alone with her. What kind of courtship is that?"

"What would you know about proper courtin'?"

Jakob had never said anything mean to her. Jakob was always kind, always offered a loving pat on the hand or shoulder, a strong arm to lean on. Time after time, his quick, devil-may-care wink had stolen her breath. He'd never spoken to her like this.

Not until he'd met Lydia.

Peine bit the tip of her tongue as hard as she could, and blinked a tear from the corner of her eye. "Jakob," she said with a convincing tremble in her voice, "I only want the best for you. For you to be happy."

"Hey," he said softly, and stepped to the rail beneath her. He covered her hand with his, and a jolt shot up her arm. "I'm sorry. I'm pleased with your concern."

He turned those blue eyes up to her, and her heart flip-flopped. She blinked hard enough to release another tear. He did care! She knew he did! "How will she ever adapt to this god-awful life, Jakob? She's never been outside that church town, never seen what the world and men are like."

Jakob backed away and settled his hat over his forehead. "I won't mislead her about what this life is like. Whether or not she wants to come will be up to her. I can't make Lydia do anything she doesn't want to do."

Lydia's name on his lips pricked Peine's ire. The sound was like salt in a fresh wound. Why wouldn't *Lydia* want to come? He was perfect, wonderful. But he was Peine's. "Why her, Jakob?"

Jakob picked up his boots and shrugged his broad shoulders. "I'm not sure." He looked at his boots. "These need a good polishing before I meet with her father."

Disgusted, Peine flounced through the kitchen door.

Lydia hurried along Church Street, her head swimming with imagined scenes of the life she and Herr Neubauer would have together. She thanked God for sending Jakob. Her prayers were not the serene praises and petitions they had been a month ago—she even thanked God for the fire, a trial turned blessing.

Men's voices came from behind the heavy closed door at the rear of the church. She knocked.

"Enter." Her father sat behind his massive cherrywood desk, and in a chair before him sat Jakob. Jakob stood when she entered.

"Sit, Lydia," her father said. "I thought you should be present. You have spent time with Herr Neubauer, and I think he has made a decision."

Lydia and Jakob exchanged confused glances. He remained standing until she took the straight-backed chair next to his.

Jakob cleared his throat. "I thought we could talk alone, *Vater* Beker." He gave Lydia an apologetic glance.

"There is nothing to hide. This is not the church of Germany. You need not confess your sins to me." Etham smiled benevolently through his neat black beard.

Jakob hung his hat on his knee and spread his palms on his denim-clad thighs. Lydia wiped the dampness from her own hands beneath the concealment of her gray skirt.

"I want to marry your daughter, and I'd like your approval. I'm a sober man. I can take care of her—"

"Marry my daughter!" Black eyes swung to her. "Lydia, did you know of this?"

She nodded mutely. It had seemed so logical, so preferable, when she spoke with Jakob alone, when she dreamed of their future together. Here, in her father's study, years of bending to his will and fearing to do anything else crowded in.

"This was . . . not what I anticipated." Etham ran a hand through his hair. "I assumed your interest in the colony led you here to join. You must give me a moment."

Jakob nodded.

Lydia sat meekly, twisting her skirt.

Her father's obsidian gaze lifted to hers. "What is your wish?"

Her wish? She willed surprise from her expression. Coaxing her voice from her constricted throat, she lowered her gaze. "I wish to marry Jakob. I believe the Lord allowed the fire to bring us together."

Her father remained silent for long minutes. His chair creaked as he leaned back and then forward again, thoughtfully. "I can think of no objections to a union. . . ."

Lydia's heart dared to lift in preparation for his words of blessing. *Oh, thank you, Lord!*

"As long as Herr Neubauer signs the articles of agreement and pledges himself to the Lord and the Society—"

"Wait a minute," Jakob said, interrupting him. Two sets of dark eyes fixed on his face. He raised a palm in a negative gesture. "I never said anything about joining the Society. I'm a farmer, and I—"

Etham lunged from his chair, slapping his hands flat on his desk. "You attended meetings and accepted our hospitality for naught? You came only to seduce my daughter?"

Jakob stiffened. A muscle in his lean jaw jumped. "I didn't *seduce* your daughter. Just because I wasn't born in a brick house and raised here doesn't mean I seduce women! I asked her to marry me, for God's sake!"

"You will not curse in front of her." Etham pulled himself up straight. "My daughter will not marry outside of God's will. A child of God she is, one of the chosen. We do not marry outside the brethren. If you intend to remain a heathen, nothing further do I see to discuss."

Grief sliced into Lydia's heart. She, too, had assumed Jakob wanted to become one of them. *He hadn't.* Disappointment thickened in her chest and throat.

"You think you've got the corner on God, *Vater* Beker? You look down your nose at me, and you don't know me. You're judging me an unfit husband because of my religion." Lydia recognized the anger in his rigid shoulders.

"What religion?"

Jakob leapt to his feet and swatted his hat against his thigh. The muscle in his jaw jerked while he composed himself. Cringing inside, Lydia peered from beneath her lashes. The room's atmosphere had grown volatile. *Jakob. Oh, Jakob. Oh, God.* "I want to talk to Lydia before I leave."

Etham walked to the door. "Five minutes." The door clicked shut behind him

Chapter Four

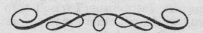

Flooded with shame, Lydia fought the tears smarting behind her lids. She refused to look up. She stared at her lap, and two shiny black boots came into view.

"I didn't realize you'd expect me to join the colony."

His husky voice pierced her soul. Her chin trembled.

"Lydia."

She turned her face away from him.

"Look at me."

Why? So that she could memorize the face she'd never see again? So that she could brand the exact color of his sky blue eyes and fair hair on her heart forever? So that she could gauge his height and the breadth of his shoulders, marvel one last time at the sun-kissed hue of his vibrant skin? So that she could ensure suffering the exact measure of her foolishness for eternity? No.

"Lydia, I never meant to hurt you. I guess it was foolish thinking our marriage could've been worked out so easily. Have you changed your mind about marrying me?"

Twisting her skirt in her lap, she struggled to sort out her wretched feelings, horrified that she'd misinterpreted his intent and thus embarrassed them both. If only she'd realized! If only they'd discussed his intention beforehand, before coming to Father.

"Sorry I am to have misled you. I . . . I didn't think. I wasn't certain of . . ." Her quavering voice faded away.

His hand touched her shoulder, and she jumped. Quickly he withdrew it. "Is he right? You can't marry me because I'm not one of the brethren?"

"This is my home, my people."

"You're too good for me?"

"Nein!" She met his eyes, and wished she hadn't. Blue and ice-cold, they chilled her with their intensity. She didn't want to remember them like this.

"Come with me, then."

Had she heard him right? She stared at her clenched hands, blinking back tears. Go with him? She wanted to. *Sie Gott,* she wanted to! Her father would never give his permission. How could she leave her grandmother? How could she make that choice in this instant?

As a child, she'd fallen from a ladder while dusting lamps in the service hall. The fall on the hard wooden floor had knocked the air from her lungs, and she'd been unable to breathe for terrifying minutes. That was what this choice felt like. Her mouth opened. She forced words out. "I . . . cannot."

A floorboard creaked as Jakob shifted his weight. Seconds passed, and his eyes bored into the top of her head. She refused to look up again.

His boots thundered across the carpeted floor. The wooden barrier slammed shut. Raising her apron, she buried her face. Hurt and disappointment hollowed an aching void where her heart had palpitated only moments before. Why had God sent Jakob to save her from the fire and given her a second chance? Why had a union with him felt so right? Was he saint or sinner? She had seen only what she wanted to see, neglecting even concern for his salvation. Remorse filled the agonizing cavity in her chest, a weight so great and unfamiliar that it frightened her. She dried her face, lifted her chin and forced herself to breathe.

It's not too late! I could catch him! She could run out that door and—and what? Come face-to-face with her father? Twenty years of self-denial and obedience were not easily cast aside. She sat rigidly for several minutes before her father entered.

"I am sorry you suffered this indignity. The sinful nature is a powerful force, and not to be dealt with lightly. We trusted Herr Neubauer's motives, but the serpent disguises himself in many forms, Lydia. You have been sheltered from his deceitful ways until now."

Her skin burned with humiliation.

"Perhaps it took an Outsider to open your eyes. It may be a blessing in disguise that will instruct you in the future. We must pray diligently." Etham sat in the chair next to hers, and together they bent at the waist and prayed. For what, Lydia wasn't sure.

He had to go back.

Jakob perched on a nail keg in the tack room, surrounded by the familiar smells of neat's-foot oil, leather and horses. His canine companion lay at his feet, snoring lightly, her chin resting on his booted toe. Rain poured from the sky and thunder shook the barn rafters, and he busied himself sharpening tools and oiling harnesses. Doves chirred in the loft beyond the tack room door. Working the land fatigued and satisfied him at the same time. Even though a body was pushed to its physical limit, the tedious hours still left a mind free to explore.

Absently he reached down and stroked the dog's silken ears. He had pictured a wife sharing these days and nights, making the labor seem worthwhile. He pictured Lydia in the kitchen, in the garden, in his bed... He remembered her delicate profile against the glowing gas lamps, her rose petal-soft skin and the intoxicating fragrance of her hair.

He envisioned their own house, children, Sunday dinners and picnics in the meadow, where it sloped down beneath a stand of eastern hemlock. Perhaps she needed time to examine her vision of the future. He had waited this long, he could be patient a little longer. One thing was certain: *Vater* Beker's word wasn't enough. Jakob would settle for nothing less than hearing from her own lips that she no longer wanted to marry him. She couldn't have changed her mind so easily. The distress on her face that evening still haunted his nights.

Could he convince her to come? He'd seen eagerness in her eyes, a spark of life none of the other colonists had. But was she different enough from her family to choose a life with him? He wanted her and it was a want bad enough to mellow his indignation.

As soon as the rain stopped, he would clear the road for one last trip to Accord.

With a grudgingly repentant heart, Lydia sought to restore her former role in her family and community. Working for the good of the whole, she strove to win her father's approval and God's forgiveness, suspecting that the latter would be easier. Her work was done with a strength born of an anger she could neither vent nor recognize. Another sin could not be compounded upon the last.

Each day she put in her full schedule at the bakery, sat with the women during supper and service and joined her mother and her sisters in the housework each evening. At the nine-o'clock bell she went to her cot and prayed, asking God to take away her confused feelings for the Outsider. Sometimes her prayers lasted until the early hours of the morning. The next day she began all over again.

Orderliness had always been security. The Society's purpose had always reassured her. Solitude had been familiar. Never had she been hungry, or cold, or burdened.

Until now. Until Jakob.

Assigned the task of cleaning the number two dormitory, Lydia sat in the open doorway with a cup of tea after the bell for *Vesperbrot*. The view was slightly more stimulating than that from the bakery. Main Street was the site of the town store, the apothecary's and the hatter's. Few men and women were walking between the businesses.

Three unmarried women arrived home for the afternoon break. Lydia moved away from the doorway, her thoughts touching on each woman. How did they resign themselves to their unmarried state? She pictured living here, where no children laughed or cried, no voices spoiled the silence and no small shoes lined the kitchen wall.

Instead of fearing that life on earth would end before she had experienced a shred of life, she now dreaded the prospect of *living!* The prospect of growing older with no hope of her own family, only the Society.

Resuming her window cleaning, a shout came from the street. "Fräulein Beker!"

Lucas Dürer stood on the walkway below. "*Vater* Beker sends you home to sit with your grandmother."

She hurried home and found the old woman's dark eyes dull with pain. "Grandmother."

"What are you hiding from me, child?"

"I'm not hiding anything." She knelt beside the cot.

"Is my pain hidden because I don't talk about it?"

"Nein," Lydia whispered.

"What is the pain you're not telling me?" Rose Beker's thick gray braid lay like a rope across her shallow chest.

Lydia knew better than to deny her Grandmother. She sighed. "I didn't tell you because I was . . . I am ashamed."

"What would such a flower have to be ashamed of?"

"I became . . . distracted by the Outsider. I thought of nothing but the idle promise of a life with him, and believed he wanted to become one of us. I was wrong." Here, only here, in this tiny, barren room, was she free to express her fear and uncertainties.

"Did he deliberately lead you to think he wanted to be a Harmonist?"

Lydia's emotions had been so painfully near the surface that she hadn't considered his. She remembered Jakob's words vividly. *I never meant to hurt you. It was foolish thinking our marriage could've been worked out so easily.* Hurt and embarrassment had turned her thoughts inward until she hadn't listened. Perhaps if she'd been able to think it out, to talk to him without humiliating tears threatening . . .

"He is kind and good," she said, realizing as she spoke that it was true. "He did not mislead me. His proposal was sincere, but . . . he didn't realize how different we are, how impossible a union was."

"Do you love the young man?"

Lydia's eyes met their amber-flecked match. "Love is something one must learn, and there was no time."

"I know what your father says." Grandmother clucked reproachfully. "What are *your* feelings?"

"I think I might have loved him. I wanted to." She drew a deep breath, leaned forward and closed her fingers lovingly over her grandmother's twisted hand. "I've placed it behind me. Don't worry."

"You cannot go back to life as it was before. You're not untouched."

"I will go on."

"With your joyless life?"

Joyless. What a perfect word. "You were happy here."

"Because your grandfather was here. Sometimes we must follow our instincts, our hearts."

Lydia's heart fluttered curiously.

"Promise me one thing, child."

"Of course." She'd jump off a cliff for the old woman.

"Look at *Meier* Neubauer with your heart, not with your father's eyes."

"I doubt I shall ever look at him again in any manner." There was something incredibly sad about saying those words. Opportunity had laid itself at her feet. She'd had a chance to shed the suffocating mantle of the colony and climb on the back of Jakob Neubauer's horse. What held her? Responsibility. Obligation. Duty. To whom? She looked into her grandmother's gold-flecked eyes. "I must concentrate on fulfilling God's pleasure, not mine."

"What if marrying him pleased God?"

"Impossible." The word, her father's word, was out before she thought about it. As always, Grandmother's odd ideas unsettled her. She gazed down, tenderly. "Close your eyes. You need to sleep."

She pulled the rocker beside the cot and sat, a unique thought rolling across her troubled mind. *Could* God's will and hers really be the same?

Anton entered the bedroom, unbuttoning his shirt. "What are you making?"

"A new shade for the baby buggy." Peine adjusted the lacy white fabric on her lap.

"A what?"

"I said, *a shade for the buggy!*"

Anton studied her briefly, then tossed his shirt over the back of a chair.

"Please don't leave that there."

He poured water into the porcelain bowl.

"Did you hear me?"

"I heard you," he replied, his back to her. As a child, a nearly fatal case of measles had left him deaf in one ear. The hearing loss had never been a problem—until Peine. His family accepted, compensated, forgot. But his wife criticized, mocked and reminded—ruthlessly.

Drying his face and shoulders, Anton turned. "I need to run into town in the mornin'. Wanna go?"

"No."

"Got any letters to mail?"

"No."

He took a fresh shirt from a drawer. "Have you written your ma since you've been here?"

"I have."

"Not that I've noticed."

Peine leaned over the side of her rocker and plucked a spool of thread from her sewing box. "Put your shirt on."

Deliberately he tossed the clean, folded shirt on the bed. "Don't you s'pose she wonders how you are? Wouldn't you like to take Nikolaus to meet his grandma sometime?"

"No!" She stabbed the needle into a wad of material and tossed it on the bed. Standing, she snatched his dirty shirt from the chair and, after rolling it, placed it in a woven basket under the bureau, with the rest of the soiled laundry. "I've written her. Jakob took a letter for me the other day. I don't want to go to Pittsburgh. There's nothing there, and I don't wish to discuss it."

Anton ran a brush through his hair and dropped it on the washstand. Jakob again. Always Jakob. Anton would have had to be deaf in both ears, and blind to boot, to miss the attraction his wife had for his brother. Nothing he could say or do equaled Jakob's words and accomplishments. He watched

Peine place his comb and brush in perfect alignment. "How come you're not helping Annette with supper?"

"I was, but I didn't feel well." She sat and resumed her sewing, avoiding looking at his bare torso, avoiding the hated scar on his shoulder. It was V-shaped, the result of a barbed-wire-fencing incident a few years back. Another example of his many imperfections.

Anton stretched out on the bed, hands behind his head, and studied her. She was pretty. Not as pretty as he'd first thought, but pretty. At first he'd tried hard. He'd flirted and courted, thinking they needed to get to know one another. She hadn't responded.

Her fair skin was clear and delicate, her gold hair luxurious and shiny. Beneath her satiny rose dress, her body was lush and warm. Immediately his own body responded, and he cursed it silently.

She endured his lovemaking. Just like she endured everything else—the farm, the work . . . him.

He knew she was disappointed. She was a city girl, born and bred. Undoubtedly she missed the social life, pretty dresses and friends, but whenever he offered to take her visiting, she flatly refused. He was at a loss on how to please her. And lately it had become less important to do so. But he couldn't let that happen.

He thought of Nikolaus, whom he'd passed as he entered the house. Playing on the porch with his grandfather, his son had beamed and clapped his hands delightedly at Anton's appearance. The child needed a strong family. Two loving parents. For him, Anton would work on his relationship with Peine. He stood and shrugged into his shirt.

Lydia had been assigned to extinguish lights, straighten benches and stack hymnals—chores to keep her hands and mind busy. She finished her tasks and left the assembly hall, pulling the door closed behind her. The night was warm, and a light breeze sighed through the poplar leaves and lifted her skirt's hem.

"Lydia."

Thinking the voice was a trick of the wind in the boughs overhead, a sound contrived by her own traitorous imagination to lure her thoughts back to the subject she sought to forget, she walked on.

"Lydia, please." The masculine voice was as unmistakably near as the blood that pounded in her ears. She stopped and hugged her Bible against her breast as she turned.

"Jakob." He was so tall! How had she forgotten? A luminous white shirt encased his chest and shoulders, and the moonlight emphasized their breadth. She fought the urge to touch him, to reach out and assure herself he was real. "What are you doing here?"

"You need to ask?"

The quiet voice was so achingly familiar that she fought back tears. She'd thought never to hear it again. "Walk with me, in the other direction, where my father won't see us."

He followed her lead, falling into step at her side. Frightened of her response to his nearness, she held the Book protectively against the front of her dress. *Oh, Jakob, please. Don't do this to me. I want to forget, but I can't.* "I didn't expect to see you."

"Did you think I'd just go home and forget?"

"I didn't know."

He plucked a sprig from a hanging branch and twirled it between his fingers. "I don't want to forget about us. At least not till I've done my darnedest to work it out."

Church Street fell behind them. They walked without speaking through the residential section, the gas lamps defining their shadows in yellow halos. They passed the footpath, but continued walking. Somewhere beside the goose meadow he took the lead. Their eyes adjusted to the dark, and they found a waist-high fence to follow.

Jakob stopped.

Lydia took another step before turning toward him uncertainly. They were alone.

"Did you have time to think?" In the radiant moonlight he slid the fingers of both hands into his pants pockets and leaned back against the rail fence.

She'd thought of little else but his tall form in his white shirt, his sun-gilded hair and skin. She'd wondered a hundred times what would have happened had she walked out of her father's study beside him. What would life be like in his world . . . life with him?

"I've had much time to try not to think." Her heart struggled against the confines of her breast until her extremities tingled and her head grew light.

"What'd you try not to think about?"

What life would be like here. Without you. "The rudiments of the world."

"Oh. One of your father's inspired messages."

Was that a mocking smile? She would never admit that her father had used that phrase this very evening. "Are you ridiculing?"

"Sorry."

She lowered her arms, relaxing her defensive posture. The breeze pressed her skirts flat and carried the orchard's aromatic smells to them. She had tried for weeks to banish this man from her thoughts, and now here he was, tall and self-assured, standing before her as though her yearning had conjured him from thin air. She hadn't erased even one tiny shred of him from her memory. She doubted she ever could.

Everything about him was familiar—but better, much better than the vague reverie she tried to stifle each sleepless night. The reality was lofty and strong and solid, carrying the unmistakable scent of leather and horse. His pale hair shimmered ethereal in the moonlight.

"What do you want?" She couldn't play games with him. She wasn't coy or self-assured.

"I want you to marry me." There was no hesitation, no question, no doubt, in his reply.

The night folded its sultry, star-studded silence around her. There was no sound but that of her thudding heart. One part of her wanted to throw her head back and laugh out loud with joy, while another part—the rigidly disciplined part—wished the heavens would reach down and swallow her up, send a chariot as they had for the prophet Elijah. "You still want to marry me?"

He pushed away from the fence. "Nothing has changed, Lydia. I still feel the same. I want you for my wife."

"But my father—"

"I only care what you think, what you want." He pulled his hands from his pockets and closed his fingers around her upper arms, his face inches from hers. It was impossible not to look at him, not to search his shadowed eyes and feel the strength emanating from him. "What do you want, Lydia?"

Everything. To be your wife. To have your children. To be here for my grandmother. His grasp was light. It was easy to pull away and step back. She seized the fence for support, mind racing and heart pounding. She'd thought she wanted her father's approval, and when she realized Jakob was unwilling to join the Society, her only choice had been to satisfy herself with life in the colony. When she spoke again, her whisper was unsteady. "I don't know."

But now...now he had made it clear that she *did* have another choice! One that would overturn the world as she knew it. She could defy her father's wishes, turn her back on the only people and home she'd ever known and give up her secure life to leave with this Outsider. This...man. *Jakob.*

His long hair had been trimmed since she last saw him, but still curled over his collar's edge, shining pale and silvery. She detected a sunburn on his smooth skin, his shiny, defined cheekbones. Even in the dark, she knew the color of his pure blue eyes. Only her youngest sister, Faith, and Grandmother had ever before stirred strong feelings within her. But these...these feelings consumed her, tugged her heart toward the unthinkable choice.

"I've never thought of what I want before. Only what is right, what God wants, what my father wants." *Look with your heart, not your father's eyes.* Her grandmother's words came back to her. Her eyes saw the man before her. Her heart once again experienced the thrust his nearness brought.

"I can wait a little longer." He stepped in front of her, trapping her against the fence. "But not too long."

She held her breath.

With the gentlest of touches, he laid his palm along the curve of her jaw, fingertips grazing her earlobe, and she knew he must feel her heart racing in that telltale pulse point. "Think about what Fraülein Beker wants to do with the rest of her life. I'll be back for your decision."

He moved slightly, and Lydia experienced the unnerving sensation of falling. Her body jerked as if she were suddenly awaking from a dream, and she gripped the fence behind her for balance, one hand pressed flat against her racing heart. Her Bible fell at Jakob's feet.

Slowly—ever so slowly—he skimmed his fingertips along her jawline, drawing them away. That touch, that gentlest of touches, branded her with its rightness. Told her she wanted— needed—more. He picked up her Bible, handed it to her, and left.

He was offering everything she longed for. The chance to see all the things and places she dreamed of. The opportunity to marry him, to live somewhere new and exciting, to bear his children.

Lydia's skin tingled where his callused fingers had stroked. Did she have the courage? Could she bear to leave her grandmother behind?

The night sky was filled with stars, big and bright and close enough to touch. Many nights she had admired them, feeling small and unimportant under the canopy of God's handiwork, and wondered about people in crowded cities and busy towns who saw the same auroral light. But tonight there were no other people in the world. Only her and the tall Outsider who wanted to marry her and was willing to wait for her decision.

Wait for her decision! Did she have the power to do it? Her entire life, she had been told what to do, what to think, what to wear. She had been given no choice in the food she ate, the tasks she performed, the books she read.

Now she faced the biggest decision of her life, and—Lord help her—she knew what she wanted.

Chapter Five

"Father. Have tea with us." Lydia pumped water into the teakettle and placed it on the stove. Grandmother sat at the table, her shawl wrapped snugly around her bowed shoulders, even though the evening was warm.

Etham hung his hat on a wall peg and settled himself at the table. "Lydia, I am concerned about your distraction from your daily work."

Rose pushed her cup aside, as if to rise, but at Lydia's beseeching look, she stayed.

"It is time you married. Some believers best serve God unmarried, devoted entirely to Him, but the rest must have a husband and children to devote themselves to."

Oddly enough, Lydia had reasoned the same thing. Deliberately she avoided her grandmother's eyes.

"Peter Schuler is a match for you. I spoke with him today. Or Lucas Dürer. You work well together."

Speechless, Lydia glanced at the old woman, who was staring intently into her teacup. Rose's gaze lifted and met her granddaughter's, revealing a dark displeasure.

Worked well together? Peter Schuler or Lucas Dürer for a *husband?* Lucas's boyish blush came to mind. Then Peter's somber gray gaze. Yes, nice young men. Both suitable. Dependable. Faithful. Predictable. And chosen by her *Vater.* She tried to imagine Lucas touching her, wondered if moonlight on Peter Schuler's neat hair would set her heart to racing. Did her father want her to say, "Yes, I will take that one," as if she were selecting an apple from a barrel?

Grandmother spoke up. "She must have time."

"Of course she may have time. Perhaps there is another Harmonist she prefers. In any case, her sin must be acquitted—immediately." He stood. *"Vielen dank."*

The two women stared at the wedding china, fine china cups and saucers decorated in a rich, flowing blue flower-and-scroll design, until he was well out of hearing distance.

"What are you thinking, Lydia?"

Lydia took Grandmother's mottled hand and massaged it lovingly. "I am confused when I think of Jakob."

"And when you are with him?"

Her smile was spontaneous. "He...unsettles me, but it is comforting to look at him, to hear his voice. I want to hear it always. When I thought he would join the colony, I was beside myself. I asked God to take away the feelings, but He doesn't. Why are these feelings wrong?"

"They're not wrong, child. It's the way a woman should feel about the man she will marry."

"But marriage to an Outsider?"

Tears welled up in the old woman's eyes, and she gripped Lydia's hand with surprising strength. "I call you 'child,' but you are a grown woman, with hopes, wants and needs. Don't stifle them for an unsatisfactory life. You will always feel that part of you is missing."

"What are you saying?" Was Grandmother encouraging her to turn against her father's wishes, to defy everything she had been raised to believe in?

"Follow your heart. Weigh these new feelings. No matter which choice, you'll lose something. Measure the gain against the loss. Perhaps God hasn't removed those feelings because they are His will."

Sleep did not come easily. Balancing the options always narrowed down to the same two choices; Jakob, or her family and her home. Exhaustive prayer and self-examination brought a plague of discordant dreams. Work was her only relief, giving her hands and mind purpose for another day. Not until the appointed evening, following worship service, did the scales tip toward her answer.

Jakob! She ran to where he waited, and without a thought to propriety or onlookers, threw her arms around his neck and pressed her face against his crisp collar. "Jakob," she whispered, as fervently as any prayer.

His body tensed in hesitation. Slowly his hands circled her waist, their heat penetrating the fabric. Lydia caught herself in surprise and stepped back.

Glancing over her shoulder, he pulled her behind a row of young hemlocks. He released her hand, and they studied one another as their eyes adjusted to the darkness.

"Have you thought about us?"

"I have thought of little else." Her face flamed at her forwardness. He waited for her answer. "My father wants me to marry and take my mind off worldly desires."

"Meanin' me." He snapped a twig from a branch and toyed with the needles. "Will marrying someone else take your mind off me?"

Lydia was comforted that he couldn't see the color she knew radiated from her face. She couldn't forget him in a thousand lifetimes. "I think not."

He scraped needles from the twig, and they fell to the black earth at his feet. "Will you marry me?"

Grasping her shoulder gently, he turned her toward him and pulled her closer, without touching his body to hers. His hand was heavy and strong on her shoulder, and he smelled faintly spicy. He curled his fingers under her chin, his knuckles tipping her face toward his. Lydia watched his face, anticipation striking a chord of forbidden excitement. Lowering his head, he touched his lips to hers. They were warm and firm. Her eyelids drifted shut. His breath fluttered on her cheek; hers stopped.

She knew then, at the touch of his gentle lips drawing her breath away, that there was something more. Something more than choosing a husband because of convenience or suitability, more than marrying a man because of his particular faith or lack of it. This feeling, this soul-deep feeling of rightness when Jakob's mouth moved over hers in a questioning, first-taste kiss, proved it. Her breathing resumed, irregularly, like the beating of her traitorous heart.

"You're the only woman I want to marry, but...if you don't want me, I'll leave you be."

Lydia's heart leapt in her chest. She fought the desperate urge to grip his shirtfront and cling to it for all she was worth. *Don't leave me here!* The singles dormitory loomed like a black-shrouded prison. When everything had been weighed and considered and worried over, her heart allowed only one answer.

"*Ja,* I will marry you." The soft words surprised them both. In the moonlight, in front of God and plain enough for Jakob to see, she smiled in pure elation, the weight of the past weeks replaced by an unexpected buoyancy.

Jakob placed his palm along the side of her face. "I'll be a good husband, Lydia."

"I know." *Husband!* The word, and the intimate way he said her name, stirred something to life inside her. Husband. His hand held her head still. For a breath-stealing moment, she thought he was going to kiss her again, but he released her and ran the hand through his moon-kissed hair. "I must tell my father," she said.

"I'll go with you."

Lydia would have preferred to wait another day, but Jakob wouldn't allow it. Though he'd been determined to convince her to marry him, deep down he'd half expected her to refuse, and he hadn't dared consider the possibility of losing her. That spontaneous hug, and her confident answer and smile, assured him she wanted to marry him. This unspoiled woman with the angelic face wanted to be his wife!

He wanted to embrace her, squeeze her forever and carry her away before Etham could manipulate her. But he knew the importance she placed on facing her father.

Inside, their footsteps muted by thin carpet, Lydia led the way to her father's study. Etham glanced up from the books on his desk. "You are no longer welcome here."

"I'm not here for your approval." Jakob stood stiffly at Lydia's side, a few protective inches ahead.

Lydia raised her hand plaintively. "Please, Father. May we sit and speak civilly, like Christians?"

He composed himself visibly, positioning himself in his leather chair. "Speak."

Lydia perched on the edge of a straight chair. Jakob pulled another close, hoping his nearness would encourage her.

"A decision I have made that will greatly displease you, and I regret that. If there were another way I would have it so. I want to marry Jakob."

Jakob savored the hard-earned words, knowing how difficult they were for her to speak, loving the fact that she meant them.

A vein stood out on Etham's forehead, and he gripped the edge of his desk with white knuckles. He glared venomously at Jakob. "How dare you take my daughter from her home!"

Jakob opened his mouth, but Lydia jumped to his defense.

"He is not taking me away. I go willingly, no matter what. The choice of how difficult this will be is yours. I wanted to tell you, to try to make you understand—"

"Enough!" His fierce shout silenced her. Black, black eyes bored into hers. "*Sie Gott*, if you stop now you will serve only a fair probation, and—"

"*Vater*." Lydia's voice was soft, tortured. Were her heart and soul the same? Something tender tore inside Jakob. Could he ever make this up to her? "I will marry Herr Neubauer."

"You will give up home, family, everything for this... *Outsider?*" He spat out the word as if it were bile.

Lydia lifted her chin, as though willing her voice not to quiver. Etham made it sound as if she were throwing her life away. Jakob's heart skipped a beat. Her father was wily. He knew how to bend her. Jakob wanted to shove his fist down the man's throat, but Lydia had to do this herself, her own way. *Stand firm, darlin'. I'll make it all worth your while, I promise.*

"His home will be mine. I do not give up my family—"

"You will! You will be no more welcome in Accord than he is. If my words have missed your heart, hear God's words. 'Be ye not unequally yoked with unbelievers.' "

The nine o'clock bell rang. On the street, the crier led the chant. "Another day hath ended...." At home her brothers and sisters were tucking themselves into their cots, and down the hall from them her grandmother lay on her cot.

Lydia forced herself to envision the tiny, sterile rooms of the singles dormitory, to imagine lying on a cot night after endless black night. No husband, no children, no home. Life *here* would be hell!

She looked into Jakob's pale eyes. With his unwavering blue gaze, he willed her to stand firm.

It's my decision.

The freedom was heady. Exhilarating. All her life she'd waited for it, longed for it. She steeled herself and spoke from her heart, as her grandmother had admonished her to. "I repented, but God didn't remove these feelings. I will marry Herr Neubauer."

A flicker of anger—or was it hurt?—leapt into her father's eyes and then disappeared. "He has blinded you. Evil often disguises itself in handsome clothes."

"Jakob is not evil."

"The truth falls on deaf ears." Deliberately he closed every book on his desk and made a neat stack of them. "If you live outside the Lord's will, you are not welcome here. You forfeit what would rightfully have been yours. The bride box, the wedding quilt, the dishes, all of it. The *Mitgift* belongs to Rachael. She is now my eldest daughter."

Pain knifed through Lydia's chest, cutting off her breath and her sense of belonging. She would take nothing into this marriage—not her father's blessing, not God's blessing. Not the delicate china dishes that had been carried over from Germany by her great-great-grandmother.

"I will talk with Herr Neubauer alone," *Vater* said.

Distraught, she studied her father's familiar features. He would not meet her eyes. Numb, she stood.

Jakob walked her to the door. "I'll come for you in the morning. Unless you'd rather go with me now."

"*Nein.* I will tell my family goodbye and be ready."

Jakob closed the door and turned back to Etham. "You'll be sorry for that."

"Not as sorry as you!" Etham thundered. "Your punishment will be a thousandfold for taking an innocent!"

Unstirred, Jakob stood before the desk. "I'm shakin' in my boots."

Etham lunged to his feet. "I am aware of what you want. She is young and beautiful, and you have had unholy thoughts since the first time you saw her."

"Is the way you treat Lydia the way you think I should treat her? You slice her off the family like a wormhole on a tomato. I respect her. I'll provide and care for her and make her a decent husband. I've waited long to choose a wife. I'm not gonna do anything to ruin her life or mine."

"You have a few years on her in age, *Meier* Neubauer," Etham said, stressing the farmer's title as if it were an insult. "But you are far ahead in carnal knowledge. She is pure. Innocent. She has never been exposed to a coarse, worldly man driven by his own lusts. Your desires are unheard-of, unseemly! She will be obedient and meek, because it is our way, but she will never share your crude desires. She will be revolted. Remember that!"

Etham's words nicked Jakob's confidence. He shook his head slowly. "You can't keep her here. Accord isn't a prison."

"I will pray for her to see the light. You will regret this, Herr Neubauer. She will never adapt to your life."

Jakob turned and walked to the door, then paused with his hand on the knob. It was too late to turn back, even if he had wanted to. Lydia had taken a stand against her father. She had defended *him* against her father's insults. Lydia had chosen him. She was his now. Praying he deserved her confidence, he looked back at the man. "We'll prove you wrong."

The following morning, Jakob gripped Lydia's arm above her elbow and assisted her ascent onto the sprung buggy seat. Not once did she look back. Her feet had carried her down the footpath to where the springboard, hitched to the team of horses, awaited. Holding herself in control, she smoothed and adjusted the deep blue skirts of her best dress over her lap, checked the already precise bow of her Norman cap under her chin, tugged the jacket front of her close-fitting spencer together and then—and only then—did she turn her head.

Jakob clucked to the team. They leaned into their harnesses, jerking her backward with the motion. She caught her balance and snapped her head forward.

The horses drew them swiftly past the rows of Lombardy poplars lining the street, and her mind focused on the wagon wheels rumbling over the evenly paved brick road. This was where she had dreamed of sitting, high on the seat of an Outsider's buggy, off to see sights other than those she'd seen all her twenty years. She should be ecstatic. She should be anticipating a grand adventure. Why, then, was her heart breaking?

Grandmother had been overjoyed at Lydia's decision. She'd assured Lydia repeatedly that she'd done the right thing and told her not to worry, Rachael and *Mutter* would take care of her. And they would. But a part of Lydia stayed behind in that tiny room. She felt like a traitor for leaving, guilty for the choice she'd been forced to make.

The few people on the brick paths moved with purpose and paid them little attention; no one loitered on the streets of Accord. At this midmorning hour the Harmony Society had returned to their tasks after morning lunch and would work until the noon bell. No one would mourn her departure. Few would miss her. Her duties would be divided and assumed like water soaked up by a sponge. Like a lizard that grew a new leg to replace a severed one, her absence would barely be noticed. So unimportant was she that she left behind no void, no space that had been hers alone.

At the end of Church Street, Jakob slowed the horses for the turn onto Main. They passed the town store, the ropemaker's and the bakery.

Lydia looked long and hard at the bakery. The familiar warm smell of yeast and bread was a sad-sweet joy and she tried to take it all in at once, to remember it all just as it was this day. The sun pronounced the uniform redness of the buildings and nurtured the lush grapevines banding them.

They crossed the stream bridge and pulled up onto the road that would take them away from the colony. *This is real,* Lydia chanted inwardly to combat the dreamlike quality of leaving her home. *This is really happening.*

"Are you certain?"

She turned and found Jakob studying her, gauging her reactions and the very real threat of tears. Wild daffodils cascaded down a ravine past his shoulder, their golden beauty lost to her. *Was she certain?* The time for deliberation had passed. She had considered and reconsidered. Which pain was the greatest? Losing her birthright and her father's blessing? Not seeing her brothers and sisters? Deserting Grandmother? Or the emptiness, the void in her life, if she never saw Jakob again?

She studied the way his tilted hat shaded most of his face, and glanced at the enormous hands holding the supple leather reins, then back at his face. "I'm certain."

He relaxed visibly. Was it so important to him, then? He gave her a wry smile. "I don't know if I can make up to you everything you're leaving behind."

"I don't know if it's wise that you try."

She had known her father wouldn't relent. Even in the beginning, when she'd unreasonably hoped he would accept Jakob as a fellow German, she'd known deep inside that he would not—could not. His faith and commitment were strong, and he was not swayed by emotion. Not even when that emotion was love for his daughter.

Soon Accord was miles behind them. A wheel hit a deep, dry rut and bounced them in and out, jarring her teeth. She gripped the edge of the seat and turned to check on her meager belongings in a tiny corner of the springboard.

"We'll be stoppin' in town for necessaries. Think of what you'll be needing." Jakob seemed to sense her appraisal of those possessions. He flicked a deerfly from the rump of one of the horses with his whip.

Her spirits revived at his words. A town! Alert, she sat straight on the seat and studied the narrow, meandering road for as far as she could see.

Necessaries. She mulled the word over. Anything she had ever needed had been provided by the colony. It was a matter of pride for the tailor or shoemaker to note when someone needed an article. Since belongings were shared, shabby or worn-out clothing reflected on the whole. Children were not only reprimanded by their parents for scuffing shoes or ruining clothes, but by their classmates and playmates, as well, since all was community property. She had never wanted for anything. Necessities were shared, and tastes were Spartan.

Jakob's family undoubtedly had everything they needed to cook and keep house. What more would there be for her to concern herself with? Instead of voicing these nervous thoughts, she asked, "What town?"

"Butler. We're almost there."

Lydia immediately drew her attention to the small buildings ahead, and a flutter began in the pit of her stomach. *A town!*

Few of the unpainted wooden structures were over one story tall, and the main street was nothing but dirt, which blew up in clouds of dust under the horses' hooves, but to Lydia the sight was astounding. Were there people in all those buildings? she wondered. What were they doing, wearing? Fascinated, she scanned the shops and offices, reading their identifying signs. A livery, an eatery and a clothing store caught her attention. Wooden troughs stood in front of buildings with railings. Jakob drew near and stopped the springboard.

He tied the reins to the brake handle and leapt over the side with an ease of motion surprising for a man his size. He took a small bucket from under the seat, filled it with water and let each horse drink. Only after putting the pail away did he turn to her and raise his hands.

Lydia wavered, uncertain of his intention and hesitant about those huge hands coming in contact with her person on the street.

"Stand and lean out. I'll lift you down."

Tense, she stood, automatically sweeping the wrinkles from her full skirt. Her hands hovered in the air, as if about to play a melody on an invisible piano.

Jakob cocked his head up at her, squinting into the bright sunlight, waiting.

Leaning forward from the waist, she redistributed her weight. Jakob seized her waist firmly and effortlessly, and lowered her to the boardwalk. As quickly as he had grasped her waist, he let go and took her arm.

The imprint of his strong hands seared her ribs, but their footsteps ringing on the boardwalk distracted her. A few storefronts away, he ushered her through an open doorway into the dim recess, a potpourri of sights and smells assailing her senses before she'd taken more than a few steps. Jakob strode noisily across the dusty board floor and approached a counter.

A tiny, aged woman on the other side of the menagerie of notions peered curiously at Lydia through gold-rimmed spectacles. "Never seen you afore, miss. New here?"

"Elsie, meet Lydia Beker. She's going to be my wife."

The old woman's brows shot above her spectacles, and she pursed her pruny lips before she gave a curt nod. "Don't say! Right nice ter meetcha. Gotcher se'f a fine catch here, missy." She cackled, apparently unperturbed that her question had gone unanswered. "Be all ya kin do ta keep 'em Neubauer boys full a vittles and in clean dungarees."

Lydia deciphered her words slowly. Jakob touched her arm. "I'm gonna pick up some things in back. Look around. Elsie, help Miss Beker with anything she wants, while I give Ned an order."

Lydia raised her hand, as if to call him back. Her voice stuck in her throat. Feeling more vulnerable than she ever had in her life, she watched his broad back disappear. She lowered her hand.

What would she say if he came back? He was a stranger to her, too.

Chapter Six

Lydia turned to orient herself in the cramped, overcrowded room. Each inch of floor and wall was stacked in a haphazard display of every imaginable—and some never imagined—items. Stingy paths wound between barrels, boxes, crates and bags. Never had she eaten anything not grown or raised in Accord by the Harmonists. She knew who milled the grain, who harvested the vegetables, who dug the potatoes, had helped with those tasks herself on occasion. Where had these foods come from?

Stacks of stiff dungarees, rows and bolts of innumerable fabrics, ribbons and lace littered countertops and shelves. Unusual hats with ornate trims, hats of every size and shape topped a loft cabinet, dust apparent on their brims. Never had she worn anything not made by Accord's tailor or shoemaker or hatter. Her incredulous gaze took in rope, harnesses, tools and an assortment of unnameable items hanging from nails and pegs in the ceiling beams. In awe, she fingered a length of yellow satin ribbon.

Jakob sauntered over to her side. "Like that?" His tawny hair held a ridge where his hat belonged.

"It is pretty."

"Want a yard?"

She looked at the trim skeptically. "Whatever would I do with it?"

"Wear it in your hair."

She gauged his sincerity. What kind of woman or occasion warranted the adornment of ribbon? "I don't—"

"Elsie, a yard of this yellow ribbon. What else?"

She lowered her face in embarrassment, having no idea what he expected of her, or what, if anything, she needed that she didn't already have. Neither did she comprehend the cost of material things, never having had occasion to know value in dollars and cents. "I know of nothing," she said.

"Look at me."

She did. That betraying muscle in his jaw twitched.

"I promised I could provide for you, and I can." He led her to a counter displaying a variety of jars and bottles in dozens of shapes and sizes, the labels decorated with flowers and fancy script.

Lydia followed like an obedient child, uncertain of his expectations, yet understanding that his pride was involved.

"Annette and Peine have these notions litterin' their dressing tables. Isn't there something here you want?"

She read a few labels. Cold cream. In a jar? What kept the cream from turning sour? Toilet water. One groomed with this tainted-looking water? "I have no dressing table," she stated, relieved of having to make the decision.

Jakob shrugged his broad shoulders and led her to the yard goods. "How about calico for dresses?"

Who sewed these fabrics into garments? she wondered. The few dresses she'd been rationed would be serviceable for many years. However, if it pleased him, she wouldn't deny him, even though the purchase was an extravagant waste. *"Ja."*

"What color do you fancy?"

There were colors and materials she'd never seen. "Never could I decide. Please select."

From the bottom of a pile he withdrew a soft, pale yellow material decorated with tiny white flowers in delicate chains. Another stack yielded a vivid green cotton, and at her smile he added a sheer white muslin. The hovering Elsie approved his choices, too.

"Can you find trim to go with the green?" he asked.

Lydia nodded at the wide, snowy-white eyelet held against her green dress material. Elsie chose thread and inquired if Lydia wanted needles, bringing a card from under a counter. The dawning realization that *she* would be expected to create garments out of these supplies terrified her. What if Jakob knew how few abilities she possessed? Jobs in the colony were specifically assigned. She was a baker. Nothing more. How could she tell him?

Purchases stacked on a counter, Elsie figured the debt on a slate, and Jakob added a paper-wrapped bar of lavender soap to the pile.

He paid with coins counted from a leather pouch and carried the wrapped bundle out the door, adding the package to the assortment of bags stacked in the springboard.

Lifting her by the waist, she grasped his corded forearms and balanced herself. Looking down into his face, she was disconcerted by his charming smile. Beneath her fingertips, his arms didn't tremble beneath her weight. She marveled at how long he held her suspended without growing tired. At last, almost reluctantly, he stood her in the springboard.

The ride to Butler had taken nearly three hours, and the stop at the mercantile another hour. The day's anxiety had taxed Lydia. The horses leaned into their harnesses, and her back and neck ached with the strain of holding herself upright against the lurch and sway of the wagon.

"To your farm how much farther?"

Jakob withdrew a long object from behind the seat: yellow pleated fabric half covering a wooden handle. A white ruffle with limp fringe adorned the handle side. He pointed the object at her. "An hour or so."

Accepting the proffered gift, she contemplated it.

"It's a parasol."

"Oh."

He shifted the reins to his left hand and took the parasol back. He knew the secret, and the yellow material blossomed into a saucer-shaped shade on a pole. He held the parasol at an angle that prevented the burning sun from reaching her. "Your nose is pink."

She accepted the gift this time with greater appreciation, rewarding his thoughtfulness with a gracious smile. She'd never had anything of her own before. Something brand-new, and purchased with her in mind. In delight, she watched the fringe bob and sway with the wagon. "Thank you, Jakob."

He grunted and gave the horses his attention.

More farms fell behind them on the last stretch of road. Green and yellow stretched ceaselessly, graduating into softer hues, line behind line. They crossed a swollen stream, and the cool spray the horses hooves threw up was a glorious, welcome relief. The water was clear and flowing, colored pebbles and tiny darting fish visible in the sparkling sunlight. Her senses were filled to overflowing! She'd waited so long! She'd imagined the rest of the world so many times, she'd been half-afraid that reality wouldn't meet her expectations. If only she could share the wonder of it all with her grandmother.

Her stomach lurched as she anticipated arriving at Jakob's home. *Please, allow them to like me,* she petitioned God. *Help me get through this day.*

As far as her eyes could see was more land, sky and wildlife than she'd ever known existed. The sun, in all its radiant glory, tasted like freedom.

"Beautiful it is." Heat and weariness forgotten, she caught Jakob studying her impulsive reactions, and her cheeks burned hot.

The unhurried road led past a tiny whitewashed church, its steeple housing a bell.

"That's where we'll get married."

She stared long and hard. The church was one-sixth the size of the church in which she had attended services three times each Lord's day since she was a week old. *Wherever two or more are gathered . . .* Size was irrelevant.

The road became noticeably smoother, less jarring. Grass grew as high as the wagon wheels on both sides of the roadbed.

They topped the rise, and the Neubauer homestead lay beyond. Her home now. The horses, Gunter and Freida, obviously knew they were home before she did, and stepped up their pace.

The horse barn was the dominant building. The house stood two stories tall, with pillared porches on three sides and a stone chimney. Behind were a small log house, a privy and several outbuildings. Fields to the south and west showed varying shades of growing corn, grain and hay. Obviously the Neubauers owned acres of rich, fertile land and worked them well. Three men meant no hired help.

Lydia felt as though she'd traveled thousands of miles to another continent, as different as this was from the sequestered colony of identical buildings she'd left. Jakob slowed the team at the house. No grass or flowers grew in the yard, or anywhere near the house. Chickens ran squawking from the horses, who pranced impatiently, eager to get to their feed.

A small gathering appeared on the shaded porch, and two tall men advanced down the stairs. Lydia recognized Jakob's father on the porch with the women.

Jakob bounded from the wagon seat, then turned and extended his hands. Rather than let the moment grow awkward, Lydia stood on rubbery legs, her stomach tied in knots, and leaned out. His widespread palms spanned her waist, lifting her easily to the ground. Her legs threatened to let her fall, but Jakob kept one strong arm wrapped around her waist. *Lord, allow them to like me.*

"Lydia, this is my brother Franz. Anton you've met." Like Jakob, they were large and fair, with gregarious smiles and huge, callused hands.

Franz, the tallest and with the sharpest features, had sparkling blue eyes and sideburns riding the angle of his square jaw. His eyes smiled when he did, and he immediately reached for her hand. "Welcome, miss." He fished her bags from the back of the wagon. "I'll take these up for you."

Anton had darker eyes, deeper-set, more contemplative. He smiled and greeted her. "Pleased to see you again."

Anton led the team up the center drive. Jakob took her elbow and led her up the stairs onto the cool porch. "You remember Pa."

"Herr Neubauer."

"Happy to have you here, *fraülein.*" Johann's seamy face crinkled into a smile much like those of his sons. Instinctively she knew she would feel comfortable with this man.

Without waiting for an introduction, a russet-haired young woman came forward and took her hand. "You must be hot and tired. Come have a cold glass of lemonade. I'm Franz's wife, Annette, and I guess you've met Peine."

Peine wore her bright golden hair in an elaborate puffed style and amply filled out a shiny pink dress. Lydia had never seen the color on anything other than a flower. The garment had a tight bodice and frothy lace standing up around a revealing neckline. Peine ran her gaze over Lydia's clothing and cap in a manner that said she found them lacking. She smirked, and entered the house.

Lydia didn't have time to dwell on her disturbing rejection. Annette led her past a large room jammed with clusters of furnishings. Peine sat near Nikolaus, who played on the floor.

Jakob at her elbow, Lydia followed Annette past furniture, lamps and decorated boxes. Framed pictures hung on every wall. Each table surface was littered with odds and ends, from shells and doilies to figures of small animals and children.

"Here, sit and take off your bonnet." Annette pulled out a kitchen chair and scurried to fill a glass. Something in Jakob's manner must have alerted her. She paused, pitcher in hand. "I'm sorry. I just want to make you feel at home, and I could do that with a lot less fussing."

Much of their language was peculiar, with a different rhythm, stronger consonants and quickly rolled *R*s. Theirs was an accent from a dialect Lydia had never heard. Annette spoke so quickly; Lydia hung a sentence or two behind.

Her eloquent eyes spoke a language of their own when she turned to Jakob.

"I'll carry your lemonade upstairs and let you rest. Franz took your things up."

"I'll bring water so you can wash," Annette offered, drawing a bucket from under the basin.

Jakob ushered her into an upstairs bedroom and placed her glass on a polished oak washstand. Lydia stared at the enormous bed. They would be married in three days' time, and would share this bed. An odd sensation fluttered in her chest, and jittery warmth seized her belly.

She turned to discover Jakob watching her in the washstand's oval mirror. Their eyes met. Something hot and unexpected passed between them, and she dropped her gaze.

"If there's anything you need, holler."

She nodded.

"This is my—our—room, but I'll be sleeping in the loft until . . . for a couple of days."

"*Ja.*"

"Lydia." He turned from the mirror and faced her. "I know this is hard. I want you to feel comfortable here." He looked at the toe of his boot for several seconds. "This is your home now." He met her gaze.

"*Danke.*"

"Want some help unpacking?" He gestured toward her satchel, near the door.

She shook her head, embarrassed at the thought of him seeing her personal clothing. "*Nein.*"

"Well, then." He pointed to a chest of drawers. "I cleared half the drawers for you. See you at supper."

She nodded.

Alone in Jakob's sunny, airy bedroom, Lydia slanted a glance at the astounding bed. In the settlement, everyone except babies slept on single cots. This bed was a piece of furniture, raised off the floor on posts six inches in diameter. Sturdy ropes visibly threaded in and out of holes in the oak footboard and supported a thick mattress that sprung back when she poked it. She peeled back the edge of the coverlet. What an enormous amount of work to create a place for sleeping! She sat on the mattress to test its firmness, then lay down and noticed there were small casings filled with feathers at the top of the bed to rest her head on. And—oh! The height! How strange to lie so far from the floor!

The ceiling was painted, and the walls were freshly papered. An enormous bureau stood against one wall. She couldn't resist jumping up and opening the drawers. Jakob's clothing lay in neat, folded stacks. She felt like a thief invading his personal property, and she quickly shut the drawer.

The small door set under the eaves drew her interest, and she opened it, peering first one way and then the other into a long, slant-ceilinged storage space. More clothing hung on a wire strung across one end. Trunks and boxes were stacked in an orderly fashion at the other. Boots and shoes, small kegs and cigar boxes lined the shallowest portion of the wall space. The tiny room was well lit by a floor-level window.

Whatever did Jakob need so many possessions for? A shiny new wire stretched taut between two nails caught her attention. For her clothing, undoubtedly. She hadn't a tenth as many garments as it would hold!

Annette entered with an enormous porcelain pitcher of water, linens and the bar of soap Jakob had purchased. Unwrapped, the soap gave off a delicate flowery scent.

A different world this was, emphasized even more by the first meal they shared with her. They ate in the enormous kitchen at an oak trestle table flanked by benches and spread with a bright red cloth. The fried chicken, potatoes and beans smelled wonderful. Jakob sat close beside her.

Johann nodded to Anton, and heads were lowered.

"Lord, we thank you for this day and this family. Thank you for bringing Jake a wife. We were startin' to worry. Bless our crops and lands. Bless this food You gave us to the nourishment of our bodies. Amen."

Heads bobbed up and bowls were being passed before Lydia realized the prayer had ended. She glanced discreetly from one Neubauer to the next. Johann was absorbed with eating his meal, but the others had difficulty controlling their curiosity and met her eyes occasionally. In Accord, supper was eaten in the assembly hall, the men and women separated.

Having eaten chicken only baked or boiled, she heartily enjoyed the rich, flavorful crust. She watched in amazement as Jakob and his brothers consumed piece after piece, piling the bones high on their plates.

Appetites sated, Annette whisked plates away and replaced them with bowls of heavy applesauce cake seasoned with nutmeg. Lydia declined the coffee Annette offered her.

While the men talked of the tools they planned to sharpen that evening, Peine shot Lydia a look of animosity. The open expression of disdain shocked Lydia.

Seated at the far left, Peine still wore the bright pink costume, evidence that she had not fried the chicken. Her baby, tied into a wooden high chair with a dish towel, squashed his portion of cake into a sticky mess on the scarred wooden tray. Lydia couldn't help but smile at his rapt expression as he drew circles in the goo.

"That's Nikolaus," Jakob offered. "He's something, isn't he? I can't look at him while I'm eatin'."

"He's a fine one to talk," Franz interjected. "The rest of us can't watch *him* eat!"

Anton chortled from his side of the table, and in the blink of an eye Jakob plucked a chicken bone from the red tablecloth and tossed it directly past Lydia's face. Franz intercepted the bone and took aim. Annette snatched it from his fingers and fixed a warning frown on her husband. "You'd better wash up. You have tools to work on."

The look Franz gave his younger brother said, "We'll finish this later." He stood and sauntered to the sink. Twirling the dish towel between both hands until it wound around itself, he snapped his wife on the hip.

Lydia watched in awe. She couldn't believe Jakob had thrown a chicken bone across the table! What an ungentlemanly thing to do!

As if sensing her disapproval, Jakob apologized. "I'm sorry. C'mon. Let's go sit on the porch."

"But the dishes—"

"Not tonight," Annette ordered. "You'll have plenty of chances to do dishes, believe me. Go on. Peine will help, and I'll join you later."

Peine stiffened and watched them leave the room. *Her* Jakob had brought another woman home! Obviously discouraging words had little effect on him. Lydia was a pathetic threat, however. Starchy as she was, she'd get a good look at these gauche farmers and run back to her church family. If not, Peine thought with a poisonous little smile, she'd point out the reasons why the woman was unsuitable for Jakob. She was innocent, naive.... She'd be easy to dislodge.

Jakob led Lydia through the house and onto the enormous porch that stretched across the front of the house and down one long side. Ushering her to a cushioned wooden chair, he excused himself. "I'll get more coffee."

Left alone, Lydia studied the yard in the twilight. The light from the windows added a faint illumination across the wide porch. There were no other houses for miles, no other people.

She felt quite small and alone. A rapid scratching sound caught her attention.

The sound grew louder, approaching from the side porch. The sound neared and stopped. Lydia stared in growing trepidation at the corner of the house.

An enormous long-legged, shaggy animal stared back at her. Her heart leapt into her throat, and she feared her supper would follow. Eyes glittering black, the snout-nosed animal sat on its furry haunches, its long, fleshy pink tongue lolling out the side of its grotesque mouth as it panted. The animal resembled drawings of wolves she had seen in books, but was larger, and a thousand times more intimidating.

Wondering what the chances were of escaping the animal, Lydia decided against sudden movement. Slowly she drew her feet up onto the seat of the chair. Moving an inch at a time, she stood on the chair seat. One eye on the wolf, she looked hopefully for somewhere to escape. She prayed Jakob would return, but at the same time feared for his safety if he did. The wolf watched her stretch one leg in a most unladylike manner, grasp a pillar for support, pull herself up and stand on the narrow wooden rail. The animal stood below her, its nails clicking against the wooden porch floor.

Round brown eyes stared down into deepest black.

The wolf easily lifted its front paws to the banister at her feet, rising to meet her. Lydia screamed in terror. Unaffected, it sniffed the toes of her shoes. Its long tongue darted out and tasted the leather. Heart pounding, she screamed again, the sound bloodcurdling even to her own ears.

Chapter Seven

"Get down, Jess!" At Jakob's commanding tone, the animal sat back on its haunches. A tiny sound escaped Lydia's throat, her only outward acknowledgment of Jakob's presence. Her eyes remained on the "beast."

"Come here!" The animal padded obediently to his side. Jakob stepped closer to Lydia, his wary gaze lifting a considerable height, since she stood four feet above him on the railing. She reached for his shoulder, but then snatched her fingers back.

"Lydia? Are you all right?"

"I— It—" she stammered.

"Jessie's our pet. She's a dog."

Johann, Franz and Anton appeared from the side yard. Annette and Peine stood at the corner of the house, drawn to the source of excitement, also.

Jessie rolled soulful eyes from one Neubauer to the other. Then, seeming to lose interest in the entire party, she thumped her tail on the porch floor and moved out her leg for a long scratch at her black-and-brown fur.

Searing heat spread up Lydia's neck and cheeks. They thought her a complete fool! How ashamed Jakob must be! "I—I am sorry. The d-dog frightened me."

She extended one foot to step down. The dog stood and took a step. Instinctively she grasped Jakob's shoulder.

"Jessie! Stay! She's curious. She won't hurt you." Disbelief must have been apparent on her face. "Anton, take her around back, will ya?"

For a startled moment, Lydia thought Jakob referred to her, but Anton climbed over the side of the porch rail and coaxed the wolf-dog away. Before the family dispersed, Lydia detected a mocking smirk on Peine's face.

Jakob took her hand from his shoulder, pulled her arm around the back of his neck and lifted her into his grasp. One muscled arm hooked behind her knee, the other wrapped around her back. He carried her easily against his hard chest, her eyes scant inches from his chin. Her breast pressed against his. She sensed him studying her face, and self-consciously lowered her lashes. Slowly, fingers lingering at her waist, he lowered her to the floor.

"You've never seen a dog?" He gestured for her to sit and seated himself opposite her.

"It looks like a wolf."

"You'll get used to her. She helps with the cows."

"*Ja?* What does she do?"

"Keeps them from straying when we're bringin' them in for milking."

"I can milk a cow."

"No!" He grinned mischievously and pretended to give her an amazed stare.

"I milked our cow every evening."

"Can you make butter?"

"*Nein.* That was not my job. The milk is turned in each morning—except our family's share. We requisitioned butter from the town store."

"I was only teasing."

"Why do you do that?"

"Do what?"

"Say things to mock."

"I didn't mock. I only mean to make you laugh, have a little fun."

They looked at one another, then away. His sense of humor was foreign to her. As he was. As his home was. Lydia studied the road she'd traveled. Long shadows of scattered elms lay across the drive in wavy lines, because of the grass growing up the center, where wagon wheels left it undisturbed. "My abilities are unimpressive. I wish to be useful."

"I'm impressed. I don't think Annette can milk, and I know Peine can't. It's a . . ."

"A what?"

"Well, men usually do the milking."

"Oh." Was it disgraceful to do a man's chore? She decided not to boast of her skills, if any. The things she'd learned to do might be inappropriate for her new life. She had a wealth of education, but her knowledge would be of little use to her as a farmer's wife.

Wife! In three days she would be *married* to this man! Her thoughts rushed back to the room upstairs, to the enormous high bed, and something wild burst into an enthusiastic fluttering in her chest.

Jakob leaned back comfortably, raised his long legs and rested his feet on top of the rail. His dungarees were faded but clean, and his boots, though worn, had been polished many times. His blue chambray shirt covered a broad chest; the sleeves, rolled up past his elbows, revealed muscle-corded arms with a pale covering of flaxen hair. The hair on his head was a shade lighter, and long, falling over the collar of his shirt. He had an animated face, grinning and guileless one moment, honest and attentive the next.

When had she ever pondered a person's appearance? Surely he had chores, like the others. "Am I taking you away from something?"

"Yes." His relaxed gaze turned to her, and he grinned. "Thanks."

Her heart did a reverse somersault. He always managed to say something confusing, and each time he did it reaffirmed how peculiar his thinking was in comparison to hers. He spoke more slowly, more clearly, than the women, and she was grateful for that, but understanding the words and comprehending their meaning were two different matters.

The sun had set nearly an hour before, and Jakob had escorted her into the parlor, inviting her to sit on a love seat. He settled beside her. Lydia didn't know where to focus her attention in the overstimulating room.

Annette appeared, her apron gone. She had changed into a printed navy-blue dress, tailored tight at her narrow waist with a pleated and embroidered white inset at the bodice. Her smile offered Lydia a welcome.

A low table in front of the love seat held a wooden tray, and Annette poured cups of steaming black coffee from a warming pitcher on it. It smelled like nothing Lydia had ever known. She accepted the cup handed her. She watched Jakob. He blew on the steaming liquid, took a tentative sip, blew again, then drank.

Following his example, Lydia did the same. Acrid and bitter, the drink burned her tongue. Annette settled herself in a stuffed chair near the fireplace. One or two at a time, the rest of the family migrated to the source of activity. Lydia declined when a fresh pot was passed, having barely managed to finish her first cup.

Jakob caught her stifling a yawn. "You're exhausted. Go on up."

"There's a well of hot water on the step-stove," Annette offered. "If you need anything else, just yell."

"Danke, und gute Nacht."

Good-nights echoed. Only Peine didn't respond.

As she directed her attention to mending the small shirt in her hands, Peine listened to Jakob escorting Lydia up the stairs. A spot of crimson appeared on the fabric, and she stared at the tip of her finger. Contempt diminished the physical pain of the needle's prick.

Lydia had made a fool of herself over the dog. Good. Jakob treated her like a child. Why couldn't he see her for what she was—a holier-than-thou fanatic? Her meek manner was so utterly convincing that the entire family was taken in. All but Peine. She'd locked horns with Lydia's kind before, and it would be a challenge to do so again. Lydia Beker would not fit into this family. She would see to it.

"What is that song?" Lydia glanced up from the potatoes she was peeling.

Distracted, Annette answered absently, "Turkey in the Straw." She dropped the knife she held and left the room abruptly, returning minutes later with a tissue-wrapped package.

"What is this?"

"Open it."

Carefully wiping her hands on one of the hemmed flour sacks the Neubauers used for kitchen towels, Lydia accepted the package. With great care, she unwrapped the almost translucent paper from a flat box. Slowly she removed the lid and folded back another layer of the same tissue. Inside lay pieces of stark white, daintily crocheted . . . She looked to the other woman for enlightenment.

"It's a lovely wedding custom. The bride wears something borrowed." Annette handed the pieces to Lydia. "The collar and cuffs are mine. They'll look stunning on your dark blue dress."

Lydia examined Annette's tawny eyes for anything other than generosity, but saw only kindness. Unspoken but understood was the implication that her drab blue dress, though still inappropriate for a wedding in the Lutheran community, would be improved by the dainty accessories. Lydia was many inches taller than Annette, and this offering was no doubt the only solution.

"I have another surprise, too."

Lydia followed her toward the stairs. On the other side of the doorway, she nearly ran into Annette's back. The other woman drew up short, saving herself from a collision with Peine.

The blond woman stood erect, her chin tilted in a defiant manner. Lydia stepped next to Annette. Peine's green eyes smoldered. She glowered from one woman to the other, resting with an eerie battle light on Lydia. Peine's gaze raked her from the tip of her cap to her shoes, without so much as a change in expression or a flutter of an eyelid. She made no move to step aside. Annette led Lydia around her.

On the landing, Lydia turned. Realization dawned. Peine had been standing on the other side of the doorway, listening to their conversation.

Annette's room was much the same as Jakob's, but embellishments made the space seem smaller. The bed was massive, but without thick posts. A wardrobe stood against one wall, round boxes stacked on top. An enormous embroidery hoop holding a half-finished pillowslip lay on a Windsor rocker.

Jakob had been correct. A dressing table, as he'd called it, adjacent to the window, stood littered with squat jars and tall bottles, combs and brushes, hairpins, buttons and beaded collars. The room had a powdery, floral scent, completely feminine. In contrast, Franz's dusty boots stood under the washstand.

A colorful quilt in a tulip design draped the bed. Annette picked up a frothy spill of elaborate lace. Three white combs were sewn into the braided white silk crown she offered. "Another tradition—something old. This veil was Franz's and Jakob's mother's. I wore it at my wedding."

Lydia allowed her to flutter the lace about her shoulders and arrange the veil on her head, but her cap prevented Annette securing the combs.

"I can fix your hair so the veil will stay."

Lydia stared at the white lace against her dark hair and dress reflected in the standing oval mirror. How different she looked! Occasionally she had glimpsed her reflection in the small mirror that sat on her grandmother's chest of drawers; never had she seen a full reflection. How wonderful she felt wearing the feminine accessory! "Is it the custom?"

"Every bride wears a veil, but few are this beautiful."

"I don't wish to embarrass Jakob. *Danke.* I will be pleased to wear the borrowed gifts." She removed the veil, and Annette placed it in a huge trunk constructed of dark wood with a carved heart-and-rose design at the foot of the bed. Lydia ran her fingers over the polished surface.

"It's my dower trunk. My father made it for me when I was nine or ten."

"You are fortunate."

"Do you know what a dowry is?"

Lydia's dark eyes filled with sudden tears. "I know."

Annette touched her arm. "Did I say something wrong?"

"*Nein.* You are kind." Struggling with the flood of tears, Lydia turned her face away.

Annette offered her a delicately scented handkerchief. "I'm sorry if I—"

"My own thoughts disturb me. I must remind myself that material possessions are unimportant."

Annette drew her to the high bed's edge.

She had given no thought to the enormous task before her, Lydia thought. Everything was so different! Torn from one way of life and thrust into another, how could she hope to fit in? How would she ever learn it all? What if she embarrassed Jakob? What if he regretted asking her to come?

"To this marriage I bring nothing," she said at last. "None of the things a man expects. None of the familiar things a woman likes to keep near. I have nothing to offer Jakob." She dabbed the handkerchief at the corners of her eyes. Temporarily burying her disgrace in the confusion of moving and settling in, she was unable to stifle the humiliation any longer. She'd been cheated by her father's denial and his refusal to accept her marriage. Alienated by her own people, she wondered if she *could* fit in, or if her awkwardness would be a disappointment to Jakob.

"Nonsense! I just met you, but I can see why Jakob chose you. Not for anything you carry into the house, but for what you carry inside. Here." Annette touched her own breast. "You're a beautiful person, Lydia, inside and out. You'll make Jakob happy. He didn't need a wife to bring things. What could he possibly need?"

Lydia managed a watery smile. What *did* Jakob need?

Annette touched her soft, scented cheek against her new friend's. "I'm glad you're here."

"I was afraid I would have no one to talk to. My grandmother was—is—my friend."

"Well, you have me now. And Jakob."

Lydia smoothed the handkerchief with trembling fingers. She would do her best. She would not let Jakob regret his proposal. She would not embarrass him. That she promised.

The morning of the wedding, Annette and another young farm wife, Charlotte, whisked Lydia into a tiny room behind the pulpit area. Annette coaxed her into removing her cap and letting down her hair.

Charlotte watched in delight as Annette transformed the wavy sable tresses with the aid of an enormous roll of dark, tangled hair—a rat, she'd called it—and smiled at the horror on

Lydia's face. "You'll have to start saving hair from your brushes and combs to make your own."

Lydia nodded, noting how the women used the rats to create rolls and add height. Charlotte wore her red-gold hair in a shiny twist, wispy curls cascading onto her neck.

Annette placed the billowy white veil on her sister-in-law-to-be and adjusted the already perfect collar and cuffs. She handed her a delicate bouquet of violets and rhododendron. Lydia didn't know whose hand shook more.

The pews were full on both sides of the tiny church, men and women sitting together. The sea of unfamiliar faces took Lydia aback. A gay assortment of hats—the costume sort, not practical daywear—adorned the ladies' heads. Reverend Mercer stood resplendent in flowing white robes, a bloodred stole hanging down the front. A huge, ornate gold cross on a chain lay heavily on his chest. In his hands he held a Bible, for which Lydia gave silent thanks.

Towering over the minister in a black suit, a pleated white shirt and a familiar string tie, stood Jakob. Lydia held her breath. His hair was freshly clipped and brushed back from his tanned face in sun-bleached waves. Easy smile lines appeared at the corner of each eye—he was a splendid-looking man. Hesitantly she released her breath and smiled into his eyes. The quavering organ music stopped.

The minister read a prayer, and the congregation repeated some of the lines. He asked the bride and groom to kneel and repeat the confession, leading them slowly.

"O almighty God, merciful father..."

Lydia's father preached on the Rappites' exodus from Germany. Her faith had been opposed to many facets of the church of Germany, this rite being one of them. She shuddered, imagining her father's reaction.

Seeing her slight trembling, Jakob took her slender hand reassuringly in his work-hardened one. His sky blue eyes rested on her face, and, at the touch of his hand, her heart flipflopped in her breast. This ceremony united them for life! There was no turning back.

Individually, they repeated their vows. Jakob first, his voice mellow-timbred and clear. "I, Jakob, do promise to love—"

How could he promise that? "—and to cherish you, to bear with each other's infirmities and weaknesses—" *Oh, would he be burdened with her weaknesses?* "—to comfort you in sickness, trouble and sorrow." *At least she never got sick!* "I do promise and covenant to be thy loving and faithful husband." His promise brought tears to her eyes and a lump to her throat. "In plenty and in want, in sickness and in health, for better or for worse, as long as we both shall live."

Lydia's softly accented voice brought a gentle smile to his lips with "to be thy loving and faithful wife." He placed a slender gold wedding band on her trembling finger. The minister pronounced them man and wife, and gave Jakob permission to kiss her—in front of the entire congregation!

Her shock must have been evident, for he tugged her close with the hand he still held, and pressed his lips against her cheek. The veil hid the contact from the congregation's view, and the crowd murmured their approval.

"I now present Mister and Mrs. Jakob Neubauer." Friends and neighbors stood and applauded. Mortified at the attention, Lydia lowered her head and allowed her new husband to escort her from the church.

Peine clenched her jaw until her molars ached. Anton took her elbow, and she screamed inside. Her beautiful Jakob kissing that—that plain, pious *dishrag!* How could he have married her? Try as she had, Peine hadn't convinced him that that large, dreary wallflower wasn't for him. She plucked Anton's hand from her arm and stepped ahead of him.

Within the hour, springboards, wagons and buggies dotted the Neubauers' dooryard. An area near the kitchen offered shade for tables and food, while a protected spot farther out was allotted for kegs—and a good portion of the menfolk. Before Lydia knew it, she headed a line, Jakob at her elbow. He filled her plate and led her to a blanket spread away from the crowd.

"Where did the food come from so quickly?"

"They've had it ready all mornin'," Jakob said. "These shindigs are the highlight of the season. Sharing food and friendship is important. We work hard, and we like to play hard when we get the chance. Wait until the music starts." He bit into a chicken leg and winked.

"Will they play 'Turkey in the Straw'?"

He grinned. "Is that a favorite of yours?"

"I don't know. I should like to hear it."

"Then you will." He tipped his cup at her. "Eat."

She picked at her food. Three young boys ran past them playing a game of tag, and frenzied barking echoed across the dooryard. Jessie, tied with a length of rope to a white pine tree, leapt on her tether. Lydia knew she was the reason the poor dog had been anchored to a tree for the past three days. "Jessie hates me."

"Naw, she just wants to play with the kids."

"May she?"

She watched him enjoy a slice of bread that had most assuredly not been baked by Annette. "You want me to set her loose?"

"I feel sorry for her."

"I think she'll stay clear of you, but just in case, you can always shinny up this tree." He tilted his head, awaiting her reaction, and learned she could stare him down. He shrugged his shoulders and loped down the decline. On one knee, he took Jessie's head between both hands and said something softly into her face. Jessie's tongue bathed his chin and jaw adoringly. He grinned and scratched her ears.

Loosed, Jessie raced after the boys, her ears flopping.

As the afternoon wore on, beer flowed through the men's steins and mugs and they chose teams for the games. When Jakob was drafted, Lydia stood on the sidelines with the women. Most of the ladies had exchanged their elegant hats for more practical slat bonnets, which kept the sun from their faces. Annette offered the use of her bonnet, and Lydia gladly exchanged the veil.

Jakob was one of the four men who formed a large square. Two men, one of them Anton, stood inside the square. "What are they doing?"

"*Mosch Balle,*" her sister-in-law replied, watching with anticipation.

Corner ball? The men outside the square tossed a hard-looking rubber sphere. Faster and faster the ball flew, until at times Lydia lost track of it. Men and children on the sidelines yelled. Abruptly a burly man threw the ball at Anton, in the center. Anton dodged; the ball bounced across the square and another player caught it. Again the ball whizzed into the center, where the second man avoided it. Again and again the men threw the ball, until it struck Anton on the shoulder with a solid thunk. He staggered. The crowd cheered.

Players swigged beer from their steins and began again. Lydia was mortified at the sight of Jakob standing as a target in the center of the square. His own brothers were tossing the hard ball back and forth, preparing to strike. She couldn't look away.

A forceful pitch sailed through the air, aimed high. Jakob twisted out of reach. The thrower left the field amid good-natured jeers. The players shot the ball between them until once again it was "hot." Lydia flinched at each attempt to strike Jakob. He ducked and dodged, but, inevitably, a well-aimed ball flew into the center and struck him on the thigh.

The farmers shouted wildly, laughing and making ribald comments concerning the groom. Jakob accepted a kerchief from Reverend Mercer and guided Lydia toward the tables. He drank a glass of tea, refilled it and drank again. She kept her lashes lowered.

Never had she seen rough play, or play of any manner for that matter. Never had she heard crude comments, or seen women moving among men as equals. Never had she watched uninhibited fun, heard genuine laughter, or known freedom and spontaneity in an inconsequential activity. How amazing! How forbidden and frightening!

"Something wrong?"

She shook her head and sipped tart lemonade from a fruit jar. Jakob wiped his face and neck and ran long fingers through his hair.

"Are you mad because I left you alone?"

"*Nein*, Jakob. I did not . . ."

"Go ahead."

"I did not like to see you hit."

He almost laughed, but caught himself. "We play *Mosch Balle* all the time. For hours, sometimes. It's harmless."

"Does the ball hurt?"

"Naw. Well, yeah, it hurts, but that's just part of the game." She sipped her drink.

He looked over the populated dooryard and lawn and tucked his fingers in the pockets of his trousers. "I won't play if it bothers you."

Lydia looked up and waited until his blue gaze flitted uncomfortably to hers. He would endure the men's teasing to please her? "Don't be foolish. You will play."

"I'll tell you what—I'll do my best to see that I don't get hit." She offered him a wry lift of one brow.

He tossed his head back and laughed.

The melodious sound insinuated itself into Lydia's heart. Laugh lines creased each side of his mouth and eyes, as she'd expected. She caught her breath and managed to look him in the eye. "I can see you do your best now."

Impetuously he took her hand. Her fingers were cold from the jar, and he kissed the backs of them. She didn't know how amusing she could be. He was pleased by his family's warm acceptance. He'd hurt for her when she left her own people. Everything was new and frightening, but she took it in stride, even her unexpected, though endearing, reaction to Jessie. He wanted to teach her everything, to teach her how to have fun and enjoy life. Although uncertain how to proceed, he swore he'd do his best to please her.

"We're going to be happy together, Lydia." Still smiling, he released her hand and enjoyed her blush.

It wasn't long before the musicians brought out their violins, dulcimers and banjos. Couples paired off for square dancing. Watching in wonder, Lydia tapped her toe. "We have only brass instruments in the colony. These songs are faster and lighter than hymns."

Jakob studied her lovely dark eyes.

"I thought music purely for worship. This is for . . ."

"For fun," Jakob supplied.

"*Ja.*"

"Are you having fun?"

Her eyes widened. "Am I?"

He took her hand. "Want to learn the steps?"

She shook her head. He led her around the dancers to where the musicians stood or sat on crates. They finished the song, and he took a violin from a gray-bearded man.

"You play the violin?" she asked as he tucked the instrument under his chin.

"Fiddle," he corrected. He tapped his foot and led the measure, the others joining in. She beamed with delight. "Turkey in the Straw!" Halfway through the song, he handed the fiddle back to its owner and took her hand.

"Do you know the words?" she asked.

"The words?"

She nodded.

"To the song? Well . . . yeah."

"Will you sing them?"

Shifting his weight from one leg to the other, he glanced around self-consciously and pulled her away from the musicians. He cleared his throat.

"Well, I had a little chicken
and she wouldn't lay an egg,
So I poured hot water up and down her leg!
The little chicken hollered,
and the little chicken begged.
Then the damned little chicken
laid a hard-boiled egg . . ."

She laughed out loud.

Jakob watched newly animated features light up her guileless face. The setting sun highlighted the gold flecks in her distracting eyes. Her abandonment revealed even white teeth, and her beauty tightened an unexpected coil inside him, bringing a smile to his face. This lovely, unaffected woman was his bride. Tonight he would sleep not in the hayloft, but in his own familiar bed, with his own unfamiliar wife. How long he had waited! Warmth, beyond that which the summer evening created, flushed his skin and seared his vitals. *Wife.* He had a wife. He prayed he was ready to be a husband.

Chapter Eight

Peine watched them, envy as green as her emerald dress coiling in her vitals. Lydia's laugh and Jakob's tender, adoring smile were knives in her breast. How could he look at her like that? She was nothing! Nobody! And he was the strongest, most handsome man on the lawn. Watching his long-legged lope, seeing how effortlessly he dodged and evaded the hard ball, emphasized more than ever how right he was for Peine. A man like that needed a woman who was his equal. She was satisfied to see a tiny, aged woman break up their absorption with one another.

"I swear, young Neubauer, you look as pleased as a hog set loose in a sweet 'atater patch!"

Lydia smiled politely. "You've come a long way from your store, ma'am."

Jakob couldn't help but grin.

"Weddin's a big to-do in the county. Nobody misses the gatherin' no matter how far 'tis. Good vittles."

Jakob looked pleased. He had finger-combed his unruly hair. His tanned face and neck glowed with perspiration. Lydia surprised herself by wondering what the skin beneath his damp shirt would feel like to touch.

Jakob touched her elbow and spoke to Elsie. "Excuse us. Thanks for comin'."

Dancers dipped and swayed in time to the music, stepping lively in individual pairs. The newlyweds watched from the sidelines. Jakob visited with a barrel-chested neighbor.

"Are you just going to stand there like a bump on a log?"

Lydia turned to Peine. "I beg your pardon?"

"It's a tradition for the bride and groom to dance together. I've never attended a wedding where the couple didn't dance the first dance."

Lydia glanced at Jakob, but he wasn't listening. "I do not know how."

"What did you say?"

"I said, I do not know how to dance." Several heads turned their way, and Lydia's cheeks reddened.

Peine snorted and fanned herself with her accordion-pleated fan. Her head had been pounding all day, the sun and heat intensifying the throbbing pain, the gaiety and festivities grating on her nerves.

"I thought as much. Tell me..." She waggled the fan under her uptilted chin. "What *do* you know how to do?"

Lydia was obviously flustered, and her gaze fell to Peine's shoulder. "I am a baker."

"Mmm..." Peine murmured with a distracted nod. "Did you make the dress you're wearing?"

"Nein."

"Mrs. Schelling is wearing a lovely dress. The blue shirt-waist with the silk braid? She's an excellent seamstress. Her daughter was, too." Peine shook her head in what she hoped was a pitying manner and fanned herself. "Sad."

Lydia ventured into the snare. " 'Was'?"

"Yes. Poor girl died. So young, too."

Lydia's expression grew tender, and Peine delivered the final thrust.

"Jakob was heartbroken. I don't think he ever got over it," she said in a conspiratorial whisper.

Wide, amber-flecked dark eyes beseeched her. "What do you mean?"

"Why, that's Sylvie's mother. Sylvie was the girl Jakob was going to marry. He did tell you about her, didn't he?" Peine flicked the fan closed and flapped her hand. "Well, water under the bridge. Forget I mentioned it."

Lydia sneaked a surreptitious glance at Jakob, who was listening to the farmer. Peine hid her smile. The dancers had dwindled. Many of the women were packing their baskets and crates. The party was over.

Jakob would sleep with this plain sparrow. Peine envisioned him beside her in bed, kissing her. Touching her. Resentment mounted, bitter and brooding.

Her thoughts harkened back to her own wedding night, and her initiation into intimacy. The night wouldn't have been solely an act of endurance if she'd married right. If the husband in that narrow berth had been Jakob.

"I trust your mother explained everything, and that you're not too frightened about the marriage act." She leaned toward her. "Some men are more demanding than others, but you don't have anything to worry about with Jakob." Peine smothered her desperate anger and willed herself to smile sweetly. Lydia might be here for now, but she wouldn't last long.

Thoroughly confused, Lydia started at Jakob's touch. Ashamed of her reaction, she refused to meet his eyes.

He gave a sidelong nod. "Time to say good-night."

The tables had been dismantled and their planks carried to the wagons. The evening had grown dark, and the children were tired and dirty. It was milking time, and those with herds had chores.

She took the arm he offered, and together they thanked, waved and accepted congratulations until only a handful of friends remained.

Jakob joined the men carrying lanterns to the barn, and Charlotte came for Lydia. Annette met them at the back door. "I haven't seen you for hours! Are you exhausted?"

Lydia was. Each of the other women carried a pail. They led her upstairs, into Jakob's room, and poured steaming water into a long, dark metal tub shaped like a coffin.

"We usually bathe in the kitchen, so this is a treat for you," Annette explained.

Embarrassed, Lydia accepted the towels and soap handed her, noting the other women's clothing. Charlotte wore a soft skirt in a vibrant shade of green, belted with a sash of the same fabric. Her blouse was snow white, with long, slender sleeves and a high neck edged with delicate filigreed lace. The front was a marvel of tiny tucks and pleats, each stitched into place with shiny white embroidery thread. A row of minute pearl buttons ran down the center into her waistband.

Annette wore another feminine dress with a tiny waist and a white embroidered bodice inset. Both women were lovely and fashionable, and Lydia felt like a mud hen in comparison. Immediately she was contrite. Such vanity!

These women had attended many weddings, seen many brides. Both had experienced marriage themselves. They knew what was expected of a woman. Had Jakob been embarrassed by her dress, her mannerisms, her social awkwardness? Would he find her inadequate tonight, too?

"Kind you both are." *Jakob had wanted to marry someone else?* Tentatively, she met Annette's tawny eyes and wished she could voice her fear and uncertainty. "I owe you much."

Annette touched her cheek. "You don't owe us a thing. Just be happy, and make Jakob happy."

Make Jakob happy. Lydia watched them leave the room. Laying the soap and towels on the washstand, she idly studied her reflection in the beveled oval mirror. Tall and incongruous, she looked and dressed nothing like the fashionable women she'd seen today.

Some men are more demanding than others. Nothing to worry about with Jakob. What did that mean? And how did Peine know?

Lydia pictured him, tall and agile, dodging the hard ball that afternoon. He was a large man, a man of physical strength and vibrant health. He had a loving family, a comfortable home, a prosperous farm and many friends.

Make him happy? She hadn't the faintest idea how.

Franz and Tom Simms sat atop a rail in one of the empty stalls. "Join us, Jake?"

They passed a jug of corn liquor, and he shook his head. "Aw, come on," Tom coaxed. "It'll take the kinks out."

"Nah. Doesn't settle too good with me."

Franz jumped down and hung the pitchfork he'd used on a hook. "He's afraid he'll get numb and miss out on something tonight."

The two of them laughed, and Jakob shook his head good-naturedly. He remembered the pails of milk near the barn door, and carried two toward the house.

The light was on in his bedroom window. Anticipation gnawed at his insides. She was getting ready for bed. Tonight, when he climbed those stairs and stepped into his room, he wouldn't be alone. Lydia was waiting. His wife. The wife he'd waited so long for. No longer would he lie alone and hear his brothers' hushed whispers down the hall. Never again would he simply dream of the woman who'd one day be his.

Etham Beker's taunts rang through Jakob's head. *She is pure. Innocent. She will be obedient and meek, because it is our way, but she will never share your crude desires. She will be revolted.*

He wondered what her hair looked like. He imagined her without her proper dress, crocheted collar and cuffs, dared imagine her without anything on at all.

He'd thought about it before. Oh, how he'd thought about it! That aspect of their relationship would fall into place, like everything else. He'd proposed, and she'd accepted. He'd brought her here, and they'd married. Now the time was at hand, and he was annoyed with this uneasiness.

Jakob shook off his misgivings. He wet two dish towels at the pump, covered the pails and set the buckets in the well until morning, when the women could get to them, and rejoined the men. He'd give her—and himself—a few more minutes alone. Now that the moment was finally here, what would she think of a man she'd seen scarcely a dozen times climbing into bed beside her?

How close was her father to being right?

Perched on the edge of the mammoth bed, a white satin sheet folded on her lap, Lydia idly smoothed the corner. It was the first gift she had ever received, and she'd hidden it beneath the clothing in her leather satchel. The precise knots and stitches of embroidered thread told a story of obvious care and love. Intricate roses and tiny doves winged their way into each corner, testifying to time and thought on her behalf. Over and over the question bubbled to the surface of her logical mind: Why would

Grandmother expend such energy on a sheet with a distasteful purpose?

Tears stung behind her eyelids at the thought of Grandmother's gnarled hands threading the tiny needle, snipping thread with her silver embroidery scissors and tying knots in acute pain. The night before leaving Accord, Lydia had watched those hands place the snowy-white satin in her own and seen them linger a moment too long, as if letting go were difficult.

"What is this?" she had asked.

Rose Beker had made her familiar, slow way to her rocker. "A maiden-sheet. A bridal cloth. In my family it was the tradition for the bride's mother to make a bridal cloth for her daughter. My mother gave me one just like it when I married your grandfather."

Lydia had unfolded the slippery fabric and discovered that the cloth was backed with white flannel. The material had fallen open to its full size. She'd blinked in surprise. The sheet was a third the size of a bed sheet, and square, with exquisite stitches at each corner. "Whatever is it for? It is much too small for a cot or a bed."

Grandmother had set the creaky chair to rocking and replied with candor. "For centuries a bride's purity was a necessary virtue. Among royalty, proof of her innocence was required. That was the sheet's purpose. After a time it became a tradition. And a convenience. The cloth protects the linens from being soiled on your wedding night."

Lydia had considered the implication, and a wary uneasiness had gnawed at her calm demeanor. Opening her eyes wide, she'd fought a sudden urge to drop the cloth like a red-hot skillet. "What do you mean? Soiled by what?"

The old woman had given her a tolerant smile. "There is a little blood the first time, child."

"Oh." White-faced, Lydia had imagined the snowy-white cloth stained with her own blood. She'd sagged onto the cot.

"Don't let your imagination run away with you, Lydia," her grandmother admonished. "Jakob is a gentle and sensitive young man, and he cares for you. It is simply a moment's discomfort which you will soon forget. But," she'd added with a meditative smile, "it is a lovely tradition."

Now under her still fingers the fabric was damp with perspiration. Lydia glanced down, her confidence wavering, her nerves taking over. She forced herself to stand, lay the sheet aside, peel the down tick and fold the sheets back. With steady hands, she spread the flannel-backed satin across the bed, pulling the top bedding over it.

Jakob's bed still seemed enormous and far from the ground. Even after having slept on it for three nights, she was unaccustomed to its size and height. She undressed and quickly bathed in the coffin-tub before donning her nightdress and braiding her hair into a long plait that hung down her back to her waist. Blowing out the lamp, she lay in the darkness and waited.

With the shade pulled, even the bright moonlight didn't penetrate the upstairs room. This was the latest she had ever gone to bed, and she missed the toll of the bell and the cry of the watcher.

Everything was different, but she'd known it would be. The marriage ceremony would have worked her father into a lather! But the games and joking would have brought smiles to Grandmother's wrinkled face, and her siblings would have swooned at the fried chicken and the pickles and desserts.

Staring into the darkness, Lydia folded her hands over her stomach. She had to relearn her entire life, and yet not compromise her beliefs. Could she juggle the two? Frightening, too, was Peine's hostility. What reason could the woman have to dislike her so?

Acclimatizing herself was a daunting proposition, but she couldn't turn back now. She'd made her decision. She was different, yes, but she was determined to learn and be accepted. Tonight she would give Jakob no cause to regret marrying her. She'd do her best, even if she had to grit her teeth. Oddly, remembering his kisses, his touches, she didn't think she'd have to. Against every teaching she'd ever known, she liked the touch of Jakob's lips on hers, his hands on her arm or at her waist, his unique scent....

In the room below, the back door closed soundly. Her heart fluttered, and her pulse quickened.

It was their bedtime custom, she had learned, for the last one in to bank the fires and lock the doors. There had been no locks in Accord.

Two sets of boots sounded on the stairs. One continued down the long hallway after low voices murmured good-nights outside the door. Her mouth went dry.

The door opened and closed, and lanternlight danced long shadows across the papered walls. Jakob rested the lantern on the high dresser before backing up to the wall jack near the door and removing his boots. One by one they hit the floor with a solid thunk. He sat on the bed and took off his stockings. From the corner of one eye, she observed him removing his string tie and shirt.

Lydia felt as though she were balanced precariously on the edge of a cliff. The least provocation would send her plummeting into space. Every panic-stricken nerve in her body screamed silently. His weight lifted as he stood and moved to the washstand. He washed with the warm water she had thoughtfully dipped before her bath.

Jakob blew out the lantern, and it guttered and spat. Thick blackness enfolded them, intense, formless. The unmistakable sound of him removing his trousers was followed by dipping and shifting as the mattress took his overwhelming weight. Lydia's heart thumped up into her throat. She prayed she wouldn't faint.

"What's this?" His voice held mild surprise, and she knew his bare skin had met the cool satin.

Her heart thrummed from her throat into her ears, and red blotches sprang up in the enveloping darkness. Her chest lurched, but she said simply, "A maiden-sheet. My grandmother gave it to me."

"What for?" Pleased that he was as ignorant as she had been, she barely noticed his bluntness.

"For...tonight."

"Oh." Apparently he wasn't as untutored as she, because he asked no further questions, but lay perfectly still beside her. She heard him swallow. The faint smell of firewood drifted across the pillows, and she knew he'd been the last one in, giving her time alone. Was it consideration for her modesty, or was he as unsettled as she?

"Lydia?"

She jumped at her softly spoken name, and immediately felt foolish. *"Ja."*

The uncertainty in her voice tore at him. A wife shouldn't jump at the sound of her husband's voice. He wanted to reassure her, to take her in his arms and gentle her like a frightened colt. He wanted to tell her they would learn this facet of their marriage together, that he had to learn to be a husband as much as she had to learn to be a wife, that they would discover the way together. His mouth felt as if he'd eaten a bucket of sand, and his arms rested like lead weights at his side.

They lay side by side beneath the coverlet and the awkward blackness. The only words that came to mind were those of her father—admonishing words, piercing Jakob's hopes more deeply now than they had the day they were spoken. He was afraid to go too quickly, afraid to impulsively rush in and frighten her. The soul-subduing voice rang through his head: *She will be obedient and meek. . . .*

Jakob lay thinking how small she was. Not tiny—in comparison to other women, she was tall. She was fragile-boned next to his strapping frame, and delicate-skinned. And innocent, so innocent.

Jakob hesitated, afraid of making a wrong move. The man was supposed to lead, to have confidence. He was almost certain she knew nothing of what was to happen. It was up to him to put her at ease and pave the way for her acceptance, but what did he know? The weighty responsibility clashed with desire that had escalated all day; his mind and body dueling for victory. He had to learn to be a husband. It was imperative they get off to a good beginning. He swallowed again, and wished he could see her face, tell her with his eyes how he felt. Words could never lend the emotion he wished to convey.

"Lydia," he said, forgetting he'd said it before. "What I feel for you is good. I want to share my life with you and make a home for us together. I want us to be happy. I'd never hurt you. Do you know that's the truth?"

She remained silent.

"Are you afraid of me?"

Her breast thumped erratically as though there were a wild bird trapped inside. Her hand, clamped on the edge of the down tick, cramped. "Not of you."

"But you're afraid?"

His sensitive question brought tears to her eyes. *"Ja,"* she whispered.

"Me too." His words hung in the cavernous blackness overhead.

"You?" she asked. Whatever did this imposing, steel-sinewed man have to fear? She needed to rearrange her thinking to imagine Jakob afraid of anyone or anything. His image, tall and solid, browned by the sun, came to mind. He'd even stood toe-to-toe with her father, facing him without flinching! "Whatever are *you* afraid of?"

Flat on his back, he directed his quiet words to the darkness above their faces. "That you'll hate me. That you'll learn to . . . that I'll be unacceptable."

A bittersweet drawing at her throat brought a lump bobbing up. Her cheek muscles contracted, and tears rolled down her temples into her hair. A confidence. Voicing his fear proved his trust in her, and she sensed he'd never before been so painfully honest with anyone. "Never could I hate you, Jakob. I chose to be your wife."

Her voice trembled. How strange that trying to reassure him comforted her.

His bulk shifted and he turned toward her, his breath against her face. "I think we're only nervous. It's probably normal."

She struggled to interpret the underlying message in his words. "This is—uncommon for you, Jakob?"

His voice, when he rediscovered it, was no longer quiet. "Of course!" The words shot out before he caught himself. "What'd you think? I sleep with women all the time? I waited for you."

She stumbled over her next words. "I do not know—I just thought—I thought, since you are an Outsider, that . . ."

"That only Harmonists have morals? That all men are alike and can't control themselves?"

She'd made him angry. Mortified at his bald words, she regretted having doubted his integrity. *Was* that what she thought? *"Es tut mir leid, ich verstehe nicht—"*

"I can't understand you."

"Sorry, I am sorry. Forgive me—"

"Oh, Lydia." He groped until he found her hand at the edge of the tick and drew it to his face. "There's nothin' to forgive. Let's not argue over something as special as this." His lean cheek, beneath her palm, was warm and decidedly firm—a wondrous new sensation. The slightly rough texture it had taken on since his morning shave was discernible as his jaw moved against her fingers when he spoke. His thumb guided her wrist in his easy grasp, and he turned his face into her palm. Firm lips brushed a kiss into her damp flesh, and a shiver ran up her arm into her shoulder and spread throughout her body. Her senses thrummed.

The lengthy caress changed hues, and his tongue slipped out to taste her petal-soft skin. Her hand jerked in his gentle hold, and a gasp escaped her lips. She slid her hand to his warm neck, and Jakob lowered his face and kissed her cheek, as sweetly as he had after the reverend pronounced them man and wife. "Thanks for today," he said into the damp hair at her temple, his breath summer-warm.

A great swelling emotion radiated, sweet and calming, until she lay content in his arms. She knew then, without a doubt, that she could learn to love this man as a wife loves a husband.

His breath fanned her cheek. He kissed her mouth... lightly...reverently...encouraged by the way she relaxed against his chest.

Through the fabric of her nightdress, he found her breast, his large palm unmoving, learning her shape and size and the beat of her heart beneath. Lydia lay perfectly still, not daring to move and forgetting to breathe. At last he moved his fingers and, with a tentative exploration, discovered her texture beneath the cloth. He brushed the sensitive skin, and her nipple puckered beneath his touch. Her involuntary reaction shamed her.

His breath on her skin was hot and rapid. *Walk in the spirit and ye shall not fulfill the lust of the flesh....* Since God had created humans male and female, this act must be necessary, she thought. Lust was the sinful aspect.

"Do you want me to stop?"

"*Nein.*"

Uncertainly he sought the hem of her nightdress, his fingers grazing her skin and sending shivers skittering along her legs. He inched the fabric upward until she shifted her weight to assist him, her heart racing. His hand brushed her bare thigh, and she jumped.

"It's okay."

"*Ja.*"

"What do you want me to do?"

"Whatever must be done."

"I don't want to hurt you."

"I am prepared."

"But you're shaking."

"So are you."

"Tell me if I hurt you."

"It is over quickly." She fervently prayed her grandmother was right.

Chapter Nine

He obeyed and lifted himself above her, his body heavy, his skin warm and electrifying. She held her breath, and he engulfed her with his bulk, his hard strength taking on a life of its own in the dark. His hair-roughened knee urged her soft thigh aside. Unfamiliar stimuli quickened her senses. After twenty years of touch deprivation, she responded with breathless anticipation to every inch of his skin against hers. Jakob was exhilarating, a fiery intoxicant she needed to indulge in.

Her blood pounded at an alarming rate, and her heart cracked against her rib cage. He nuzzled her ear, and gooseflesh skittered across her shoulders. Her hands found no safe place to light, so they fluttered in the darkness before cautiously lowering to his back. His heated flesh burned her palms, and she gasped a tiny noise of surprise and revelation. Nothing had prepared her for this. Nothing could have.

She wanted to melt in his heat, to be consumed by his strength and weight. Her taut body quivered expectantly; an entire lifetime of self-control and passivity warred inside her. "Is it all right to want this?"

Slowly Jakob raised his head.

She hadn't realized she'd said the words aloud.

She has never been exposed to a coarse, worldly man driven by his own lusts. Etham Beker's words rang in Jakob's head. His attempt to penetrate her body lost its drive. Lydia needed time. Time to get to know him so that she didn't feel she'd done this important thing with a stranger. Or a brute.

He made a strangled sound deep in his throat and pushed himself away. Falling back on the cooled sheet, he flung his arm over his head, the knuckles of one hand rapping the wall.

"Jakob?" she whispered, voice trembling.

"Sorry. I just can't," he replied raggedly. *Pure... innocent... obedient and meek... will be revolted...* Jakob squeezed his eyes shut and fought the crazy urge to seal his hands over his ears. She was everything her father said she was... touchingly naive... submissive... and frightened.

He'd frightened her. Silently he petitioned God not to allow Etham Beker's predictions to come true.

"Was it... is it me?" she asked. "Something I did?" *Something I didn't know how to do that I should have? Oh, God, no. Don't let him be disappointed with me! I'll try harder! Just let me know how.* Body quaking, her inadequacy tore at something vital, her ignorance rendered her more vulnerable than ever. Bruised inside, she ached.

"Hush." His huge hand swooped from the darkness and smoothed her hair away from her forehead in a soothing gesture. He drew the bedclothes up and tucked them around her. "It's been a hell of a week. Today was long and tiring. I know it wasn't easy for you. You're tense, and we need time to relax." He paused. "I can't hurt you."

She pinched her eyes shut, and he stroked her hair. Discovering the dampness at her temples, he brushed her cheek with callused fingers. "Did I hurt you?"

His unselfish concern was more than she could bear. Her ignorance and fear had robbed him of his right as her husband, yet still he pacified her. Shamed, she turned her face to the pillow.

He patted her shoulder awkwardly. "Hey... please don't." Leaning on one elbow, he kissed her temple. "Don't turn away. Forgive me?"

His gentling tone, more than his words, comforted her. Blackness surrounded them, cradling them in its concealing wrap. Jakob turned, his weight shifting and wringing groans from the bed frame.

What must he think of her? Was he concealing anger? Disgust? How did men and women go through with what they'd attempted and still face one another? No wonder Father Rapp had considered the institution of marriage unnecessary! Angry with herself, Lydia took her frustration out on the concept of marriage.

"Get some sleep. We've got our whole lives ahead of us." He rolled to his back, adjusting the tick around them.

Discreetly Lydia tugged her cotton gown down around her legs and nestled her cheek against the cool pillow. Jakob's form, next to her in the soft bed, was the greatest hindrance to relaxation; the absence of the bell tolling the hour, the intimate blackness and the unfamiliar house were nothing compared to his awesome presence.

Never had she shared a bed. It was not the Society's way. Never had she shared the warmth of a confined space or been near enough a man to detect the scent of his skin and hair, hear his breathing, touch . . . lie against . . .

The night was endless darkness painted with the uncanny memory of Jakob's skin, his breath against her ear, his lips on hers. His soft snoring, though barely perceptible, was as loud as gunfire because of its peculiarity. In time she drifted into a light sleep, waking often to orient herself and listen to her husband. Each time a knee or an elbow came in contact with skin, she was alert.

At dawn, she drifted off. The other side of the mattress dipped heavily, and Jakob stood, stretching.

Pale gray light sufficiently exposed him as he stood, and Lydia's curiosity overcame prudence. Large as he was, his body was supple and graceful; long legs, narrow hips and a solid waist flared up toward a tanned torso to his well-proportioned back and shoulders. He ran long fingers through his mussed hair and washed his face with the cold water in the porcelain bowl. Taking clean dungarees from a drawer, he stepped into them.

Lydia closed her eyes and sensed him as he neared the bed. A moment later, she heard him retrieve his boots and leave the room. Downstairs, the stove lids clanged and the back door closed.

The bridal sheet was a mass of shiny wrinkles, rumpled, but as pure a white as ever. Lydia snatched it from the bed, folded it and stored it in the linen chest, wondering how many of her ancestors had had only a few wrinkles to show after their wedding nights.

Peeling potatoes in the sunny kitchen, Lydia watched Annette punch down a puffed lump of dough while humming. A streak of flour graced her chin, and beside her apron four perfect white fingerprints accented her colorful skirt. Her sweet expression and the wordless tune captivated Lydia.

"What is that song?" Lydia poured water over the potatoes and set the enormous kettle on the stove.

Annette glanced up from the loaves she shaped. "Hmm . . . 'My Grandfather's Clock.' "

"Are there words?"

"Yes, of course, but don't ask me to sing them. I'm not as musical as Jakob." She grinned and smeared lard in the corners of a pan with her fingers.

Embarrassed, Lydia bent and retrieved a potato peel from the floor.

A few minutes before dinner, Peine arrived. She tied the baby into the high chair and set plates and forks on the table with a flourish. Ignoring Lydia, she merely acknowledged Annette's presence by allowing her space to carry bowls of food to the table.

The men arrived promptly and washed in turn at the kitchen sink. Last, Jakob slid onto the bench next to her.

"How was your mornin'?"

"Fine, *danke*. Yours?"

His eyebrows lifted at her courteous reply. "Mine was all right."

Franz jabbered to the baby, and Johann spoke to no one in particular about a stump he'd tried unsuccessfully to burn out.

"I helped fix the meal," Lydia said.

"Smells good." Their elbows bumped as they had at breakfast, when she'd tried to ignore his closeness. Now she had no choice but to look at him. He gave her an encouraging smile.

"You were up early this morning, Jakob." Peine's syrupy voice broke into their exchange. "Seems to me you might have taken the opportunity to sleep late. I'm sure no one would've minded.''

Anton's look could have charred the bacon, but Peine ignored it. ''Doesn't seem right for you to hurry off to do chores on your first morning as a married man.''

Uncomfortable silence brought heat flooding into Lydia's cheeks. She was mortified at the attention drawn to them. Everyone's thoughts had surely turned to the newlyweds' intimacy on their wedding night. Was there any way they could know that nothing had happened? Of course not. And even if they all thought things had transpired as they should have, she didn't know which would be more embarrassing.

''Jake?'' Johann nodded at his youngest son.

Jakob caught her hand and bowed his head. ''Lord, thank You for Your bounty on our table and in our hearts.'' He squeezed her fingers gently. ''We're grateful for Your loving kindness. Bless the hands that fixed this food, and bless it to our bodies in Jesus' name. Amen.''

Lydia looked at her husband. He released her hand and reached for the basket of rolls. Peine's indelicate comments were politely ignored. The family gave their attention to the meal.

The manner in which this family prayed disturbed her. They addressed God in a relaxed manner and the next moment resumed conversation with someone else. In one light, the regularity of their table blessings pleased her, yet in another, their casual treatment seemed indifferent. What must God think of their prayers? What must He think of her sweeping along with them in their rush to move from one activity to the next?

They seemed to think the hurry worthwhile. It gave them time in the evening to simply do as they pleased. No chores, no cooking or cleaning or laundry. She had believed since childhood that idle time gave Satan ground on which to stake his claim and work his wicked ways. When she voiced these fears to Jakob, he'd said he didn't think God had a problem with him taking time to sit on his porch and enjoy the fruits of his labors.

That night Jakob suggested they go for a walk. Crickets chirped, and a favorable breeze tousled his hair and kissed her skirts. They strolled toward the pasture where Gunter and Freida grazed. Sensing Jakob, the pair approached and leaned their heads over the wooden fence in greeting. Jakob spoke softly, scrubbing their thick necks with his long fingers. He walked a short distance, picked up fruit under a tree and returned. He extended his palm, and Gunter greedily accepted the apple.

He pressed an apple into Lydia's hand. "Come on, she won't hurt you."

Reluctantly she held it, following his example. He offered Gunter another piece of fruit. His hand curled slightly around the apple, and the huge nose lowered, the enormous flexible lips curled upward. The horse's long teeth closed over the apple.

"Go on, try it."

The other horse was waiting patiently. Timidly Lydia raised her hand.

"Nice girl," she managed, her voice unsteady. Freida bobbed her enormous head once before lowering it, and Lydia jerked her hand back, the apple falling to the ground. Freida rooted along the bottom of the fence with her nose.

Jakob's hearty laugh eased her discomfort. She retrieved the apple, saw the animal's baleful brown eyes rolled in her direction, and gave it another try.

She was given no time for hesitancy. Her husband stepped behind her, cupped his hand under hers and lifted. Higher, higher, higher, until the proffered fruit had her hand in what seemed to her great jeopardy. Struggling against his strength was useless. She could only watch the ponderous head lower, the gigantic lips open, the teeth . . .

No sound escaped her lips. Freida's muzzle, amazingly soft and delicate, brushed her palm. The beast chewed a safe distance away, and Lydia's heart beat again. As her body relaxed against Jakob's, she grew aware of the exact opposite reaction in his. He lowered her arm, but kept her hand encased in his. He wrapped his other arm securely around her waist so that the entire length of her body molded against his.

It was an intimacy she'd never shared, that she'd never known people shared. An intimacy he had every right to as her husband. This, and more . . .

He eased his hold until, though she was still within his lenient embrace, she could move away any time she wished. Against her shoulder blade, his heart raced. She remembered the disturbing touch of his hand brushing her leg in the enveloping darkness of his bedroom, his hair-roughened thighs against her skin, the searing heat, and his undeniable silken hardness.

The memory embarrassed and intrigued her at the same time, and she realized she wasn't as afraid of him as she was of her reaction to him. Her heart swelled as it always did when he was close.

It seemed they stood that way endlessly, neither of them wanting to pull away first, until Freida came searching. The horse nuzzled the front of Lydia's dress, pushing her backward. Jakob steadied them both, and they stepped apart. He retrieved Freida's other treat and fed it to her.

"You're no lady," he chastised, though the horse crunched unconcernedly.

Lydia raised her brows, temporarily misunderstanding who he was speaking to.

His mind was elsewhere. "Someday soon," he said with conviction, "we're going to have our own house. We'll plan it together."

"Our own house?"

"You didn't think we all intended to live together forever, did you?"

She guessed she had. She wouldn't mind a house of their own. She wouldn't have to suffer Peine's hostile looks. Leaving Annette would be another matter. She knew little about taking care of a household, and was afraid of failing Jakob. His expectations were lofty, and she didn't want him to regret bringing her here.

"Where will we move to?"

As if sensing her apprehension, he pointed in a westerly direction. "Only over the ridge. I'm not taking you away from here."

She looked at him, and then away.

"Don't you like the idea? We won't fit in one house with more children, you know. You can help pick a spot for our house. I'll build it just the way you want it. What would you like?"

What would she like? Lydia raised her hand and pressed her fingertips against her lips girlishly. She couldn't remember having been asked that question. Her hand fell back to her side. "May I have a flower garden?"

He smiled and leaned from the waist to pluck a long stem of grass and stick it between his teeth. "Anything you want."

Her own home? It seemed too good to be true! She recognized the prosperity of the land he worked, but, divided among the Neubauer men, how far could their profits go? "Is not a house costly?"

"I've been saving, and I might take a job."

"A job!" Strolling across the meadow, she stopped in alarm. Jobs were in cities! "Where?"

"A railroad. There are steel bridges going up all over Pennsylvania. There's time to plan, so don't worry."

If he went away to work, would she go with him or stay here? He tried to make light, but a knot of apprehension settled in her belly. She *would* worry! The Neubauers were not her family, and they would not take Jakob's place if he left. He was all she had. They barely knew one another, but already her security depended on him.

She was a fish trying to survive on dry land, and Jakob was her only means of survival. Suddenly she wanted him to need her as badly as she needed him. She lacked the instinct to know what she desired in their relationship, but the seed had been planted and she'd see it to fruition. The same intangible germ had inspired Grandmother to leave her parents and her assured life and cleave to her husband.

Whither thou goest... Lydia recalled her grandmother's frail voice reading from the Book of Ruth. If Jakob left, she wanted to go with him.

She turned guileless eyes on him, and Jakob caught his breath. Lord, she was beautiful, her delicate ivory skin the perfect foil for her rich, dark hair and eyes. Her expressions remained unguarded and charmingly youthful, enhancing her unique, naive appeal. Jakob experienced a primitive need to protect her, to wrap her in his arms and keep the world from touching her innocence.

Ironically, it was *he* she needed protection from! She'd been safely cosseted, sheltered from this strange, overwhelming world until he'd pitched her into it.

A needle of guilt pricked, the thread of conscience weaving in and out of his desire. He struggled to snip the nagging sensation. A clean, feminine scent clung to her. The soft, enticing feel of her skin through her clothing intoxicated him. She was natural. Chaste. She was his wife.

He faced her. Her head fell back to keep his gaze. Taking her shoulders gently, he urged her toward him until their lips met with heart-stopping reverence. With an almost holy purpose, he tasted her, aroused further by the knowledge that he was the only man ever to relish her sweetness. He deepened the kiss, gentling her with light caresses on her upper back until she relaxed against his chest. He withdrew slightly, his lips nipping hers. His teeth touched her lip briefly. He tasted her with the tip of his tongue, kissed her in enticing nips to the corner of her mouth and back in patient chains.

Lord, how he wanted her! He was as intrigued as the first time he'd set eyes on her. More so. Now she was his wife. The title ignited his blood.

He lowered his hands to her spine. She slid her hands under his arms and seized his shoulder blades, clinging with unexpected response. Her touch through his clothing strengthened his passion. He loved her taste, the feel of her soft breasts pressed against his chest, the way she stood on the tips of her toes to avail herself of his mouth. Never had he wanted anything more than he wanted to peel her dress away and touch his face to her skin. Smell her flesh, taste it. She taxed every ounce of restraint to the limit. Instead, he severed the kiss, pressed her head against his chest and remembered to breathe.

He had known it would be like this.

She hadn't.

Beneath Lydia's ear, Jakob's heart pounded erratically, his breath unsteady. She loosened her grip on his back, realizing she'd clung to him to keep from folding to the ground.

It was nothing like she'd anticipated. He gave to her unsparingly...lavishing...enriching...until she felt as pliable as dough. Her lips throbbed warm and wet from his kiss. A languid sense of privation buzzed within her vitals, and she regretted that he'd stopped. If only she could have had this bubbling glow the night before....

Leaning away, Jakob took her face between his hands, his affectionate smile flooding her with additional warmth. He hugged her against his broad chest, then released her and took her hand. They walked, neither of them noticing the sunset. Fireflies dotted fields that would sparkle like the night sky in another hour.

Jakob spoke again of the house they would build together, his voice wistful, yet confident. His excitement about the layout and the building was contagious. "Tomorrow we'll ride over the ridge and map it out. What d'ya say?"

"I say...I say it is Sunday."

"We'll go after church." They turned back toward the farmhouse, where long rectangular spills of light streamed from the parlor windows.

"In Accord—" She stopped. Perhaps he was sick of her constant comparisons.

"Go ahead. I want to hear."

"In Accord there are three worship services on Sunday, and we spend the remainder of the day doing chores."

He swatted at a mosquito on his wrist. "The chores are always there. Sunday is a day of rest. During planting and harvesting we work every hour of light until the crops are in. But that's just one season."

A day of rest! However did they pass the time without a normal day's chores? "Different it is here, Jakob."

"I know. But different is just different, not bad."

She glanced up, still tasting him on her lips, remembering his length pressed along her back. So far, different wasn't bad at all.

That night Jakob came to bed in the darkness. "I haven't courted you properly," he said in that deep, mellow voice for her ears alone.

"Nein?"

"No."

"How does one court 'properly'?"

"Well—" he paused, as if considering "—a couple does a lot of hand holding and moonin'—"

"What is moonin'?"

"Staring into each other's eyes and sighin'."

That brought a giggle.

"And then they move on to kissin' and huggin'—"

"That we've done."

"Are you going to let me finish a sentence?"

She giggled again.

"Are you being coy?"

"I think not."

He laughed. "I think not, either—too. Which is it?" On top of the down tick, he found her hand, and threaded their fingers together. "By the time they get married, the couple knows each other. As well as they can without actually . . . being married. They get a chance to share likes and dreams."

"Jakob?"

"Hmm?"

"Did you not share dreams with me tonight?"

They lay side by side, hands clasped, talking into the darkness. "I guess I did. What about you? What've you dreamed about?"

Lydia took a relaxing breath. A Harmonist was not encouraged to dream. Thoughts other than the educational or vocational were unnecessary. Her father did the thinking and planning for the colony.

"Come on, didn't you ever want a handsome prince on his trusty steed to carry you off?" he teased. "Or did you imagine finding the pot of gold at the end of the rainbow?"

"That is ludicrous. A rainbow has no beginning or end. It is not physical, but a reflection."

Silence.

"Jakob?"

"You've got me there."

"Where?" His laughter was a deep baritone rumble that brought a smile to her lips. "What is so funny?"

"You." His hand tightened on hers, and the mattress dipped dangerously, rolling her toward him. He wrapped her shoulder in his arm and pulled her against his softly matted chest.

Lydia inhaled his clean male scent. Did her lack of common knowledge actually amuse him? Living in Accord, had she missed out on something other women, women like Peine and—and Sylvie—inherently knew?

"A dream is something you've always, always wanted. Isn't there something?" His deep whisper rasped behind her ear.

She closed her eyes, and a shiver rippled up her spine. Of course there was something she had always, *always* wanted— one of the reasons she had chosen to marry him and leave her family. "*Ja.* There is something."

"What?"

"A baby."

Chapter Ten

His breath caught. Under her ear, his heart thrust instinctively. His hand on her shoulder caressed gently. "I want children, too, Lydia."

"*Ja.*" Strength radiated from his arms and chest, and she remembered him carrying her from the burning bakery, knew the ease with which he could lift her from a wagon or force her hand to a horse's mouth. She recalled him tall and agile, dodging the *Mosch Balle* during the game, scoffing at the idea that a blow from the ball was painful. She recognized the controlled strength within the gentle man, and knew he could take her if he chose. She knew, too, that she wouldn't resist if he did. Wished, in fact, that he would.

He didn't.

He stroked her shoulder through her nightdress, snuggled her close and left her wondering.

The next morning's worship service consisted of a congregational confession, words of inspiration from Reverend Mercer and singing. Oh, the enthusiasm with which these people sang did her heart good! Most of the hymns were familiar, and those that weren't were easy to follow in the hymnal Jakob held for her. She stood or sat at his side, whichever the service called for, and heartily joined in. On the high notes, when others backed off, heads turned at the spine-tingling volume coming from the otherwise inconspicuous young woman. Jakob smiled proudly and held her hand.

At dinner he sat with his thigh pressed significantly against hers.

"These are delicious! What are they?" Franz took an extra helping of the side dish, a buttered cross between noodles and dumplings.

"*Spatzle,*" Lydia replied.

"Don't recall ever havin' 'em before." Johann took the bowl from Franz. "Sure are tasty, *fräulein.*"

The others murmured agreement.

Lydia blushed under the family's compliments, at last hopeful that she might fit in. "*Danke.*"

Jakob winked at her.

"Some of us watch our figures." Peine made a production of distastefully pushing the *Spatzle* around on her plate with a fork. "They look greasy."

"Don't pay attention to her," Annette advised Lydia after the men retired to the front parlor and Peine disappeared, as was her habit. "When she learns she can't get your goat, she'll quit trying."

Lydia balanced a stack of plates on the table's edge. "I don't have a goat."

"*Ach!* I always forget. I mean, get you riled. Upset you. Hurt your feelings. She does it deliberately, you know. Try to ignore her insults."

"Why?"

"Why ignore her?"

"Why does she behave that way?"

"I can't begin to imagine. All I know is, don't take anything personally. She resents the whole world."

"How sad."

"You amaze me." Annette gave Lydia a tender look before rapidly shaving off a chunk of acrid-smelling soap into the pan of hot water. "Let's hurry with these. Franz promised me a trip to my sister's this afternoon, and I don't mean to miss a minute of it."

Lydia carried the scraps to the chickens.

Jakob hailed her on her return to the house. "Are you ready to go?"

"Go?"

"To see our house. Or do you have something pressing to do?" He quirked a sandy brow.

"No. I mean, *ja!* I will be ready in a moment."

Minutes later, she waited on the wide drive from the barn, enjoying the frivolous shadow of her parasol as she twirled it. The sound of hooves approached. She turned, seeing her husband astride Freida.

"Where is the wagon?"

"Franz and Annette are taking it to her sister's."

"How will we travel?"

He patted the folded blanket behind the saddle. The makeshift seat seemed a great distance from the ground. "You want me to ride up there . . . on the horse with you?"

"Got any other suggestions?" Guiding the reins to one side, he walked Freida to the porch. "C'mon. Climb up here and get on behind me. You can balance on the rail."

His eyes, shadowed by his hat's brim, teased her daringly. She looked from his face down the drive and back, considering how badly she wanted to go.

Hesitantly she climbed the porch steps. She stared Freida in the eye for a full minute. The horse seemed to size her up in return.

Jakob stifled a chuckle.

Resolutely she collapsed the yellow parasol and handed it up to him. From a chair she stepped onto the railing, balancing against a column. Taking Jakob's hand, she used her other hand to gather her skirt. Throwing her leg over Freida's back, she landed clumsily behind him. He steadied her with one hand and soothed the animal sidestepping uneasily beneath them. Lydia wrapped her arms around his waist, clinging to him while he spoke to her in the same calming voice he used with the horse.

"That's not so bad, eh? You'll get used to it."

It wasn't so bad after all. The horse carried them both effortlessly, covering ground with an easy gait. She had an excuse to wrap her arms tightly around Jakob, to discover his incredibly muscular torso and smell his clean hair and clothing. Once he glanced down and covered her hand with his, and happiness inflated her heart, bringing a smile to her lips.

A quarter-mile west, they came to a grassy clearing, bordered on the south by a natural windbreak of pyramid-shaped hemlock. Here and there, stately maples dotted the landscape. Jakob tied the horse to one and helped her down. His hat swept the scene in a proud arc. "What d'you think?"

"It is lovely!" Her thighs sore from the ride, she barely managed to keep up with his long-legged stride across the level ground. "Where is the house?"

"About here, with a well there. A stream runs right back of those trees."

"And the garden?"

"There. Full sun all day."

"And a flower garden I'll plant along the entire side of the house. The chickens will have to stay in their pen."

He caught her against his chest and hugged her soundly. "I'm sure you'll keep the chickens in line."

Leaning back, she looked up into his vibrant blue eyes and realized the enthusiasm they'd just shared. She wanted to share more with him . . . so much more . . . if only he'd let her. "It's a beautiful place for a home."

"I've been here a hundred times, but it's never looked as good as it does today. It's beautiful because you're beautiful."

"You are teasing me again?"

He squeezed her shoulder. "Lydia! You're beautiful! You were the prettiest woman in church this mornin'."

Frowning, she pulled from his embrace. Her father's accusing words reminded her that he believed Jakob to be motivated by lust. An unfamiliar warmth pooled inside her. Dark, hot thoughts of her sensitized skin brought a quivering burst of pleasure. As good as Jakob made her feel, was it right to encourage his preoccupation with her? How vain she was to enjoy his flattery! "It is not important what we look like. All that matters to God is on the inside."

Allowing her to wander away from him, Jakob plopped down in the shade of one of his maples. "Like a potato, eh? Not much to look at on the outside, but they sure taste good when you're hungry."

She smoothed her skirts and sat near him. "Now I know you are teasing me."

"Am I? Maybe I'm just hungry." He pretended to take bites from her ear and jaw, and she laughed, then pressed her palms against his shoulders to push him back. No match for his strength, she tumbled to a reclining position on the soft grass. Jakob's healthy, sun-kissed face loomed over her, the maples' silvery green underleaves forming a sun-dappled canopy above his golden head. The laughter died in her breast.

His eyes rested on her parted lips. "Are you sayin' you would've married me if I was a toothless, leathery old critter with squinty eyes?"

She watched his mouth as he spoke. Instinctively she sensed underlying desire tugging at them like a magnet. There was something almost wicked about Jakob's mouth. Something dark and mysterious, and completely intriguing. She was afraid he wouldn't kiss her. "There is nothing wrong with squinty eyes."

He moved toward her and kissed her eyelids, her brows and her temples. Her heart pounded so fast the leaves were a silver green blur above his head. His lips touched hers in a feather-light brush.

A thousand fireflies fluttered against her ribs.

"I'm...glad...you're...not...toothless," he said, punctuating each word with a kiss. "How would you eat Annette's bread?"

The smile she almost formed was cut off by a kiss burned against her lips. Slanting his mouth over hers, he adjusted his weight on an elbow and framed her jaw with his hand.

Sensing her hand at his side, he lifted and spread her palm against the side of his face. Her fingertips caressed his lean jaw, his coarse sideburns and his amazingly soft earlobes.

"Oh, Lydia..." He pulled his mouth from hers and dropped his face into the hollow of her neck. Minutes later, he kissed her prim collar and rolled onto his back, folded his hands behind his head and gazed up into the arching branches. Beside him she sat and tucked stray wisps of hair under her white cap. What was he afraid of?

Last night he'd savored the delicate lavender scent of her hair against his face, stroked the diminutive bones beneath the warm satin skin of her shoulder and recalled the many nights he'd gone to his room alone while his brothers took their wives to the rooms they shared. He'd known a deep satisfaction. He wasn't alone anymore, and last night that had been enough.

Now he didn't think he'd ever get enough of her. But he was afraid. Much as he'd tried to dislodge the sapling of uncertainty Etham Beker had planted, it had taken root. Lydia's incredible naiveté, her unsophisticated outlook and her fresh delight in simple things, reminded him of her innocence at every turn.

He knew what he feared—she would be meek and yielding, because it was her character, but she would be disgusted, as her father prophesied. Jakob had hoped and dreamed and planned for marriage for as long as he could remember. Dreams of a house and family were based on their compatibility.

"Lydia . . ." he began.

Her forthright gaze met his.

"You need time to trust me. Time to feel comfortable." Even though allowing her that time was frustrating him beyond endurance.

"I trust you, Jakob."

"I guess you do." She'd come with him, hadn't she? "But I don't want to frighten you."

Their gaiety evaporated in the sunshine like dew on a hot morning. Both of them watched Freida cropping grass, lost in their own concerns.

He felt her touch his hand and turned it over to envelop hers. At last he stood and pulled her to her feet. "Time for milking."

A cool breeze graced the Neubauers', fluttering the sheer curtains at the long windows. The front parlor was full that evening. More and more Lydia understood the worth of the weekly rush to get through chores and have this time to spend as they chose. The family gathered in the cluttered room, the men taking turns playing a game with black and red wooden markers on a checkered board of the same colors.

Franz stacked wooden blocks on the floor with Nikolaus. She thought of her family doing ordinary things and wondered if Grandmother missed her. Did Rachael milk the cow in the morning? Nathan wouldn't let the flower bed go untended, she knew.

Annette sat near a lantern, crocheting a lace edge on a pillowcase. "Play for us, Jakob. Nikky, want to hear Uncle Jake play?"

The baby nodded his fair head. Jakob opened a case and withdrew his fiddle.

He played tune after tune, while Nikolaus bobbed and jumped, taking turns pat-a-caking with whoever struck his fancy. Johann picked him up and executed some fancy steps. Smiling, Lydia glanced at the happy faces surrounding her.

Then she saw Peine.

She'd worn the deep burgundy dress with puffed sleeves to church, and hadn't changed into work clothes like the others. The neckline left her pale collarbone and chest bare. Around her neck she wore a band of velvet, with a round piece of jewelry fastened at her throat. She wore her fair hair swept into a faultless coiffure under which Lydia knew nested "rats."

But it was Peine's emerald eyes that caught and held Lydia's attention. They flitted from one person to another in a hungry manner, as if she needed to fill herself with their faces and actions. The most unvarnished look was the one she gave Jakob as he played, her lips parting and her gaze devouring him. Apprehension tightened a fist in Lydia's stomach.

Peine's gaze flickered to Lydia, and the mask dropped over her features. She tilted her chin and smiled haughtily, but not before Lydia saw anguished emotion. Yearning.

And she identified with it.

Jakob replaced his instrument, and Annette hurried to make coffee. Lydia followed.

Pumping water into the metal pot, Annette sighed. "I guess we'll have the muffins left over from dinner with our coffee. Everyone has to be getting sick of the same old things. I know I am."

"I don't know how to do as many things as you, but I am willing to help."

"You've been a blessing in the kitchen already. Maybe between the two of us we can experiment with some of the dried apples from last year. It's such a waste to ruin them that I quit trying. Soon the peaches will be ripe."

"I can bake *Gefullte Krapfen* or *Apfelkuchlen*. Or do they like *Apfelbettelmann?*"

Annette set the pot on the step-stove. "What are they?"

"Tartlets."

She listened as Lydia described cookies and a fluffy baked apple dish and smiled broadly. "Oh, Lydia, that would be wonderful! I'm ashamed to say I never developed much skill at baking. My mother gave up and warned me not to marry a man with a sweet tooth."

Lydia regarded her curiously.

Annette laughed. "A craving for sweets."

Serving coffee and muffins in the parlor, Annette handed a cup of steaming liquid to Jakob. "What an excellent choice you made! Your wife can bake!"

Every male voice responded with appreciation.

"We know why he chose you, Lydia," Franz said with a teasing wink. "He couldn't choke down another dry muffin."

His wife ignored the taunt and sat beside him with a swish of her skirt. She slapped her hands on her knees. "You have a niche in this household, Lydia. If your pies are any indication, I can't wait to sample the rest. Tomorrow morning the bread is all yours."

Franz and Anton hooted their approval.

Embarrassed, Lydia scanned their jovial expressions. Everyone smiled but Peine, her look of resentment prominent.

"I'm sure you had more reasons for marryin' her than that, didn't you, Jake?" Anton lifted Nikolaus onto his lap. To the others he said, "He's lovestruck."

Anton batted his lashes and rolled his eyes comically, and Annette bit back a laugh. "He doesn't hear us when we talk to him. He forgets things. The other day he walked out of the barn and tripped over the skid he left there himself! His mind is for sure not on chores, and I think—"

"Nobody cares what you think, Anton," Jakob said, interrupting him. "You told me you were going to use that skid to move barrels, so I figured you'd taken it."

"You weren't listening, 'cause I told you I had to..." Anton's voice carried on, and Lydia realized Jakob wasn't amused. She glanced at Johann, but read no alarm on his face.

Jakob leaned forward on the small sofa. "Well, you know," he bit out, "when you're looking for stuck cows, it helps to search where the mud is. That cow would've been standing up to her rump if I hadn't started on your quarter. Where'd you think she'd be? Up a tree?"

"Boys, don't get into this right now," Annette told them calmingly.

Neither of them paid her any heed.

"I swear, Jake, you're so damned touchy, I think you're brain's addled. What've you done to him?" Anton asked of Lydia, an accusing finger pointed at his brother.

"Leave her out of it." Jakob stood. "In fact...leave *me* out of it!" He stalked out the front door, the screen slamming in his wake.

Lydia stared after him, stupefied.

Franz helped his wife collect cups and plates. Together they disappeared into the kitchen.

Inordinately pleased, Peine scooped up Nikolaus and pranced up the stairs, Anton following. Lydia had looked like a frightened rabbit when Jakob and Anton shouted. Peine had learned long ago that their bickering meant nothing. Any attempt to take a side during an argument brought out their fierce loyalty. They could say anything about one another, but heaven help anyone who got in the middle. The recollection gave her an idea.

She dressed Nikolaus in his pajamas and pulled him into her lap in the rocking chair.

"He should go to bed earlier, Peine."

"Your daddy doesn't want to spend time with you in the evenings, Nikolaus."

"That's not true, and you know it. You just use him so you don't have to be with me."

She rocked and hummed.

"This marriage is a joke."

"What did you expect?"

He studied her rocking his son. Her green eyes were jewel-like, beautiful but cold. He slept with her each night, woke beside her each morning, had created a child with her, but he'd never really known her. *I expected to live happily ever after.*

"You have what you wanted," she said, cutting into his thoughts.

He snorted. "Hardly."

"Did you want your son?"

"Of course I did." *I wanted you, too. A hundred years ago, when I still had hope. I wanted a woman to love, a woman to love me. Someone to share this life with. Now I don't know what I want.*

"Well, then. You have what you wanted."

Anton grabbed a dime novel from his dresser and fell back on the bed. There was no reasoning with that warped logic.

A star winked accusingly at Jakob as he stood at the corner of the old cabin behind the house. Okay, he'd let his brother's teasing get to him. He was human. He'd overreacted. But how much strain could a man handle? He'd been holding back for days now. Weeks. Years!

He'd waited an eternity for a wife. He'd been patient. Tolerant. Gentle.

How many days and nights could he endure? Was he trying to prove something by restraining his desire for her? Was he showing her how patient and sincere he was? Or was he trying to prove to himself that her father was wrong? He'd desired her from the first. He found her attractive and desirable. What on God's green earth was wrong with that? He'd waited for her. He'd married her. How much more honorable could a man be?

Unseeing, he passed the outbuildings, leaned against a gnarled oak and gazed across the backyard toward the house. Lovely Lydia. Innocent. Attracted to him.

A wife was a heady responsibility. A responsible husband would wait. He'd taken her away from her family and security. He didn't have the right to take her freedom of choice away, too. But he wanted her more with each day. The longing and frustration tore him in two. It would be easy to take her. She'd made it plain she wouldn't resist.

But he didn't want her that way, didn't want to merely appease his own desire without thought for hers. If her father was right, he couldn't bear her rejection.

Somehow he would wait. He had to.

Johann rocked in his chair.

Uncertain of what to do, Lydia turned huge eyes upon her father-in-law. "Shall I go to him?"

"Naw. Let him stew awhile, and don't look so all-fired scared. These boys of mine been fightin' worse 'n that for twenty-odd years, and nothin's gonna change long as they're livin' together. Brothers get into a ruckus now and then. It's nothin' to fret over, Lydia."

It must be all right, if he wasn't worried. She nodded.

"What does your family do of an evenin'?"

She drew a deep breath. "After the worship service, there are chores. The children do school lessons, and if there's time after that we read our Bibles."

"You too tired to do that now?"

Surprised, she shook her head. He searched a cluttered desk and returned with a Bible, its leather binding as well-worn as her father's. Lydia scooted across the love seat and sat near his rocker.

He patted the Book's cover. "It was Wilhelmina's."

"Jakob's mother's?"

"*Ja.*"

"What was she like?"

Faded blue eyes met hers. "*Schön,*" he said at last, remembering. "Beautiful. Small...lively...and her eyes were the color of the mornin' sky on a frosty day."

Johann gazed as though he saw her at that very moment. "She gave me beautiful children. Sons. All sons."

Lydia considered these men who placed such importance on physical beauty. "Was she young when she died?"

"*Ja.* Jakob was only ten when she died of the fever. Anton had it, too, but he was stronger, and pulled through." He rocked slowly. "She was so young...it seems like those years went by faster than the years since she's been gone." He glanced at her and shrugged. "Doesn't seem fair, does it, that it couldn't of been the other way 'round?"

Quick tears welled in her eyes. He had loved his wife very much.

Realization struck Lydia, and she sat straighter on the sofa. His conversation had been in an unfamiliar dialect, but close enough that she'd understood. "You speak German!"

His still-handsome face smiled easily, weathered lines creasing his cheeks. "It's good to have someone to use it with. My folks spoke German always. Wilhelmina knew 'nough to get her by, but her family spoke the language of the new country at home, so our boys didn't learn much." He opened his Bible to the Book of Psalms. "Next time we'll read from yours. I hope it's German?"

Lydia smiled and nodded. A familial warmth spread through her heart. For the first time since coming to live with the Neubauers, she felt a sense of belonging. The only person who'd ever put her more at ease was Grandmother.

God had answered a prayer. Perhaps He didn't look with disfavor at her marriage after all.

Chapter Eleven

Lydia stood barefoot in front of the washstand, wearing her long white cotton underslip. She studied her reflection in the mirror. God hadn't taken away her feelings for Jakob. He'd given her a friend.

She thought of Jakob somewhere outdoors, perhaps in the barn, drawing comfort from the warmth and familiarity of the horses, instead of coming to her. A primitive instinct told her that his edginess was due to her failure to overcome this physical obstacle. She was failing him.

She'd been incompetent in every area of their marriage so far. She couldn't cook or sew or dance. She hadn't even known what his dog was, for heaven's sake! What had she done right? She remembered the length of his body against hers, the rasp of his hair-roughened skin—so different from hers—and a languid warmth pooled in her abdomen. He wanted her. She knew it intuitively.

Absently Lydia drew the brush through her hair and divided the length into sections. She met her own troubled gaze. This must be the thing she could do to please him. It was her wifely duty.

Jakob entered the room. He didn't ignore her partial state of undress. After carefully avoiding her for days, he studied her. His gaze lifted and met hers in the mirror. He gave her a crooked smile.

She dropped the thick plait against her breast and watched him back up against the wall and remove his boots. He straightened and unbuttoned his shirt.

He dropped the shirt. "Why do you do that?"

She stopped wrapping the tie around the end of her braid. "Do what?"

"Weave your hair in that rope to sleep."

"I have always worn it this way. My mother and grandmother wear theirs this way. My sisters, too."

"Family tradition, hmm?" As was his habit, he carried the lantern from the top of his chiffonier and placed it on the washstand. He stood so near, she smelled woodsmoke in his hair. His anger seemed to have disappeared. He reached for the front of her slip, and she froze, fingertips gripping the washstand. He lifted the braid into his palm.

In the mirror she watched breathlessly as he held the plait of hair, measuring its length, stroking it with his thumb. With his other hand, he unraveled the piece of fabric she hadn't tied. He ran long fingers through her hair, a section at a time, higher and higher. Stepping behind her back, he loosened the hair at her nape, his fingers massaging her scalp, working out tension. When her hair had been freed, he speared his fingers to her scalp, spreading the dark tresses over her shoulders like a silken cape.

"I've wanted to see you like this." His black-velvet whisper sent her heart skittering in her breast like a wild bird. Their eyes met in the reflection—hers self-conscious, vulnerable, his somber, resolute. Strong hands continued stroking, contouring her shape through her hair, caressing her back, kneading her shoulders and neck. Languid contentment oozed through every cell of her being. She'd been deprived of human touch her entire life, and now she reveled in the honest pleasure.

He pulled her back against his length, and she closed her eyes. His rigid stance warmed her from her knees to her shoulders, and an apprehensive trembling began in her stomach and flowed outward until she feared her legs would refuse to support her. "Jakob."

"Hmm?" he murmured through the hair behind her ear.

A shiver rippled across her shoulder and down her arm. His warm breath tilted her world on its axis.

Jakob's heady attack on her senses increased her resolve with an almost frightening passion. He desired her. He'd chosen her over any other woman. She tamped down a sprouting of guilt that she should feel such pride. She would not let him down. "Will you kiss me?"

His hands stilled on her shoulders. His patience was worn beyond endurance. He didn't know if he could kiss her without wanting more. The texture of her fragrant hair, the scent of her skin, the feel of her woman-soft frame, assaulted his senses and inflamed his body. Holding back was the most exquisite torture he'd ever known.

She faced him. "Jakob?"

"Lydia, I don't know if it's such a good idea, what with you standing here like that, and—"

"Don't you want to kiss me?"

An internal flame lit his blue eyes. "I want to kiss you. And a whole lot more."

"Let's find out. Let me do this. For both of us."

His heart thundered against his chest. Though determined to wait, he'd come to her already inflamed, wanting. Her words intensified his desire painfully. Once he started, he knew, he'd never stop. "Are you sure?"

"I'm sure."

Jakob's pulse throbbed everywhere.

"Bitte."

The word was a solid punch to his gut. *Please.* He framed her face with his palms, spearing the hair at her temples with his fingers, and turned her face up to his.

She was his wife. She wanted him. He owed it to both of them to seal the vows they'd made, to discover the wonder of how marvelously they were created man and woman, to place the uncertainty and anxiety behind them so that they could work on other aspects of their relationship.

He kissed her with a passion that only hinted at the desire he'd held in check for so long. She slid her fingers inside his gaping shirt and flattened her palms against his bare chest. His skin quivered at her glorious touch.

With an impatient shrug, he slid out of his shirt and blew out the lantern.

Ignoring the fact that she hadn't finished undressing for bed, he tugged her restrictive underslip over her head. The stitches popped in the seams. Her satin skin sparked a flame beneath a mountain of kindling. He pressed himself against her long-limbed body, the tiny noise she made tearing at his gut and inflaming his desire at the same time. Her father's oppressive warnings loomed, but Jakob banished them from his mind, from his body.

He wasn't sure which of them led the other to the bed. Jakob removed his denims and pressed her against the soft mattress. "I've waited so long for you, Lydia."

She was soft, intoxicating. He needed her more than he needed to breathe. He kissed her mouth, hungry and urgent. Her hip was firm, slender. He caressed it, savoring the texture of her skin—softer than a newborn calf, softer than a baby chick. A shudder passed through her.

He was on fire. The scent of her body, the gasp in his ear, propelled him over the edge. She cried out when he filled her, and the sound brought him both pleasure and pain.

Jakob strove to purge himself, to drive her father from their bed and end her anguish quickly. She felt better than good. She felt wonderful—soft, warm, exquisitely tight and enveloping—and he'd waited so long. He hurtled toward an inescapable peak and, with a convulsive groan, clenched a fistful of silken hair and pressed his face hard against her jaw.

He shuddered and rolled to her side, his heart thudding against her shoulder. Too quickly, his thoughts cleared and focused. Oh, God, what did she think? Had he been clumsy? Probably. Had he hurt her? Obviously. Would she regret her quick decision to marry him? Dear God, he hoped not. "I'm sorry."

A clumsy silence enveloped them.

"Jakob?"

"What?" His voice was a rasp.

"Will I have a baby?"

He groaned again, this time at her ignorance. Did she think that was it? She'd suffered the indignity and earned the reward? "I'm sorry to tell you it's not that easy. It can take a lot of times."

"Oh."

The silence of the house buzzed in his ears. Through the open window, a cow bellowed for her calf. "Jakob?"

What now? "What?"

"I didn't find you unacceptable."

A painful lump swelled in his throat and refused to go up or down. She'd remembered his confession that first night. His fear. Unconvinced, he squeezed his eyes shut against the self-condemnation swelling in every cell and tissue of his traitorous body.

"I'm sorry," he whispered, knowing it wasn't enough, wishing he'd known how to make it better for her.

Later, he wondered how she could sleep. In abandonment, her hair fanned his pillow like a sleek skein. The first light of day cast its gray illumination, and he awakened after what seemed only minutes of rest. He turned, the stubble on his chin catching strands of her hair. He fingered the tresses, cool satin beneath his fingertips. She lay on her side, facing him, her hand curled palm up between them. One long strand of hair had fallen across her face and caught on her barely parted lips. Her skin was pink with the warmth of slumber, and her breathing was even and shallow. She was so young. So vulnerable. So utterly desirable.

She belonged to him. He knew at last the bliss of a man and woman's joining. And the knowledge only made him want her more. But what of her? What was her reaction?

His own selfish desires had taken her from her home, and placed her in a culture she knew nothing about. How could he hope to replace her family and their comfortable life? Did he have the right to push himself on her, too? She'd done it to please him, he knew that, and he'd been so eager to hear her suggestion, he'd needed little encouragement. How unfair that she had to suffer in order to fulfill the most sacred act of marriage. In order to get a baby.

The thought of her carrying his child made him hard and ready all over again. Guiltily the groom pushed his weight from the bed and stood, watching his bride sleep. He was gone before the first rooster crowed.

* * *

A whirlwind of bustling energy, Annette packed a basket with jars of vegetables, a tin of muffins and a baked chicken. "I'll be gone all morning," she said to Lydia, who watched from the sink. "Bitsy McKenna has been bedridden, and has no daughters to do chores. I'd like to stay and put things right, if you don't mind getting dinner alone."

"I'll take care of everything."

"Well, then," she said, glancing around, "I'll be off." She plucked her slat bonnet from the rack of hooks on her way out the back door.

Lydia boiled water and carried the heavy kettles to the washtub on the back porch. Shaving lye soap into the water, she swished it with a stick and refilled the kettles for the next tubful. A handful of garments went into the tub, the heavy lid was fastened down and she maneuvered the long wooden handle, working the paddle inside the tub.

Challenged by the task, Lydia worked the stick back and forth, back and forth. She would be proud to accomplish the task well and know that she was capable of assuming her share of the workload. Her arms ached into her shoulders and back as she fed each piece through the wringer and began again. The endless task left plenty of time for her thoughts to wander, remembering every detail of the night before. Her own fear and bewilderment . . . and then . . .

The perfect sense it had made.

How wonderfully she had been created in order to accommodate her strapping husband! Yes, it had hurt at first, as Grandmother had promised, but not for long . . .

She remembered the tension, the solid strength of his powerful body, and excitement bolted through her. Was pride at his uncontrolled desire for her sinful? The aspect of marriage she had been resigned to in order for God to give them children no longer seemed unpleasant.

Along with the sense of wonder billowed confusion over Jakob's reaction. He was sorry. What was the cause of his regret? What was there to forgive? In her ignorance, had she missed something important, something he understood and was displeased with?

Belatedly she thought of the satin sheet folded neatly in the trunk at the foot of the bed, and was relieved to launder the sheets in private.

She lugged the baskets of clothing and bedding to the line and hung them. Perspiration ran from under her wilted cap. Dampness circled under her arms. Her apron and dress were soaked to her skin when she encountered Peine at the kitchen door.

Peine ran a critical eye over the detestable creature. The sounds coming from Jakob's room last night had cost her a night's sleep. How could he want this bedraggled frump? Didn't he realize what he was doing to her? To them? The thought of Jakob's mouth and hands on this person lobbed hatred into her heart. Jakob would be hers, no matter what it took! Obviously she'd have to help him recognize his mistake.

She appeared cool and fresh, golden hair hanging in waves to her shoulders. Her gaze assessed Lydia's wilted form, and the smudges of stove ash on her cheek. Lydia prepared for an icy snub.

"I just settled Nikolaus for a nap. Would you care to take a cup of tea with me?"

Trying to suppress her surprise, she followed Peine into the cool kitchen and melted onto a chair. *"Danke."*

"Sugar?"

"Please. I haven't had tea since I arrived."

"These men like their black coffee, and we do seem to cater to their wishes, don't we? I keep a tin in the pantry. Help yourself whenever you'd like."

"Danke—thank you."

"Why do you always wear your cap?" the other woman asked as they sipped their tea.

"It's the custom in the community I come from."

"Does Jakob like it?"

She hadn't considered what he thought of her cap, though she knew her dresses were not as becoming as the other women's. "I don't know." She considered herself an embarrassment. "Does it make me look different?"

"Well, it does set you apart. Men like to see a woman's hair. It's one of our feminine attractions."

"Ja." Absently Lydia massaged her sore shoulder, feeling the ache all the way down her spine.

"Could I see your hair?" Peine's extraordinary green eyes scanned Lydia's cap. Lydia removed it and sat straighter as Peine came around the table. "It's lovely!" she crooned, her voice as sweet as the tea. "All you need is to learn to arrange it more fashionably, and it would look quite nice."

Peine always looked elegant and feminine, and if she was willing to make friends, Lydia was certainly more than ready. "Will you show me?"

"Sure. Let's run upstairs." Lydia followed.

Peine's and Anton's room was infinitely tidier and better organized than Annette's and Franz's. There wasn't a speck of dust or an item out of place. Even the crisp white curtains at the windows seemed immune to rustling by the late-morning breeze. Peine pointed out Nikolaus, sleeping in the cast-iron crib, and sat Lydia down at her methodically arranged dressing table. She plucked the pins from her hair, and it fell in lustrous waves.

"First of all," she instructed in a quiet voice, "you must learn to save hair to make rats."

"I know about rats."

Peine took her own brush and pulled it through Lydia's hair. It felt wonderful—the bristles against her scalp, another person's skillful touch.... Lydia's eyes drifted shut.

Peine experimented with a few styles, none of them pleasing her. With a finger under her chin, she studied Lydia. "I don't know," she said, disappointment in her voice. "It's too long and heavy to work with. Perhaps if it were a little shorter..."

Lydia considered her reflection doubtfully.

"The latest styles are fashionably shorter. Think how pleased Jakob would be if you looked like the ladies in Pittsburgh!"

Lydia knew she looked different from the Outsiders. Even her speech set her apart. Here with the Neubauers, *she* was the Outsider! If she fit in better, perhaps Jakob would be more pleased.

The deciding factor was the pleasure she imagined on his face when he saw her looking more like the women he was accustomed to. He would be happy that she was adjusting more and more to his world. "Do it."

A long time later, discarded lengths of hair lying on the floor around them, Peine curled a dark tendril around her finger and let it spring back against Lydia's temple. "Sylvie had beautiful hair, and she wore it down most of the time. Jakob always liked my hair like this."

Lydia met her eyes in the mirror.

"I was right, wasn't I?" Peine asked.

"About my hair?"

"About Jakob. I told you there was nothing to worry about. He's gentle with you. Treats you respectably."

Lydia's mind screamed silently, fearing what Peine might say or ask. Her chest constricted.

"He's a hell of a man. It's a shame you can't really appreciate him. Wives are respectable, and respectable women don't enjoy seduction."

Was that why Jakob had been sorry? What was her response supposed to be? Dare she ask?

Her mind reeled at the implications of what Peine had said. Sounds of the team came from the drive. Men's voices floated through the open windows. Lydia's gaze met Peine's in the mirror. Her heart slammed in her throat.

"Oh! I haven't prepared dinner!" In horror, she ran from the room, nearly tripping on the stairs before reaching the kitchen in a panic. She searched the pantry for the quickest thing she could put together. Voices in the side yard increased her alarm.

Franz was washing at the sink when she returned to the kitchen with a cured ham.

Jakob entered the room.

Ten feet apart, he and Lydia regarded one another. He barely surveyed her rumpled, stained gray dress. What caught his attention was her hair, unbound. She wasn't wearing the cap she was never without. He took a hesitant step closer. The soft arrangement of hair seemed out of character, incongruous with the unkempt condition of her dress. Another step, and a sick, sinking grief pierced his hungry belly. Hair that had once hung to her hips now barely reached past her shoulders. She had cut it!

"Your hair..."

She gripped the ham with white knuckles.

"What have you done to your hair?"

"I cut it. Do you like it?" She placed the ham on the table.

Ashamed, Jakob couldn't have felt more pain if she'd kicked his heart. Her hair. Her lovely, sensuous hair. "I wish you hadn't felt you had to do it." He hardened his expression to cover the hurt, and moved to the sink.

Jakob ate sullenly, refusing to look at Lydia. All morning he'd thought of nothing but the night before. Even now, with his brothers scattered around him, he experienced a quickening in his abdomen when he indulged in thoughts of marvelous dark hair spilling around her slender shoulders. The scent, the texture and the sight were stimulants, inflaming him beyond reason. No, he probably hadn't the finesse to understand how to make love to a woman. He'd undoubtedly been clumsy and unskilled. And she...

She had been so repulsed, she'd chosen to rid herself of the catalyst that had pushed him over the edge.

Jakob kept his eyes on his plate, not joining in the stilted conversation. Lydia picked at a slice of ham. The dark scowl on her husband's ordinarily pleasant face frightened her. His displeasure deflated another bubble of hope. Would she ever know how to please him? How to fit in?

Emotions rioted within her: shame at her inability to be a good wife, embarrassment that she had neglected to put out a simple meal before they arrived and had to watch them eat ham, cheese and milk for their noon meal. Annette always had a hot meal ready, but vanity had kept Lydia from her task. Silently she asked God to forgive her pride and selfishness. Fear that she was none of the things Jakob expected of a wife came out the victor. Exhaustion, too, took its toll, and tears threatened.

Johann finished his second sandwich and pushed away from the table, thanking her. Jakob and his brothers followed him out the door. Peine was the only person in good spirits. "I'll clean up. You go change," she offered.

Lydia took advantage of the rare opportunity. The hateful reflection in the mirror was more than she could bear. She hastily pinned up her hair and pulled on a clean white cap.

She had to get away. She needed some time to herself. Time away from this house and the contents and inhabitants that reminded her of her difference at every turn.

She walked in the opposite direction from the men and spotted a stand of trees beyond the outbuildings. It was a fair walk, and when she reached the shade she turned and looked back on the house and yard. The line full of clothes flapped accusingly in the warm breeze. They were probably dry, and she should be folding them.

Tears she'd held back during dinner erupted in a wave of anguish. She cried for fear that she was a poor substitute for the woman Jakob had really wanted to marry. She sobbed the frustration she fought at every turn, and somewhere during the sobs she cried out her homesickness for Faith and her grandmother, miles away. Had she done the right thing, coming here? Would Jakob grow weary of her incompetence and wish he'd never brought her?

Lord help her, she had enjoyed last night. She had enjoyed her husband's hands on her skin, the closeness, the incredible beauty of the way God had created her to be his wife. She craved him. His touch. His smell. She'd felt wonderful . . . wanton . . .

Jakob had been sorry.

Respectable women don't enjoy seduction.

She was obviously not a respectable woman. Jakob's reaction had confirmed her initial fears that wanting him was sinful. Had she lured him, knowing he wouldn't resist, and now he resented her for it?

In the shade of an ancient hemlock, she knelt and prayed out her anguish. Drawing strength from her Lord, she set off determinedly for the house. She couldn't do anything about her hair now. It would grow, but like everything else she faced, it would take time.

She couldn't change last night. She wasn't Sylvie, but she was here. She would make the best of things and fit in. She would find a way to please her husband. And she would find a way to visit her family in Accord.

Chapter Twelve

"It's so hot Jessie's fleas aren't biting."

Jakob paused in his Saturday chores and sat beside Lydia on the shaded side porch. At her feet sat a basket of apples, and two more waited near the back door. The task took little physical effort, and in the July heat Lydia welcomed a chore in the shade. A trickle of perspiration rolled down her spine under her gray dress and apron.

"This is a good time to take a job on the steel bridge," Jakob said. "It'll be at least another six weeks before the crops are ready, and I can earn a sizable amount by then."

Lydia's gaze jerked up from the apple she was peeling. This was it. She had hoped against hope he wouldn't take a job. If things were more comfortable between them, would he want to leave so soon?

She studied him. Earlier, he'd discarded his shirt. It was distracting to see her husband and his equally brawny brothers in a constant state of half undress. They never came in for meals without shirts, but the first several times she had come upon them in the yard, she hadn't known where to look. Now she allowed herself to admire the tawny mat of hair on Jakob's tanned chest, the well-toned muscles under the sleek golden skin of his upper arms and the long-fingered hands resting idly on his dirty dungarees.

Her gaze lifted and found him watching her. Heat tingled in her cheeks. "You will leave soon?" she asked as a distraction.

"At the barn dance tonight, I'll ask where the bridges are going up."

She looked back at the knife in her hand, and resumed peeling apples. She didn't want him to leave her here, but what could she do? Obviously he'd made up his mind about earning money for the house.

Lydia was lonely already. If he was leaving for several weeks, she needed to see Grandmother. A pesky fly buzzed, circling Lydia's ear, and she waved it away. "To you I want to talk about something."

Jakob leaned over and plucked several slices of fruit from the bucket at her side. "Hmm?"

"I would like you to teach me to ride Freida."

He chewed and studied her. She'd never asked anything of him before.

"If I could ride, I could visit my family."

"You can't ride all that way alone. It's not safe. Anything could happen."

"What could happen?"

"You could fall and get hurt. It could be a long time before anyone found you."

"You could fall when you ride, too, but that does not stop you."

"That's different. I've ridden my whole life."

"There had to be a first time."

"Other things could happen. The whole world isn't good and God-fearing like the people where you were raised."

"But, Jakob—"

"Lydia! You're beginning to sound like—"

Expectantly she waited for his next words. "Like what?"

He sat forward testily in the wooden chair. "Like a wife!"

The paring knife fell still in her lap. Seeing the telltale muscle in his cheek jerk, she knew it was unwise to argue. "If you intended to insult me, you did not. I'm proud to be your wife. I'm only sorry to constantly anger you."

Worry, and something else, shifted behind his eyes. His stubbornness annoyed her. Lydia turned her attention to the task before her. The silence lengthened. Had her persistence pushed him too far? Well, she'd discovered she could be stubborn, too. She'd never known that before. Peelings dropped into her lap. The knife made a crisp sound each time it sliced through the apple. Jessie appeared after a nap in the shade, and padded sluggishly across the porch, giving Lydia wide berth.

Finally, Jakob scooted his chair closer. He reached across the remaining space, placed the knife on her apron and pulled her hand to his face. He pressed the backs of her fingers against his lean cheek.

"I didn't intend to insult you. *Es tut mir leid.*" He said the words in German against her knuckles.

The moment stretched poignantly into the sultry summer afternoon. What an intimate thing it was to have her fingers against his lips, his warm breath creating a foolish flutter in her breast. His blue eyes were an icy contrast to his deeply tanned skin. He kissed her fingers, tasted each, turned her hand over and kissed a spot in her palm that aroused a tightness low in her abdomen.

"Mmm, you taste good. A little cinnamon and you could be a strudel." She smiled, and he tugged her hand until she leaned toward him. "Mad at me?"

His face scant inches from hers, she dropped her gaze, only to discover his broad chest sprinkled with hair the color of corn silk. "*Nein*—no."

"How do you say 'beautiful'?"

"*Schön.*"

"*Es tut mir leid, schön weib.*" Tipping her chin up with his fingers, he covered her slightly parted lips with his own, gently at first, then pressing firmly. His apology, as well as his kiss, pronounced the tremulous flutter within her breast. His lips tasted sweet from the apple he'd eaten, but salty from his perspiring skin. He deepened the kiss, and she fought for breath, reminded of the sensation she'd experienced when the bakery's storeroom exploded. It was as if the air had been sucked from a room.

She forced herself to breathe, thinking of the weeks he'd be gone. She touched the hair at the back of his neck. Her fingers slid into the soft thickness and prolonged the kiss, holding him with gentle persistence.

His kisses created wonderful and wanton feelings. Greedy. Strangely disquieting. That she enjoyed this intimacy surprised her. His lips, hungry and mobile, turned her insides to liquid. She wanted more of him. She needed to open herself fully and take all of him she could. When he was gone, she would need to remember this moment.

Respectable women don't enjoy seduction.

Embarrassed by her unconcealed response, she pulled away. He leaned back to look at her, keeping her hand tucked in his. Her other hand drifted back to her lap. His eyes were translucent, like two pieces of sky seen through cracks in a roof.

Jakob. Jakob, I don't know how to fix this thing between us. I don't know how I should think or feel, I just know what I want. I want you. And I need you to want me.

"What are you thinking?" He watched her pinkened lips as she answered.

"Jakob, I want to tell you . . ." Her lashes swept her flushed cheeks.

He tipped her chin up with a thumb. "What?"

"I am sorry for cutting my hair and making you angry."

A rock sank in the pit of his belly. He should be the one apologizing.

"I thought it would please you if I looked like the ladies in Pittsburgh."

Her tongue darted out to nervously touch her upper lip, and the rock moved elsewhere.

"I know I'm not fashionable, and that I don't know how to behave or what to—"

"Lydia."

Her dark eyes scanned his face. "Ja?"

"What are you saying?"

"Just that—that I wish to please you more than anything, and I seem to make a fool of myself each time."

He took a second to reevaluate his assumptions. "Do you mean you cut your hair because you thought I wanted you to look like a city woman?"

At her blush, he squeezed her hand reassuringly. He ran his thumb over her bottom lip, tormenting himself with the erotic satin texture against his coarse skin.

She blushed more deeply than before. Taking a strand of loose hair, he caressed it between his fingers. His knuckles grazed her neck and cheek, holding her gaze with his. Her lips

were slightly parted, and still moist from the kiss they'd shared.
"You don't know what you do to me."

"What?" she asked.

He shook his head and gave her a wry grin. *You make me
hard and crazy. You turn me inside out, and I love the torture.
You make me want to build you a house and make you a baby.
I don't trust myself anymore, and I'm angry and frustrated all
the time. You make me want to carry you off someplace alone
and do all the things I've dreamed of doing.*

"I've never met anyone like you" was all he said. "I don't
want you to be like anyone else. I like you just the way you
are." Smelling like apples and sun-dried cotton.

"Is it good?"

What he felt for her was so good that the thought of her
taking a horse in his absence filled him with terror. He closed
the distance between them, cupping her delicate chin in his
palm. Sylvie's life had been taken by a horse, and the thought
of such a thing happening to Lydia—he couldn't even think
about it.

Closing her eyes, she met his lips, and he kissed her lazily,
savoring her taste. She hadn't cut her hair out of disgust or re-
vulsion. She'd tried to please him, as she always tried to please
him. Guiltily he realized how homesick she must be. He hadn't
done a very good job of fulfilling his promise to court her. He'd
have to fix that. "Yes, it's good," he whispered against her lips.
"Very good."

Peine dropped the dining room curtain into place and leaned
back against the wall beside the window.

Kissing her! *Kissing* her!

She hit the papered wall at her side with a fist. Damn her!
Nothing had been the same since she came. Lydia wasn't going
to get away with this. Jakob would have to see her for what she
really was—a conniving holier-than-thou moment's pleasure.

Taking a deep breath, Peine pushed away from the wall and
stood where she could see through the slit between the two lacy
panels.

Perhaps he did have some sick crush on the girl. Who knew how long he'd been without a woman? Well, it wouldn't do. He needed some help figuring out what he really wanted.

Peine smiled and turned away from the window. She was the one he wanted. He loved her. Always had. First Anton had been in the way, and now this little bitch. Anton wasn't a problem; she could handle him. Lydia was the one who was becoming a problem.

Peine thought of the dance tonight. She would keep her eyes and ears open, stay close and see what opportunities the night offered. She'd come up against greater forces than Lydia Beker and come out the victor. She could handle her, too.

Early that evening, Jakob entered their room, and Lydia glanced up in surprise. Until now they had avoided dressing at the same time. He was dressed only in denims, and his wet hair dripped on his bare shoulders. His wife surveyed his bare chest with a blush, bent to tie her shoes and prepared to leave.

"Don't go," he said, hoping it sounded more like an invitation than an order. He crossed to the washstand. She perched on the bed's edge and watched him dry his hair and shoulders with brisk movements. He bent at the knees and combed his hair in the mirror.

Removing a crisp white shirt from his chest of drawers, he examined the arrow-straight creases in it. "You've been doing these, and I haven't thanked you."

"It is not necessary."

He hung the shirt carefully on the bedpost and took her hands, urging her gently until she stood. When he didn't have his boots on, her eyes came level with his chin. "I know how hard everything has been for you. You've done a good job. There's still so much work ahead, and sometimes I think it's unfair..."

The thought died away before he could voice his insecurities. He'd taken so much from her, and he had so little to offer in return. That was why the house was important. So far his plans had progressed as he'd hoped. She was the wife he'd wanted, and he would build her a house with the flower garden she wanted. He would make her happy. Then they could begin their family. Releasing her hands, he draped his arms loosely around her waist.

"What is unfair, Jakob?"

She smelled of lavender, clean and feminine. She intoxicated him, but he was still almost a stranger to her. *Time, Neubauer. Give her time.* "That all the other women will look like pigweed in a posy patch next to you."

Her hands came up so that her fingers rested on his arms, and her innocent touch sent immediate signals throughout the rest of his body. Gently he pulled her closer, until the lower halves of their clothed bodies met. Her soft form molded against his willingly. Her hair was cool and satiny beneath his fingers, and he buried his face in the dark tresses and inhaled deeply. Her body trembled.

Jakob removed his hands from her hair and grasped her upper arms, holding her away from him. His gaze flickered over the hair covering her shoulders, and he thought of her cutting it to please him.

Of course she was submissive; meekness was the backbone of her character, her beliefs. If she had chosen a husband within her colony, how would he have treated her? Just how chaste could a husband be?

He pictured her married to a dark-haired tailor or ropemaker in somber blue clothing, and a fierce possessiveness counteracted his misgivings. Hating the helplessness that smothered him, he pulled her close, needing to brand her as his own. His lips covered hers, hard and demanding—no evidence of the gentle kisses they'd shared that afternoon.

Punishing her for his own wretched frustration, he kissed her hard, using her startled gasp to plunge his tongue into her mouth and seek every conquerable depth within. She recoiled. He knew the instant she wanted to pull away. Gratified in some perverse way, he released her abruptly and reached for his shirt.

Lydia caught her balance, seized the bedpost and lowered herself to the edge of the bed. Jakob shrugged into his shirt and grabbed his gray snakeskin boots.

"Jakob?"

He paused in the doorway without looking back over his shoulder.

"Are you angry with me?"

An uneasy silence stretched across the room. She didn't deserve to be treated this way. Finally he turned and met her stare. "No. I'm not angry with you." He looked at the floor. "I'm angry with me."

"Why?"

He shook his head. "I'm not sure." He turned until he met her dark, confused gaze. "I'm sorry, Lydia. Let's just forget it."

With that, he left the room.

Chapter Thirteen

Impromptu tables fabricated of planks and sawhorses supported enormous quantities of popped corn, cookies and baked goods. One held a wooden keg of beer with a spigot at the bottom. A bucket on the floor caught the brew that drizzled over the sides of steins and mugs. At one end of the building stood a platform made of skids end to end and laid with flat planking. Both sets of doors were open to the sultry summer breeze; the space in between had been swept clean and scattered with sawdust for dancing.

Lydia took it all in with jittery anticipation. Next to her, Charlotte straightened and absently tucked her royal blue blouse into the waist of her full print skirt. Wound through her red-gold hair was a matching ribbon. A short time ago, Lydia couldn't have imagined a woman who wore adornment in her hair. "Your blouse is lovely."

Charlotte touched her collar in a pretty gesture. "Thanks. I used a blouse of Annette's for the pattern. I still have the paper, if you'd like to borrow it."

"*Danke,* but I don't know how to sew."

"Didn't your mother teach you? I'm not being critical," Charlotte hastened to add. "I just wondered."

"No. For pleasure my grandmother sews. In the colony the tailors provide garments. Each person has one job only. I was a baker."

Charlotte's friendly hazel eyes were sympathetic. "Farm life must be hard for you."

"Not hard. Different. But I'm learning." She watched the musicians warm up. Jakob tuned his fiddle and joked with the men, lanternlight glinting off his fair head.

The other woman touched her sleeve timidly. "I'd be glad to show you how, if you wouldn't be insulted."

"Insulted?" She smiled and touched Charlotte's hand. "Grateful I would be!"

Several couples moved onto the sawdust-littered floor and stepped to the lively music as a barrel-chested fiddler called out obscure directions. Men and women moved together in orderly circles, like patterns on a quilt. Tom swept Charlotte onto the dance floor in a swish of bright blue skirts. Lydia watched in fascination.

A half-dozen lively tunes later, Jakob left his place on the stand and threaded his way to Lydia's side. He filled his stein from a keg and took a long thirsty drink. "Are you ready for the Virginia reel?"

"Your pardon?" Lydia cocked a brow, still uncertain of his mood.

He gestured with a long arm toward the dance floor, and slicked the foam from his upper lip with his tongue. The action brought to mind his harsh kiss earlier, the shocking thrust of his tongue into her mouth. Lydia's heart lurched.

"*Nein* . . . No."

"*Ja*. There's no time like the present. I insist." He thumped his stein down on a nearby table and grabbed her wrist, pulling her toward the dancers who were squaring off for a fresh round.

"Jakob, no. Please."

He took her trembling hand in his. "Hey! This is fun! Don't look so scared!"

The music began, a lively rendition she didn't recognize. Heart pounding, cheeks scorching, Lydia watched Jakob and listened to the caller. She didn't comprehend "allemande left" or "do-si-do." Just when she thought she understood "swing your partner," the couples separated. Men moved to the ladies at the opposite corners.

Her elbow locked with Tom Simms's, and she stepped on his feet twice. Feeling awkward and gauche, she wanted to disintegrate into the sawdust on the floor. After an eternity, the song ended.

Jakob tried to catch her hand for another set, but she evaded him and ran toward the rear doors. "Lydia, wait!"

"Nein, Jakob."

"Dance with me."

"No."

"Jake!"

"Hey, Neubauer!" Several voices called Jakob back to his place among the musicians. "We need ya for this—Jake!"

Outside, Lydia watched billowy clouds chase a quarter moon and leaned back against the rough barn siding. Her pulse pounded in her temples. She'd looked ridiculous! Her drab blue dress, lack of grace and clumsiness all marked her the "Outsider." She wanted to evaporate into the summer-smelling night air.

"Thirsty?" She turned at Annette's voice. Her sister-in-law handed her a sweating jar of lemonade.

"Thank you."

She leaned against the barn beside Lydia. "You all right?"

Lydia nodded.

"Men can be tactless sometimes."

Had everyone seen her humiliation? Did Annette feel sorry for her? Lydia couldn't bear to know the answer to her own question. She sipped the tart lemonade. "What is Jakob doing?"

"They dragged him back to his fiddle. Let's go try Bitsy McKenna's cookies."

"I don't know, Annette. I—"

"Come on. You can't stay out here forever." Annette drew her back into the festivities. With her and Charlotte suggesting ideas for dresses and blouses, Lydia's discomfort waned. Charlotte introduced her to everyone who passed by, and Lydia tried to remember names and faces.

As the night wore on, she found herself standing by Anton, and together they watched Franz and Annette gracefully executing the steps of the quadrille. As she watched them, sadness struck Lydia again.

Annette seemed happier and more content with her life than either Peine or Lydia. A vague discomfort raised itself within her. The uncomfortable emotion crept stealthily into her awareness, like a barn cat slinking in with a mouse.

Stabbed by secret envy, Lydia looked away and struggled to bury the sinful feeling. Annette possessed the missing something she herself so desperately wanted.

Peine clung to the arm of a handsome young man, the latest in an ever-changing stream of males who had asked her to dance.

"It's really easy, you know."

Lydia turned to Anton.

"The square dance. The calls tell you what to do, and you can watch the others if you get lost."

She understood a few of the singing calls from her observations during the evening. "What's 'cross over'?"

Her brother-in-law explained the term, plus "allemande," "meander" and "shuttling." "Come on, I'll show you."

"Not here." Panic rose in her chest.

"Outside." He led the way through the rear door. Where they could easily hear the calls, Anton patiently showed her the steps. Gradually her hand relaxed in his, and she began to anticipate the next command. She ran into his back as they do-si-doed; he steadied her with a laugh, and they tried again. Anton's matter-of-fact directions and easy laughter drew her into the festive spirit. She grew more comfortable with her easy-going partner and the dance.

Jakob drained his stein again and wiped his mouth on the sleeve he'd rolled to his bicep. He owed his light-headedness to the stifling heat in his airless corner of the barn. His watchful gaze narrowed as Anton took Lydia's arm and led her into the throng of dancers.

They stood side by side, holding hands, before the music began, and Jakob strangled on an unwholesome gulp of jealousy. She'd fled from him, but accepted his brother's invitation! Lydia curtsied and clapped her hands gleefully. Jakob's stein was full once again, and he lifted it to his lips. Envy, that great, blinding tyrant, had its hooks in him.

During a break, he discussed bridge locations with other farmers, one eye on Lydia. She, Anton and Annette fanned themselves, laughed together and had a good time—without him. He was unaccountably hurt. She had a good time with his brother, but held herself stiff as a rake handle when he was around.

"She doesn't mean anything by it." Peine refilled his stein again. "I've seen you watching them, but it's harmless."

He took a long swallow.

She fluffed her golden hair off her neck and patted her cheek with a lacy handkerchief.

The green talons gripped Jakob's senses.

Peine trailed the handkerchief across her pale chest, which was exposed by a low neckline, and dragged her long-lashed gaze over Jakob's face. "She seems to be having a wonderful time, doesn't she?"

He squinted from her to his smiling, laughing wife. Behind him, the musicians picked up their instruments and settled themselves. He drained his beer and slammed down the stein.

Crossing the floor in angry strides, he grabbed Lydia by the arm and pulled her out the door. "What do you think you're doing?" he berated, digging his fingers into her arm.

"I don't— I don't know what—"

"Jake! What's the matter with you?" Footsteps sounded on the drive beside them, and Anton reached for his brother's shoulder. "What the hell—"

Jakob jerked back, knocking Lydia off balance. She stumbled, and Anton steadied her. "You're not playing with a full deck tonight, little brother. You've always danced with my wife, Jake. Why shouldn't I— *Oof!*"

Jakob silenced his brother by hurling a shoulder into his belly, gratified to hear a whoosh of air escape Anton's lips. Anton fell back, gripping the front of Jakob's shirt, bringing Jakob down on top of him. Legs and arms flying, they rolled in the dirt at Lydia's feet.

She sidestepped. A few mildly interested observers appeared in the doorway. In the light from the barn, Lydia spotted Peine. A triumphant look lit her face.

Jakob was on his feet again, his expression almost one of regret. But it was too late. Anton swung a fist. Jakob ducked and lunged. Anton jumped to the side and lifted a knee into Jakob's ribs.

Jakob held his side and panted, glaring at his brother. Lydia watched in horror, unable to move. "Jakob!" She ran to his side. "Stop! Stop this at once!"

Closed-fisted, he made the mistake of glancing at her. Anton saw his opening and caught Jakob's jaw with his fist, knocking him backward. Jakob tripped over a tree root and landed on his backside in the dirt—hard. Lydia cringed and held her breath.

"Come on, you drunken turd!" Anton taunted. "I whupped you when you were ten and I can whup you now! What're you so all-fired mad about? You don't have the sense to show a lady how to dance before you lead her onto the floor in front of fifty people! You wanna pound me 'cause I showed her how? Come on!"

Jakob scrambled to his feet and swayed. Anton stood in readiness, feet sprattled.

"Jakob. Please." Lydia tried to reason with her husband. "He wants your goat. Don't give it to him."

Through a haze of anger and alcohol, he gaped at her as if he'd been hit in the face with a dead fish.

Anton dropped his fists and chuckled deep in his winded chest. The chuckle grew to a guffaw. "Your goat," he chortled. Another gale of laughter overtook him, and he convulsed with laughter. "She said I want your goat!"

Amazingly, Jakob laughed.

Peine and the others drifted back into the barn, where the music was still in full swing. Both brothers turned, and their laughter died on their faces at Lydia's expression.

Humiliation festered until it became full-blown anger. She clenched her fists at her sides, as if she, too, could have hit one of them. Her expression obviously sobered them both.

Jakob started toward her. "Lydia—"

"If belittling me is the solution for your childish confrontation, then I am useful. My poor use of your language is not as degrading as full-grown men fistfighting in the dirt. Disrespectful it is to hit another person. If you're not ashamed of yourselves, I'm ashamed enough for you. To be the wife of a man with no self-control is not something I am proud of.'' She whirled and marched around the corner of the barn.

No one followed.

In the darkness, Lydia found her way to the wagon. Nearby, Gunter and Freida chewed clumps of grass. Surprisingly, she didn't feel like crying. The longer she stood there, the more her anger abated, to be replaced by remorse. *"Ach,* how could I have said those awful things?'' she said aloud.

Lightning bugs danced sporadically in a beanfield beyond the house. Her impudence had finished her this time! A woman *never* raised her voice to a man! Never questioned his integrity, or challenged his authority. Her mother had never dared challenge a word or action of her father. Lydia had never heard a woman speak that way. Jakob had been lenient up to this point. But now? What would happen now?

Footsteps sounded in the gravel behind her. She tensed. The form wasn't tall or broad enough for Jakob, and she sighed in relief. Annette again.

''You all right?''

''No, I've done something awful!'' The first tears threatened. ''I said terrible, insulting things to Jakob and Anton.''

''So I heard.'' At Lydia's questioning look, she explained, ''Peine told me.''

''They'll never forgive me.''

''Of course they will.'' She chuckled. ''They may even thank you. You didn't say anything the rest of us haven't tried to, believe me. If they behave like children, they deserve to be treated like children.''

Unconvinced, Lydia shook her head.

The notes of ''Turkey in the Straw'' wafted through the warm night air. Annette convinced her to return.

Johann coaxed her into dancing and remained with her while they packed. Jakob lifted her over the side of the wagon, as always, but she snatched her hands away from his hard shoulders as soon as he released her. He rode beside her in stony silence while Johann drove the team.

Franz and Annette snuggled in the far corner, and Anton and Peine exchanged harsh words that were barely disguised by the jingle of harnesses and the rumble of the wagon wheels. Nikolaus slept soundly on a quilt near Annette, oblivious of the emotions raging on both sides of him.

Once in their room, Lydia poured warm water into the basin and washed quickly. Peine's and Anton's angry words carried down the hall. Jakob opened and closed the door, and the voices momentarily grew louder. He stripped off his shirt with an economy of motion, flung it toward the woven basket, and missed. Lydia backed away from the washstand, giving him a wide berth. He took the cloth she'd used and scrubbed at his upper body. Beads of water glistening on his shoulders in the lanternlight, he turned his frosty blue gaze on her. Lydia wilted, moving closer to the bed's edge.

"I didn't like what you did," he growled. He towered over her where she perched tentatively on the side of the bed.

Lydia's heart pounded in alarm. "I don't know what you mean."

"Dancing with Anton," he said roughly. He flicked her shortened braid over her shoulder and tapped her collarbone, enunciating each syllable. "I didn't like it. You didn't want to dance with me, but you had a gay time with him."

He blew out the lantern, and his trousers hit the floor. She scrambled to her side of the bed, drawing the sheet protectively under her chin.

"Jakob..." She blinked in the sudden darkness. "I did not know you would find it inappropriate. Many others danced with partners who were not their mates."

He snorted.

She'd been grateful to Anton for teaching her to dance. It had been enjoyable! For once she'd blended in with the farmers and their wives, no longer sticking out like a misfit....

Jakob turned onto his side, away from her. The bed seemed larger than ever.

What on earth had gotten into Jakob to make him behave this way? She suspected he'd drank too many steins of beer, but there had to be something else. An idea dawned, and she rolled the possibility over in her mind, as though savoring a rich pastry on her tongue. "Jakob?"

"What?"

"Are you feeling jealousy?"

Dead silence met her straining ears.

"Jako—"

"Yes, dammit!" He flung himself onto his back. "Are you happy?"

Her entire body relaxed, and she smiled. "Yes. I believe I am."

The darkness assumed a friendlier countenance. Perhaps another prayer had been answered; perhaps she was learning to understand this unusual, emotional Outsider and his world better than she thought.

He rolled toward her and found her hair in the dark. Gently he smoothed it back from her forehead in a caress that eased her worried heart and closed her eyes with a weary sigh. "I'm sorry," he said at last. "I drank too much and lost my temper."

He pulled her close, and she snuggled against his firm chest, inhaling his yeasty scent. Yes, she was learning. "You have no reason for jealousy," she whispered.

A soft snore was his only reply.

The following morning, Peine smiled and pulled on a slender pair of white gloves. She stroked the lace fingers from tip to base, working them into place. What a pity to waste the exquisite ensemble on Sunday-morning church service. She detested church. But she would look good for Jakob. She picked up her drawstring handbag and preened in the mirror.

She resented every "saint" gathered there—especially the women. The men went to please their wives—or the town council. But the women went to gather forces, to garner information and ammunition so that they could blast the rest of the sinful world with pious warnings and judgments.

She practiced her butter-wouldn't-melt-in-her-mouth smile. Pompous idiots, all of them! But she was above them. She had them all fooled. It was a particularly good morning, however, despite the fact that Anton had persisted with his unwanted affections the night before.

She placed her hand on her abdomen and smiled.

Everything was going along as planned.

Maneuvering Lydia into the position of coming between the two brothers had been a stroke of genius. Jakob would soon realize his mistake. He would know they couldn't be together with *her* in the way. Soon he would come to his senses, and she would have Lydia exactly where she wanted her. Gone.

Chapter Fourteen

A bridge was going up across the Susquehanna River near Williamsport, far to the northeast near the base of the Bald Eagle Mountains. Lydia looked at the spot on the map Jakob showed her. Over halfway across the state of Pennsylvania! A three-day trip from Pittsburgh by train meant Jakob would have to leave at the end of the week.

He looked up from the map on the kitchen table and seemed to read the uncertainty in her eyes. "It's not that far. Only six weeks, and I'll be back."

Six weeks. Her finger traced the railroad tracks, creeks and cities along the route. So far! Farther than she'd ever dreamed of going. She was already lonely. He was her family. Was it so easy for him to leave for so long?

Jakob folded the map into a neat triangle. Sunday dinner had been cleared away, and Franz and Annette had gone to visit her sister. Anton was taking his frustrations out on the hills of firewood behind the barn, and from the sounds of it, he already had a sizable amount split and stacked. Lydia hadn't seen Peine since church.

"Time for your lesson."

She raised her gaze. "Lesson?"

"You want to ride. Get your bonnet."

Surprised, she did as she was told. What had prompted his change of mind? Did this mean she'd be seeing her grandmother soon? Lydia listened attentively, and Jakob explained the procedure for saddling and harnessing the horses. He showed her how tight to make the cinches, how to adjust the stirrups and which side to mount from. When both horses were saddled, he laced his fingers together and indicated that she should step into his palm. She pulled on the saddle horn, and he lifted. It wasn't a graceful mount. She wrestled with her skirt, revealing a great deal of calf.

Jakob pretended not to notice as he raised himself into Gunter's saddle with an ease she envied. He showed her how to control the horse with gentle tugs on the reins and appropriate pressure of her knees. Using those leg muscles took some getting used to, and by the time they reached the house site, her legs were so stiff she couldn't get down alone. Jakob reached for her, and she slid into his arms, letting him catch her with one arm behind her knees.

She gazed into his eyes, unable to look away. She wanted him to kiss her, to fix whatever this thing was between them. She needed him to look at her the way he had before he consummated their marriage, before disillusionment clouded his eyes. She wanted another chance. He allowed her feet to slide to the ground, and she wobbled away from him, toward the shade of a tree.

Freida raised her nose and nudged Lydia's back. Her already weak legs buckled. She sprawled, in an unladylike fashion, on the ground, her skirts trapped beneath her, her underskirts and an immodest expanse of both legs revealed. Scrambling to cover herself, she sat where she'd fallen, too tired to argue with her overworked legs.

"You okay?"

"Yes." She saw him trying not to smile.

Overhead, a blue jay called to its mate. Jakob knelt on the grass and studied the expanse of afternoon sky. She envied his effortless ease of motion, admired the way the sun filtered down through the trees and dappled his broad shoulders. She would miss him.

A painful prick, like that of a thorn or needle, stung Lydia's hip. Another needlelike pain bit the small of her back, and another pinpricked her waist. "Ow!" she cried out in alarm.

"What's wrong?"

"I don't know," she said, squirming to scratch at the flaming spots. "It feels as if there's a thorn inside my dress, but I can't find anything to pull out. It moves around. Oh!"

Helplessly he watched for several seconds. "Something must be biting you. Turn around."

Too uncomfortable to object, she turned her back and allowed him to unbutton her dress. "Hurry!"

Another sharp sting pierced her side. With her frantic help, he peeled her dress down and peered inside her cotton underslip. "I see the welts. Untie the front."

He tugged at the narrow shoulders of her undergarment, and she complied, dropping it to her waist, baring herself, too intent on stopping the stings to notice. He searched the folds of fabric. "Here."

He held an insect between his thumb and forefinger—a huge winged ant. Flicking it away, he said, "Fire ant."

Lydia clutched her clothing against her breasts, vulnerably exposed to the warm afternoon sun and Jakob's perusal. Behind her, Jakob stared at the silken white skin of her long back, studying the bumpy column of vertebrae where it dipped into the folds of bunched fabric at her hips. Her narrow waist flared into smooth, rounded buttocks, two dimples on opposite sides of her spine.

"Is it bad?"

"What?"

"My back—the bites. They sting." She scratched her hip.

"No, don't do that." He stopped her hand. "We'll have to go back to the house and put something on them." Purposefully he turned her sleeves right side out. She twisted at the waist, poked her hand through the armhole of her slip, and Jakob got a heart-stopping view of a full, creamy white breast with a dark, puckered nipple. That brief sight speared him with desire. Roughly he helped her into the dress and buttoned it quickly. If he'd had anything to say, he couldn't have talked; his tongue stuck to the roof of his dry mouth as it was.

Back at the barn, he tutored her relentlessly, hoping to take her mind off the inflamed and itching stings and his off that disturbing first sight of her skin. He showed her how to walk and cool the horses, and how to use fresh hay to dry their coats before taking a stiff brush and finishing the task. He measured water and feed, explaining all the while that the horses' care and comfort always came first. They were a valuable and indispensable asset to the farm and not to be treated otherwise. Finally, hoping exhaustion would claim them both, he sent her upstairs while he dipped cold water from the well.

Jakob splashed his face and neck with water, the effort having no more effect than spitting on a forest fire. He was going up those stairs to see her body in the light again. And not touch her? He stuck his entire head in the bucket and came up sputtering. Why not touch her? *She's my wife!* He heard a peculiar noise in his own throat. She was the gentlest of women. The best of women. He remembered his callow attempt at making love to her—like a green schoolboy starved for her flesh—and hot shame washed over him anew. He couldn't go on like this.

In their bedroom, she stood in her white slip, and her hair had fallen from its confinement down over one shoulder.

"Wash." He poured water into the basin and busied himself with towels and ointment while she obeyed. He led her to the edge of the bed and took a deep, cleansing breath, steeling himself for another glimpse of her uncovered body. "Turn around." He coaxed the garment from her shoulders past her waist. "You've been scratching."

"I feel foolish," she said, and flinched when he dabbed cool, sticky salve on her skin.

"Nothing to feel foolish about. Everybody gets bit sooner or later." He lifted her tangled hair and searched out bites. Loose tendrils clung to her slender white neck. He wanted to nudge them aside with his nose and lay his lips on the soft, fair skin.

"Here." She raised her arm. Sure enough, welts trailed across the velvety pale skin of her side. He tried to concentrate on getting salve on the red spots, but his attention wavered to the underside of her breast, where she clutched her slip fiercely, concealing herself. The swell of her flattened breast had a shadow underneath that dried his mouth until he forced himself to swallow. He wanted to press his face against the freshly washed lavender-scented skin, to touch his tongue to that shadowed crease between her breast and rib and . . .

She turned to him, an innocent expression in her gold-flecked eyes, and he knew his own expression was as guilty as . . . sin. Her dark gaze was luminous and questioning. "Jakob?"

His name on her lips was more than a question. It was an invitation. He dragged his gaze from her eyes to her full, slightly parted lips, then to her hands, clenched on the white cotton over her breasts. With calm, deliberate movements, he let go of the ointment tin and reached out, pulling the garment away from her. At first she resisted, but then her arms slackened. The material peeled away and fell. He turned her shoulders and looked at her body for the first time.

Her breasts were full and rounded, dark-tipped, with nipples that pebbled as he watched. He skimmed the backs of his fingers up over her ribs, smoothed them in a back-and-forth motion under the swell of one breast. Her skin was as soft and delicate as a baby's. Pure white against his dark hands. He cupped one breast, testing its weight in his palm.

Sliding down, he knelt next to the bed, circled her ribs with both hands and laid his face in the soft, fragrant valley between her breasts. He inhaled deeply, absorbing her heady woman's smell. Her hands fluttered to his shoulders, and he felt them tremble through his shirt. God, she was beautiful! Beautiful . . . his beautiful wife . . .

He would have this much, just this much. Let her get used to him, to his hands on her skin. He wanted more. So much more. But even this sweet torture was better than nothing at all.

Rubbing his face against her petal-soft flesh, he gloried in her scent and texture. He needed her. He wanted her, with a possessiveness that scared him. But more than that, he wanted her to desire him—not merely to submit because she was afraid or meek, but to need him as fiercely as he needed her. Almost roughly, he hugged her, pressing his face against her upper chest, then dragging his lips to her throat.

Lydia's heart beat wildly. Hard enough for him to feel the rhythm under his mouth. Her pulse surged. Her body flowed against his and her fingers tightened on his muscled shoulders. Strong, solid arms held her tightly. His brawny masculinity made her feel altogether feminine and wantonly desirable. She would have liked to give credit to the salve for taking away the bites' sting, but Jakob's overpowering nearness and his burning lips on her skin were the real balm. Hands splayed across her spine, he relaxed his arms' hold.

"Jakob..." she whispered against the top of his head. She wanted to tell him how empty her life had been before him, how empty life would be while he was gone, how enormous his bed felt when he wasn't beside her. She didn't want them to part without a wonderful memory. Something deep inside her needed some part of him, craved a shred of satisfaction to soothe the loneliness ahead. "Jakob?"

He pulled back and gazed up at her. His ruddy face and clear blue eyes, and her own breasts, were in her line of vision. She felt herself blush. He didn't take his eyes from her.

She forgot her nakedness. Forgot the subject she'd wanted to discuss. Forgot everything except Jakob. Her perusal fell to his slightly parted lips. He raised himself from his knees to kiss her, and she stood to meet him. His kiss was anxious, almost insistent. One hand found the side of her bared breast, and he inhaled sharply.

Heart pounding, she waited. *Touch me! Yes, touch me!* She silently begged him to satisfy her longing, to envelop her, begged for every breath he took to be hers. She leaned into him.

Jakob's hands spanned her ribs, buffed the delicate skin of her sides with callused palms, then obligingly covered her breasts. With maddeningly slow and gentle fingers he brushed feather-light, over the hardened tips. Her eyes fell shut, and her lips parted on a gratified sigh. Ah, the pleasure his touch brought....

"Lydia..." he said, breathing against her mouth and changing his hold as if to guide her to the bed.

She slipped her hands down his shirtfront, stilling him, wanting to divest herself of the rest of her clothing. She couldn't get close enough to him.

Jakob did it for her, as though reading her thoughts. Clumsily he jerked the slip down over her hips and watched the underclothes puddle at her ankles. An unidentifiable emotion flickered in his eyes. His heated gaze burned a path from her legs and belly across her breasts, and back to her lips.

With jerky movements, he unbuttoned his shirt, shrugged out of it and unbuttoned his trousers. Lydia spun, yanked back the quilt and knelt on the bed.

Behind her, his belt buckle hit the floor. An instant later, he wrapped his arms around her in a possessive embrace. Flesh against flesh sent a shudder of pleasurable sensation to every nerve ending.

His knees bracketed her hips and he pressed himself along her back, tugging her hair aside and touching his face to the curve of her neck.

Lydia closed her eyes and concentrated on every inch along her back and buttocks where his skin touched hers. She had never been touched, had never known this closeness, this satisfaction. Nothing had ever felt so good, had ever captured her attention so intently that the rest of the world ceased to exist.

With a hesitant palm, she reached over her shoulder and touched his face, then laced her fingers in his hair. He turned and pressed his mouth against her fingers, took the tip of one between his searing lips, and her stomach quivered.

She turned from the waist and met his mouth with her own. He kissed her eagerly, intent on his purpose.

"Turn now," he said against her lips, and she did, lying back against the pillow at his urging. He flowed down over her, his weight a solid pleasure. Sweet, pulsing desire overbalanced thought and reason, and Lydia welcomed him into her body.

His kiss was prayerful, crushing, his body graceful, deliberate. As though she were a long-sought-after treasure, his hands bracketed her face, then her hips. Hot and greedy, Jakob's fervor burst with a groan and an all-over shudder.

He buried his damp forehead in the V of her neck and shoulder and struggled for air, his heart pounding against her breast. Minutes later, he pushed himself away, not meeting her eyes. "I didn't mean for that to happen."

Puzzled, she tried to read his face. "Are you sorry again?"

"Are you?" he asked, instead of answering.

What had seemed so lovely and natural only moments before now made her uncomfortable. She'd grown too confused to sort out any of her feelings. She only knew she felt robbed and baffled. "I'm sick of sorries," she replied.

Jakob stood and tugged on his dungarees and shirt. Without a backward glance at her or the mirror, he picked up his boots and stalked from the room.

Lydia pulled the sheet from its moorings and wrapped it around her before stepping to the washstand.

The reflection shocked her. In total disarray, her hair fell in a tangle over her shoulders, pins protruding here and there. Her lips were a deep rose, swollen from his kisses. Pink patches of abraded skin dotted her neck and chest. What had just happened?

Through the bedroom window drifted the bellows of the cows coming near the barn for milking. It was broad daylight, and she'd behaved like a . . . like a what? Was that what displeased Jakob? Should she be setting standards of proper behavior?

Shameless! Lydia applied herself to her hairbrush with purging strokes, and tortured her hair into a severe knot. He was disappointed with her, and she with herself. The marriage bed was one thing, used for the purpose intended, but lust was quite another. No doubt he was shocked that she'd allowed him such liberties, and in broad daylight!

She pressed a wet cloth against her flushed face and ran her thumbnail over the bristles of his ebony-handled hairbrush, some undefinable yearning still shimmying through her veins.

But still she would miss him. Oh, how she would miss him . . .

Lydia lay staring into the darkness overhead. Even in his absence, she could almost hear Jakob's boots hitting the floor. The rustle of his clothing was nearly audible. The bed ropes would creak as they took his weight. The scent of firewood would be in his hair. Where did he sleep? What did he eat? Did he miss her?

The first week had been unbearable. At the dinner table, Lydia's gaze had raked over Jakob's empty place as a tongue sought a sore tooth.

She'd taken his place at milking, though the brothers' eyebrows had shot up dubiously the first night she appeared with her sleeves rolled back. But when her buckets were filled as quickly and efficiently as theirs, they'd shared a contrite expression. She'd appointed herself the job of feeding the chickens and hogs each morning.

Today had been exhausting, and she should have been able to fall asleep. She and Annette had picked apples and peaches, peeled and sliced them and strung them on long, heavy lengths of thread, draping them over one entire side of the porch to dry. After milking, the evenings stretched before her, and she often wished she could sew or embroider like Annette. Instead, she used Annette's recipes, putting up pickles, relishes—anything to occupy herself. Anything to fill the minutes and hours. And still she missed him.

Every night, she recalled each detail of their intimate encounters. The night Jakob had spread her hair over her shoulders and coaxed her onto this bed. She'd been determined to fulfill her marital obligations. The afternoon he'd soothed her with salve and inflamed her with kisses and touches.

The memory of those encounters robbed her of sleep.... The scents. His own blend of man and musk and bay rum. The sights. Corded, flexing muscles, hair-dusted limbs, chest, belly...

The sounds. Oh, yes, the sounds! Frustrated groans, the intimate, slick sounds of ravenous mouths and slippery— Warmth other than that left over from the sweltering day burned a hungry yearning straight to her core. Lydia couldn't have said which plagued her more—the sultry heat of the night, or her lonely aching for Jakob.

Jakob turned on his side, the bedroll offering scant cushioning between his hips and the hard ground. He threw an arm over his ear, hoping to block out the snores of the other men in the enormous tent, and tried not to think about his soft bed and his softly rounded, lavender-scented wife. He hadn't grown accustomed to the smell of his own sweat and that of fifty-odd men. That day he'd stood in mud up to his knees for nearly ten hours, unloading steel girders. Every muscle in his body burned, and his shoulders were sun-scorched, but the work was worth it.

He'd return with enough money to purchase the supplies needed to build their house. Once they had their own home, things between them would work out.

The morning he left, an awkward silence had stretched between them as he carried his bags out to the springboard.

"If you need anything just ask Annette or Franz. I left money in the top drawer. It's yours to do whatever you want with."

Holding herself straight and tall, she'd nodded.

"Don't take up with one of the other fiddle players while I'm gone." Two were in their sixties, and the other was a happily married father of seven.

She'd managed a smile. "I think not."

Her hair had been caught up in a roll on the back of her head, yet loose wisps had already framed her face. She hadn't worn the white cap that morning. He'd watched her expression as she struggled for composure, and wished he knew what to say to reassure her that everything would be all right.

"It won't be long. I'll be back before you know it." He'd kissed her then, quick and hard, and she'd felt the lump of steel beneath his jacket.

Her dark eyes had widened. "A gun, Jakob? A gun you are taking?"

"Just a precaution, nothing to worry over." But her betraying expression had told him she would. She was probably imagining bandits, train robbers, muggers and wild animals right now. He reached across the short space to his belongings and touched the small bag of dried apples she'd sent with him. He'd eaten her loaf of bread the first day.

He rolled onto his back and tucked his palms under his head, experiencing the now-familiar reaction of his body to thoughts of her. He stifled a groan. There was nothing wrong with him. He was a normal man with a healthy desire for his wife. Now he knew the feel of her skin, knew her scents and textures, knew the dark color of her nipples and how they pebbled when he brushed them with his face. He savored the memory of her perched on the bed, her upper body exposed to his senses, and remembered the exquisite feel of burying himself deep within her and appeasing his years of loneliness and denial.

He tortured himself, remembering her kisses, her body. But it was such sweet torture. He pressed his knuckles into his eyes and erased the image. Lord, he was selfish.

Instead of behaving like a rutting schoolboy, he should stifle his own desires and think of her pleasure and her needs. Perhaps if he took a little time ... made her want him as much as he wanted her ...

Someone on the other side of the tent grunted and rolled over on his hard pallet. Jakob closed his eyes and willed himself to sleep. It wouldn't be much longer. If he hung on a little longer, he'd be home with his wife. And when he was, he'd start over again. He'd show her how caring and gentle he could be. He hadn't done so great this far. He'd rushed her and probably frightened her, but he'd learn. He had to.

With Johann's help, Lydia's riding lessons continued. Mounting got easier, though she had to stack crates near the corral fence to step from. After each lesson, she walked and groomed Freida, and gave her carefully measured portions of feed and water.

"You're a good rider, Lydia!" Peine's musical voice called as Lydia returned from the barn one Saturday afternoon. Lydia shaded her eyes with a hand and spotted Peine in a shady corner of the porch. Nikolaus was playing with wooden blocks at her feet. *"Ja?"*

"Oh, yes! You're every bit as good as the men."

Lydia perched on the railing and gazed out across the dooryard, toward the corral. "It's an enjoyable freedom. I can go as fast or as slow as I like, turn Freida in any direction I choose.... I like riding."

"It will be nice for you to visit your grandmother. I'm sure you miss your family," Peine cooed.

"I do."

"You must be worried about her health."

"Yes."

The other woman laid aside the small book she'd been holding. "You probably want to see her while you still can. You'd never forgive yourself if you didn't get to see her one last time."

Lydia snapped her head back and found Peine's wide green eyes filled with sympathy. A picture of dark, pain-filled eyes formed in her mind, and a lump filled her throat. What if Grandmother's health had failed rapidly? She must see her before—before any more time passed.

She gazed toward the eastern horizon. "I'm not certain of the way. When Jakob brought me here, we came through Butler, but I know there's a direct route."

"We have the map."

The thought of visiting Accord was frightening and exhilarating at the same time. *"Ja."*

They were in the kitchen, their heads bent over the unfolded piece of paper when Charlotte Simms poked her head in the door. "I brought my piece bag."

Annette removed a basket of apples from the table. "We'll teach Lydia to sew!"

Lydia smiled. "I can make a dress!"

Resentment filled Peine, and her temples throbbed. She watched the activity from her end of the trestle table. Sipping tea, she listened to every word spoken. Perhaps goading Lydia about her drab clothing had backfired. If she dressed tastefully, she might look half-decent. She would have to use another method to discourage her. Not to worry. The girl's downfalls were endless. And she was such a forgiving sap!

Chapter Fifteen

Alone. Lydia had never been so alone or so far from civilization in her life. She glanced down at the saddle holster bearing the rifle Johann had forced her to bring.

The dusty road had taken her an alarmingly long way before she reached the fork. Knowing nothing of the measurement of miles, she watched for landmarks and took the right fork, studying the trail behind her so that it would look familiar on the return trip. She'd felt oddly alone ever since she'd reached the end of the long drive and looked back on the homestead, laid out as she'd seen it the day she rode in on the springboard next to Jakob.

Elation overpowered anxiety at the prospect of seeing Grandmother. In the fields to her right, the corn stood tall, its husks rasping in the pleasant, dry wind. It was nearly harvesttime, and time for Jakob's return. It seemed he'd been gone forever. Grasshoppers sprang from the stalks into the air as the horse disturbed them. Determinedly Freida cantered on, oblivious of their agitation. The sun rose higher in the morning sky, and a lazy warmth soaked into Lydia's skin and bones. Freedom was a heady sensation.

On the other side of the stream, she dismounted, stretched her legs and allowed Freida a drink. Once down, she knew she'd made a mistake; she'd never get back on the horse without help.

Taking the reins, she walked, chastising herself with every step. After ten minutes, a weathered stump presented itself. Lydia glanced toward heaven and gave thanks. She would remember the lesson.

The ride had taken so much longer than she'd thought it should. Grass, trees and sky looked the same for miles and miles—everywhere, for all she knew! She could easily have veered off in the wrong direction and become hopelessly lost. The sun grew hot. Lydia dabbed nervous perspiration from her face and neck. She was almost regretting her rash decision by the time she recognized the stand of beech trees, several of which had been blown over in a storm and lay decaying against the ground. Relief flooded her, and she exhaled her pent-up anxiety in a whoosh. Allegheny County.

At the hill's crest, a warm familiarity suffused her breast. Lydia filled her gaze with the straight streets, the perfect, box-like blocks of buildings and trees.

The beast beneath Lydia shifted her footing. The church bell pealed across the countryside, and an involuntary shiver ran up her spine. *Vater.* Inwardly she cringed at the thought of him discovering her. Her eyes sought the church, where he was at this moment. Where he was every morning, cosseted in his study. She counted ten bells. Two hours until dinner.

Heart hammering, Lydia rode into Accord, opposite Church Street, turned into the livery and slid from the saddle, glad she'd chosen to dress like an Outsider. Herr Grunewald greeted her without interest.

"I'll be stayin' about two hours. Please care for my horse until I return from shoppin'," she said, head averted, adopting the Neubauers' clipped speech. From the reticule Peine had loaned her, she withdrew two of the coins Jakob had left and instructed the livery man on precise amounts of food and water. She handed the coins to him. "Thank you."

"*Danke.*"

She passed the common quickly. Not a brick had changed, not a blade of the carefully cut grass, not a flower or herb. No weeds grew in the bed she had planted beside the house. Just as she'd expected, there was no outward sign of her absence.

At the door of her childhood home, she hesitated, listening for voices, then pushed the door open. From long habit, she removed her shoes. The kitchen of the two-story brick house was cool and dim, and spotlessly clean. Chairs stood at attention around the empty table. Though the room was painfully familiar, its lack of furnishings and utensils now seemed odd and . . . somehow lonely. The oppressive lack of life and laughter hit her squarely for the first time.

Lydia hurried along the hallway, her heart pounding in anticipation and her silky green skirts rustling in the silence of the house. The disturbing scent of cedar from her parents' room triggered memories of her quiet, nondescript childhood. Gray memories. Bland memories, like food with no salt or spice. Nothing like her new memories.

Grandmother's door stood open. Lydia peered inside. Her grandmother, small and pale atop the colorful bridal quilt, stared back at her. Dark eyes met, and a dawning smile creased the old woman's face.

"Child . . ." she said softly.

Tears stinging her eyes, Lydia knelt at her grandmother's side. They embraced before she drew back to look into her wrinkled, well-loved face. With gnarled fingers, her grandmother untied the bow beneath Lydia's chin. Lydia removed the bonnet and tossed it and the reticule on the floor.

"You look different. . . . Your hair . . ." Her grandmother's voice trailed away.

She looked exactly the same. A little thinner, perhaps. The ever-present shawl was wrapped around her bony shoulders, and the thick gray braid lay across her chest. Acute regret tinged Lydia's voice. "I wish you didn't have to be alone all day."

"When you have lived as long as I, you appreciate peace and quiet."

The comment was for her benefit. The colony offered immeasurable solitude, no matter what age one was. Her strength and selflessness roused Lydia's admiration.

"Rachael comes at noon," Grandmother added in a subtle warning. "What is life like on your farm?"

Lydia's gaze took in the modest, uncarpeted room, and her mind insisted on making comparisons. No hatboxes stacked as high as the ceiling, no beaded collars or feminine scents. Not one picture of her beloved husband.

"It's good, but sometimes I'm so frightened that I'll never fit in." She described her new relatives, the house, the friends she'd met, and told of her learning experiences with chores, cooking and sewing. Rose chuckled.

"Tell me," the old woman asked, eyes dancing with animation. "Do you plan your own days?"

"Basically, yes. Annette has shown me the chores and how to do them, but I work in any order I wish."

"If it suited you to put off a chore until the next day, you could?"

"*Ja.*"

Grandmother gave her a satisfied smile. "And *Meier* Neubauer, child? What is it like being his wife?"

Lydia straightened and sat on the edge of the cot. What was it like being Jakob's wife? She took a deep breath. "I have made it sound like I'm learning self-assurance, but it's not so. I'm afraid I'll never learn to please Jakob."

"He is a demanding husband?"

"No! No, he is kind and patient, but he should have married someone who knew how to dance to the quadrille, how to dress in lovely clothes, how to sew . . . Someone who learned to plan meals and iron clothing from her mother, like Annette, not a wife he has to instruct in every facet of the most simple functions."

Grandmother rested her frail hand on Lydia's arm and fixed a probing gaze on her. "Has he said this is an inconvenience to him?"

"*Nein.*"

"Do you think your background had never entered his mind before he asked you to marry him?"

"*Nein, I—*"

"Is he a man who makes impulsive decisions and then later regrets them?"

"Grandmother, I know what you're trying to do."

"Have you considered the possibility that Herr Neubauer was attracted to you for the very reasons you think he regrets marrying you for? My guess is he's the envy of every man who knows him. What man wouldn't enjoy the opportunity to teach a wife to do things the way it pleases him?"

"But I don't please him! There is a feeling I get...something I sense . . . that he's uneasy. Uncomfortable with our relationship."

"Comfortable doesn't come for years and years, child, and you wouldn't want it to. All newly married couples have things they must work out, even if they come from the same background and faith."

"Did you and Grandfather?"

"Goodness, yes! But I wouldn't have traded one of those differences for anything."

Lydia smoothed her new green skirt over her knees. How could she express the fears and inadequacies plaguing her? How could she say her husband's touch stripped her of thought and reason—that, in fact, she craved it? As long as she could remember, she'd lived with the elusive feeling that something was missing in her life. She'd been determined to change that by marrying Jakob and fulfilling that need. Yet the yearning remained. Still just out of reach was the answer she couldn't formulate the right question for. That feeling was still the same.

Grandmother patted her hand. "What, Lydia? What can make a flower such as you unhappy?"

"Grandmother . . . is lying together for reasons other than . . . creating a child . . . a sin?"

"Foolish girl. God created a woman for Adam when he was alone in the garden."

" 'The pleasures of the flesh are—' "

"You're going to quote Scripture to me?" Paper-thin eyelids closed for a long moment, as if she were searching for the answer inside, before flying open again. "He pleases you? Is that what the torment is over?"

Lydia felt herself blush, and her grandmother's voice grew stronger.

"I've never spoken a word against your father, but there is a limit to how much I can see and not speak the truth. This . . . fanaticism he's developed over the years is not healthy for any of you children!

"Why do you think we left New Harmony in the first place? They had done away with marriage! Father Rapp said we couldn't marry, and Matthäus knew marriage was a part of

God's plan. Think of it! Think of how perfectly your bodies fit one another. Didn't God create us in a most miraculous way?''

"I *have* thought that," Lydia agreed.

"It's as natural to take a man to your body as it is a baby to your breast. Your grandfather and I were married because we loved one another. What we shared will only be bested by the rewards awaiting us in heaven . . . and I cannot wait to see him there." Her chin trembled. "Why did you go? Why did you leave, Lydia, if you're not going to change? Do you think Jakob will love you because you wear that green dress and have butchered your hair?"

Lydia's mouth fell open in indignation. She *had* changed! She wasn't the same wistful girl Jakob Neubauer had flirted with over coffee in the bakery. She'd had enough courage to make the daring decision to leave her home and become his wife. She had changed, hadn't she?

Lydia wrestled with her grandmother's words. Was she right? Had she changed or not? "Just because I wish something does not mean it is God's will."

"The same goes for your father. Just because he wishes something doesn't make it God's will. Do you remember when I told you to follow your heart? God is in there, guiding you."

Lydia's brow furrowed in thought. Was Grandmother right? Did she dare to hope to enjoy all the aspects of her life with Jakob?

The time passed rapidly, and before she realized it, she had to bid her grandmother goodbye. She brushed the soft, dry cheek with her lips and held her bony hand until the last moment. Tight-throated, she gazed at her grandmother's beloved face. The tenderness she'd always seen was evident, yet there was something more. A resignation. A fulfillment.

"I'll die happy knowing you love him, Lydia Rose."

Lydia spread her hands on the quilt she'd once thought her heritage. A bolt of grief slammed through her, and her chest constricted. She should be here, spending these precious last days and hours with her. The inevitability of her death didn't make it any easier to deal with. It was unfair that Lydia wasn't free to sit here all day and all night if she wanted to! She choked back a sob and hugged her grandmother goodbye.

As she rode home, the afternoon sun, high and hot, baked her through her layers of clothing. When she came to the stream, she was sorely tempted to dismount and cool her hands and face in the refreshing water, but she sat her saddle and allowed Freida to dip her nose in the water for a drink.

God had sent Jakob to save her from the fire for a second chance. Her Jakob was not the serpent in disguise. He was a godly man. To think otherwise was impossible.

She watched intently, and the landmarks guided her return trip. At the fork that marked the last trail, Freida lifted her tail and ears, and it was all Lydia could do to keep the horse from taking off at a dead run once they reached the main road running past the farm. At the end of the drive, she gave up and simply hung on.

Exhausted from the day's heat, the long ride and her own turbulent emotions, she wiped the animal down with fistfuls of hay and walked her around the corral the way Jakob had shown her. *Jakob.* The chore evoked memories of the day she'd been stung and the deliberate way he'd forestalled climbing the stairs and tending her bites. Lydia used the curry brush, measured food and water and dried and hung the saddle and tack. For the first time she wondered if he was as ashamed to admit his feelings as she. That first night—that very first night, he'd expressed his inadequacy....

"How was your ride?" Annette was taking in laundry.

"Exhausting. Do I have time for a bath before supper? I smell like a horse."

"Go freshen up. I can't wait to hear about your visit."

That night Lydia blew out the lantern and tried not to listen to the angry voices drifting up from the darkness in the yard below. Peine and Anton. Again. Why did they waste precious time arguing? She would be content just to have Jakob near. She lay atop the lofty bed, the now-familiar longing engulfing her. An insoluble knot of yearning ached in the hollow of her breast.

A string of curses volleyed across the dooryard. Peine's snapping voice shouted vile names. Shocked to the bone, Lydia pulled Jakob's pillow over her head. She lay on her side and drew herself up into the tiniest ball she could manage, wrapping her arms around her knees, her nose pressed into the nightdress covering them.

Blocking out Peine's unrestrained voice, Lydia pictured Jakob. She remembered his supple form as she'd glimpsed it the morning after they were married. The memory glided through her body, squirmed, swelled, ignited her longing for him. That one afternoon was vivid in her mental register of disturbing encounters. The feel of his silky hair against her flesh, his rough cheek stroking her breasts. She'd felt . . . worshiped.

And then, as always, he'd withdrawn. Had he been shocked at her compliance, as she'd thought, or was there perhaps some encouragement she'd neglected to offer? In her ignorance, had she committed an offense? Somehow, Lord help her, she didn't find their intimacy as objectionable as he did. Jakob. *Oh, Jakob.* She squeezed her eyes shut and her thighs together, hoping to escape the overwhelming burden. She prayed for strength and guidance—and sleep.

Peine glanced up from hanging her freshly laundered underthings on the clothesline. Picking up the empty basket, she made her way to the house. In the kitchen, Lydia and Annette were excitedly discussing Jakob's return. Lydia sounded like a child anticipating her birthday. What a fool! Perhaps it wasn't plain enough yet that Jakob wasn't for her. Annette left in search of jars to put her berries up in.

"When will he be home?" Peine asked.

Lydia pressed butter into wooden molds. "He left the bridge site yesterday, and he will be in Williamsport for a day or two, then in Pittsburgh a day. That should make it about Saturday."

With a swoosh of her blue damask skirts, Peine dropped into a chair and selected a sugar cookie from the plate in the center of the table. "Humph. After three days, his carnal desires should be satisfied."

Lydia looked up. "What do you mean?"

"I *mean,* there are women in the cities who can be bought. Women who make it their job to know ways to please a man." She gave Lydia her most worldly expression.

Lydia's hands stopped shaping the yellow butter and dangled lifelessly over the half-full mold. "Do you mean harlots?"

"Nicer name than some I've heard." Peine rose and picked up Nikolaus's clothing from where she'd dropped it after a particularly messy breakfast. The girl was such a chit. Had all her knowledge come from the Bible?

"But that is adultery! Jakob would never—"

"Honey, don't say 'never' when you're talking about a man. All men sample the wares." And Peine knew better than most. She'd lived in the rear of a brothel most of her formative years. She'd learned exactly what went on. She knew the so-called "respectable" patrons. Why, she was even aware of the going rates! "How do you think the profession manages to flourish?"

"No." Lydia resumed her task. "Not Jakob. He's honorable."

Still not convinced, eh? "Oh, come on, Lydia. Where do you think he learned how to do all those exciting things? By being honorable? You're not naive enough to think he's never been with other women, are you?" Yes, she probably was. "I know better."

She watched as her words effectively cut Lydia to the quick. "And—" she paused for effect, in case that wound hadn't been fatal "—local word had it Sylvie Schelling was pregnant when she died. Jakob was her beau."

Lydia slapped the tabletop. "Why do you say these things to me?"

Peine turned a saintly emerald gaze on her. "Don't you want to be friends? Women talk about these things. If you'd rather not, I'll comply. I'll try to remember you're not just another friend. You're different."

Upstairs, she pressed her fingers into her lower back. She couldn't be rid of that amazon soon enough! Already the pull of her abdominal muscles had given Peine an unbearable backache. She imagined Jakob rubbing away her misery with his big, work-worn hands. The possibility had dimmed since Lydia's arrival. She wanted that girl far from this place. She wanted to scream and rant and cry.

But no, she wouldn't cry. She hadn't cried since she was nine and her mother pulled away in a fancy carriage belonging to one of her string of "friends." Oh, yes, Peine knew what paid women in the cities did for men.

All-consuming rage had filled her that autumn afternoon as the dry leaves crackled under the wagon wheels. The vehicle had pulled away from Savannah Stockwell's, and she'd retreated to the two bleak rooms she'd shared with her mother.

Born of her anger had been a determination to get as far away from the dreadful city as she could, never again to be known as "Peine in the butt," the kid nobody wanted. Citizens had looked down their sanctimonious noses with disdain; classmates had treated her with contempt. Pious church ladies had pointed fingers and called her names. But worse, far worse, had been the occasional adult who looked at her with pity, as if she were a starving kitten to be put out of its misery.

Aloof, and too wrapped up in herself and her callers to bother with a troublesome child, her mother had driven Peine, the only person who ever truly cared for her, away. Exactly when the grief had turned to hate, Peine wasn't sure. She'd cloaked herself in hatred and anger, using the twin emotions as a defense against the hurt of a father who couldn't be trusted and a mother who couldn't love her.

One person had seemed to care, and had treated her with concern and dignity. Reese Tippet. A middle-aged businessman with a grown son who'd moved west. He'd owned several respectable—and some not-so-respectable—businesses in Philadelphia.

Peine had met him while doing chores at the Sedgewick Boarding House. He'd had a small office on the bottom floor, and a room upstairs. Reese had taken an interest in the beautiful but remote child, discovered her domestic situation and dedicated himself to seeing that she didn't follow in her mother's footsteps.

Initially Peine rejected every gesture of friendship and attention Reese Tippet offered. She knew men, knew what they wanted and how they went about it. Never having had anyone care enough to talk or listen to her, she was suspicious of his every word and action.

But he was kind and patient. He was lonely, she learned later. And wealthy, she learned much later.

She saved every cent she earned doing chores at the boarding house and threw herself into her studies. She was determined not to need anyone's approval or pity or friendship, and it was more than a year before she realized Reese actually liked her. She worked and saved, aided by opportune jobs Reese secured for her.

At fifteen she had her own room in the respectable Sedgewick Boarding House. Though it was wonderful to get away from her slovenly mother who'd become a drunk, other boarders—the sanctimonious Gerta Ridley in particular—held her in disdain. Gerta studied her over the top of square wire-rimmed spectacles, using each and every opportunity to shame and humiliate Peine further.

At dinner Gerta shared Peine's upbringing with each guest and new boarder, and made a point of sitting in the farthest chair from her, moving deliberately aside whenever Peine passed.

With no family and no friends, save one, Peine worked and studied on her own until she graduated. Reese presented her with a check for her first year's college tuition. Halfway through her first semester, a stray bullet during a holdup at the local bank killed him, and she lost the only friend she'd ever had.

When she was nineteen, her father returned to Pittsburgh, and though she wouldn't have recognized him, he found her and wormed his way into her unembellished life. Through a tiny crack in her armor, he struck a responsive chord: a remote, carefully shelved desire to belong, to have a family, to give and receive love.

Until he could find work, she put him up in the boarding house. They took their meals together, rented carriages for Sunday drives, shopped in fashionable stores and finally, hesitantly, Peine stopped hating and enjoyed his dashing company. The right job never quite came along, but they enjoyed themselves. In the back of her mind, she realized her savings were dwindling, but she was convinced he would repay her as soon as a position opened up. What he did for a living wasn't quite clear, and later she asked herself why she'd never wondered.

The New Year dawned, and she didn't have tuition. Her savings had run out. All she had left were two rooms and her father. One fall morning, as she awaited his arrival in the dining hall, the proprietor informed her that her father had checked out.

Across the table, Gerta Ridley wore a smug grin.

Peine ate her breakfast as if nothing were wrong, and afterward went out for a newspaper. Reese was gone. Her money was gone. Her father was gone. Again. She needed a job.

But she never cried.

A week later she saw Anton's article in the Pittsburgh *Gazette*. After a sleepless night, she posted a letter. A week later, the response came, along with money to buy whatever she needed. She didn't need much, but she spent it anyway, on dresses, jewelry and hats. She'd set that backwater farmer on his ear.

Anton showed up at the boarding house and took her to dinner. He was handsome enough, nice enough, and he was her ticket out of town. She didn't want to linger in Pittsburgh and risk having him talk to people at the boarding house or chance upon someone who knew her mother. She cast aside his suggestions that they get to know one another better. She took care of last-minute business—including a midnight visit to Gerta Ridley's room—and they were married the following day, spending their first night together on a train.

Peine glanced at Nikolaus, who was sleeping soundly in his crib. Anton was crazy about the child.

She stepped to the window and watched Annette carrying a basket across the yard. Franz had married her because he loved her, not because he wanted children and no one else was available. Not like her and Anton.

And Lydia, she thought with contempt. The naive little Bible-thumper didn't know the power she held in her holy hands. Jakob had fallen all over himself since he'd found her. Heaven only knew what the attraction was. Lydia was pretty enough, for a gray country mouse. But she was artless, ignorant. That, of course, was in Peine's favor.

Peine wanted Jakob for herself. After the years of suffering alone, the years of persecution, she deserved him.

Anton had brought her to his home, their marriage certificate tucked in his bag. One look at Jakob, and disappointment had swept through her veins. Jakob, not Anton, was the man she wanted. Jakob was meant for her.

After living with the family for a time, she appreciated Jakob more than ever. He was always willing to stop and talk with her as Reese had. His ready smile reminded her of Reese, too. They were the only men she had ever trusted. Jakob understood her moods and was less critical than Anton. He was perfect. And he'd been unmarried.

Until now. Until Lydia. Gullible, naive Lydia.

Not for long. Peine smiled. She could dislodge Lydia. All she had to do was discover the right toehold. Jakob was hers.

Chapter Sixteen

None of Lydia's chores held her attention, and she found herself repeating tasks. At meals she picked at her food, finding the empty space between her and Johann cavernous. At night she lay awake in bed—Jakob's bed—her thoughts rife with doubt and self-doubt.

Each time she pictured him, his expression the day she'd cut her hair superimposed itself over the face she wanted to remember. Grievous disappointment. Curious vulnerability. And something else she couldn't pinpoint...

She'd sensed it since the morning after that first time, after she understood the act of becoming one flesh. If only she'd known what was expected of her! If only she'd been able to sew pretty dresses and wear them before he left. If only...

None of that mattered now. Jakob was honorable. He would not lie with a harlot, no matter how dissatisfied he was with his wife, even if she'd been his second choice.

Saturday morning she told herself the same thing while milking. A warm liquid stream hit the back of her hand and splashed up onto her nose. She jerked in surprise.

"What's the matter? Suck a lemon for breakfast?"

She returned Franz's grin and dabbed at her nose with her sleeve. "Just thinking."

"Wonderin' where that brother of mine is?"

"Which one?"

He laughed. "We know where Anton is. He's still in the doghouse! I mean Jake."

"I didn't know Jessie had a house. Whatever is Anton doing in it?"

Franz laughed heartily and aimed the cow's teat at her with a devilish grin.

She shrieked, and the stream of milk caught her neck and shoulder.

"He's comin'! Jake's comin'!" Johann's call from outside the barn caught her attention.

Lydia set her pail well away from the cow and straightened, automatically tucking in loose hairs. She dried her neck with her apron. "See now? You've got me smelling like a cow!"

Up the incline toward the barn rumbled a brand-new springboard, loaded as high as the driver's head and covered with a tarpaulin. Two massive black horses with white blazes pulled the wagon. Perched high on the seat was indeed Jakob. Lydia's heart smiled in welcome.

The team reached level ground. He reined them in and pulled the brake, his eyes on his wife's face. Hesitantly Lydia moved to the side of the wagon. Would he be glad to see her? If he didn't acknowledge her properly, she'd die.

Jakob leapt from the seat, sweeping his hat from his head. His fair hair shone gold in the morning sun, the breeze catching it like tassels in a cornfield. He needed a haircut. His face and neck were darker than ever, burnished the color of teak by the sun. He removed a worn pair of leather gloves and stood staring at her.

She was beautiful. Just as he remembered. A rosy blush complemented her fair skin, and beguiling tendrils of dark hair lay against her neck and temples. Lydia. She was tantalizing, even in her day dress, with perspiration glowing on her cheeks. He'd wanted to bring the world home for her, buy her a lifetime of happiness and wrap it with himself. He'd been an emotional washout since before he left. Now he was going to fix that.

With sudden haste, he pulled her against him and held her head near the steady beating of his heart. God, she felt good. She was strong and warm, smelling faintly of bread and— cows? Releasing her, he turned to his waiting father and slapped him on the back.

Johann hugged him in return. "You're home sooner than we thought."

"Yeah. I got my shopping done and left without sleepin' last night."

Unconsciously Lydia caught the sleeve of his jacket, her wide eyes on the mysterious covered load on the wagon. At the slight tug on his wrist, Jakob turned. "Help me."

She was quick to assist him in removing his jacket, eager for his touch, no matter how insignificant. He unstrapped his leather holster, laid it and the gun under the wagon seat and gestured proudly toward the pair of ebony horses. Their coats glistened with sweat in the sun. "What do you think?"

"Where did you get them?"

"A ranch this side of Pittsburgh. Blaze and Carolina." The horses' ears pricked up at the sound of their names. "Aren't they beauties?"

The muscles beneath the shirt on his broad back undulated as he unharnessed the team, speaking softly to them, running his hands over their necks and flanks. He wore an unfamiliar pair of black suspenders crisscrossed over the damp, wrinkled white fabric of his shirt. Being so close and not touching him was like drowning. Lydia wanted to run her hands over him the way he did with the horses. He reached under Carolina's belly, and his shoulders pulled the material of his shirt taut. The thought of another woman touching him sliced her heart into ragged shreds. "May I walk her?"

He turned, squinting into the sun, and her tortured heart skipped a beat. "Sure."

Together they walked the pair around the barn and corral, leading them into the shelter of the shady building. Lydia brought fistfuls of hay and wiped the animals down while Jakob poured feed and water. The anxiety she'd been repressing for two days bubbled near the surface. "You were shopping, then?"

"Yes." Amusement lit his expression, and she lowered her gaze. Doubting him left her plagued with guilt. She felt adulterous herself, felt she was harboring sordid uncertainties.

Franz had finished with the cows and carried the buckets out of the barn. Jakob forked hay from the loft down the chute into the troughs and closed the horses in their stalls, and then his hot gaze returned to her. Silence ensued, swallowing the space between them. Jakob faced her, feet apart, and regarded her with steely-bright eyes.

Quick-springing expectancy soared through Lydia's veins, gaining momentum when he stepped toward her.

He caught her around the waist and pulled her against his hard body. "I missed you."

Three words! Three words made the difference between night and day. Between misery and ecstasy. Jakob buried his face in her hair. Running his hands up her arms, he bracketed her jaws, pulling her face up to his.

No wonder the animals stood docile beneath his attention. He was tall and magnificent, and his touch was incredibly exhilarating. His body radiated the warmth of the afternoon sun. He'd missed her! "I missed you, too."

Her confession came easily after his. Her hands, uncertain as always, fluttered in the air by his hips. Before she could decide what to do with them, he stepped back and smiled at her. "I'm hungry."

She wanted him to fold her into himself and hold her in his goodness forever. Hiding her disappointment that he hadn't kissed her, she returned his smile and ran to prepare him a meal, pleased that the other women were elsewhere. She sliced bread, fried sausage and warmed biscuits left from breakfast. Just as she held eggs over a skillet, Jakob treaded through the back door, his arms laden with packages wrapped in brown paper and newsprint. He steadied the pile and sat it on the table.

She stared. "What are those?"

"Your presents," he replied matter-of-factly. "Smells good. Is it ready?"

She cracked the eggs into the hot skillet. Never could she recall eggs taking so long to fry! At last she heaped his plate and placed it before him.

He'd washed at the pump, and his sleeves and hair were damp. Taking a buttered slab of bread, he bit into it. "Mmm... Missed this, too," he said around a mouthful. A teasing gleam lit his eyes. "Well?"

She tilted her head.

"Going to open your presents?"

As if he'd fired the starting gun at a race, Lydia plopped down on the bench across from him and picked up the first package. The string was difficult to untie, and impatiently she reached for the bread knife. Inside a red velvet-lined box were a silver thimble and a tiny pair of matching embroidery scissors, sunk in wells of fabric. She touched them cautiously with her index finger before taking them out and holding them in her palm. "Thank you."

He nodded. She read the importance of these offerings in his eyes and sensed instinctively his desire to please her. She opened a box with a hinged lid. Inside nestled a gold-plated signet bracelet. The rolled band opened with a spring and closed snugly around her wrist. The signet top bore a flat heart with curlicues on either side, and her initials engraved in roman script: L on the left, R on the right, and a dominating N in the center.

"Oh, Jakob, this is beautiful." Her eyes filled with guilty tears. Tears of remorse. While she'd unjustly doubted his fidelity, he'd had her initials engraved on a gold bracelet. His fork paused, hovering in the blur of her tears.

"I hope those are happy tears."

I was miserable without you, Jakob. She could only nod.

She unwrapped a soft green belt with a filigree buckle, followed by an ivory fan, and ribbed cotton-and-wool vests and drawers. Pink-faced, Lydia glanced at him.

"You'll thank me this winter, when you see how cold it is on the way to church."

Three pairs of black cotton stockings were next, with elastic tops and ankles. Fabrics followed. Lydia ran her fingers over various textures of fancy figured flannelettes, fine cambric percale, dark red chambray, slick black sateen, heavy German calico, white shimmer crepe de chine and bleached table damasks. Mentally planning Jakob a dark red chambray shirt and herself a white crepe blouse, Lydia discovered a royal blue fabric at the bottom of the package.

She slid it out, unrolled it and ran her hands across the cool satin. On a spring morning only months ago, she'd wistfully imagined a dress made out of material like this. A dream. A fantasy she'd conjured up to relieve the boredom and monotony of colony life. So much had changed since then. So many dreams had come true. Life here was far from boring. Her reality was bewildering. Exhausting and sometimes painful, but never boring. "Oh, Jakob..."

Jakob drank in her wholesome candor, sharing her lingering smile. He was glad to be home, glad to be near her. Though he was hard-pressed to know just how to work out the physical aspect of their marriage, he'd determined to try.

"I can sew now."

He was paying attention to the delicate bow of her upper lip when the import of her words sunk in. "Now? You can sew *now?*"

"Yes! Charlotte and Annette taught me. They are both good friends." A length of string wrapped around her thumb, forgotten, the end trailing across the tabletop.

Why hadn't he realized she couldn't sew? How thoughtless of him to purchase material she had no idea what to do with! He'd wondered why she hadn't made herself dresses. "Why didn't you tell me you didn't know how to sew when I bought the fabric?"

Dark eyes scanned his face. *I was afraid you'd regret marrying me.* "You did not ask."

He grinned. "I didn't, did I? Could you tell me things sometimes, even if I don't ask?"

She whisked his plate away and replaced it with a cup of steaming coffee. Her weaknesses far outnumbered her strengths. It wouldn't be easy to share them. "I'll try."

The uncertainty in her reply troubled him. He'd been so starchy and headstrong that she'd been afraid to tell him she couldn't make dresses. No doubt there were other things she hadn't voiced. He'd have to assure her he hadn't married her for her domestic skills.

But hadn't he? At one time he *had* considered the help she'd be around the farm. He hadn't wanted a lazy wife like Peine, but Lydia was far from lazy. Thinking of the help Lydia would be to him had been part of his justification for wanting to bring her here. Later he'd told her he didn't care about those things, and he'd meant it.

Lydia sat limply on the wooden bench, surveying the pile of new belongings. She raised her eyes to his. "Why did you spend your hard-earned money on gifts for me?"

Jakob looked at his coffee mug. Why? Because he'd spent every waking hour for the past six weeks thinking of her and wanting to please her more than anything. Because he hadn't done a very good job of offering himself to her. Because he wanted to start over again and do it right. "I wanted to. I promised to be a good husband and provide for you."

He rose from the bench and walked around the end of the table, seating his hip next to hers, his body facing the other way. He took her chin in his fingers and held her face close to his. Lydia's heart do-si-doed within her rib cage. His fingers on her chin were hard and callused, like she remembered. It pleased him to give her these things. How could it be sinful to feel pampered and cosseted on such an occasion? It pleased her immeasurably to think of him shopping for her. "Thank you, Jakob."

"Bitte, schön weib." His lips touched hers gently, and she tasted coffee. His hand slid from her chin into the hair at the back of her neck, his mouth widening over hers.

She forgot the dishes in the sink and the wagonful of supplies as he kissed her with disturbing reverence. The kiss had been conceived during long, empty nights over the past weeks, and was born now as she rediscovered her emotional thirst. Her heart caught in her throat, hindered her breathing. Oh, how she had missed him!

"Ah, Lydia." He breathed her name against her ear, fluttering wisps of hair. He took her shoulders and held her at arm's length. "I have to unload the wagon."

"May I help?"

"Come on." With childlike enthusiasm, they scampered outdoors.

How he had packed it all in one wagon, she couldn't fathom! Barrels of nails, doors and windows, a stove, lamps, lanterns, paint, plaster, wire, tools, rope, a pump, an enamel sink, a steel bathtub, hinges and doorknobs and bits and bridles burdened the wagon.

Perspiration dotting his forehead, he handed her the last package. Inside was a woven jacquard lap robe with a heavy knotted fringe. "You'll thank me this winter."

"I'll thank you now." She stood on tiptoe and kissed his damp cheek. His face pinkened considerably, and she doubted it was from the sun or the exertion. Lydia took secret satisfaction from the knowledge that he wasn't immune to her aggressive show of affection.

She discovered a cache under the wagon seat. A dozen bars of soap, ranging from oatmeal to clear glycerin and buttermilk. She smiled. She had a husband who bought soap rather than using homemade lye. The more she learned about him, the more she . . . loved him?

Dinner was a celebration, everyone caught up in having the family once again complete. Jakob's steady, familiar voice asked the blessing, and he squeezed Lydia's hand.

By midafternoon, it was obvious that lack of sleep had taken its toll on him. His face was drawn and dark, and his buoyant mood diminished. He barely ate any supper, a sure sign of exhaustion.

Lydia touched his wrist with her fingertips while the others enjoyed dessert. "Why don't you go up and lie down? You're worn out."

Jakob half smiled. "You don't mind?"

"Of course not. Rest."

He closed his fingers over hers on his wrist. "Will you check the horses for me?"

"Yes." Pleased that he trusted her with the chore, she dropped her gaze to his fingers. Almost regretfully, he pulled his hand back, bade the family good-night and with one backward glance at his wife, climbed the stairs.

Later that evening, Lydia found the massive pair of horses resting in their stalls. She spoke soothingly and offered them each an apple. They munched placidly, sniffing the front of her apron. She scraped their massive foreheads with her fingertips, as she'd seen Jakob do, sensing that it would be a familiar gesture.

The magnificent pair was a symbol of Jakob's desire for independence. He was weaning himself and Lydia from the extended family, preparing for the day they moved into their own house. The step was easily recognizable as part of his plan for them, the one he'd spoken of so wistfully.

Low voices floated through the front parlor on her way past. The lantern cast a swinging shadow across the stairway walls. In their room, she rested it on the washstand. Discreetly checking to make certain Jakob was indeed asleep, she slipped out of her undergarments, bathed her body and dressed in her thin cotton nightdress. Perching on the bed's edge, she studied her husband in the glow from the lantern, reassuring herself with his presence.

He slept on his back, one hand on the sheet at his hip, the other in a loose fist on her pillow. She had never seen him asleep. His muscled arms and shoulders were bronzed from hours of work in the hot sun. The broad expanse of his chest was unmistakably disconcerting, the fuzzy hair golden in the lantern's glow. She wanted to delve her fingers in and ruffle it, feel the texture of his bronze skin beneath her fingertips.

His weary face was relaxed, his breathing even and his eyelids appeared to flutter in slumber. The taut skin over his cheekbones seemed kissed by the summer sun. If he woke at this moment, he would see desire in her eyes. Maybe he would take her chin in his fingers and pull her face to his. Maybe he would make up for every day they'd been apart.

It was perhaps unfair, yet it was still gratifying, to postpone blowing out the lantern so that she could relish the fact that he was lying in this bed again. She took his hand from her pillow and held it a minute longer than necessary before laying it at his side.

He was home. For tonight, it was enough.

Though he slept soundly and was unaware of her, his solid presence comforted Lydia. More than that, it was a joy. She'd longed for this night. Her chest filled with an ardent, all-consuming tenderness for this husband who'd worked weeks in the blistering sun to bring her gifts and buy materials for a house. Their house.

Today he had reminded her of the promises he'd made months ago in Accord. He had promised to be a good husband, to provide for her, to see that she never regretted her decision and . . .

He'd pledged faithfulness.

She reached her hand toward him, then withdrew. Overcoming her hesitancy, she slid a single finger over his wide forehead and his tawny brow, down his long nose and across his full upper lip. His lips parted, and his hand returned to her pillow. She picked it up and laid her palm against his, comparing. His hand was considerably larger, work-hardened, with a sprinkling of golden hair on the back.

She remembered his fear that she would find him unacceptable. Never! He was strong and tender, outlandish and beautiful. He had taught her how to laugh and enjoy life. How ironic that she was the unacceptable partner. If she woke him now, he might pull her beneath him in the lamplight, might stroke her with callused palms, might plant his seed within her—

If only Lydia knew how she displeased him. She tried her best to talk and dress like the women he was familiar with. She would try harder, and offer encouragement for his touch.

Without disturbing him, she tiptoed to the oil lamp and blew. It guttered, spat and went out, the smell of the wick threading a trail across the darkened room. She lay down, and Jakob turned, fitting his long body against hers. She could willingly lend encouragement. The thought provoked quavery delight. She found his hand and held it to her breast until sleep took her.

Jakob placed his fiddle case under the seat of his new springboard and leaned against one of the wheels, whistling. From his jeans pocket, he withdrew the watch he'd bought in Williamsport and flipped it open.

The rest of the family had gone ahead a half-hour ago. With his own rig now, he was staying behind to wait for Lydia. How unlike her to take so long getting ready! He didn't want to be late for the dance at the Karssens'.

What was she doing, anyway? He was idly rechecking the harnesses when the front door closed and she stepped off the porch. A flattering green dress with a snowy-white tucked and embroidered bodice emphasized her full breasts and narrow waist. He stared for a full minute after she reached the wagon and waited for his assistance.

The green kid belt he'd given her drew attention to the soft curve of the hips below. His body responded immediately. The dress was a far cry from the uncomplimentary grays and dark blues she normally wore. In those drab dresses, behind the concealment of her starched and prim white aprons, she was lovely. But in this dress . . .

Lydia was breathtaking.

Beneath a matching bonnet with white eyelet trim, her hair hung in glistening dark ringlets past her shoulders.

"You're beautiful," he said at last.

"Thank you." Her cheeks pinkened. She reached both gloved hands toward him and brought him to his senses.

"Oh, here." He spanned her waist with his hands, lifting her into the wagon. A perfectly gentlemanlike thing to do, but he was no gentleman. Climbing up beside her, he adjusted his dun-colored hat on his head, and gave her sidelong looks from beneath its brim, thinking of the heavenly body beneath the dress. And he'd been so exhausted the night before. She'd lain right there beside him during the night, and he'd slept through it!

Not tonight! Her subtle lavender fragrance incited his senses. Not tonight.

Lydia was easily coaxed onto the sawdust-sprinkled dance floor. Jakob taught her a few new steps, feeling desire and anticipation flowing between them. Every dance, every comment, was an opportunity to touch her. He watched her devotedly during his turn on the musicians' platform. Lydia danced with Johann and deliberately stayed clear of Anton.

As usual, the heat in Jakob's corner was oppressive. After ten o'clock he walked outdoors to clear his head. Returning from the outhouse, he saw Lydia framed against the open doorway. His breath caught.

Slowly walking toward him, Lydia used her new white fan, which proudly lifted her hair from her face with each arc, the tiny silver spangles on the edge of the fan shimmering in the moonlight. She looked like any other young woman he'd seen in the cities and the community, except that she was more beautiful. For a fleeting moment, Jakob wondered if she could lose her unique identity and blend right in with the others.

Her speech reassured him it was impossible.

"Darf ich bitten? Das ist für Sie." She extended a pint jar of lemonade.

"Danke." He accepted the jar. "What did you ask?"

"If you'd like to dance."

"It's hot in there. I drank a couple of beers, and I need to clear my head."

"You promised you were a sober man, Jakob."

Jakob jerked his gaze up. She fanned her lifted chin furiously and gave him a look that on any other woman would have been considered coy. She was teasing him! He laughed sheepishly.

"Come. Walk with you I will," she offered.

He drained his glass, and she slipped her arm through the crook of his. They strolled the Karssens' long drive, enjoying the breeze whispering to the leaves in the treetops. Cicadas chorused from tall grasses on either side, growing louder as they reached a grove of fruit trees.

They continued along the roadway. The unmistakable earth-smell of tomatoes wafted on the summer air. "Feeling better?"

"Um-hmm..." was his noncommittal reply. "What did you do while I was gone?"

"Your papa taught me a card game. I wish I could have known your mother."

"Yes, well, she was..."

"Schön."

"Beautiful. He told you that."

"It seems you Neubauer men place quite an importance on the physical attributes of your wives."

He shrugged. "We're just appreciative."

"Perhaps you're flatterers and bull-throwers."

"Bull-throwers?" Jakob chortled. "Where'd you pick up that one?"

"Anton."

"I should have known. I wonder if it was safe to leave you alone with my family for six weeks. Gambling and cursing! What other transgressions did they lead you into?"

"We were *not* gambling, and that wasn't a curse word." She tipped her face up to his, her body rigid. "Was it?"

His hands closed over her upper arms. "Close."

"How close?" His hands flexed in an enticing distraction.

"As close as we're standing right now."

"Really?"

His face was clearly defined in the moonlight. Brazenly Jakob pulled her against him and tasted her parted lips. Palms flat on her back, he pressed her body against his. His chest was rock-solid against her breasts.

Lydia's eyes closed, and she leaned into his embrace, welcoming his kiss, a heart-stopping kiss, like the ones they'd shared that lazy Saturday afternoon so long ago. She wondered for a moment why it was tomatoes she smelled and not apples.

Jakob's tongue drew a silky line across her lower lip and tested the satiny inner skin of her upper lip. Unprepared for the erotic assault, she involuntarily withdrew an inch, her thumbs pressing into his biceps. He would have no part of her retreat. One at a time, he placed her hands around his waist, then curled her tighter against the hard length of his body. Through his shirt, her fingers traced the muscled contours of his lower back. His insatiable mouth slanted over hers. His tongue searched, probed, until the import dawned and she allowed him entrance into her mouth. His satisfied groan told her she pleased him.

The knowledge was heady, and she reveled in it for long, poignant minutes. He ran his hands over her back, up and down her sides, then slid them upward and framed her jaw.

"Let's go home," he whispered hoarsely.

Chapter Seventeen

"Now?" Blinking to orient herself, Lydia gazed into his shining eyes.

"Now." He tugged her hands and led her back the way they'd come, almost at a run. "Wait by the horses while I get my fiddle."

"And my bonnet."

"And your bonnet." As if they were embarking on a long journey, he folded her against his chest and kissed her fervently. "I'll be right back."

She touched her burning lips and watched him lope up the drive. He hadn't kissed her like that before he went away. She stood near the team of black horses and wished she knew how to hook up the wagon traces. Her shoulders trembled, and she crossed her arms over her breasts, feeling an odd sensation there.

Jakob's boots pounded up behind her, and she whirled to face him. He handed her the fiddle case and bonnet, and she pulled her hat on, tying the ribbons loosely under her chin. She delighted in the sounds of him fastening the leather traces and chains to the wagon, his low, familiar voice mellowing the horses, while having an entirely different effect on her.

He grasped her waist and lifted her, his hands lingering on her soft leather belt before he jumped up beside her. The night air cooled her heated face, and the horses pulled them toward home with agonizing slowness.

They didn't speak, but sat side by side, their shoulders rubbing with the lurch and sway of the wagon on the rutted road.

Finally the road became smoother, a sign that their destination was near.

"I have to put the horses up."

"I'll help."

Jakob set the brake and leapt down. Lydia waited, anticipation jangling in every nerve ending. Coming around, he reached for her, catching her about the waist and pulling her full weight against him. She slid, gracelessly, down his body until she dangled, her feet inches from the ground, her green dress bunched between their bodies.

Unmindful of her immodest condition, Jakob made silent promises with a chain of kisses along her jaw and across her lips. A delicious shiver slid down her neck and shoulders and tightened her breasts. Next to them, the horses stamped and whinnied. Reluctantly Jakob released her and bent to the traces.

Lydia smoothed her dress down, then took Carolina's short lead and walked her into the barn. Jakob brought Blaze, and together they wiped and brushed the new team. She assured him she could see to the feed and water while he pulled the wagon into the barn. He left the double doors open and lit a lantern outside the barn to guide the others.

He tugged her toward the house with an urgency that said he wouldn't be denied. She experienced a flash of awkwardness. Everything had seemed spontaneous and natural back at the Karssens', but nearly an hour had passed. She knew what he had in mind to do, and she wanted all of it to feel as natural as his kisses. This time she had to encourage him. This time she must please him.

The lantern Jakob carried bobbed golden light up the staircase. Shadows stretched and shrank, teasing like playful children. The lantern's journey ended at the chiffonier. Lydia fumbled with the ribbons beneath her chin. Jakob tugged at them and then tossed the bonnet carelessly on her trunk.

He claimed her mouth and left no doubt in her mind that he could create the same tumultuous pulse that he had at the dance. Her heart beat energetically, every cell screaming.

His lips trailed across her chin and down her throat, plucking, nibbling, tasting. Lydia's head lolled back, and she stared wide-eyed at the ceiling. *Please don't let me disappoint him again.* Clumsily he searched for pins in her hair, and when she reached back to loosen the cascade he turned her away and impatiently unbuttoned her dress.

"Do you want this, Lydia?" His breathy voice rasped at her ear. "I don't want to do anything you're not ready for."

She turned back to him and raised her fingertips to the strong line of his tense jaw. "*Ja.* I am ready for this."

His gaze surveyed her bare shoulders and the hair fallen over them. Almost reluctantly, he reached over to the lantern, plummeting the room into sudden darkness. Unerringly he found her and peeled her dress and underclothes to her waist.

"What's this?" His fingers met soft cotton and eyelet. "You didn't wear this before."

"It's a chemise. Annette said ladies wear them under their clothing."

"And drawers!" He chuckled, dropped to his knees and peeled down the drawers to land wherever the rest of her clothing had gone. He pressed his face against her stomach and breathed deep.

His whisker-rough cheek awakened wonderful sensations against skin wrinkled by the restricting underclothes. Turning his face, he rubbed her belly and breasts with his chin and nose. Lydia almost purred. He stood, his lips finding hers, and backed her toward the bed. She tumbled, heedless of the coverlet.

She pushed his shoulders, gently. "Jakob."

"Lydia?"

"Jakob, your shirt."

He raised himself, impatiently. His belt buckle hit the floor. "Damn!"

Another frustrated curse, and the ropes creaked. His weight left the bed.

The familiar thud of his boots was music to her ears. One hit the floor, followed by another. The rustle of his clothing sent a shiver up her spine, and she scrambled beneath the sheet.

Returning to the bed, he threaded his fingers through her hair, spread it across the pillows and buried his face in the tresses. He rolled to his side, pulling her with him, his eloquent mouth kissing her eyes, her nose and her brows with feather-light reverence. His steel-strong arm beneath her held her close while his free hand stroked her shoulder. His callused palm, buffing her silky skin, sent delightful shivers rippling from shoulder to knees. The contrast between his rough hand and his soft, warm lips sent a deeper tremor pulsating through her.

Jakob cupped her breast, and she stopped breathing. His gentle fingers provoked an involuntary shrinking and tightening of the sensitive skin around her nipple. He kissed her, his mouth coaxing her to breathe again. She yielded to the caress of the fingers that were provoking an exquisite response from her body.

His tongue teased hers, probing her lips and retreating once she parted hers to him. At last she comprehended the inarticulate message and hesitantly returned the bold kiss.

Jakob groaned and pressed himself against her. She reveled in his imposing size and weight, and in the effect she was having on him. He skimmed her flesh with his palm, dragging the sheet down with his wrist. Reaching the silken curve of her hip, he kissed her fiercely.

"Ah, Lydia..." Her name was a sensuous lament against her open mouth. "I want to touch you all over... feel you all over me...." Against her ear, his low-pitched murmurs of praise and magic tumbled, spreading a delicious glow through her veins.

"Jakob," she whispered, arching her neck against his mouth. The welcome caress of his hand moved from her breasts, across her belly, down to her thighs. Lydia's eyes closed, and her breathing grew shallow.

"Say it again." Jakob bit her jaw, her chin, hampering her control.

"Jakob," she whispered. He touched her experimentally. She gasped and trembled.

Boldly he pulled her beneath him, flattening her breasts. She welcomed him, and marveled again at how perfectly God had made her body to accommodate him. She wondered if the thought of creating a baby even entered Jakob's mind. How, when they matched so perfectly in all the imperative places, could this be sinful? It couldn't be.

Jakob's mindless excitement was sheer joy to her. Every nerve ending, long denied a loving touch, shrieked for gratification. She dared to run her hands across his back and hips, and the well-toned muscles quivered beneath her palms. His reciprocal movements increased. He arched, groaned against her neck and shuddered convulsively. His energy subsided, and Lydia embraced him, proud that he'd chosen her.

He adjusted their bodies and lay against her side, his head pillowed upon her breast, his thundering heart slowing against her ribs. She gloried in the feel of his thick silky hair under her chin and between her fingers, and allowed herself a weary smile. She hadn't disappointed him. This time she had pleased him, she was sure.

Her body teemed with all-alive exhilaration and inexplicable warmth, still attentive and tender, but not unpleasant. An astonishing realization bloomed within her heart and mind.

"I love you, Jakob," she whispered, fluttering the hair on top of his head. Had she said it in German or English? It didn't matter. He was already asleep.

"It's time to get dressed for church."

For the first time, Lydia had to wake Jakob. His eyelids flickered, and a frown furrowed his brow. He squinted against the sunlight streaming through the open window. Lydia was already dressed and stood brushing her hair at the washstand. She wore festive yellow, as bright as the sun streaming through the window. The dress had a wide white sash tied in a perky bow on her backside.

The thought of the green dress she'd worn the evening before thrust into his memory, and recollection flooded him.

Good Lord! He'd been as randy as—

Lydia patiently worked tangles from her dark hair, tangles he'd no doubt put there with his tumbling and fumbling. She caught up both sides of her hair with the tortoiseshell combs he'd bought her, leaving the back to hang free in loose waves. She turned from the mirror and picked up the small handbag, looking toward him expectantly.

His gaze caught the tip of a gray snakeskin boot lying on its side. He refused to meet her eyes. God, he'd been in such a hurry. He was what Etham considered him to be—a coarse, worldly man driven by his own lusts.

Lydia glanced over her shoulder at the mirror, and an abraded patch of pink skin under her jaw caught his notice. His stubble had irritated her delicate skin. Had he hurt her in other ways? Had he been rough?

He'd been thoughtless, of that he was certain. After all his careful thinking and planning as to how he would introduce pleasure to her, he had rushed her home to bed! Night after night at the bridge site, he'd considered and imagined, and then he'd taken her selfishly! She deserved better.

Did he have it in him to behave better? Self-disgust filled him at the thought of the impatient desire that boiled within him when he kissed and touched her.

"Is anything wrong?" The worry in her dark eyes touched him. And then he understood. She didn't know any different. Every small bit of knowledge she had about marital relations, she'd learned from him. And in his own ignorance and lust, he'd let her down.

"Nothing is wrong," he assured her. "I've got a headache from sleeping too late."

"I will bring you a powder."

"No. As soon as I eat, I'll feel better." He sat at the bed's edge. He could tell she still needed some reassurance. "Want to pick me out a shirt while I wash up?"

She smiled and hurried to comply.

Downstairs, Anton and Johann were seated at the table, sipping coffee and talking. Peine, wearing a bright lemon-colored dress with a scandalous neckline, swept out of the room, carrying with her a freshly dressed Nikolaus and the heavy floral scent of perfume. The look she gave Lydia was positively scathing.

"I saved you some pancakes and bacon," Annette said from the sink.

Franz appeared in the doorway. "We took care of the horses for you this mornin', Jake. Thought you might like a leisurely sleep-in. Hurry, or we'll be late for church."

"Thank you," Jakob said to his retreating back.

Lydia poured him a cup of coffee and sat beside him.

"Want to do something after church?" he asked.

"*Ja.*"

"What would ya like to do?"

She looked up at him. "I would like to ride one of your new horses."

"They're *our* horses."

"Then I want to ride *my* horse."

"In that pretty dress?"

He had noticed! She smiled. "Of course not."

Lydia had never changed clothes as fast as she did after church. Wearing a gray day dress, she reached the porch out of breath.

Annette, idly rocking the wooden swing, tossed Lydia her bonnet. "Here, take this."

"Thank you." The family sat in the shade of the porch, Johann and Franz engaged in a checker game.

Jakob cantered down the drive on Blaze, Carolina in tow. He reined in, and dust shrouded the animals' forelegs. "Ready so soon?"

She smiled and tied Annette's bonnet under her chin.

"There's no stopping her when it comes to riding," Peine called in a musical voice from the wicker chair she lounged in. "She's gotten so good, she'll be riding circles around the rest of you!"

Lydia gave her a half-hesitant smile and stepped to the railing. Jakob steadied the prancing beast.

"Why, Jakob—" Peine's voice pierced Lydia's concentration as she secured a foot in the stirrup "—perhaps you'll let her take one of the new horses to go visiting, like she took Freida."

Jakob's head swiveled, and he looked at Peine, then back at his wife. His eyes narrowed under his hat's brim. "You rode Freida to go visiting?"

"Yes."

"Where?"

"To Accord."

Carolina grew restless and sidestepped. Jakob crowded her back into place. "Get on."

At his gruff command, Lydia pulled her weight up and threw her leg over the saddle. His telltale jaw muscle jerked. She accepted the reins from his gloved hand.

Gemlike blue eyes bored into hers. "H'yah!"

She leaned forward and dug her knees in, moving with the horse. The shimmering noonday heat had barely passed, the sun was still high in the sky and the air was dry and windless. Grasshoppers and other insects sailed into the air when the horses' hooves disturbed their feasting. Carolina was harder to manage than the docile Freida, but Lydia accepted the challenge.

Bonnet flung back on her shoulders, she rode hard behind Jakob until he drew up at a summer-dry creek. Jakob dismounted and reached for Lydia, roughly pulling her down in front of him. She steadied herself.

"You deliberately rode to Accord after I told you not to. Were you alone?"

"*Ja.*"

"Yes, what?"

"Yes, to Accord I went, and yes, I went alone."

Taking Carolina's reins from her hands, he turned sharply and stalked away.

Lydia ran several steps and caught up with him. "Jakob, I—"

He swung back to face her, his palms flung outward. "I told you we'd go together! I said it wasn't safe!"

"But I practiced like you said, and I was careful. Your papa went over the map with me. He taught me to load and shoot his rifle. He wouldn't have let me go if he thought there was any danger."

"Careful doesn't mean a thing!" He slapped the reins against his long thigh. "I didn't want you to go alone!"

"Jakob, you frighten me when you're angry. I did everything exactly the way you taught me. Even when I was hot and tired, I took care of the horses first."

Still holding the reins, he allowed the horses to pull him toward a trickle of water they found in the dry, cracked creek bed.

Lydia followed beside him, growing angry herself. Peine had made a point of sweetly telling him that Lydia had gone. She had managed to make the news sound like a compliment directed at Lydia.

Did his horses mean more to him than she did? They must. Feeling as emotionally parched as the hard ground beneath her, Lydia held his gaze. Every time she gained a little ground, she slipped right back. Two steps forward, three steps back.

She stepped in front of him.

He seemed to look uncomfortably toward the horizon. He studied his palm and slapped the reins against it.

Overhead, an eagle soared gracefully, then disappeared. Lydia swallowed.

Her gaze fell to the front of his shirt. *Oh, Jakob. Jakob, take me in your arms like you did last night, and everything will be all right.*

Last night she'd slept contentedly, his head resting on her breast, his fingers tangled in her hair, believing she'd at last measured up, that she'd responded in a pleasing manner. Now he was angry with her again.

They were both hot and sweaty. His shirtfront had grown damp, and the top of her head burned under the sun. She pulled the bonnet back up on her head.

Jakob relaxed his posture and dropped his gaze. He took a deep breath and calmed himself. If anything had happened to Lydia, he didn't know what he would've done. She had been foolish to take that chance with her safety. She had no idea the type of person who could chance upon an innocent like her.

He studied the cracked earth at her feet, struggling with the reason he feared her taking the horse alone. The odds of such an occurrence happening were slim, but it had happened once, and it could happen again.

"Lydia."

She met his gaze.

"When I was very young, I was engaged to a girl."

She nodded. "I know."

"How?" he frowned.

"Peine told me."

Peine? What business was it of hers? He shrugged away the question and went on. "She snuck out of her room on her way to meet me one night. In the dark stable, she chose the wrong stall."

His wife touched his arm.

"A stallion no one had been able to control kicked her to death."

Tears formed in Lydia's rich, dark eyes.

Jakob knew it wasn't his fault, wasn't anyone's fault. It had been a horrible accident. But in the far recesses of his heart, he'd hefted a load of guilt. Sylvie had been in love with him— fearful, yet eager to please. At his insistence, she'd been on her way to meet him. In a hurry, and hiding in the darkness, she'd made a fatal mistake.

"I waited for over an hour," he said softly. "I thought maybe she'd fallen asleep, or that her father had found her out." He shrugged. "I didn't find out what had happened until the next day."

"I'm so sorry," Lydia whispered.

He wiped a tear from her cheek with his thumb.

"I'll never let anything happen to you, Lydia. I thought you were safely tucked away at home while I was gone. Now I find out you were riding all over the county, putting yourself in danger." He glared up at the afternoon sky. Mad at himself, he had taken his anger out on her.

Catching him by surprise, she stepped forward and pressed her face against his damp shirtfront. A little sob escaped her. "Why didn't you tell me?"

He felt her hands clutch at his waist, and he wrapped his arms around her, in spite of the blistering heat. "What's done is done," he said at last. "We won't talk about it again."

"Then you forgive me?"

He couldn't help but smile, knowing he'd forgive her anything if she smiled or touched him or turned that liquid gaze upon him. "If you forgive me."

She smiled. *"Ja."*

"Let's get out of the sun." Handing Lydia the reins, he knelt and made a cradle of his entwined fingers. "Step up."

Lydia obeyed, settling on Carolina with a natural grace and spurring the animal. Jakob found himself strangely impressed. She accomplished everything she set out to do, from the complete upheaval of her life to the simplest chore. He admired her. What measures would she take to get to him if someone kept them apart? Her loyalty and love for her grandmother was obvious. If only she felt that way about him. He snorted in self-derision. If only he'd given her reason to. He prompted Blaze with his heels and caught up to her.

It soon became apparent to the family that Peine was pregnant. Uncharacteristically, she grew more animated with each passing day. The unfashionable attire she'd taken to wearing didn't dim her look of pleasure. Where she'd been sullen and withdrawn at meals in the past, she now spoke cheerfully and made a semblance of helping serve and clear.

She made a special point of speaking to Jakob, brushing against him, touching his hand or arm. He always spoke kindly to her. The smiles he offered were hers alone. She accepted them and tucked them into her slim collection of happy moments. Beneath her heart she carried a secret.

While cutting the wheat and hay, the men didn't return to the house at noon. Lydia and Annette took turns carrying meals to the fields, giving themselves an opportunity to watch the progress of the harvest.

Chaff filled the air, their noses, their clothing. The men's skin dried out; their hands blistered. They worked their backs and muscles to the limit and ate cold suppers. Franz and Lydia milked, the others returning to the fields while daylight lasted. All the Neubauers slept hard and wakened early.

Annette and Lydia worked as hard and long as the men. Even Peine was obliged to assume her share of the tasks. In huge kettles of boiling water, they blanched corn on the cob, cooled it and cut it off, then spread it in thin layers on framed sections of screen wire. They covered the corn with cheesecloth and allowed the sun to dry it. The kernels had to be stirred and brought in at night until completely dry. Then they were funneled into cloth table-salt bags and the bags sewn shut.

The women picked the remainder of the apples, though there were already bushels stored in the fruit cellar.

"Do we have to peel and dry all of them?" Lydia asked.

The look on her face made Annette laugh. "No. I'll show you."

They poured bushel after bushel into a shallow depression in the yard. Johann brought a bundle of hay and spread it over the pile, then covered it with boards for weight.

"When it snows," Annette informed her, "they'll keep all winter."

Noon meals were of sumptuous fare—Lydia's fresh fruit pies, corn on the cob, sliced tomatoes, fresh vegetables and cabbage slaws.

Late one afternoon, Lydia was churning butter in the shade of the side porch. A putrid smell wafted across the dooryard to her nostrils. "What are you doing out there?"

Standing at a rough-hewn worktable in the yard, Annette looked up from the lard tin she'd been peering into. She measured a powdery white substance and added it, stirring with a stick. "It's an old recipe of my mother's. I always keep it on hand. This'll do everything from shampooing hair and removing grease to killing bedbugs."

"Bedbugs?" She wouldn't care to shampoo *her* hair with it!

A cloud of dust and chaff appeared to the east. Minutes later, a wagon became visible above the churning haze thrown up by galloping hooves. The horses were moving so fast! It wasn't nearly time for the men to eat or milk. Apprehension tugged at the hollow between Lydia's breasts.

"Annette?" she called, her breathing shallow.

Her sister-in-law followed Lydia's gaze, reached for a rag and briskly dried her fingers.

Lydia ran down the porch steps. Their eyes met and exchanged a wordless message. Something was wrong.

Chapter Eighteen

The wagon barreled up the drive, Johann driving the team, urging them on with a leather whip. Behind him, in the wagon bed, two fair heads bobbed. Where was the third?

The wagon drew to a halt in the dooryard, and the women ran around the horses. Franz knelt on a layer of hay, and Anton held his hat to shield the sun from Jakob's face. Jakob lay flat on his back, one knee raised, a broad hand splayed on his chest.

Lydia hitched up her skirts and climbed the wheel spokes, clambering over the side. Frantically she searched for the life-ebbing blood she expected to see flowing from her husband. There was none. What was wrong?

His dungarees were covered with chaff and dust, and his shirt was missing. His brothers helped him sit, revealing the damage. Red, swollen welts massed his face, neck and chest. "Jakob?" she asked, fear in her voice. "How—?"

"I can stand myself," he grumbled, and did. Lydia ached to touch him, to assure herself of his safety, but his surly manner held her in check.

"Bees, *fräulein,*" Johann explained.

Anton leapt over the side of the wagon bed and took off at a dead run for the corral. Lydia and Franz flanked Jakob as he stepped over the box down to the ground. With a shaky stride, he made his way, unaided, into the house.

Annette pumped water and rattled pans, her familiar efficiency comforting Lydia.

"Upstairs," Franz urged.

Lydia ran ahead and pulled back the coverlet. Like an arthritic old man, Jakob sank onto the bed's edge. His face had swollen more in the time it had taken to climb the stairs. The welts on his chest had erupted into an angry red. He bent to his boots and grimaced.

Franz aided him, and Lydia propped both pillows behind her husband's head, urging him back. He lay down and looked up at her. One sky blue eye had disappeared behind the puffy flesh of his eyelid, and the other threatened to do the same. Seeing him that way twisted something undeniably painful inside her chest. She hid her distress with a tender smile.

Annette bustled in with a bucket and cloths. "Well water is the coldest we have. I hope Anton thinks to get ice while he's fetching the doctor."

How long did it take to ride to town and back? Johann handed Jakob a glass and uncorked a bottle with his teeth. Amber liquid jerked from the bottle into the glass. The potent smell of the liquor reached Lydia's nostrils; she hoped it brought relief. Jakob drained the glass in seconds. Johann refilled it, and Jakob drank again, more slowly, grimaced and exhaled.

"How bad is he?" Jakob asked from between puffed lips.

"Pretty bad, son."

Lydia grabbed Johann's wrist. Who else had been stung? All the Neubauers were accounted for. "Who was Jakob asking about?"

"Blaze. Jake was pullin' the mower. Cut right into a nest in a fence row. Them bees swarmed all over the team. They was squealin' and tryin' to run away. Jake stood up and held on. Nothin' more terrifyin' than a team of fine horses out of control with a machine in gear! Only Jake's gumption in standin' all them stingin' bees kept that from happenin'. You did fine, son."

Jakob's prized horses! Lydia's agonized gaze took in the knotted, swelling skin of Jakob's bronzed chest. "You didn't have your shirt on."

Jakob moved his misshapen lips, but his father spoke for him. "He had it on. We used it to squash and scrape off the bees."

Lydia fought a wave of nausea.

"Let's see to the horses, Pa." Franz coaxed Johann from the room.

Annette and Lydia bathed Jakob's swelling flesh. On her way out the door, Annette pushed a foul-smelling concoction at Lydia. "Cover the stings with this."

Alone with him, bowl in hand, Lydia regarded his shirtless chest and was reminded of how he'd tended her minor bites without hesitation. She steeled herself and masked her apprehension, dipping a cloth in the bowl.

"Lydia?"

"*Ja.*"

"I haf bites on my legs." He gestured with one swollen hand. "You'll haffa hep me outa my pants."

Thus far, their intimacy had been in spontaneous bursts of passion, and nothing had prepared her for this. Lydia blushed furiously, but set the bowl on the bedside stand. With trembling fingers, she bent and fumbled with his belt and his button fly. Hands lying useless at his sides, he lifted himself, and she struggled with the well-worn denims. She discovered, as she had only surmised on laundry days, that he didn't wear his drawers on sweltering summer days. She discovered, too, that his golden brown tan ended in a definite line; the skin below his navel was as pale as her own.

Her fingers innocently brushed him, and they both discovered that a sizable amount of pain and fever was no deterrent to his ardor. Lydia's face flamed, probably as red as the welts on his chest. Her first glimpse of his distended manhood expanded her chest and set her fingers trembling. Heart thumping a hard, fast beat, she yanked the denims off the end of the bed, draped the sheet over him and turned away to pick up the bowl of poultice.

After a full minute, she forced herself to turn back to him. His eyelids were closed. His ears and his beloved face were swollen almost beyond recognition. A tiny sob escaped her throat. "Oh, Jakob..."

"Is's awright, hon," he told her comfortingly.

Gently she spread the cool poultice. Few spots, mainly on his lower body, remained unscathed. By the time she finished, he'd broken into a sweat and lay shivering. Wiping her hands on a towel, she knelt at the side of the bed and prayed, hands clasped, head bowed, until the door opened an hour later.

The doctor, a beefy Norwegian in his early fifties, walked with a marked limp and spoke in a voice too mild for his abrupt manner. He washed his hands in the bowl, plopped his bag down next to Jakob's leg and leaned over him.

He dipped a finger in the poultice Annette had prepared and tasted it. Grimacing, he nodded his approval.

He produced two corked brown bottles from his bag. "This is for the infection," he pronounced, "and this is for the pain. Every four hours. Where's the horse?"

Lydia's chin dropped. She watched him prepare to leave. "*Herr Doktor?*" She stepped between the doctor and the door. "How is he? What's wrong—exactly?"

"Poisoned."

"Is he— Will he be all right?"

"Some folks get a bad reaction and die. Then again, I've seen others keep working like nothing happened. Depends on the body's tolerance." That said, he snatched up his bag and left.

Shocked by the doctor's careless attitude, Lydia blinked. She glanced at Jakob. His face was a grotesque parody of its usual handsome self. Die? Her Jakob could die? She refused to give the paralyzing thought credence. Tears gathered in her throat, but she swallowed them and unconsciously wadded up fistfuls of her skirt.

Jakob squinted through his slit of an eye. His lips barely moved when he spoke. "Thum bedthide manner, huh?"

She relaxed her hands and blotted the corners of her eyes with her apron. "Don't talk. It hurts your mouth."

"I've been thtung before, and I'm thtill here."

Not this badly, Jakob. "I'll get a spoon for your medicine."

He slept then, awaking an hour later. She leaned forward in the rocker Johann had carried up and studied him with concern. What little she could see of his eyes, they were focused and clear. "Are you hungry?"

Jakob nodded and swallowed. His lips had cracked and bled, the tender skin stretched beyond endurance. Lydia dabbed them with a soft cloth and coated them with petroleum jelly.

She fed him soup and a glass of milk. "Wha' did the others haff?" he grumbled.

"Don't think about them. Think about getting this inside you." She wiped his chin and held a napkin underneath for the next spoonful.

He turned his head. "You're treatin' me like a baby."

"Do you want to do it yourself?"

"Yeth."

He did, making a worse mess than she had. His bloated fingers refused to hold the spoon, and soup dribbled across his chest. Lydia took the bowl, wiped his chest with a washcloth then dried it.

She fed him the last spoonfuls. Jakob started to object, but the look in her eye warned him off. She tended his lips again and cleared away the tray.

Jakob spent a bad night. In the depth of the night Lydia changed the cold cloths on his head by the soft glow of the lantern. By morning his fever had broken. The day that followed went much as the evening before had.

Unused to idle time, Jakob grew surly. Lack of activity kept him from sleeping well, and by the third day he was refusing the medicine. His crossness wore Lydia's patience thin.

Midmorning on the fourth day, Lydia entered their room carrying a pitcher of water and his shaving gear. Seated at the foot of the bed, Peine glared as if Lydia were the intruder.

"We'll speak later, Jakob." Peine paused in the doorway, studied him, then quit the room, the heavy scent of her floral perfume lingering.

Lydia laid out a towel and handed Jakob his shaving articles. She observed his long, bare form under the sheet. Peine had to have noticed, too. The muscles of his wide shoulders and arms undulated beneath the bronze skin as he lathered his face and neck. What business did that woman have in her husband's bedroom?

Holding a mirror for him, she perched on the bed's edge. Peine always spoke as if she knew Jakob better than Lydia did. "Do the two of you talk often?"

"Two of who?"

"You and Peine."

He tilted his head back and peered in the mirror. "We live in the same house. We're bound to talk once in a while."

"In here?"

He glanced at her from the corner of his blue eye, which was bluer than ever against the white lather on his cheek. Turning his attention back to his task, he drew the razor up his neck. "She just asked how I was feeling."

Her gaze perused his golden shoulders and broad chest, and she wondered at the uncomfortable feeling Peine's presence had evoked, wondered why the thought of her sister-in-law looking at his unclothed body irritated her so.

Her gaze returned to his face and found him looking at her. He'd caught her studying his body. He winced, and a spot of red grew on his chin.

Lydia removed the towel and razor against his grumpy protests. "You look better," she said, as if she'd been appraising his stings.

He tilted his chin and assessed her with his head tipped back while she applied the razor to his neck. "The way I looked bothered you?"

"Yes!" How could he think not?

"I thought it didn't matter what we look like on the outside. All that matters to God is on the inside, remember?" His breath fluttered the hair on her forehead.

"That's different," she replied, and glanced at his lips.

"You even said that there's nothing wrong with squinty eyes."

"You know perfectly well that I meant however one looks *naturally* is unimportant."

"And I've looked unnatural?"

She didn't reply. His pulse beat at the base of his throat. She loved his eyes, his chin, all of him. She loved him. She'd wanted to cry at his disfigurement.

"What could be more natural than the birds and the bees?"

Lydia stuffed a wet towel into his hands. "What do birds have to do with any of this?"

He chuckled, trying not to move his sore lips, and washed his face. He'd seen her look at his body, and he could have sworn he'd seen something akin to appreciation sparkle in her eyes. "I suggest you wait in the hall."

"Why?"

"Cause I'm gonna wash this foul mess off." He lathered a washcloth. "Unless you want to help, that is." He saw her consider it, watched indecision flit across her delicate features. It was cruel of him to dare her, but day after day lying abed in pain had soured his disposition. And what did he have to lose?

Maybe she'd stay.

Lydia stood, confusion creasing her forehead.

Maybe she'd wash his sore but wanting body for him. Jakob reached for the knotted sheet at his hip, and remembered her embarrassment when she'd helped him out of his dungarees. Her fingers twitched against the folds of her skirt, awakening excitement in the pit of his belly. She spun and left the room. He grinned.

He appeared in the kitchen, wet hair slicked back, dressed in his work clothes and boots.

Lydia took one look and knew his intent. "Jakob Neubauer, you're not going to work in the fields today!"

"Who's gonna stop me?"

Hands on hips, she faced him. "You still have poison in your body, and the sun might be harmful to your bites."

Annette tactfully slipped from the room.

"I'm fine. I can't lay in that bed another minute. It's harvesttime. I need to work. Are you going to fix me something to eat, or do I have to do it myself?"

She'd been taking him his meals regularly. Why did he act as if she were neglecting her duties? She yanked the breadboard from a peg and astounded herself with the irreverent thought of hitting him over his hard head! Instead, she hit the table with a spiteful sound that surprised both.

Jakob ate the sandwiches in silence, drank two cold glasses of milk and grabbed his hat.

"Lydia."

She turned from the basin.

"*Danke.*"

His voice was sincere, and the word spoken in her language, as if just for her. His eyelids and lips, though improved, remained pitifully scarred. Her anger toward her thickheaded husband softened. *"Bitte."*

Lydia paused in the tedious chore of maneuvering the paddle stick on the barrel washer. A whining sound caught her attention. She listened. Maybe she imagined it. No! There it was again.

At the bottom of the steps, she cocked her head. On her hands and knees beside a chokeberry bush, she peered under the porch into the darkness. Her eyes adjusted, and she made out the eerie glow of a pair of eyes staring back at her.

Startled, she prepared to back away, but the whine came again, pathetic and thin, accompanied by a rhythmic thumping on the hard-packed dirt.

"Jessie?"

The dog's tail whacked the earth in reply.

"What's wrong? Come out here so I can see you." After considerable coaxing, she urged the dog out. Jessie blinked against the harsh sunlight. Lydia saw that the tender, thinly haired parts of the dog's face and ears were covered with knots. Her nostrils were swollen shut. Compassion brought tears to Lydia's throat. Jessie licked her cheek and nose with a dry tongue. "Oh, Jessie. Poor girl."

Lydia dragged the reluctant animal across the threshold into the kitchen, where she bathed her bee stings and coated them with Annette's poultice. She spread an old rug in a shady corner of the porch, and filled a bowl with cold water, placing it near the dog. Just as she turned back to her laundry, a shot rang out across the dooryard.

The reverberations echoed between the outbuildings, across the dooryard, and dissipated into the sunny afternoon sky. Lydia blinked in surprise and ran toward the terrible sound of an animal's scream.

She could only see blue shirts and dun-colored hats through the corral fence. Coming closer, she recognized Jakob and his father, and at their feet lay Jakob's prized black horse. Blood trickled from a neat bullet hole in the white blaze between his eyes. His lips were foam-flecked, and his massive limbs jerked reflexively.

Once again she saw Jakob smugly driving his new team up the drive that first day, remembered the pride with which he'd shown her the animals, the care he'd taken with their feeding and grooming. She stared at the horse's shiny dark coat, the hide Jakob had lovingly run his hands over time and again, and her heart broke.

"Oh, Jakob," she whispered.

Jakob turned his head toward her, holding his lips in a straight line. Seeing the misery in her eyes, he didn't trust himself to speak. Listlessly he held the gun at his side, as though it weighed hundreds of pounds. The animal's front legs twitched intermittently.

"He had to do it, *fräulein*," his father said. "We waited for Jake to get better so he could decide. The critter was sufferin'."

Lydia moved to his side. "Oh, Jakob, I'm sorry."

Her dark, tormented eyes almost finished him. He bit the inside of his mouth and fought his overwhelming discouragement, not wanting her to see his weakness.

Consolingly she touched his forearm. He glanced at her hand on his skin. She needed to touch as much as he did. He wrapped a strong arm around her and pulled her against his hip, handing his father the gun at the same time.

Lydia pressed her forehead against his shirtfront. "I'm so grateful you're safe."

With his other arm, he hugged her.

"Jessie is sick, too," she told him.

He leaned back to look at her. "Jess?"

"Yes, but I washed her and put salve on her stings. I think she'll be all right."

Jakob pulled her shoulders away from his chest and stared at her. "You doctored Jessie?"

She nodded.

He would have liked to see that! The way those two avoided one another? Compassion had overcome fear—another accomplishment for her. He hugged her again, rightfully proud.

Automatically, Lydia circled his waist with her arms, returning the embrace.

"Thanks, darlin'." The task of moving and burying his horse didn't seem quite as bitter as it had moments ago. "See you at supper."

Later that afternoon, Lydia selected apples from a full barrel in the pantry. She performed the task routinely, her thoughts centered on Jakob's distress. How hard it must have been for him to watch the horse suffer, then to shoot him squarely between the eyes and watch him die.

Apples again. She didn't care if she never ate another apple as long as she lived! Perhaps she could cook them together with some pieplant and bake a cobbler. She filled her apron, snatching up the corners and squeezing her way between barrels. The porch door squeaked, alerting her to the presence of someone she couldn't yet see. Shifting her grip on her apron, she paused in the doorway.

Franz, in worn work clothes and dusty boots, stepped behind Annette, who was dropping doughy dumplings into a steaming kettle of noodles. He closed blunt fingers over Annette's shoulders and pressed his face against her damp neck. Embarrassed, Lydia backed farther into the pantry's shelter.

Covertly Lydia watched as Franz slowly slid his hands down his wife's arms to her hips. His touch lingered caressingly, then glided to grasp her buttocks through layers of dress and petticoats.

Unconsciously Lydia lifted and tightened her grip on the bundle of apples. She knew she should turn away, or make her presence known, but for some unexplainable reason, she just watched in fascination.

Annette turned to face him. Her arms lifted, and she laid her wrists over his broad shoulders. The spoon in her hand dripped chicken broth down the back of his shirt, but only Lydia seemed to notice. Franz grasped her hips again, pulling her flush against his body, and their lips met in a bold kiss.

Lydia's heart thrummed in an alarming staccato beat, leaping into her throat and choking off her breath. Annette seemed as eager for her husband as he was for her!

Her sister-in-law gripped the back of Franz's neck with her free hand. He kneaded the fabric of her skirt. Palms dragging, his slow touch inched from her hips, across her waist and up to the starched front of her dress.

His coarse, work-worn hands pressed Annette's breasts upward in almost angry circles. She saw no humiliation, no discomfort, on Annette's pink face. Rather, tenderness shone from her eyes when the kiss ended. Franz's face was as flushed as hers. Their noses touched in playful intimacy.

"Meet me in the tack room tonight?"

Annette laughed, and he slid his arms around her, hugging her energetically. The wooden spoon clattered to the floor, and he stepped back to retrieve it for her. She thanked him, and the promise in her eyes caught at Lydia's heart.

"I'll be there."

The tart, fruity aroma of the apples she gripped penetrated Lydia's senses. She felt each lump pressed against her own breasts. Guiltily she lowered the apron and stepped back, allowing the dimness in the pantry to envelop her. She sank against the rough wall, resting her head on the planks. Sweet, sweet Annette, with her daintily embroidered bodices and hankies and pillow slips. Annette, whose soft, pale skin smelled of lilac water. Lydia imagined Annette and Franz, heads together on those delicate pillow slips, the scent of lilac water on their fevered skin. She pictured them in the privacy of the tack room, against a backdrop of saddles and bridles.

And she smiled.

"Lydia?" She jumped, and an apple shot from her apron and rolled across the floorboards. Franz bent to pick it up and reached questioningly for her arm. "Are you all right?"

"No! I mean, yes. I'm fine."

"You gave me a start, leaning against the wall that way. Sure you're feelin' okay?"

Embarrassed, Lydia accepted the apple. This was the same man she'd milked with, alone in the barn night after night for weeks. He hadn't suddenly sprouted horns. "I'm just a little tired."

He followed her to the table and watched her roll the fruit onto the surface. "You took good care of Jake. I know he's cantankerous, but . . . the horse, ya know."

"I know."

"Get some rest tonight."

She smiled into his kind face. "I will. Thanks."

The door opened and closed, and Annette hummed a cheerful tune. Tendrils of dark hair curled attractively around her ears and high forehead. Her fair skin glowed with a faint sheen of perspiration. She was lovely. What man wouldn't be smitten by her fair beauty and gentle manner?

Lydia wanted—no, craved—what Annette and Franz had.

There was a way to learn that missing element. If she had the courage. If she wanted a real marriage, a home and a family, she had no other choice. Ignorance stood in the way.

She looked down at the growing pile of peels and cores on the table. Quavery warmth meandered through her veins.

She would ask Jakob.

Chapter Nineteen

Lydia breathed a sigh of relief at the passing of the harvest. She no longer milked morning and evening. Once again the family ate supper together—a welcome interlude in the daily routine. Whereas before she'd considered their evenings a sinful waste of time, Lydia had learned to deeply appreciate the relaxation and companionship.

Tonight Jakob had played his fiddle, and she and Johann had taken turns dancing with Nikolaus.

"We'll check the animals," Franz said. He and Annette left the room hand in hand.

Lydia snuck a sidelong look at Jakob. Franz's hands on Annette's starched dressfront popped to mind, and she envisioned the two of them in the barn, kissing, touching. Warmth curled in secret places within her, and she found herself watching Jakob's dark hands.

Idly he shuffled a worn deck of playing cards. He met her eyes. "Tired?"

"No."

"Still think I'm damned for those few games of euchre?" The corner of his full lips turned up, teasingly, and she thought of him kissing her.

"Maybe." She gathered Nikolaus's wooden blocks.

"Wanna try to beat me at checkers?"

"All right."

Jakob located the game, and they excused themselves and went up to their room.

"Are you concentrating, Lydia?" he asked after effortlessly beating her four games straight.

"Hmm? No, I think not." Lying on her stomach, she rolled and smoothed a wad of skirts trapped beneath her.

Jakob steadied the board on the bed. "What're you thinkin'?"

She looked up into his fathomless blue eyes. Whenever she'd asked him questions, he'd been forthright. She knew he appreciated honesty, so she prepared to say what she'd been thinking. She felt her cheeks grow warm. "I was thinking about what Annette and Franz are doing in the barn."

Jakob's lips parted, accompanied by a total lack of reply. A tinge of pink ruddied his deeply tanned cheeks.

"What do you think they're doing?" she persisted.

He busied himself, arranging red checkers on her side of the board. "I don't know."

Color high in his cheeks told her he did know. "Do you think they play checkers?"

The side of his mouth turned up, but he refused to meet her eyes. "I doubt it."

Lydia won the next game, but not because she concentrated any harder than before. She jumped his last king. "Jakob?"

Apparently thinking it safe now, he met her eyes.

"I want to ask you something."

"Lydia." He pushed his long frame from the bed and picked up the board and checkers. "I don't . . ." He set the game on a chair next to the door.

She sat at the bed's edge, her skirt rumpled carelessly beneath one knee.

He shifted his weight from one foot to the other, his glance skittering from the mussed bed and back to her. He plowed a hand through his hair. "Okay." Pulling the chair over, he plunked down in front of her. "Ask."

She entwined the fingers of both hands and gathered her courage. "I'd like to know what you apologized for."

Minutes ticked away in the silence of the room. Down the hall, a door closed. "What do I do wrong, Jakob?"

He swallowed, as if trying to bring some moisture to his dry mouth. "Nothing that I know of."

Lydia's pulse hammered in her throat, constricting her voice. "But . . . I don't know . . . how to please you." She twisted her hands in her lap, wanting to cry over her inability to express herself. "I can tell you're unhappy and angry each time . . ."

Her voice trailed off, and she felt herself blush furiously.

"Don't." He raised his big hand and scrubbed his face, then kneaded his neck.

"Is there . . . something about me? My body? Something I don't understand how to do?"

This time his mouth opened, as if he were *trying* to say something. Something hard to say? Something painful?

"I realize it was unfair of me to place such emphasis on having children. There's really no hurry, and if I—"

"No!" His knuckles tapped against his pursed lips momentarily. He stood and paced to the window and back again. Sitting on the edge of the chair again, he took her hand. "No, Lydia. You're beautiful. You're perfect in every way. What bothers me is what you must think of me. I had it all figured out when I was away. I planned it so differently."

He'd thought about these things while he was gone? Hope glowed in her heart. "What did you plan differently, Jakob?"

His gaze skittered away. He stared at her hand in his, frowned intently, and softly cleared his throat. "I promised myself I'd go slow and easy with you. I wanted to make up for . . . everything, but none of it was good for you. I wasn't gentle or caring like I should've been."

"You're gentle and caring all the time, Jakob."

"No, I'm not," he told her. "I'm selfish. I always get . . . I . . ."

She leaned forward and squeezed his fingers.

"I feel like I'm too rough, in too much of a hurry." He snorted. He'd been too eager, not the least bit gentle. He'd wanted her so badly, waited for so long. Too long. Everything about her felt so good, so right. Her nearness set him aflame. "Thank God you don't have anything to compare it to."

She stared at him in bewilderment. "My grandmother said we would work it out. That it's natural and good. I think so, too."

Jakob made a religious inspection of her face, studied her hair, her dress. His heart zigzagged in his chest, and for one chaotic moment he wondered if he heard thunder. *She will be meek and obedient, because it is our way....* Again her father's taunting words crowded against hers. "Don't say that just to please me."

Her dark eyes filled with pain. "Jakob, would I say something I didn't mean?"

He grasped her upper arms in his strong hands. Her dark eyes opened wide, but he saw no fear there. He saw trust, and an imploring glow. Her gaze dropped to his lips, smoldering with earnest longing. His heart beat wildly.

"What are you saying?"

"You please me. I want us to have what Franz and Annette have."

His wife wanted him, *enjoyed* him. Intense relief rolled down his body, oozed into his pores in a song of awakening. Joy took up the descant, trilling through his veins, cleansing him for another, more vibrant shock of emotion. Desire. Want for her chased everything else into silence.

Their eyes were scant inches apart. Her shoulders trembled, and he relaxed his grasp.

"Jakob?" she whispered.

He had compared her to Sylvie. Yes, she was pure, like Sylvie. Fearful of God's retribution, like Sylvie. She wanted to please him, as Sylvie had. But there was something else....

Something about her was not at all like Sylvie. He ran his thumb across her shoulder, and her eyes smoldered. He moistened his lips with his tongue, and color suffused her cheeks. Their gazes met, and he could see the pulse at the base of her throat hammering.

Lydia responded.

That was the difference. He had desired Sylvie, but she had never reciprocated. He'd carried that guilt around for so long it had become part of him. Guilt like a pocket watch he set in the morning and kept in his pocket all day, checking it regularly. Guilt that her naive wanting to please him had inadvertently sent her to her death.

Lydia had been an innocent, but she'd come to his home willingly. And she'd submitted to him willingly. Maybe he *was* a coarse, worldly man, but maybe she didn't mind. He'd asked himself how long he would let Etham Beker stand between them, and now he knew.

"Lydia, you really thought you made me unhappy?"

She nodded, and tears filled her luminous eyes, tearing at his heart. She was still an innocent. Still so good and pure and forgiving. And she always would be. His desire for her couldn't sully her pure heart. And her desire for him—his body responded at the thought—her own desire, only made her more beautiful, more desirable.

He shook his head, more in wonder than in denial. "There's nothing wrong with you. You're beautiful. Your body's beautiful. Just thinking about it drives me crazy. I've been wild for you since the first time I saw you."

Her eyes darkened. His mouth closed over her slightly parted lips. He kissed her with an intensity that warmed her, seared her, melted her. He slanted his head and changed the pressure he coaxed her mouth with. She opened her lips, accepting the velvety caress of his tongue against hers. He wrapped his arms around her shoulders and pulled her upward until they stood, their mouths separating.

Boldly Lydia placed her hands on his shirtfront and measured the rapid beating of his heart. Tenderly he again covered her lips with his, gathering her closer in his arms. Lydia raised her fingertips to touch his lean cheek, and felt the widening of his jaw as his mouth opened over hers. His tongue probed the inside of her mouth, tampering with sensations she hadn't known she could feel. He'd kissed her before, but he'd never kissed her like this! Since that first enlightening kiss in the pasture, there had been tender kisses, sweet kisses, and a few warmer, more imaginative kisses. But this...this all-consuming, hungry, unsatisfying... This was what she'd yearned for, yet with it, he created an even greater wanting.

He dragged his lips from hers, dotted damp kisses across her chin and throat. Warmth suffused her body in a liquid outpouring. "Jakob?"

He murmured an unintelligible reply against her ear.

"Touch me."

Jakob's lips rested against her earlobe, and his breath fanned her neck. With deliberate slowness, he turned her away from him and unbuttoned her dress. It pooled at her ankles, and he turned her to face him. Tugging at the satin ribbon on her chemise, he lowered the fabric, exposing the creamy skin of her upper chest.

Through the soft material, he cupped her breast and lifted it until it swelled above the fabric. He lowered his head and kissed the skin that was revealed. Her breath caught in her throat, then escaped in a shuddering exhalation. His tongue, hot and wet, aroused her every nerve ending, and she buried her hand in his thick hair.

Without leaving her breast, he slid her chemise to her waist and unlaced her muslin drawers. Her garments fell to the floor. The lantern cast a soft glow across her skin and hair. Jakob removed her shoes, and slid her stockings down her legs.

She stood before him. His gaze darkened with desire at the sight of her bare form; his reaction was a heady delight. She reached for his shirt and unbuttoned it. Jerking it aside impatiently, he slid his fingers into her hair. Pins dropped on the floor around them. Raking his fingers through the tresses, he spread them across her shoulders. Through the silky veil, he caressed her.

"I love your hair, Lydia."

"Jakob, I am sorry."

"Don't be. It will grow."

"I only wanted to please you. I thought if I looked like the ladies in Pittsburgh—"

He groaned, and molded the shape of her breast. "I don't care a straw about the ladies in Pittsburgh. I want you just the way you are."

She arched her throat to his lips.

"Ah, Lydia..." His tongue touched her skin, drawing a sharp breath from her.

That was the way she wanted to hear him say her name—as a lover's song of praise, a whispered chant of adoration. Her eyes closed. She shuddered. *"Ja, mir gefallt...sehr gut, Mann."*

"You like this?" he attempted to translate.

"Ja."

"Mir gefallt sehr gut, Weib."

She smiled through giddy tears. "You're a fast learner."

He yanked the coverlet off the end of the bed, and raised the sheet, urging her beneath. "Do you want the lantern out?"

Her gaze lingered on his broad chest. *"Nein."*

She watched him remove his trousers, glad for the glow of the lantern, glad to see her husband's masculine beauty, glad to understand the mysterious secrets of this ancient ritual.

He lowered himself beside her, his heated arousal sliding against her sensitive hip. Lydia's heart pounded, her body alive and expectant. He touched her bottom lip with the tip of his finger. "What's this?"

The slide of his skin against hers had her undivided attention, and she had to focus on his question. *"Die Lippe."*

He kissed her lip where he'd touched it, then slid his hand across her shoulder and brushed her hair aside. "And this?"

His chest hair grazed her breast, and her nipples tightened in response. *"Die Schulter."*

Dipping his head, he pressed a kiss on the rounded curve of her shoulder. He lifted her limp hand and indicated the blue-veined skin of her inner wrist. "And this?"

Her gaze fixed on his damp lips. *"Das Handgelenk."*

"Das Handgelenk is a mouthful, *ja?"* His mouth opened wider, as if he'd swallow her hand, but he settled for a wide, sucking nip on her wrist. One bared breast fell under his attention. "And this?"

She held her breath in anticipation. *"Die Brust."*

He didn't disappoint her. Lowering his face, he nuzzled the silky white skin. Her heart stopped. Lydia had to force herself to breathe.

"Schön," he murmured against her warm flesh. His kisses triggered shivers that skittered upward, across her neck and shoulders. His tongue skimmed from one breast to the other, and his mouth fastened on the waiting peak. Warmth flooded her.

Lydia gasped at the sweetness of his mouth on her flesh, arching into the exquisite sensation. Her hands strayed naturally across his hard wide shoulders and his upper arms. He rained kisses across her chest and belly, rubbed his face against her tender skin. Branding kisses up her torso, he nuzzled the curve of her neck.

Breath ragged, he kissed her. He brushed her hair aside and stroked her smooth skin, his rough palms a gratifying contrast. She craved his touch.

She framed his jaw in her hands as he kissed her, his skin firm and pleasantly textured. Her thumbs detected the hollows in his cheeks as his tongue sought hers. Lydia opened her eyes and enjoyed his gilt hair and brows in the lamplight. Caught up in the newfound treasure of shared enjoyment, wanting him to feel every bit as encouraged and wonderful as she did, she ran her palms eagerly over his shoulders and back. The muscle beneath was brawny and solid. His biceps were granite-hard but mobile beneath tanned skin as he shifted his weight.

His mouth moved across her lips to her chin. His breathing grew agonized. She pressed her head back into the pillow and afforded him a path across her neck and throat. He moved his hard, hair-roughened body against her from breasts to knees. Lydia ran her fingertips across his beloved face, remembering her distress when his features had been swollen with stings.

"Schön," she murmured in praise, and though the apricot glow of the lantern had dimmed, she thought she saw him blush.

He kissed her with single-minded passion, his thigh boring between hers. Lydia's knees fell apart naturally, and he moved over her, burying himself in her, reverently, unsparingly. Lydia closed her eyes and reveled in the fact that this strong, beautiful man wanted her. His strokes were long and languid.

He took his time kissing, touching, inflaming. Her hands found the taut skin stretched over his hipbones, and his movements grew deliberate. Lydia arched her body to meet his urgent rhythm, a glorious, unbearable tension coiling within her. With splayed fingers, she speared the tawny hair on his chest, felt the tumultuous beating of his heart beneath. She saw the pleasure on his face and welcomed every inch of his forceful thrusts.

Something hot and wonderful grew and burst within her, sending delicious, throbbing waves of pleasure spiraling outward from the place their bodies joined. She knew then what he'd wanted to give her, what she'd ached and waited for. And she knew, too, that they had shared something good and special. She stopped a sob in her throat and blinked back tears.

He groaned and fell heavily against her side.

Lydia stroked the damp cornsilk hair from his forehead, while against her ribs his heartbeat slowed and steadied.

"It is good, Jakob?" she whispered.

He raised his heavy head and reassured her with his eyes. "*Est ist gut,* Lydia. *Sehr gut.*"

Lydia awakened to the familiar creak of the bedropes. Water splashed in the porcelain bowl.

"I'll get warm water for you, Jakob." She sat.

"No." He pushed her back against the pillows. "I'll get it for you after I'm dressed."

His hands were warm on her bare shoulders. She smiled. "Silly."

"I'm not silly. I'm smitten."

She looked at him doubtfully.

"By your beauty." He caressed her collarbone with his thumb.

She loved him. She hadn't hoped to feel this way about him. About anyone. Ever. "Are you flattering me again?"

"That's praise. Haven't you ever read the Song of Solomon?"

"It was never in my studies, no. What does it say?"

"'Thou hast ravished my heart, my sister, my spouse! How much better is thy love than wine! How fair is thy love, my sister, my spouse. Thy lips, O my spouse, drop as honeycomb: honey and milk are under thy tongue.'"

Her eyes widened. "Jakob! That's in the Bible?"

He dropped his hands. "Yup."

"It's as poetic as *Romeo and Juliet!*"

"You've read *Romeo and Juliet?*" he asked, his eyes wide with disbelief.

She propped herself against the pillows and adjusted the coverlet across her breasts. "I read a few of your books while you were building bridges."

"Your father'd have my hide."

She agreed with a giggle, their newfound comfort with one another a secure joy.

He kissed her temple, and her thoughts centered on the night before. As if his hand remembered, too, he glided it along her side and rested it on her ribs, beneath her breast.

"I was scared, Lydia." His candid blue eyes diverted her thoughts from his hand. "I thought maybe you regretted coming here with me. Life was perfect where you came from. Here, people hurt, fight, say mean things. I carried you from Eden to an imperfect world. I was selfish."

Lydia's chest ached like an empty stomach at his words. "I have friends here, Jakob. I've learned to enjoy life."

"You were happy with your family, and if I hadn't come along, you would've been satisfied. You didn't know any other life was out here."

"You're not selfish," she began, uncertain how to express the things she wanted him to understand. "My life was not perfect before I met you. I didn't have anything—except my grandmother and sisters, and even that pleasure was forbidden. I was lonely."

She took his other hand from his thigh and threaded her fingers through his. "I tried to be satisfied with my life, but there was something missing. A few months ago I couldn't have told you what that was." Lydia grinned. "A few days ago I couldn't have told you what that was."

"Now you know?"

"I think so." She tilted her head. "I can't even think about what my life would have been like if God hadn't led you to Accord. Can you believe that was merely a coincidence?"

"No," he answered softly, and smiled.

"I was scared, too," she admitted. "I thought you were sorry you'd ever brought me here. Like…I was an oddity at first, and then you realized how inept I was, how I would never fit in."

"Oh, darlin'." He pulled her against his bare chest. "I want you happy. You're not like anyone else I ever met, and I don't want you to be." He hugged her soundly. They absorbed one another's warmth for several minutes, and at last he pulled away. "Hungry?"

She nodded.

"Me too. My belly's rubbin' my backbone. Think you could make one of those cinnamon cakes with blueberries?" He tugged a pair of dark trousers on.

Lydia gathered her clothes from the floor. Her mahogany hair, in glorious disarray, tumbled across her shoulders. As she straightened, the dark tips of her full breasts peeked through. Jakob's gaze lowered to the curve of her waist and gentle swell of her hips.

"If I don't leave now," he said, his voice thick with desire, "we'll be late for church. I'll fetch your water."

Lydia smiled at his retreating back, feeling incredibly feminine and desirable. He wanted her. He wasn't sorry he'd brought her here.

She picked up her hairbrush and turned to the mirror. Gathering her tangled hair over one shoulder, she studied her reflection without shame. He thought her beautiful. Was she? Her skin was clear and fair, her waist small, her legs long. Her attention focused on her breasts, and a familiar wave of sensation tingled in her limbs and breast. Jakob had touched each place she saw in the mirror. He had buried himself in her, and enjoyed her. Pleasing him pleased her. Could life get any better?

Jakob's ardor didn't wane after services and the ride home. At dinner she buttered him a slice of bread, and her fingers grazed his as she handed it to him. He jerked his gaze to her gold-flecked eyes. The message there tied his abdomen in knots. She smiled, and he raised the bread to his mouth and took a deliberate bite. She rewarded his intimation with a subtle darkening of her eyes.

After the meal, Jakob stood and tossed his napkin down. "Wanna go for a ride after doing the dishes?"

From the corner of the table, Peine glared at them.

Lydia scraped plates into a lard tin. "I'll finish up here and meet you in the barn."

"Jakob's looking tired today, don't you think?" Peine asked after he'd gone. "Do you think he's up to all the activity so soon after his accident? He may have poison left in his body." Today she wore a frivolous pastel dress enhanced by delicate lace at the neck and sleeves. A matching ribbon threaded through her wavy golden hair. As usual, she avoided the clean-up tasks.

"I think Jakob has recovered," Lydia replied. "From the activity I've witnessed, I'm sure he knows his own capability." She extended the lard bucket by the handle. "It's your turn to take the scraps out, isn't it?"

The other woman stiffened. Lydia stepped closer, hoisting the pail practically under Peine's nose. A full head taller, she smiled down. Fire flashed in Peine's emerald eyes, but she accepted the scraps.

The back door banged shut behind her. Lydia and Annette exchanged amused looks, a vision of Peine mincing up to the swill barrel in her party frock dancing between them.

Lydia chose her yellow dress to ride in. Even though it was impractical and would require laundering, the dress reflected her buoyant mood. She threw her shawl around her shoulders and ran to the barn.

Gunter and Carolina stood saddled and waiting. Jakob cradled his fingers for her, and she mounted. They rode along the stream, then crossed a stubbled field. The horses carried them across their grassy clearing. "Next year we'll be living here."

The thought was more appealing than it had ever been. All alone with Jakob. Her husband. Lydia turned her face into the soft breeze. The nights were cool enough now that the sun felt wonderful during the day. "Yes."

"The bedroom will be right here." He guided them to a spot only he could have identified, then turned, awaiting her expression.

She envisioned the two of them in their bedroom, sleeping side by side, perhaps waking in the dark of the night to come together as they had last night. She smiled.

They walked the horses through the stand of hemlocks, and leaves fell around them, drifting past their heads and shoulders. Jakob dismounted, helped her down and tethered their mounts to a low branch.

Lydia didn't notice the blanket he untied from the back of his saddle until he flapped it open and let it float upon a bed of fragrant needles. Tossing his hat down, he stretched out on the blanket and patted the spot next to him. She gathered her skirt and sat.

"Ooh, lumpy." She shifted an inch.

"This is heaven compared to where I slept on the Susquehanna."

"I thought about you every minute, and wondered where you slept."

"I thought about you every minute, and I slept in a tent full of stinkin', snorin' men."

"No wonder I'm an improvement."

Jakob rolled and placed his head in her lap. "When did you learn to tease?"

She ran her fingers through his sun-bleached hair. "One comes by it quite naturally in this family, don't you think?"

"What did you think when you thought about me?"

She curled a lock of hair around her fingers. "About kisses on the porch the day I peeled apples. About that day you put ointment on my back."

"Oh, yeah…" he groaned. "I thought about that day a lot." He closed his eyes. "I wanted you so badly."

"I missed you terribly, Jakob." Lydia thought of the ungrounded misgivings she'd had the night before he returned, too ashamed to tell him she'd allowed Peine to plant seeds of doubt in her mind. "And, Jakob?"

"Hmm?"

"A baby doesn't matter that much now."

He reached up and skimmed his fingers along her jaw. "We'll have one. We'll have our house full of babies." He removed her bonnet and pulled her down alongside him. "I mean to see to it."

Lydia closed her eyes and surrendered to his soul-piercing kiss. He worked his lips over hers with incessant pressure, pressing her head back against the blanket. Her clamoring heart betrayed the effect he had on her. She accepted his kisses hungrily, greedy for the dazzling feelings he created within her. Something in her chest expanded, and she curled her arms around his neck and kissed him back.

Jakob groaned and pressed himself against her thigh. Lydia recognized his excitement through their layers of clothing, and felt his fingers groping through her hair, plucking pins. His mouth awakened every nerve ending along her neck and jaw. He covered her breasts with his hands and bit the tender flesh under her ear. The pressure of his body against hers, combined with his ragged breathing, thrilled and disturbed her at the same time. It was early afternoon, broad daylight, and bedtime was a long way off.

"Jakob," she breathed.

"Hmm . . ." he mumbled against her throat.

She stared at the sun filtering through the branches overhead and melted as his tongue dipped into her ear. "What are you doing?"

"Kissin' you." He covered her mouth again, running his tongue across her teeth. "I'm fulfilling every dream I had lying awake nights in that tent."

Her eyes widened. "What are you planning?"

His eyes smiled. "I'm planning to take this pretty dress off you so it doesn't get mussed up."

Lydia shoved against his chest and sat bolt upright. "Here?"

Chapter Twenty

"Now?" Her dark hair tumbled over one shoulder. She stared at him incredulously.

"Yeah. Here...now."

She looked away from his face and scanned the clearing, then studied the sloping hill to the west. Jakob could see her misgivings. Eyes dark with passion, she studied his expression, his mouth. Her own lips were pink and swollen from his kisses. He watched her indecision transform into desire.

Her smile was hesitant. His was instant.

He kissed her again. Reaching for the buttons of her dress, he unfastened them.

Her hands stopped him. He looked at her, a questioning frown knitting his brow. Slowly she reached forward and unbuttoned his shirt. Peeling the fabric open, she slid her hands inside and stroked his chest.

Jakob closed his eyes and gloried in her touch. He loved the feel of her hands in his hair, on his skin. "Your touch is heaven."

Her hands stilled. Opening his eyes, he questioned her with them.

"My grandmother said the only thing better than this is heaven."

"Wise woman. Don't stop." He tossed the shirt behind him. "Kiss me."

Lydia pressed her lips against his chest. Her lips were cool against his feverish skin, his heart quick-beating beneath them. A timid kiss beneath his ear set his blood on fire. Her lips plucked at his jaw, his cheekbone. Her face swam before him, her breath fanned his mouth.

"Kiss me," he whispered.

She did, and he wrapped his arms around her and folded her against him. Breast to breast, knee to knee, their breathing rose and fell in rapid harmony. She shuddered as he pushed her dress from her shoulders, but she stood, fingertips resting on his bare shoulders, and stepped free of it. The dark circles of her nipples showed through the snowy-white chemise. She was beautiful. She was eager, in her own naive manner, and her response set him on fire. He covered her breasts with his hands and kneaded, stroking her taut nipples through the fabric with his thumbs. She hugged his head against her midriff.

Impatiently Jakob urged her down on the blanket and lay beside her, his trouser-clad leg wedging between her knees. He tugged the satin bow between her breasts and untied it, reaching inside the material and sating his hand with her fullness. He dipped his head and tasted the exquisite blue-veined skin. A sound escaped her throat, and her shoulder lifted, as if she were offering herself more fully.

He found the drawstring and untied her drawers, skimming his hand down her belly and finding her slick feminine warmth. She gasped and dug her fingers into his shoulders. Unmercifully Jakob seized upon her reaction and continued the caress. His lips traveled from her breast to her mouth and back. The scent of her hair and skin intoxicated him. He wound a skein of hair around his wrist and rubbed it sensuously across her breasts, his cheek and lips.

Together they tugged off his boots and trousers. He tossed her drawers on the pile and lowered himself over her. She gathered him close, opening herself to his silken thrusts. The trees were a green-and-gold canopy overhead, an occasional leaf dropping unnoticed. Beneath the blanket, dry leaves crackled, needles snapped, the sounds lost in a chorus of mingled breath and murmurs.

Jakob forced himself to rest. Raising himself above her on long arms, he took a deep breath.

"Jakob?" Her hand raised, and she touched his cheek questioningly.

He took her hand, brought her fingers to his lips and spoke against them. "I want it as good for you as it is for me."

"It is, Jakob. I—"

"I asked Franz, and he—"

"You what?"

"I wanted to know how I could make it better for you—"

"You talked to Franz about *this?*" She attempted to squirm out from under him, but his body pinned hers to the earth. He had spoken to his brother about this most intimate detail of their marriage? What on earth had he asked him? Told him? "You spoke to him about *us?*"

The inflection in her voice assured him of the ultimate betrayal. "No, of course not. Hold still. I wasn't born with all the answers, just because I'm a man. He was the logical person to ask, so I did."

Lydia's eyes were huge. They widened even further as Jakob moved within her. Unable to help herself, she was intrigued. Franz and Annette certainly seemed blissful, and—her breath caught in her throat—Jakob's exquisite movements soothed her embarrassment. It couldn't hurt to have an open mind.

He watched fascination replace initial mortification. "Trust me?"

She nodded.

Grasping her hips, he rolled onto his back and, without separating from her, settled Lydia on top of him. Taking her hands, he placed them on his solid chest. The gold ring that made her his glittered in the sunlight. He guided her hips until she caught the rhythm. Her eyes fluttered closed. His hands stole inside her gaping chemise, and he swallowed hard, allowing her to stroke his desire—and her own—to mindlessness. His body arched, and Lydia leaned into his palms. The dangling satin ribbon of her chemise tickled his chest . . . his chin . . . his chest . . . his chin . . .

The supple muscles of her long legs tensed, and he opened his eyes to watch the play of emotion on her lovely face. Lips parted, breasts bobbing, she was magnificent; the embodiment of every bridegroom's fantasies. Her hair reflected sundappled auburn fire from above. Her neck arched, and she cried his name. Instantly his strong hands grasped her hips and aided her movements. He lunged upward a last time, and caught her as she fell against his chest.

He kissed her damp hair, lifted it from her neck.

Lydia's heart swelled with love and wonder, raced with a tumultuous thumping. Every ounce of her being had yearned, craved, that heart-stopping ecstasy. She pushed herself up and ran her hands over Jakob's damp chest.

How positively wanton! Midday, with the sun shining warm and wonderful on her shoulders, and she, clad only in a gaping chemise and stockings! Laughter bubbled up and spilled over, and Jakob's body quaked as he joined her.

Their laughter rose through the silver-leaved branches and echoed across their soon-to-be front yard.

"We can sit on our front porch and remember this day." He kissed her fingers.

Nearby a bird called its mate.

He twisted a lock of her hair around his thumb, a deep, warm satisfaction lingering. He traced her delicate collarbone. She wasn't small, but she was feminine. Strong, supple and made just for him. His woman. Everything was turning out the way he wanted it to. By next year they would be living in their own home.

A billowy cloud temporarily shaded the tree they lay beneath. Jakob looked up and watched a leaf drift past Lydia's hair. A needlelike prick of doubt snagged his tranquillity. He was almost afraid to allow himself the security the past week offered. It was almost too good to be true.

A strange horse was munching oats in a stall when Lydia and Jakob returned their horses to the barn. Jakob looked him over. "Never seen him before. Must be a visitor."

They cared for the animals and ran hand in hand to the house. With the sun setting, the evening promised a chill.

A handsome young man with fawn-colored hair separated himself from the others and rose from the table as they entered the kitchen. Lydia blinked. It took several seconds before she recognized her brother out of context.

"Nathan?" Whatever was he doing here?

He held his black hat in a long-fingered hand.

"This feller says he's kin of yours," Johann said kindly.

Lydia ran to wrap her arms around her brother's waist, the impulsive hug as natural as breathing. His surprise was obvious. Over her shoulder, Nathan's gaze found Jakob.

Annette turned the fire down under a fresh pot of coffee. "I offered him a slice of your mince pie, Lydia, but he turned it down."

"Thank you, ma'am," he said in his familiar deep voice. "Speak with my sister, I must."

Suddenly everyone had somewhere to go.

"Jakob, please stay," Lydia said softly. "Nathan, it's good to see you. How did you find me, and how did you get here? Why did Father—"

"Father does not know I came. Grandmother sent me. I took a horse from the stables and asked directions in Butler."

Fear expanded Lydia's chest. His defiant action needed a powerful motivation. Father would punish him severely. "What is it?" she asked, her voice barely above a whisper. "Grandmother— Is she—?"

"Gravely ill she is. *Herr Doktor* does not have hope she will live through the night."

A silent exclamation passed her lips. She saw her grandmother, small and frail upon her low cot, her gray dress barely lifting with each breath.

Nathan's eyes swam with unshed tears.

Jakob watched Lydia's hand tremble on Nathan's jacket. Her silent tears distressed him more than if she'd screamed and wailed.

"Is she in pain?" she asked.

"Dr. Klein gave her medicine. She only . . ."

"What? Tell me!"

"She only asks for you. To come here she begged me. I told her Father would not allow it, but she would not listen. What else could I do?" He blinked, looking beseechingly from her face to Jakob's. "I could not deny her."

Lydia hugged him again, and this time his arms returned the embrace. "*Danke*. You're taking a risk for me. Did you bring a message?"

"She wants you at her side."

Her shoulders slumped. She stared at the scarred tabletop. Minutes passed, and she sat heavily.

"I think perhaps she is not thinking clearly," her brother explained. "You are not allowed in the colony."

Jakob could see that Nathan wanted to reach over and touch her hand to comfort her. Rigid self-discipline rooted him to the spot.

"I will tell her I spoke with you. That you are well and send your love."

Lydia nodded without enthusiasm. A tear traced down her porcelain cheek. *"Ja."*

Jakob drew his gaze from their grieving faces and selected cups from the cupboard. He recalled himself at the age of ten, and relived the emotions he'd experienced the last time he saw his mother alive. She'd told him she loved him. He'd told her in return, and cried brokenheartedly. That last goodbye was a memory he still treasured.

"I could sneak in like I did before!" Lydia exclaimed, pressing one hand flat on the tabletop.

Nathan shook his head. "You could not. *Vater* sits by her side constantly."

She stared at the cup Jakob placed before her.

Jakob's mind churned in helpless turmoil. His wife would have to mourn without her family, without the comfort of seeing her beloved grandmother one last time, without honoring the old woman's final request.

A flicker of guilt pricked his conscience. Because of him, she was denied this human solace. She had chosen to be his wife rather than a Harmonist, and now she must pay the price. Anger welled inside him. The price was too high!

Etham Beker had done this to her. *Vater* Beker's own daughter and mother suffered because of his narrow-minded bigotry! The heartless man made decisions for their lives without considering anyone's feelings.

Jakob remembered sitting at the Bekers' kitchen table with the old woman, remembered her teasing smile. Lydia loved her grandmother deeply. She wouldn't be deprived.

Calmly he poured coffee into the cups. Anger wouldn't help the situation, and he didn't want Lydia more upset. "Lydia, pack us each a change of clothes. Use the leather bag in the closet. Find a warm jacket for yourself. Nathan, have a cup of coffee, and then we'll go out to the barn.''

Lydia stared at him in confusion. ''What? Why?''

''You're going to see your grandma.''

''But how? My father won't—''

''Your father *will* let you see her, or I'll eat my hat.''

Nathan looked at him, as if trying to picture it.

''Go on.'' Jakob jerked a thumb toward the hall.

Knowing her husband, she ran for the stairs.

A half-hour later, the three rode toward Accord in the dark. Nathan's mount had been replaced by Carolina. He gaped at his sister, who was riding astride, yellow skirts tucked under her knees. Jakob led the way, finding the landmarks even at the brisk pace in the darkness. Pausing on the rise, the horses rested briefly while the riders stared at the dim illumination from Accord's softly glowing gas lamps below. Beneath them, the horses snorted, their bellies heaving with exertion.

Tension coiled in Lydia's stomach. Her father was down there. What would his reaction be when he saw her? When he saw Jakob? God help them!

Jakob led them down the hill and directly onto Church Street. In the common, the bushes had been pruned and the flowers were gone, signs of oncoming winter. The horses' hooves clomped, a loud, hollow sound on the even brick walkways.

Jakob halted in front of the Beker house. Dismounting, he reached for his wife and bore her weight to the ground. ''Nathan will stable the horses. Come.''

He took Lydia by the elbow and led her to the door.

What would her father do when they barged in? Her heart pounded. ''Jakob, I'm frightened.''

''You want to see her, don't you?''

She gripped his hand as if it were a lifeline. She wanted to see her grandmother more than anything. ''Yes.''

''Then you're gonna. Get in there.''

''But—''

''I'm right behind you.''

Lydia took a deep breath and opened the door, blinking as her eyes adjusted to the brightly lit kitchen. *Mutter* and Rachael sat at the small table, empty teacups in front of them. They looked exactly as they always had, wearing gray dresses and prim white aprons and caps. Instead of being reassuring, the familiarity of the scene was somehow sad. Every day she'd been gone, she'd lived to the fullest, whether ecstatic, afraid or confused. She'd felt something wonderful, done something new, each day. The Beker family had plodded on day after day with neither change nor pleasure.

"Lydia!" *Mutter* cried, her happy look of recognition immediately replaced by one of anxiety. Her fair gaze observed the towering man behind her daughter.

Jakob closed the door with a firm click that said they were staying.

Rachael moved first. She pushed back the chair she sat in and stood. "*Vater* is in the bedroom with Grandmother."

Lydia recognized the warning. "Is she . . . still . . ."

"*Ja.*"

"Thank God." She tilted her gaze up to her husband's face.

"Lydia will see her now," he stated.

Rachael and her mother regarded one another, but neither of them replied.

Jakob prompted Lydia across the room into the hallway. An oil lamp with a metal reflector behind the dome hung on the wall, illuminating their path. Etham's voice drifted from the open doorway ahead. He spoke softly, but his voice became clearer. Her father stepped into the hallway and caught sight of the two intruders. He drew up short, his posture stiffening. "What are you doing here?"

Lydia opened her mouth, but Jakob spoke.

"She's come to see her grandmother."

"She made her choice, *Meier* Neubauer. She turned her back on her family and this home." He spoke as if Lydia weren't standing there.

"No, she didn't make that choice, *Reverend* Beker. You made it. You turned your back on her."

"It was my decision to make! She is unwelcome here until she sees the error of her ways, and repents!"

"Hell will freeze over first," Jakob snorted. "But she's here now, and she's going in there. Who will stop her?" His deep, quiet voice held enough threat to make his intent clear.

Behind them, Lydia sensed *Mutter* and Rachael.

Etham's eyes burned with black intensity. "All I need do is send one of the boys to ring the alarm bell. Twenty men will appear and remove you both." He stepped forward. "Make it easy on yourselves, and leave now."

Faster, Jakob stepped forward, placing Lydia behind his left arm. He faced her father, menacingly. From the concealment of his woolen jacket he removed a steel gray object and pointed it at the other man. "You'll step back into that room and stay out of Lydia's way."

A nauseating flash of vertigo swept Lydia with the recognition of what he held. She clawed her fingers into the sleeve of his jacket. "Jakob, no..."

Using her grip on his sleeve to his advantage, Jakob yanked her forward and gestured toward the doorway with the gun. "Go on."

"Jakob—"

"Get in there!"

Heart pounding, Lydia skittered past her father. Rose Beker's dark eyes greeted her granddaughter without surprise.

"Child."

"Grandmother." Lydia fell on her knees beside the sleeping cot and buried her face in the covers pulled over the old woman's sunken chest.

Obviously Etham Beker had never looked down the barrel of a .45 Peacemaker, and his murderous expression said he didn't care for the blond farmer waggling it under his nose now. He backed into the room and dropped onto the chair indicated by a jerk of Jakob's head.

Lydia felt Grandmother's breast quake and saw her seamy smile. Their hands entwined on top of the coverlet.

"I knew you'd find a way." She chuckled silently, and Lydia didn't know if her grandmother spoke to her or to Jakob.

Mutter and Rachael brought chairs. Absurdly Jakob thanked them and sat, as if he were an honored guest. Nathan returned, and his eyes widened at the sight of Jakob's generous hand leveling the Peacemaker at Etham.

"*Danke*, Nathan," his grandmother praised. "You did not fail me."

Nathan blushed. At his father's glare, he excused himself.

Rachael brought tea and *Kekse*. Jakob thanked her, and they spoke softly.

Rose slept for the better part of an hour, her fingers tucked within Lydia's. Lydia observed the darkened nails on the pasty hand, listened to the deep, tortured breathing.

"Lydia Rose," a thin voice called. "My beautiful wild-flower..."

Lydia realized she'd fallen asleep. She raised her head and smiled at the endearment.

"He makes you happy?"

As though they were continuing a conversation begun only a moment ago, Lydia replied, "Yes."

"Do not settle for less." Her pale skin seemed stretched over her teeth in a smile. "Not like he did. Not like she did."

Lydia met Jakob's eyes. He smiled, encouragingly.

"Etham, son," Grandmother said in a stronger voice, "you settled for less. You made Christine, that pretty young thing, settle for less, too. She was young once. Vibrant...a real beauty. Remember?"

Etham sat up rigidly, black eyes fixed on his mother.

"Ah, but now...your father...he wanted it all. Took everything God offered him and turned it into a joy and a blessing. Matthäus..."

It was impossible not to shed a tear at the sad-sweet way she spoke his name, as if he could hear her. Lydia pressed her lips against Rose's bony fingers, and snuck a peek at her father. He stared resolutely at his lap.

"He was tall, like you, Jakob, but his hair was dark...not as dark as mine. Etham and Lydia got their coloring from me.... Lydia got her height from him, though."

Lydia exchanged a look with her mother. Christine's pale face showed her weariness. The old woman's ramblings were taking their toll on everyone.

"I remember how he looked the day he came to get me," she continued. "We lived down by Carbon.... My daddy raised pigs on Sugar Creek. I had met him the summer before, when he and his daddy came and bought dressed hogs."

Etham stared at her as if she were hallucinating. "*Mutter*, I've never heard of those places."

"No. You have only heard the story of your father's people, who came from Germany. That history keeps our purpose firm.... My parents were from Ireland."

This new angle to the familiar story had Lydia's complete attention. "He came to your parents' home for you? How did he know you'd go with him?"

"He didn't. He said he was going to start a new town in Pennsylvania ... said he'd be pleased if I'd come along as his wife and help him build a town."

"What did you do?"

"Well, I thought he had grand plans. I didn't know if he could really do it.... I asked my daddy what he thought. He said I was old enough to think on my own." She snickered. "I was seventeen. He had seven other mouths to feed."

"So you left with him, just like that?" Lydia asked. Grandmother had been just a child! Lydia had never experienced want or hunger, and couldn't imagine a father relieved to have one less person to feed.

"Matthäus took me back to New Harmony, and we were one of twelve couples Father Rapp married. Others who were already married wanted to start over, so we came here. Lean years ... The men tried to take jobs to feed everyone until the gardens came in and the stock was bred."

Grandmother's paper-thin eyelids closed. Lydia watched the shallow movement of her chest.

"Plenty of nights we went to bed with our bellies growling," she whispered. "Nobody'd hire our men, of course." She smiled at some faraway memory of pleasure. "But we had one another."

Silence engulfed the room. Jakob swallowed so loud, Lydia looked up, and their misty gazes met in understanding.

"You children have my blessing," Grandmother said, and slipped into sleep.

Lydia bit her lip, blinked back tears and glanced at her father. Etham's hard expression seemed to fade in the lantern-light. She knew that his orderly, systematic concepts were battling with the information he'd digested. His own mother was an Outsider! To Lydia, it made perfect sense, answered puzzling questions. It explained the old woman's extraordinary comments and capacities.

Jakob yawned and idly tapped the gun barrel on his knee. He grinned at her, and she felt the warmth of his concern for her across the room. At long last she understood her grandmother's advice to follow her heart. Loving Jakob as she did, she would be happy anywhere he was. Anywhere they could be together. She recalled the vows they'd repeated after Reverend Mercer: in sickness, trouble and sorrow...in plenty and in want...for better or for worse...as long as we both shall live...

There was no room for doubt; she would love Jakob until her dying day, just as Rose had loved Matthäus.

Just before daylight, Grandmother's tortured breathing roused them all. Christine and Rachael knelt at the other side of the cot. Nathan appeared in the doorway, hair tousled. Etham sat at his mother's feet, and the gun remained inert on Jakob's knee. Lydia's chest felt as though one of the horses were standing on it, crushing her heart.

As dawn broke beyond the closed shutters, Rose Beker's agonized breathing ended in one forcefully exhaled gust. Etham gently closed her mouth with a trembling hand. Lydia stared at her grandmother's still, bloodless face and pressed the hand she held against her lips. Her father covered his face with his hands. Rachael and Nathan helped their weeping mother stand.

A pain so intense that she wanted to stand and scream hysterically stole Lydia's composure. Her mind locked on the person who had been dearest to her. The person who had comforted her childish fears, humored her youthful moods, understood and encouraged her mature dreams. Never again would those gold-flecked eyes twinkle with mirth. Never again would they see a field of wildflowers, or a pink-and-silver sky at sunrise.

Her grandmother had been her friend, her...kindred spirit. Her misery was so complete that Lydia couldn't cry for what seemed hours, though only minutes passed. When the wave hit, it crashed around her, sweeping her with it. Her body shook with great racking sobs that tore at her lungs. She clung to the lifeless hand and sobbed her grief against the patterned wedding quilt.

A gentle touch on her shoulder broke through her anguish, and she raised her head. Jakob knelt at her side, his face reflecting her suffering. Without a spoken word, she turned into his arms, clung to the front of his shirt and buried her face in his familiar warmth and scent.

He pressed her head against his chest. Etham looked up from his own quiet reverie and saw the incongruous vision. One of Jakob's hands held the gun steadily against the back of Lydia's head. The other stroked her back comfortingly, kneaded her waist.

"Lydia, darlin', don't make yourself sick."

"I am s-sick."

"I know." He attempted to lift her from the floor. "C'mon. Let's sit up."

"I c-can't, Jakob. I didn't know anything c-could feel this awful." She kept her face buried against his shirt, muffling her sobs. Her hair came loose from its last mooring, and the tumbled skein fell over his arm. He stroked it over her shoulder, his callused fingers absently working through the knots.

"You know, the apostle Paul wrote that death is swallowed up in victory. Know why I think he said that? Because death itself is the reward. Your grandma lived her whole life with that in mind. This is her reward. She's not suffering now. Her hands don't hurt. She doesn't miss your granddad. You're the one suffering. She's exactly where she wants to be."

Lydia raised her head. Her eyes, swollen and red-rimmed, beseeched him. "Oh, Jakob, I know you're right. I—" a hiccup rocked her "—remember her saying that nothing would be better than her life with my grandfather except their reward in heaven together. She wasn't afraid of dying, was she?"

"No, darlin', she wasn't."

Lydia shuddered as she inhaled. Turning in Jakob's embrace, she glanced at the slight figure on the cot. Her gaze met Etham's across the narrow bed. He looked as taken aback as she'd felt the first time she heard Jakob talk about God and quote Scripture. Jakob was not the heathen the Harmonists presumed him to be.

Etham glanced between Lydia and her husband. The three of them came to their feet. Lydia's hair hung in disarray across one shoulder and down her back. She wore a rumpled pale dress with chains of flowers in the patterned fabric. A matching yellow ribbon hung sorrily from a fallen lock of hair. Jakob had eyes only for her beautiful, tear-streaked face. The .45 hung against his thigh, where his hand had fallen as they stood.

Lydia went to her mother. Rachael turned her tear-stained face to observe her father and brother-in-law. Her eyes carefully avoided her grandmother.

"I will help you prepare her," Lydia said to her mother.

Christine nodded.

Etham and Jakob stared at one another's weary faces after the others left the room.

"Will I need this?" Jakob raised the barrel.

"Out of respect for my mother, I will not make a spectacle of her burial. You keep that...weapon...out of sight until she is decently buried."

"As long as you don't try to make Lydia leave before she's ready. She needs to be with her ma now."

Etham nodded.

Jakob had done it. He'd brought Lydia to her grandmother's bedside and seen to it she was with her until the end. Now he'd give her this time with her mother, and accompany her to the burial. It was the least he could do.

He holstered the Peacemaker.

Chapter Twenty-One

Etham had posted the time for his mother's burial: three o'clock on this splendid fall day.

Lydia and *Mutter* pressed clothing for Grandmother and arranged her hair beneath her cap, making the undertaker's task a simple one.

Nathan invited Jakob to observe the construction of the casket. The pieces of hardwood already cut and finished, the carpenter had only to assemble the box and tack in a dull black liner. As always, Jakob was impressed with the organization and efficiency of the Rappites. Afterward, he and Nathan saddled horses and rode west, across the stream. They returned for the service, their arms laden with the last of the season's wildflowers. Together they strewed them across the head of the grave.

Lydia, pale in a gray day dress and a white Norman cap, stood between her sisters. Faith clung to her mother's skirts. Jakob, in his woolen jacket the color of burnt umber, stood a head taller than Nathan. A dozen other colonists attended.

Each grave in the burial garden was defined with a border of the colony's red clay bricks buried endwise. There were no markers, no headstones, nothing to identify one plot from another. In death no one stood apart from their fellow believers, any more than they had in life. Jakob thought the special old woman deserved a more remarkable burial and resting place.

The service was entirely in German, and painfully short. Donning his Stetson, Jakob turned to follow the women and children, but noticed that Etham hadn't moved with them. He realized the unpleasant task facing the man, and compassion softened his heart.

Vater Beker placed his Bible on the ground and shrugged out of his dark blue dress jacket. He looked up in surprise as Jakob approached.

Jakob gestured toward the shovels. "This is your job?"

The older man nodded.

Jakob took off his own jacket and reached for a shovel.

Etham watched wordlessly as Jakob tossed a shovelful of earth into the hole. Another shovelful, and Jakob looked up to see a pensive and almost embarrassed look on his father-in-law's face. Etham grabbed a shovel and worked doggedly, sweat breaking out on his forehead. After a time, he leaned on the shovel, watching Jakob move dirt effortlessly, and mopped his face. "I am not a tyrant, Herr Neubauer."

Jakob raised one arm above his head and caught a trickle of perspiration from his temple with his shoulder.

"I do what I must in order to earn the respect of the colonists," Lydia's father said.

Jakob wanted to ask if they respected breaking hearts, but out of respect for the old woman in the dirt at their feet, he kept silent.

"At an early age I knew my leadership would be compared. I drove myself to be a more worthy, more dedicated leader than my father. I have not failed. Accord is a thriving, productive community. The Harmonists own major shares in two railroads. We enjoy diplomatic relations with state officials."

Exasperated, Jakob couldn't keep silent any longer. "What do you want me to say?" He packed earth with the back of the shovel, straightened, and tilted his hat back from his forehead. "'Well done, good and faithful servant?' I'm not God. I can't judge you.

"Yeah, okay," Jakob continued. "You accomplished those things, but what's important? What about keepin' Lydia from her family? Do your followers respect that? Or would they have respected a little compassion when your ma was dying? What's so sinful about a little human warmth? Your children are begging for a loving touch."

"You don't understand our ways."

"No, I don't. And I don't want to. I'll never understand not comforting someone you love with a hug. I'll never understand not showing the woman you love she sets your blood on fire." Jakob stabbed the shovel into the earth and picked up his jacket. "That's the difference between us. I admit to all those earthly things."

Jakob took a step and turned back. "And I want you to know we'll be back."

Etham's dark eyes met his. Perspiration rolled down his temple. "Will you bring your gun?"

"Will I need it?"

The older man raised his arm and blotted his forehead on his rolled up sleeve. "I will pray about it."

"You once told me I'd be sorry. Well, I'm not. Not one damned bit sorry. But I think you are." Jakob turned and strode away from the garden.

The family didn't take their meal in the main dining hall that evening. After a simple supper Lydia helped her mother prepare, Etham donned his shoes and jacket and left. Immediately the tension drained from the atmosphere.

Lydia's siblings were enthralled by Jakob, and obviously fascinated by his speech, mannerisms and clothing. Nathan asked numerous questions about plants, trees and soils.

"Jakob, how do you understand so much about crossbreeding and conserving soil?" she asked, drying a teacup.

"I went to the Agricultural University in Philadelphia for a year. Lived with a nice family, attended classes, wore shirts and ties." He grinned. "Whole ball of wax."

The look of puzzlement on Nathan's face caught his attention, and Jakob laughed. "He gets the same expression on his face you do, darlin'."

He used the endearment without thought. Lydia met her mother's eyes, and blushed.

Shyly Lydia's young brother Amos approached Jakob with a book.

"Whatcha got there, pardner?" Jakob casually draped his arm over the boy's shoulder as they both examined the pages. "Birds, eh? I like birds, too."

Lydia saw her young brother's gaze fall to the hand dangling over his shoulder, then dart up to Jakob's face in apparent worship. Her chest ached with empathy for her younger brothers and sisters, for the simple pleasure of the loving touch they'd been denied their short, hollow lives. They were starved for the attention Jakob gave them, just as she had been. Silently she thanked God for her good fortune.

"In fact," Jakob continued, "I had a bird-nest collection when I was a young'n like you. My mama found 'em in a drawer and set up such a ruckus you could have heard it clear over here. I had to keep them in the barn after that, and it wasn't near as much fun."

Caught up in the story, Faith inched closer to Jakob. "Did you have sisters and brothers when you were a young'n?" she asked, mimicking Jakob's pronunciation.

"Never had a sister, but I have two brothers."

"Did they have bird nests, too?"

"No..." He leaned back and scratched his chin, and Lydia realized she'd forgotten to pack his razor. "Seems like I remember Anton havin' a box of rocks—fieldstones mostly. A few chunks of iron ore and manganese. He kept a jar of old clock parts, too." He laughed. "Franz liked marbles. We always fought over the best ones."

"What are marbles?" Amos asked.

"Little glass balls. It's a game you play by drawing a circle in the dirt and—"

"Children," *Mutter* said, interrupting, "you must allow Herr Neubauer to rest. You have asked him questions all evening. Prepare yourselves for bed."

Immediately Amos and Faith said good-night and left the kitchen.

Jakob raised a brow at his wife. "Think our children will mind like that?" he asked when she neared.

"Not if they take after you," she whispered.

"Rachael," her mother said, "help me prepare Grandmother's room. Jakob may sleep in there, and Lydia may set up her old cot in your room."

"*Mutter*," Lydia said, "perhaps Jakob and I should go home."

"You have not slept," her mother reminded her. "Unless yo● object." Her blue gaze swept from her daughter to Jakob. Sh● seemed unwilling to let them go.

"Fine with me, if it's what Lydia wants," Jakob replied.

Lydia nodded. She and Jakob helped sort through Grand● mother's meager belongings. A long, uncomfortable silenc● engulfed them when Christine folded the wedding quilt an● placed it on the pile of bedding near the door. *Mutter*'s eye● swam with tears.

Lydia recognized her pain, and her mother's helplessness angered her. She knew her mother must be torn between alle● giance to her husband and love for her daughter, and had to b● frustrated at her inability to do anything about it.

"It's all right," Lydia said softly. "I know Father means fo● Rachael to have the quilt now. It's only a worldly possession● Why, it'll probably be worn out by the time she has children o● marrying age!"

Mutter dipped her hand into her apron pocket and with● drew a small object. In Lydia's hand she placed a tiny pair o● silver sewing scissors Grandmother had mended and embroi● dered with. Lydia closed her fingers over the scissors an● smiled. Her father would never miss them.

Christine and Rachael carried out bedding and clothes tha● would be turned in to the exchange. What a pitifully short tim● it took to extinguish all traces of Rose Beker's existence. Lyd● ia's gaze lingered on the empty coat hooks near the door, an● she patted the scissors in her pocket, taking comfort from then and from her mother's gesture. Jakob lowered his tall frame t● the cot and tugged at his boot. Lydia noticed his concerned ex● pression, brushed his hands aside and grasped his boot heel● "What are you thinking?"

He leaned back, both arms braced behind him, and pulled i● the opposite direction. "Wondering if you have any regrets."

His foot popped out of the boot, and she hobbled to catcl● her balance. "Regrets?"

Frowning, she lifted his other boot, applied the same pro● cedure and set it beside the first, gazing at his stockinged feet● She remembered helping him out of his boots the day before●

as sunlight filtered through the autumn leaves overhead, and suddenly it seemed an intimate act.

Jakob yanked the gray blanket from the cot and folded it into a tidy square, placing it where his head would lie in place of a pillow, which no one in the colony had heard of. Lydia touched his sleeve, and he turned.

"You're thinking I'm sorry about the things of hers I can't have?"

He took her hand from his sleeve and kissed her fingers. His unshaven upper lip prickled. She'd never seen him with the golden stubble. The growth lent him a reckless appearance she liked.

"I'm not sorry, Jakob. I'm glad I made the decisions I did. You've given me so much more. . . ."

He gathered her into his arms and kissed her. The minor irritation of his mustache immediately forgotten, his ardent mouth ignited a fire in her body. Slanting his head, he lifted his arms, allowing her hands access to his back. Lydia's blood tingled at an increasing rate. Images of their recent encounters inspired her to press herself against his muscled body and relish the temporary satisfaction of his hard chest flattening her breasts.

Jakob inhaled deeply and pulled his face away with an audible hiss. He breathed against her ear, held her head resting lightly against his hammering chest. "I thought I was so tired that nothing would keep me awake, but you're doin' a good job."

She leaned back in his arms and patted his rib cage. "Why, Jakob," she teased, attempting to break the tension. "Didn't you forget something at supper tonight? Where's your holster? What if my mother hadn't passed the corn bread? You could have pulled your gun on her."

Contrite, he leaned back from the waist. "I thought about it, but I forgot to bring bullets, anyway."

Her mouth fell open. "Empty it was!"

He nodded with a lopsided grin.

"Why, you . . . you . . . scoundrel!"

He laughed and released her, bringing her hand to his mouth again. This time he opened it and pressed a moist kiss into her palm. He folded her fingers as if she held something precious. "Keep that with you tonight."

Accustomed to his secure presence, Lydia realized the harshness of being separated for the night. She stepped back and glanced apologetically at the narrow cot. The thought of Jakob's bed, which had once seemed immorally self-indulgent, now seemed practical, as well as comfortable. "Sleep well."

"*Gute Nacht. Weib.*"

Her heart warmed at the word. How glad she was to be his wife. "*Gute Nacht. Mann.*"

The next morning, the Neubauers' windows were steamed over, and the kitchen was warm and inviting. Annette turned from the breadboard and wiped her hands on her apron. She gave Lydia a welcoming hug.

For once Lydia appreciated the steaming mug of black coffee placed in front of her. Her calves and thighs tingled from the cold. She told Annette about her grandmother's death.

"I'm glad you got to see her."

"Thanks to Jakob. He held my father at gunpoint."

Annette's eyes widened in disbelief. "Lydia, you're smiling!"

"The gun wasn't loaded, but none of us knew that."

"What must your family think of him now?"

"They're all quite enamored. Except my father, of course. I think he expected as much from a heathen."

Annette laughed.

"What's so funny?" Franz and Jakob entered, allowing a cold draft in.

Annette scurried to pour them coffee. "Your little brother has some imaginative ways of getting what he wants. Lydia must bring out the desperado in him."

"Or the gentleman," Lydia hastened to add.

Jakob met her eyes. He would do anything for her.

"Is someone going to tell me?" Franz asked.

"I coaxed her pa into lettin' her visit," Jakob explained undramatically, enjoying drawing out the tale.

"How?"

"With my Peacemaker."

His matter-of-fact delivery even tickled Lydia into a giggle. Franz laughed uproariously.

Jakob stretched a long leg under the table and kicked Franz's bench off kilter.

Franz caught his balance with a slap of his palms on the table. The commotion pulled in Johann and Anton, and Annette made another pot of coffee. Peine must have stayed upstairs with Nikolaus, and Lydia was secretly glad. She'd been through enough emotional turmoil these past few days. Franz told his version of the story, expanding it to outlandish proportions. Lydia relaxed and sipped the bitter brew. The men's laughter wrapped her in a welcome cocoon. The meal she helped prepare was punctuated by bursts of laughter, and the now-familiar drone of male voices.

Later, turning from the dishwater, she met Jakob's blue gaze. His look warmed her like the summer sky on an August day, and held silent promises. Promises only he could keep.

That night, Nikolaus pounded Jakob's worn fiddle case. Johann carried it to his son. Grandfather and grandson watched Jakob snap it open.

He tuned by ear, then stood and pulled the bow across the strings. For a change the tune wasn't frivolous, but a floating, passionate melody. Lydia had never heard him play so beautifully or so intensely.

"What's this song?" she whispered to Annette.

Annette, sitting with her fingers entwined through her husband's, replied, "'Beautiful Dreamer.'"

The notes died away, and Jakob returned the fiddle to its case. He sat on the floor at Lydia's feet.

"We have some news." Franz gathered everyone's attention. "We're going to have a baby."

Joy lit Annette's and Franz's faces and softened their eyes as they looked at one another. Johann beamed. Jakob clasped Lydia's hand and squeezed. A chorus of congratulations filled the parlor, with one exception.

Peine remained expressionless. Abruptly she picked up Nikolaus and carried him upstairs.

Lydia prepared for bed, hearing again the magical notes of Jakob's violin. She opened her Bible and read the passages her father had read at her grandmother's burial. Ready tears flowed at the beautiful words of the psalms. Reminding herself of Jakob's words, she cried only for herself. Grandmother was exactly where she wanted to be. Shamelessly Lydia grieved for herself and for the desolation of losing her best friend.

Jakob entered their bedroom and recognized her grief. He undressed down to his drawers and perched next to her on the bed. "You all right?"

She nodded.

He smoothed hair from her temples. "Want to talk?"

She shook her head. Stripping, he lifted the coverlet and urged her beneath it. His chest hair tickled her nose as he hugged her. He kissed her and caressed her limbs, and she cried again.

Initially, touching him had not come naturally, but now that she had discovered the sensitivity of his skin, she knew she would never stop. The muscles beneath his sleek skin were pure pleasure. She ran her hands along the planes and contours of his strong arms and shoulders. Numerous times she had admired his molded strength as he lifted, chopped wood, or simply moved in his own masculine way. He was contained strength, a phenomenal example of God's finest handiwork, the very air she hadn't realized she needed, the nourishment her body had never known it lacked.

Jakob rested his weight on top of her, his warm breath sighing in her ear, sending shivers dancing along her shoulders. He stroked her breasts and abdomen, his hands drawing expectancy and a bittersweet yearning from every cell and tissue of her, just as they'd coaxed the sad-sweet melody from his violin. Lydia reached for him, impulsively guiding him to the consummate degree of oneness she craved. Jakob filled her, and she gave herself up to the sensations he created with each kiss, each movement, each sigh against her mouth and chin. Her awareness sharpened until she feared she would burst into a thousand shattered fragments if the exquisite torture didn't end soon. She needed it to end, but wanted it to last forever.

Jakob rolled and urged her astride him, raising himself until his famished mouth reached her breasts. She ran her hands over the hard muscle of his shoulders, felt them tense as he guided her movements, lifted her weight, easily, rhythmically.

Suddenly there wasn't enough oxygen in the room. Jakob's endurance wore thin. After a rapturous pause, he turned and drew her beneath him, and they shared the gift of heavenly release.

Peine tucked a blanket around Nikolaus and turned back to the immaculate room. Her distaste for housekeeping in another's home went back to her youth at the Sedgewick Boarding House. There she had scrubbed floors, made beds, washed dishes and peeled vegetables. She had told Anton that her well-to-do parents had hired domestic help, so she'd never learned. The story of her past had been convincing, since she was mannerly, well dressed and college-educated. She kept their room tidy, but refused to touch any other.

The irritation that had grown in intensity over the past weeks now reached full-blown fury. Annette had stolen the glory from the child Peine carried by conceiving one of her own. As if it weren't disgusting enough to have to watch her and Franz behave like a couple of foolish youngsters courting, she now had to endure the cow eyes Jakob and Lydia gave one another. Their newfound bliss was no secret. The looks they exchanged were enough to blister the enamel on the cookware.

The fools! Jakob belonged with Peine! He was perfect for her! What did he have to talk with that priss about? Envy was eating a cavernous hole in her chest. She lowered herself into the wooden rocker. The baby rolled inside her. It would be too late to do anything once Jakob and Lydia built their house and moved out. It would have been so easy if Lydia had simply become disillusioned with this lifeless situation and gone back to her family.

Peine hadn't suspected her task would be such a difficult one. A picture of Jakob and Lydia in the room down the hall took shape, and her frustration intensified. She had to do something. Now! Something to drive Lydia away, once and for all!

The door opened, and Anton entered. He removed his boots, and she arranged them precisely under the wardrobe where she liked them. He tossed his shirt into the basket.

Peine knotted the belt of her satin gown over her distended abdomen and sat at her dressing table, brushing her hair.

Dressed only in his unfastened dungarees, Anton leaned over the side of Nikolaus's crib and touched the baby's soft cheek with one long finger. He stepped behind Peine and, in a rare gesture, fingered the golden hair she'd brushed until it shone. Jakob had once commented on how pretty her hair was.

"You never wear braids," Anton remarked.

Her eyes snapped in the reflection in the mirror. "Braids are common." She brought the brush down with a crack and rose to use the water basin. "You want me to look like Lydia?"

Clenching his jaw, Anton stared at the spotless surface of her dressing table in frustration and growing disgust. He strode to where she stood drying her face and grabbed the towel from her hands. "Do you ever have a kind word for anyone? Have you ever thought about speakin' to me in a pleasant tone?"

"Kind?" She yanked the towel from his hand and folded it, hanging it neatly over the stand. "What would you know about kind?"

He grabbed the towel from the rack and threw it on the floor. "This is common, that is boorish, I am impossible. All you ever do is complain. Nothing makes you happy."

"How the hell would you know what makes me happy? You certainly never tried. God, you're childish!" She bent to retrieve the towel, but he covered it with his bare foot and wouldn't move.

"Childish? What other names would you like to call me tonight?"

"You're stubborn and pigheaded, and you won't try." She leaned toward his good ear. "Did you hear that?"

"Oh, that's grand. I'm not tryin'."

Kneeling, she hit his leg with her fist, trying to dislodge him. "Move, dammit!"

"Stop shouting before you wake Nikky up with your shrewish screaming."

"I want you to hear me!" She stood to her full height, which still brought her only to his chest. When he wasn't expecting it, she shoved him backward and bent, snatching up the towel.

Anton grabbed her shoulders and yanked her to face him. He snatched the towel from her hand and threw it against the wall. Fingers tightening on her arms, he backed her against the bed.

She struggled, calling him names, and slapped at his hands. Relentless, he trapped both her hands with one of his, tugged her sash from its moorings, opened her dressing gown and pushed her down on the bed. His eyes darkened as he scanned her full breasts, spilling above the low-cut neckline of her gown. Seeing the smoldering look of desire on his face, something strangely akin to satisfaction sprang to life within her. He wanted her. She treated him terribly, but he wanted her. Why didn't Jakob want her?

Anton stared for a long time at the satiny mound of her belly beneath the gown.

Breathing raggedly, she stared back, almost appreciating the width of his chest, the crisp hair covering it, and the golden path narrowing into his gaping fly. If not for that disgusting scar on his shoulder, she could almost imagine he was Jakob. She wished he were his brother. Broader chest. Bluer eyes. No scar. Jakob talked to her. Jakob understood her sensitivity. She closed her eyes and envisioned him, and her body responded immediately.

Anton's grasp loosened, and he shook his head wearily. "Not this time, Peine."

"What?" she breathed.

"It's been like this too many times. Odds are I made both of these babies in anger."

Her eyes flew open. She raged. He was refusing her! She yanked her hands free, and slapped him, hard. "You conceited bastard!"

He sat back, watching her gather the gown across her breasts and raise up on her knees across the bed from him.

"You men are all alike! Can't you think of anything but your own prowess?"

"Peine, hush—"

"You might have made that one in anger," she snarled, jabbing a finger toward the crib where their son slept. "But you didn't have a blessed thing to do with this one!"

Anton blinked as if to clear his thoughts. "What're you talkin' about?"

"I'm *talkin'*," she said, mimicking his speech, "about thi baby." She rubbed her belly slowly, caressingly. "This love child." She flung the venom at him, sheer pleasure pulsing through her veins. "It isn't yours."

The words hung between them. Anton gaped at her in the silence that followed. A light pattering of rain sprinkled against the window. "You can't mean that."

"I mean it," she taunted. "Oh, I mean it."

"Whose is it?"

Peine lifted her chin and struck the final blow. "Jakob's."

Chapter Twenty-Two

Lydia sprinkled sugar and cinnamon on long strips of dough and twisted them into perfect knots. "Has Anton ever missed breakfast before?"

Putting water for starch on to boil, Annette shook her head. Everyone had heard raised voices the night before. "I think he slept in the barn. I heard him go out."

Lydia opened the oven door and slid the tray of pastries in. She pulled on a coat and picked up the scrap tins. "These are beginning to smell. I'll be right back."

A rhythmic pounding came from inside the barn. Thinking the men had all gone to winterize the stock tanks, she entered the building to investigate. In the tack room, she discovered Anton heedlessly hammering a pile of splintered boards on the workbench.

"Anton?"

He jerked around. "Lydia!"

Stepping closer, she saw the remains of a cradle, smashed beyond repair. She placed her hand on his shirtsleeve, and he averted his face. "Anton, let me help."

He shook his head. "You can't."

She couldn't bear the anguished look in his eyes. "I don't know what's bothering you, but I could pray with you."

"I've prayed so hard I don't know what to say anymore. If God's listenin', He's chosen to look the other way."

"Don't say that!" she said. "God never looks the other way! He's working on an answer right now!"

Anton's broad shoulders caved forward. He hung his head over the worktable, and his body quaked.

A startled minute passed before she realized he was weeping. She hated to see him so despondent. "Oh, Anton.. Anton."

She urged him backward, and he sat heavily upon the stool. She took his head against her breast and comforted him in the only way she knew, rocking him gently, kneading his back.

Minutes later he spoke against her coat. "I'm at the end of my rope."

"I'm sorry. I don't understand."

Despite his sorrow, he chuckled and lifted his head. "I always forget.... Picture someone hangin' suspended over a black, bottomless pit. His arms get tired, but there's nowhere to go. Nowhere but down."

"A vivid expression."

"Yeah." He sat back, and the stool creaked. "She doesn't love me, you know." Tears filled his eyes again. He pressed his knuckles against them. "I don't think she ever did. I can't fix things. Nobody can."

"God can."

"Not this time, He can't."

"Anton, what is so terrible? Tell me."

"I've been betrayed." He let his hands drop and tried to look at her, but couldn't meet her eyes. "I'm waiting to get angry enough so I can just beat the hell out of—"

She perceived his hesitation. "Out of who?"

Anton shook his head.

"Anton, what are you talking about?"

"If I tell you, you'll feel the same way I do. And there's no need for both of us to be miserable." He sighed and drew an unsteady breath. "But I don't know how I can not tell you."

"Tell me what?" She gripped his shoulders and turned him to look her in the eye.

"I'm sorry, Lydia."

"This is your fault, then?"

He shrugged. "Maybe. In some roundabout way."

She waited.

"Peine's baby isn't mine."

Stunned, Lydia tried to absorb his words. Of course Peine's baby was Anton's. They were married. Who else's would it be? "I don't understand."

"They betrayed us, Lydia." Desperation rose in Anton's voice.

"Who?"

"Jakob and Peine." He struggled with the words, the thought. "The baby is Jakob's."

Anton was delirious! He couldn't know what he was saying! "But that's ... impossible."

"Is it? She's wanted him for a long time. I saw it all along, but couldn't make myself believe it. Too proud, maybe."

Lydia's numb brain comprehended, slowly. Peine had wanted Jakob all along? Of course! It all made sense now. Peine knew how sensitive and caring Jakob was. That was why she had convinced Lydia to cut her hair and planted seeds of doubt about harlots in the cities. Peine—not Lydia—had been the one worried that Jakob was seeing another woman!

Peine wanted Jakob. That was why she'd told Jakob about taking the horse. That was why she'd done everything in her power to disillusion them both. Lydia had known that, but she'd been unable—or unwilling—to form the clues into complete thoughts.

However ... she had believed Jakob when he spoke his wedding vows. She knew he hadn't taken that promise lightly. "Jakob wouldn't be unfaithful to me," she said firmly.

"He probably hasn't been unfaithful to you since, but she's over six months pregnant, Lydia. It happened before you were married." Anton raked his hands through his hair, kneaded his neck and tipped his head back. He gazed morosely at the rafters. "I don't know. I don't know anything anymore."

The earth tilted beneath her feet, and her head spun dizzily. She looked at Anton, but no longer saw him. There was no air in the barn to breathe, and there was nowhere to go. Nothing to think. Only acute feelings. Swirling confusion. Agony. Betrayal. Emptiness.

Jakob's determination for a house entered her mind. Was his intent to separate himself from the woman he wanted, the one married to his brother? Had Lydia been the convenient distraction he needed to help him forget his attraction to Peine? Perhaps his conscience hadn't allowed him to continue an af fair with his brother's wife, and he'd taken Lydia as a substi tute. But, he'd told her he'd never been with a woman before Had he lied?

She wilted against the rough wood of the high table. Jakob must love Peine! He'd never told Lydia he loved her, only tha he needed her, desired her, wanted her. She fulfilled the need of his body, but obviously not those of his heart!

"Oh, my God," she whispered. The tack room blurred in he vision. Peine was having a baby. *Her* baby! The baby tha should rightfully be hers! Only days ago she'd told him a chile didn't matter anymore. But she'd fallen in love with him Hopelessly, fiercely, foolishly in love with him, and it did mat ter! It mattered very much! Mortified, she recalled Jakob' words that first time. "I'm sorry to tell you," he had replied i disgust, "but it's not that easy. It sometimes takes many times.'

Her head snapped up. She sucked in her breath. Many times With Peine?

Anton met her eyes. "You okay?"

"No." She pushed her weight away from the worktable. " don't know if I can forgive them."

"I'm sorry."

Tears choked her throat, and she couldn't speak. She nod ded and stumbled from the barn. A chill wind snaked inside the open front of her jacket, but she didn't notice. How could she watch Peine grow larger and larger with Jakob's child? How could she look at Peine again? How could she see that bur geoning mound under Peine's ample breasts without imagin ing Jakob planting his seed within her? Shock and disappointment sickened her. Impossible!

Lydia had been woefully ignorant of human nature before she'd come here. How Peine must have laughed over her stu pidity! Peine had tricked her, lied repeatedly. Jakob, too, hac lied by omission. Lydia tripped on the wooden porch stairs anc caught her balance. Did Jakob know the child belonged to him'

She steadied herself against a column. Of course he did Peine wouldn't waste a chance to bind him more securely to her Peine often cornered him for private conversation. Images tumbled over her: Peine perched on the end of the bed, her emerald eyes devouring Jakob, her golden hair flowing over her soft ivory shoulders.

Lydia gripped the back-door handle. It was too much. She couldn't stay. She had to leave.

"I took your crullers out of the oven." Annette looked up from the steaming flatiron in her hand. "Lydia! What's wrong?"

Lydia shook her head, ran past her, clambered up the stairs. Flinging open the storage door in the room she shared with Jakob, she grabbed her worn leather satchel.

"Lydia? What are you doing?"

Blindly she yanked gray dresses from their hangers and folded them carelessly.

"Lydia!"

She straightened from the floor, and carried a pair of shoes to the satchel lying open on the bed. "I'm leaving."

"Where are you going?"

Finally Lydia turned and looked at her sister-in-law, saw the pain and worry etched into her lovely face. "Where am I going?" Where was she going? She had nowhere to go. With her grandmother gone, there was no one in Accord. She couldn't go back there now. She had nothing and nowhere to run to. But she had Jakob and Peine to run *from*. "I don't know. It doesn't matter."

"Why, then? Why are you leaving?"

"Because I can't stay here any longer. Jakob doesn't love me. He never did."

"I can't believe that."

"Believe it." Lydia opened a drawer. The green kid belt and white spangled fan mocked her. No doubt the gifts had eased his conscience. She'd brought nothing to this marriage with her; she would take nothing when she left. Digging beneath lacy handkerchiefs, she found the silver coins he'd given her. Except these. She needed the coins until she found a job, a means of supporting herself, but she would pay him back. Hastily she tossed the last of her belongings in the bag and closed it.

"Lydia, please don't do this—" Annette's voice broke, and she stretched forward a hand, pleadingly, entreatingly. "You're frightening me."

Lydia hugged her. Her unrealistic dreams had been shattered. "Thank you for being my friend, for everything. Take good care of the baby. You'll be a wonderful mother."

Fleeing down the stairs, she ignored Annette's tearful question: "What will I tell Jakob?"

Jakob returned for the noon meal and glanced around. "Where's Lydia?"

Annette set a platter of biscuits on the table and turned away. "I can't say for sure."

Jakob sat, grabbed a biscuit and took a bite. "What d'ya mean? I didn't see her outside, so she's either upstairs or in the pantry. Root cellar, maybe?"

"No. She's none of those places."

Neither Peine nor Anton had come to eat either. Annette attended to Nikolaus in the high chair. Jakob glanced from his father to Franz. They looked as puzzled over the unusual circumstances as Jakob. The room seemed unusually large and quiet without the other family members. "Well, then, where is she?"

"I told you, I can't say for sure."

The biscuit stuck in his throat, and he swallowed. "But you know she's not here?"

"Yes."

Confused, he persisted. "Annette, will you please tell me what you do know?"

She faced the sink, but her hands lay idle on the side. "She's gone. That's all I know."

A nagging uneasiness wound his nerves taut. His sister-in-law's evasiveness disturbed him. The whole atmosphere of the house felt wrong.

He jumped up, bolted up the stairs two at a time and flung open their bedroom door, surveying the room. It was clean and quiet, only a corner of the bed's coverlet rumpled.

In the undereaves storage closet, her green and yellow dresses hung side by side on the wire he'd placed there for her. Her gray dresses were gone, as was her satchel. An unbearable ache knotted his chest.

Her hairbrush and pins were missing from the washstand. The faint scent of lavender lingered from her morning bath, sending apprehension curling through his belly. His misgivings stabbed a withering blow to the very core of his being. His heart thudded dully, painfully. Where was she?

Like a madman yanking open drawers, he discovered the gifts he'd bought her in the cities. Stockings, bracelet, belt, hankies, all of it lay in mute, mocking silence. Fear chilled him, and his heart thudded against his rib cage.

He surveyed the room they'd shared the past months, confused. Her Bible was gone from the night table. Alarmed, he opened the lid and stared into her empty trunk. His knees quaked, and he sank to the bed's edge.

Gone.

Lydia was gone.

But where? Why? Last night they had made splendid, all-consuming love on this bed. He'd slept with her bare limbs entwined with his, and awakened to the scent of her hair beneath his nose. This morning she'd kissed him so boisterously, he'd had to force himself out of the room and down to breakfast or he'd have taken her back to bed and learned new ways to pleasure her. The last look they had exchanged over coffee had held a promise for the night ahead. Tonight. Where would she be tonight if he didn't find her? What had happened between this morning and now?

Coming unglued, Jakob stalked from the room, his boots thundering on the stairs.

"What the hell is going on?" he shouted at the Neubauers sitting at the trestle table.

Johann glanced up as if his youngest son had shown up for dinner stark naked. Franz angled a look toward his wife.

Annette stood at the sink where Jakob had left her, her fingers gripping the edge. Slowly she turned and faced Jakob. Her tawny eyes revealed pain and a trace of tears, intensifying his apprehension.

"Where is she?" Jakob asked again, trying to keep his voice normal.

The screen door squeaked, and Anton entered the kitchen, drawing up short, as if automatically sensing the room's tension.

Annette met Jakob's eyes. Almost imperceptibly she nodded toward his brother, the gesture saying, "There's your answer."

"Where is Lydia?" Jakob growled again, this time directing the query at Anton.

Anton closed the door behind him. "I told her."

"Told her what?"

"About the baby."

"What baby?"

"Yours and Peine's."

Infinitely confused, Jakob shook his head. "What the hell are you talking about?"

"I'm talking about you knockin' my wife up."

"Wha-at?" Jakob choked.

"Don't deny it. Peine told me."

"Told you...that I got her...with child?" Jakob shook his head again, trying to clear his thoughts. Peine had told Anton that he had gotten her pregnant? Why?

Anton studied him. Jakob didn't recognize the dull despondency in his brother's eyes.

Jakob's body went slack with hurt and disbelief. "And you believed her?" he asked, incredulous.

"Yeah, I believed her. It explains a whole hell of a lot of things."

"Like what?" A creeping numbness had set it, and Jakob focused his attention on trying to understand what his brother had to say.

Anton glanced toward his father and Franz. "Just a lot of things."

"And you told Lydia this?"

Anton nodded, obviously a little less certain of his possession of the truth.

"And she believed it, too." It was a statement of fact, not a question. Jakob grappled with the information, a tumult of emotions whirling for prominence within him. Fury. Panic. Grief.

"Jakob, Peine's wanted you for a long time."

Jakob gawked at Anton in surprise, and sensed embarrassment scorching his cheeks. The accusation seemed almost incestuous!

"Are you telling me you didn't know that?"

Jakob shook his head. "She's always been nice to me. The rest of you misunderstood her." Somewhere in the back of his mind, he remembered Lydia telling him things Peine had done or said that made no sense...but he hadn't paid attention. Now more damage had been done. Was it repairable?

The two brothers stared at one another. No words were going to erase the harm that had been done. Jakob ached inside and out. His own brother believed him an adulterer! Filled with pain, and a rage so intense he couldn't see clearly, he squeezed his eyes shut. Peine had lied to Anton, and Anton believed her! After growing up side by side with him, sharing work, faith and home, Anton thought him capable of such a thing? His pride and honor were riddled with withering injury.

And Lydia... That she thought him capable of such an act after what they'd shared was the ultimate betrayal. *He* had been betrayed by her disbelief! Where was her childlike faith? Where was her trust? Where was *she?*

"I have to find her."

"She took Carolina," Anton offered.

"You let her take a horse?" Jakob's temper had reached the boiling point. "You broke her heart with a lie, and watched her go? You son of a—" Jakob drew back, gathering every ounce of anger and frustration, and hurtled his fist into Anton's jaw with bone-crunching ferocity.

Sprawled on the floor, where Jakob's savage blow landed him, Anton rolled to his back and threw an arm across his eyes. When he pulled it away, Jakob read the misery in his haunted eyes.

At the sight, he adjusted his senses from seething to determined. He unclenched his fists, and his vision cleared. Anger wouldn't do any good. He took a deep breath, regret already consuming him. Why take his frustration out on his brother? There wasn't any time to waste on Anton. He had to find Lydia. His wife was gone, and he had to go after her. There was only one place she could have gone—Accord.

Grabbing his hat and jacket, he slammed the door behind him and left his family gaping.

Chapter Twenty-Three

Roiling gray clouds obliterated the sun, and the temperature was dropping. Ominous thunder split the heavens, and Carolina sidestepped, shudders rippling down her withers. Lydia tightened the reins and spoke to her mount, hoping to comfort herself. Lightning branded the sky.

Never had Lydia been so frightened. She'd been in a rush to escape before Jakob returned or she came face-to-face with Peine. Now she recalled Johann's and Jakob's warnings about the hazards of travel. She was vulnerable without the gun they'd coached her to carry. The guns belonged to the Neubauers, however, and she wouldn't have taken one, even if she'd thought to.

The wind whipped Lydia's scarf from her head, and she tugged it back up, her cold hands fumbling with the woolen square under her chin. Carolina plodded on, following the direction Lydia prayed was taking them to Butler. She was hungry. If she didn't come upon the town soon, she'd have to stop and spend the night out in the open. In the morning she would find the town and inquire about transportation to Pittsburgh. In the city she'd find a job, perhaps in a bakery or a store, and earn the money to take care of herself. She'd send enough back to repay Jakob for the coins she'd taken.

Although her resolve was firm and her plans were in place, her mind wouldn't grant her peace. What about Jakob's reaction when he found her gone? Would he be annoyed? Guilty? Relieved? Would he immediately tell Peine they were free? Or did Peine already know? Would she be anxious to blurt it to

Jakob? She thought the lace curtains in Peine's room had fallen back into place as she steadied Carolina against the fence rail and mounted. No doubt the woman had smiled smugly from ear to ear. What a triumph, now that her rival was neatly out of the way.

Who would care?

Annette. Johann.

Tears filled her eyes again. How unfair of Jakob to plant her in his family and allow her to care for them! How doubly unfair that he'd entreated her to love him from her soul, when his heart had been taken by someone else!

Lightning forked across the darkened sky, followed by distant thunder. Carolina shied, and Lydia wished she had brought the more docile, less skittish Freida.

"Easy, girl," she said to the horse and to herself. To the heavens she petitioned, "*sie Gott*, be with me. Guide my way."

Her entire life, she'd been taken care of, provided for—first by her father and the colony, and later by Jakob. Now she had only herself and God to depend on.

Minutes later, her prayer was answered by a sound. She reined in Carolina so that she could listen. The noise was something man-made. She cocked her head and listened again. An off-key piano. Digging her heels into the horse's sides, she galloped toward the sound. Relief swept through her at the lights she spotted ahead. Now she would find a place for the night!

"Thank you, God. You alone never let me down."

Jakob jerked the collar of his slicker up under his ears and adjusted his dripping Stetson. Rain had pelted him for the last half hour, most of it managing to find its way down his collar to soak his shirt. He didn't know who he was angrier with now: Peine for the abominable lie, his brother for passing it on, or Lydia for believing it and causing him this grief and embarrassment.

Reining Gunter to a halt on the narrow brick street, he looped the reins around the post of the nearest gas lamp. He dreaded an encounter with Etham Beker, but he had to find Lydia. He glanced at the second-story windows. A dim glow shone from only one. The children would be asleep. Was his wife lying on a cot next to her sister? What would he say to her?

Fortified by indignation, Jakob loped up the walkway. His loud knock echoed into the night. Silent seconds passed. He pounded again, rousing a sound from inside.

The door opened, and Etham Beker filled the doorway, dressed in black pants and a gray shirt. It was the first time Jakob had seen him without his white shirt and tie. Etham drew himself up. He wasn't as tall as Jakob, yet with his black hair, beard and supercilious expression, he was an imposing figure. He didn't invite Jakob in out of the rain.

"I want to see Lydia."

No expression marred Etham's sober face.

"I want to see my wife."

"Beg a pardon, Herr Neubauer," Lydia's father said, his words clipped. "You have misplaced your wife?"

His words chafed Jakob's already well-abraded temperament. He stared into those fathomless black eyes and swallowed his humiliation. "My sister-in-law did something that hurt Lydia. She left the farm this afternoon, and I thought she would come here."

Etham Beker had the grace to look concerned. "No. She is not here." He seemed to read the disbelief on Jakob's face. "I do not lie." Resignedly he took a step backward, opening the door into the dimly lit kitchen. "You will have to see for yourself."

Unspoken between them was the memory of Jakob's gun leveled at *Vater* Beker's chest. Tracking mud over the immaculate kitchen floor, Jakob stopped midway.

Christine Beker stepped from the hallway and spotted him. A long, fair braid fell across her shoulder and across the front of the wool robe she wore. Soft curls hung at her ears and forehead, giving her a young, pretty look.

"Herr Neubauer?" Worry erased the soft look and wrinkled her forehead. "Is something wrong? Has something happened to Lydia?"

Jakob's heart fell in his chest. Lydia wasn't here! It was obvious that her *Mutter* was surprised by his appearance. Immediately he regretted causing her concern. "I'm sorry, Frau Beker. I was sure she'd be here."

Confusion and worry coiled a tight knot of tension in Jakob's belly. Lydia knew the way to Accord. Had she fallen or been hurt or attacked somewhere along the way? He had carefully looked for signs of her passing, but he admitted he wasn't much of a tracker. Should he double back and look more carefully, in case she lay bleeding or unconscious? Where else would she go?

"What is it?" Lydia's mother asked.

"I'm sure she's okay. She probably just went to our neighbors'."

"Did you—have a misunderstanding?" she asked hesitantly.

That was an understatement. "Sort of." He turned back toward the door. "I have to find her."

"Jakob." When she spoke his name, he stopped.

He turned back and glanced between her and her husband—the one fair as daybreak, the other dark as midnight.

"You will let me know that she is safe?"

Etham remained silent, and Jakob was grateful. He managed a smile for Christine. "I'll let you know."

He stepped back into the rain and considered the only other possibility. Butler. She couldn't have gotten any farther than that.

Though he wanted to spur the horse to a run, Jakob didn't dare, for fear the animal would lose his footing in the mud or stumble in a hole in the dark. The slow pace was doubly frustrating. Despite the slicker, he was soon wet to the skin, out of sorts and heavyhearted.

How dare she pack up her things—not the things he'd given her, but her belongings from the colony—and gallop away! After the life they'd begun, the meaningful days and nights, how could she believe he'd slept with his brother's wife? Didn't she know him? Didn't she have faith in his honor, his honesty? Why would she imagine that he would even look at another woman? He'd never given her cause to doubt him. Had he? He'd bought her all the things he wanted her to have and enjoy—material things, sure, but they proved his thoughts were of her.

He was building a house for her! That showed he was a husband who wanted to provide for her, who wanted them to have a permanent home of their own, and children to raise in it.

Jakob lifted agonized eyes to a streak of jagged lightning. The countryside momentarily lit with an eerie gray. Thunder volleyed across the muffled heavens, reminding him of another night months ago in Accord. He and Lydia had stood beneath gas lamps, raindrops sparkling on the stone benches, and the scent of a hundred flowers had assailed them. His throat constricted with fear.

What if he didn't find her? What if Carolina had thrown her and she was lying hurt or dying somewhere? The horrible memory of Sylvie's death stirred his fears to a fever pitch. A delicate young woman trampled to her bloody death by a horse. He shuddered.

What if she managed to catch a stage or a train? He'd never find her, never see her again. A heaviness he wouldn't have believed possible weighted his heart. Everything was working against him. Even the weather.

Well, rain wasn't going to stop him. He was going to find her. When he found her, he planned to confront her with each and every question and thought he'd had since leaving the farm. And she'd better come up with some good answers! Only Lydia could decide for herself what kind of man he was, and whether or not they had a future together.

Jakob reined Gunter up in front of Butler's only stable. Dismounting, he led him into the minimal shelter beside the building and rapped on the door. Receiving no answer, he pounded, finally rousing a bare-chested man who hitched up his suspenders and scratched his belly as he peered at Jakob.

"Yeah, I can put him up," he muttered, squinting at Jakob. "Two bits."

Jakob dug in his sodden dungarees for the coins and followed the man, who rolled open the stable door and led him into the fetid-smelling building. A lantern lit their way past rows of stalls.

Spying Carolina, Jakob drew up short. Thank God! "When did this horse get here?"

The man scratched his belly again and thought. "Earlier this evenin'. Lady rode 'er in. Asked me to keep 'er till a Mr. Neubaum came for her."

"Neubauer. That's me."

"That your horse?"

Jakob assured him it was, unnecessarily. Carolina nickered and bobbed her head, and Gunter returned the greeting.

"Where's the lady now?"

"Durned if I know. Paid me, that's all I care."

"Did she say anything that might give you an idea?"

The man eyed Jakob warily. "What d'ya want her for?"

Unbuckling his saddlebags, Jakob steeled his temper and said levelly, "She's my wife."

"Humph." He led Gunter to a stall.

Jakob dug for more coins.

The man closed stubby fingers around them. "Seems to me she asked about catchin' the train to Pittsburgh. Could be that's where she's gone."

Jakob left instructions and dashed out into the rain. He checked the deserted train station. He'd missed the last train by an hour, and there were no further departures posted until the following day. At Butler's one tiny hotel, the manager hadn't seen Lydia or anyone else new for weeks. Jakob checked in and carried his saddlebags to the dismal room.

He draped his wet clothing over a chair and lay on the lumpy bed. The room was as cold and silent as his heart.

Where was Lydia at this moment? Was she on that train? Just the night before, she had lain in his arms, and warmth and security had surrounded them. He thought of the closeness they had shared. He'd shown her physically how much he cared for her, how she filled his heart and mind to completion. Why would she run away now?

Before she came into his life, he'd been lonely. He'd only been able to dream of the pleasure a wife of his own would bring.

Now he knew . . . the joy of lying beside her each night, and the security of waking up beside her every morning. He knew the warm feeling of sharing a secret look over dinner or in church, and the bliss of hearing her speak his name in passion. His throat constricted with fear of never sharing those things again. He had to find her!

He couldn't imagine life without her now. Heavyhearted, Jakob slid from the bed and knelt. He thanked God for the time He'd given them together, and begged for help finding her. He prayed long into the night.

Lightning slashed across the sky. Peine stepped away from the window and perched at her dressing table. She smiled at the reflection in the mirror. Lydia was gone.

No one spoke to Peine at supper, but that was no loss. None of them cared a hoot about her, anyway. The meal was silent, Jakob and Lydia's empty places awkward reminders.

She'd wondered how long it would take Anton to spread the news. To her satisfaction, the business hadn't taken a day. It had had to happen sooner or later. Lydia wasn't cut out of the same cloth as Jakob. She was better off tucked away in her little colony. Maybe one of those gray fanatics would want her. She was better suited to that life, anyway.

Peine ran a brush through her shiny gold hair and pictured Jakob performing the task for her, his fingers slipping through to caress her neck and shoulders. They could be together now. Anton would understand and get over her now that he knew about this baby.

Of course Jakob's misplaced sense of honor had driven him to make a token attempt at pursuing the horrid girl. He would be back. And he would want her. Had she told him about the baby? She couldn't remember. Sometimes things got fuzzy these days. Time and events seemed to melt into a blur.

Peine rubbed her belly with satisfaction. Oh, yes, this time everything would be different. Jakob would talk with her, rub her back. He'd be a good father, yes, but she would come first. He'd build a home for the two of them, away from this crowded house, somewhere they could be alone. They would spend winters in front of the fireplace, and she would sew him shirts.

Thunder rattled the panes, and Peine glanced out the window into the darkness. Blue-eyed Jakob. Handsome Jakob.

Her perfect Jakob. Perhaps he would come to her in the morning.

Jakob paused in front of a Pittsburgh jeweler's and tugged up the collar of his sheepskin jacket. From under his hat's brim, he gazed into the display window, barely noticing the gold and silver rings. He'd purchased Lydia's wedding ring here months ago. The gold bracelet, too, he'd bought, impulsively, on his way home to her. *Lydia.*

He turned and examined the busy street. Carriages and wagons rumbled past, horses' hooves clomping on the pavement. Men in three-piece suits strolled alongside saddle-weary drifters. Ladies dressed in elegant bustled fashions carried matching parasols. A yellow one caught his eye, and his heart dared to lift. The woman on the boardwalk slipped her arm through that of a tall gentleman, and tipped her face up. She wasn't Lydia. How foolish of him; she hadn't taken the yellow dress.

How he wished he could share the city with her. Why hadn't he before this? These were things she'd never seen, things she'd wanted to see, and he should have been the one to introduce her to them. Instead, she walked somewhere alone. If he—*when* he—found her, he'd show her the city.

"Want a paper, mister?"

Jakob glanced down at the freckled face of a youngster and dug into his trousers for a nickel. "Sure. Have you seen a pretty dark-haired lady in a gray dress? She might be wearing a white cap and a gray shawl."

"Nope."

"Thanks anyway." He tipped the lad a penny and took the newspaper, tucking it under his arm as he walked. Five days he'd been looking for her. Five days without the slightest clue as to where she'd gone. Five days of the purest hell he'd ever lived through. He doggedly checked hotels until the proprietors assured him they'd send word if someone fitting her description appeared. He was a regular at the train station, arriving well before each departure and hounding the clerks.

Pittsburgh was a big city. He could have missed her anywhere—if she'd ever arrived. None of the railroad employees remembered her from the only train he'd missed that first night. Surely someone would remember her distinctive dress, or the oddity of a woman traveling alone.

That night he lay awake, wondering if he'd gone in the wrong direction. Perhaps he should have backtracked to Butler, scoured the countryside. Finding Carolina in the stable had proved she'd gotten that far. Anything could have happened once she boarded a train.

He'd given himself so much credit for going slow and easy with her. As if it were a sacrifice to patiently win her confidence and attentions! He'd loved every minute of it. He'd felt alive and brimming with sensations for the first time in his life. And the whole time he'd been planting seeds of trust and reassurance, Peine had been sowing her own seeds of doubt and deceit. He hadn't seen it coming.

Why would Peine say a thing like that, anyway? He never paid much attention to her one way or the other. He was friendly when she spoke to him, but didn't recognize the dark side of her the others apparently did. Was he being too rough in his thinking? Were any of Lydia's insecurities justified? If he could only find her and talk to her!

Jakob stood in the dark, staring down at the street below. His belly growled, but he didn't have the inclination to take care of it. Food couldn't fill the aching hunger inside him. Only Lydia could. One more day. He'd search Pittsburgh once more, and then he'd go home.

"You're a wonder!"

Lydia rolled piecrusts with the rapid efficiency born of years of practice and glanced up at the woman who spoke to her. "Ma'am?"

"You make that look so easy. I've never seen a body since my grandmother who could roll pastries like you do. Our breakfast crowd has doubled since you've been here!" Florence Allgood ran Butler's only boarding house and one of its two eateries. She was big and buxom, and a heart of pure gold beat within that ample bosom.

Lydia gave her a demure smile. "I think you're exaggerating."

"Well, it's not exaggerating to wonder how you can work from the crack of dawn to the setting sun without any time for yourself in between." Mrs. Allgood grabbed an iron kettle from a hook over the stove and pumped water into it.

"I'm used to hard work." Lydia shaped crusts into a row of pie plates. In Accord she'd worked the same hours with as little pleasure. She was accustomed to the role. It was one she fit into easily. When she'd discovered her money wasn't enough to buy train fare and a place to stay, she'd had to think fast to come up with a plan. The first establishment hadn't been interested, but Mrs. Allgood had remembered her from church and welcomed her without question. Lydia was grateful for the position and the room.

"You can always stay, you know. You don't have to go all the way to Pittsburgh for a job. You'd be safer, too."

"Thank you, but I must go after I've earned the money."

"Won't be long, the way you work."

Lydia nodded and grabbed hot pads. Carrying a kettle of pie filling to the table, she stirred it, reflecting. She couldn't stay here. Sooner or later in the small community, Jakob would learn where she was. Besides, hadn't she always wanted to see Pittsburgh? Lydia ladled apple filling into the crusts and mindlessly wove cinnamon-and-sugar-sprinkled strips of dough over the tops in an intricate pattern.

She stood up from placing them in the oven, and a wave of dizziness caught her by surprise. She steadied herself against the worktable.

"Customers loved your *Spatzle* last night." Mrs. Allgood spoke with her back to Lydia.

Lydia took a deep breath and closed her eyes, feeling better when she opened them. "I'm glad."

The mention of *Spatzle* reminded her of Peine's reaction the first time she'd made them for the Neubauers. Everything reminded her of Peine...and Jakob. Together. She couldn't seem to get them out of her mind. Work was the only thing that helped. No doubt Mrs. Allgood wondered why she had left her family and was headed for the city, but she didn't ask. Lydia was grateful. She didn't need any more friends to leave behind. She didn't need any more heartache.

* * *

The monotonous clacking of the train over the rails set Jakob's teeth on edge. He stared sightlessly out at the black night. Raindrops meandered down the window glass. He hadn't slept for more than a fitful hour at a time for the past week. His six-day stay in the city had stretched longer than he knew was wise, but he hadn't wanted to give up. *Lydia! God, Lydia!* Where the hell was she?

"But-ler!" the conductor called out. Jakob unrolled his slicker from a saddlebag and headed for a café. It was a two-hour ride home in the rain, and he'd need to eat.

Dodging the weather, he darted between overhangs, his boots echoing on the wooden boardwalks, and stepped in mud up to his ankles. Cursing, he ran on. Light shone through the windows of the first restaurant he came to. He shrugged out of his slicker and wiped his feet best he could.

A thin girl he recognized from church took his order. He was served stew and coffee and ate sullenly, not tasting a bite.

"Want a piece of pie?"

Jakob looked up at the slim-faced girl. Her eyes were round and friendly. "Sure. Why not?"

She plunked the plate in front of him and took away the soiled dishes. Jakob stared at the slice of apple pie.

The apples were a golden cinnamon color, and the crust was a delicate, flaky masterpiece. He guided his fork to the dessert and lifted a bite to his mouth. The distinctive taste melted on his tongue. There wasn't another who could make an apple pie like this. No one other than . . .

Lydia.

"Miss!" Jakob stood so rapidly, the legs of his chair scraped the wooden floor and teetered precariously.

The girl turned back, framed by the kitchen doorway. "Sir?"

"The lady who made the pie . . . where is she?"

Her eyes widened in alarm. "Is something wrong?"

"No! I just want to see the person who baked that pie!"

"Well, I—"

"Mr. Neubauer?" Florence Allgood stepped up behind her daughter. "Can I do something for you?"

"Awfully good pie, Mrs. Allgood." Jakob eyed the woman. He'd known her for years. Lydia was here.

"Thank you."

"I want to see her."

"Who?"

"Mrs. Allgood...we both know my wife made that pie. I..." He hesitated. "I need to see her."

Her face softened. She had no choice. "She's staying at my place. The boarding house next door. She's fine."

"What room?"

"Sixteen." She stepped back into the kitchen and returned with a key. Jakob's fingers closed over it, but she held on fast. "Don't wake up the boarders."

Jakob accepted the double warning. "I won't."

She let go, and he strode from the room, hard-pressed to keep from running. Lydia was here!

Chapter Twenty-Four

Thunder shook the flimsy building. Beneath the covers, Lydia shivered with cold and loneliness. Above the storm, a soft but distinct clicking caught her attention, and she held her breath. A stream of light poured into the dark room, and a man's shape stood outlined in the doorway. The form was tall and broad...and achingly familiar. Her heart threatened to stop.

His slicker crackling, Jakob entered the room and closed the door behind him. He removed the wet wrap and dropped it on the floor.

"Where's the lamp?"

"H-here." She raised up on hands and knees and struck a match, lighting the lantern.

Jakob blinked his eyes, letting them adjust to the light. They flickered over her nightdress and focused on her satchel, under the foot of her bed. His bright blue gaze fixed on her accusingly. He took off his hat and tossed it. "You took a foolish chance, woman."

Lydia's heart jerked into action and slammed against her ribs. What could she say? What choice had she been given?

"I've looked everywhere for you. I was scared to death something happened."

"Nothing did." Even after everything, she appreciated the sight he made, tall and formidable, his hair a shade darker than usual because it was damp. Seeing him flooded her soul with bitter joy. "There's a towel over there," she offered.

Finding it, he rubbed his hair furiously. "You're just damned lucky, I guess."

"I hardly consider myself fortunate in this situation."

"Did you stop to think before you ran off half-cocked?" He flung the towel toward the rack, but missed.

"I did nothing but think."

"What the hell happened between that last night and the next day?"

Lydia pulled the thin blanket up and clutched the cover against her chest, as if to ward off his anger, and any more pain. "I don't want to talk about it."

"Well, that's too damned bad, because we're going to!"

"Jakob, don't curse at me."

He opened his hands, palms downward, in a gesture of acknowledgment. "I'm sorry."

Jakob paced the room, then turned back to the door and twisted the lock. He was dripping wet, his boots tracking the floor.

"You'd better get out of those wet things."

He plowed a hand through his hair in outward irritation, but didn't comply.

"You'll get sick if you don't. You can wrap up in one of the blankets." *Why did she care? After all this, why?*

He conceded, struggling with a boot until she crept from the bed and knelt before him to help. Feeling his gaze on her, she lifted her own and met that vivid blue heat. Quickly she tugged the second boot off, stood them both on a newspaper near the door and wiped her hands.

"Lydia," he whispered. "Why?"

She fixed her gaze on his wrinkled bare toes. How could that one whispered word make it sound like he cared? What warped sense of duty had brought him after her, when he didn't love her? Did he expect her to throw her heart on the floor and let him trample it again?

"Why did you just run off like that?"

She scrambled back into the bed, tucking her feet and legs under the covers. Plucking at the blanket's edge, she avoided his eyes. "I couldn't stay."

"Because of what Anton told you?"

The pain in her heart hadn't reached the saturation point. The mention brought fresh hurt. "Yes."

His breath whistled between his teeth. "Damn."

She snuck a look at him. The muscle in his jaw danced like heat lightning. He unbuttoned his shirt halfway, and she averted her eyes. The sight of him never failed to touch her, and allowing him to see that would only humiliate her further. Why was he here?

"So." He padded to the window but didn't look out. He turned to her again. "You think I'm untrustworthy and a liar, an adulterer, and—what else? I must've left something out."

Lydia's body trembled before the imminent confrontation. She clamped her mouth shut so that her teeth wouldn't clack.

"Well, does that about cover it?" he asked, using the same tone of voice he used to taunt his brothers, a tone he'd never before used with her.

A tear squeezed from the corner of her eye. She couldn't bear to speak of these things. "Jakob, don't."

"Don't what? Don't mention how you didn't trust me enough to come to me with this first? You just agreed." He snapped his fingers in the air. "'Sure, that heathen husband of mine would do that.'" Fists on hips, he stomped back to where she huddled in the bed and bent over her. "Your low opinion is right touching, Lydia," he told her with a sneer. "Thanks for your confidence!"

Lydia watched him. Eyes afire, nostrils flared, he was a glorious sight. She'd missed him! Annoyance flashed in his eyes, and a kindred spark nipped at her, as well. "Are you denying you're in love with Peine?"

Stunned, Jakob moved his lips, but no sound came out. He gaped at her and finally sank to the foot of the bed. "Hellfire! What put a crazy notion like that in your head? Didn't I buzz around you like a bee to a flower until you married me? Didn't I go out of my way to make you comfortable, to meet your needs? I suffered every time I touched you, because I didn't want to put you off. I waited until you were good and ready, waited till I was ready to explode, before I made love to you. What more could I have done to prove myself to you?"

Silence hung in the tiny room. Thunder rolled above the boarding house, and rain pelted the windowpanes. Had she confused things that badly? Had she waited for words of love, when all the time he'd been showing her?

Jakob's hair was drying, turning the pale wheat color she loved. A sob caught in her throat. "But Peine . . ."

His tortured gaze riveted on hers. Closing the distance between them, he took her shoulders between his massive hands and pulled her to him. "Don't married people need to trust? Lydia, there wasn't anyone before you."

Her skin burned where his hands held her. Something in his eyes changed, melting into earnest appeal. "I promised faithfulness." The unfamiliar roughness in his tone demanded that she acknowledge his sincerity. "Doesn't my word mean something? Do you think I'd take my brother's wife and then lie about it? What kind of man do you think I am? Sometimes you're as bigoted as your father when it comes to Outsiders."

Her mind raced, but coherent thought seemed beyond her with his warm hands holding her, his beloved face inches from hers. A pang of remorse pierced Lydia's soul. How could she have doubted him?

"How could you take off and not let me know you were all right?" Heat danced in his eyes, and his gaze fell to her trembling lips. "God, you smell good." He kissed her mouth urgently, bringing a hand to the nape of her neck, where he held her firm.

Lydia watched him in the lamplight for a moment. His pale hair was a shiny halo. He coaxed her lips, and her eyes drifted shut as she allowed herself to savor his fervent kiss.

"Damn you, Lydia, I looked all over Pittsburgh for you," he said against her neck. "I was becoming a laughingstock."

"You went to Pittsburgh?" He'd been looking for her?

"I went to Accord first." He nipped at the sensitive column of her neck. "I was sure you'd go home," he said into the hair at her temple.

"I ran away from my home."

"I mean back to the colony."

"There's nothing for me there."

He bracketed her face with his thumbs and forced her to look at him. "I suppose there's nothing for you in my house anymore, either?"

"Jakob, I'm sorry I believed Anton." She slid her fingers around his wrists. "Jakob, did you ever . . . with Sylvie?"

"Never." Jakob's pale blue gaze fixed on her lips. "Never with anyone but you. I told you that."

She inhaled his rain-dampened scent, savored his breath on her cheek. His lips closed over hers in a volatile kiss.

His hands released hers to roam the contours beneath her prim cotton nightdress, eliciting a soft moan from her. Pressing her back upon the bed, he insinuated a thigh between hers, whispering how much he wanted her, needed her.

He felt so good. His hungry lips and hard body ignited her senses. Oh, how she had missed him! Despite the misery and pain she'd endured, she'd been despondent without him. Lydia skimmed her palms over his broad shoulders under his shirt, slid her hands inside and across the corn silk matting his chest.

"I'm tired of defending myself, Lydia. Hasn't living with me taught you anything?" He covered her breasts with both hands and kissed her roughly.

His tongue breached her lips, and, in spite of herself, Lydia welcomed it, met it and twined it with her own.

Jakob groaned and pulled her into a sitting position on the bed's edge. He knelt before her, his long, strong fingers fumbling with the infinite row of tiny buttons on her nightdress. She unbuttoned his shirt. He shrugged out of the bothersome material and removed her voluminous white gown. The cotton pooled at her hips and he brushed his lips against her warm skin, touched his tongue to the sensitive tip of one breast.

Nothing in this world made her feel as good as his strong, callused hands gliding across her skin, his hot tongue and lips first drawing sweetly, then ravishing, her breast. Her head fell back and she arched against him. He pushed her back on the mattress and continued his keen arousal of her senses. She shivered with delight and listened with mounting excitement to his breathless groans and inarticulate murmurs while he blazed a path from between her breasts to her neck. He nipped her chin and took her mouth feverishly.

"Lydia . . ." he said, shuddering against her lips. "I thought I'd lost you."

She took his face between her palms and kissed him back.

"I need you," he breathed into her mouth.

"I know." She sensed his urgency. He had always been a gentle and caring lover, sensitive to her every response, whether shy or certain. He interpreted and acted upon every physical message. Tonight, however, he craved a less considerate coupling, and she understood and wanted it as much as he did.

He should know how much she needed him, too, she decided. She took his hand and he stood before her. With trembling fingers, she reached for his button fly.

But Jakob performed the task for her, kicking his denims aside. He pressed himself against her, breath hissing through his teeth. She tasted his chest, and he tasted warm and wonderful...like Jakob. She ran her hands down his sides and he sucked his breath in when she found him, hard and hot against her belly.

The muscle in his jaw worked, but anger had nothing to do with it. She trembled deep inside with the love and yearning she felt for this man. She had nearly thrown everything away. Tears sprang to her eyes. "Jakob, love me now," she whispered in German. "Hurry."

The words might be foreign, but her hands spoke eloquently. Jakob responded by ensnaring her in strong arms and falling, pinning her beneath him on the bed. Powerfully he made her a part of him, his need to stamp her with his possession blotting out everything else. Somewhere in the back of his mind, he knew he wasn't gentle, but his pride allowed him grim satisfaction at the fact. Urgently he hurtled them into passionate oblivion.

Sometime during the night the rain stopped. Lydia awoke and listened to the unfamiliar sounds of the street below. Jakob lay tucked snugly along her side, their combined warmth a delicious pleasure.

What kind of man was this husband? Living with him *had* taught her much about him. He was hardworking and hardheaded, amiable and obstinate—depending on the day and the subject. The many gifts he'd given her had proven his generosity. He was persuasive—his boyish smile could convince her of anything. He was exciting; she smiled in the darkness, thinking of his titillating lips and hands.

He was eager to please her. He was a gentle, considerate lover and a talented musician. He was many things. But he was always... always honorable.

And she loved him.

Peine had lied. But since one Outsider lied, did she believe all Outsiders were the same? No more than she believed all colonists were the same inside. Wasn't that why God granted wisdom? Discretion, the ability to tell right from wrong? Her own feelings of shame and inadequacy had gotten in the way, somehow. If she had thought with her heart and not her head, she wouldn't have doubted Jakob. And she wouldn't have hurt the man she loved deeply.

She loved him and he only needed her. Needed her so much he'd sworn he didn't want to live without her. Needed her so much he'd scoured Pittsburgh. Needed her so much he'd searched her out in a storm. It would have to be enough.

In the hazy gray morning, Lydia woke to sounds of the town coming to life. She ran her hand over the empty spot beside her, and her heart sank. Jakob!

With relief, she spotted his slicker hung over the back of the chair. She bathed and brushed her hair before he returned minutes later.

Jakob dropped a paper-wrapped bundle on the bed and handed her a plate of biscuits drizzled with honey and a cup of coffee.

"Thank you." She peered at him from beneath her lashes, last night's urgent lovemaking fresh in her mind and on her skin.

He shrugged out of his still-damp denims. The bundle held new trousers, a shirt and socks, and he dressed while she ate. He placed her empty plate on a table near the door and plopped down on the bed's edge. She met his blue gaze hesitantly.

"I was so all-fired mad, I planned to drag you out of here and all the way home if I had to. I can see now that wouldn't do any good. You still wouldn't trust me. You need to decide whether or not you're coming back with me. But remember, you made a vow, same as I made to you. And think about this." He looked her straight in the eye. "What if you're going to have a baby?"

Lydia clamped her teeth on her lower lip, tears blurring her vision. Oh! How could he have known the innermost fear that she hadn't even allowed herself to imagine? What if she *was* carrying their child? The possibility had hidden in the shadows of her mind for over a week. If and when she did have a baby, she wanted a home and a husband! She wanted to share the fulfillment of her dreams.

"Jakob?"

His blue gaze lifted to her face.

"I have decided. I thought it over during the night."

His face revealed no thoughts within. "And?"

"And, I'm coming home with you."

He sat motionless on the bed's edge, his spine rigid.

Hadn't her decision comforted him? Did he want her to say more? "Not because I might have a baby," she went on. "And not because I have nowhere else to go. I believe I could take care of myself."

He nodded. "I guess you could."

"I let Peine undermine my faith in you—in myself, too, I realized. I did you an injustice, and I'm sorry." She raised a shaky hand and brushed the hair back from her face in a nervous gesture. It seemed he'd always been the one apologizing, and now it was her turn. "Can you forgive me?"

Jakob's posture relaxed visibly, and he pulled her easily against him. He nudged a strand of dark hair away from her mouth with his nose and kissed her. When he pulled back, he grinned. "I could be convinced."

He stopped the hand she splayed on his chest and twined his fingers through hers. His lips brushed her forehead. "Last night..."

Sensing his thoughts, she raised her face and kissed him. "Last night was perfect."

He squeezed her hand and pulled her tight against his chest. "I was planning to build our foundation this week, but I'd rather stay naked in this boarding house a few more days."

"There are no men allowed on this floor, Jakob. Mrs. Allgood will ask us to leave." Suddenly thinking of something, she pulled away. "Jakob, how did you get her to let you in? You didn't—?"

He brushed her hair away from her breasts and admired them while he chuckled. "No, I didn't hold a gun on her."

"Phew!" She collapsed against him again.

His expression grew serious. "Lydia."

She stared into his clear eyes, love for him overwhelming her. "What?"

"Don't ever leave me again."

Her throat tightened. He needed her. She loved him. He was strong and capable, every inch a dynamic, magnificent man. Yet he was humble enough to admit his need for her. She took his face between her hands. "You have my word." *More than my word, Jakob. You have my heart... my soul... my everything....*

Chapter Twenty-Five

A bright green buggy, the wheels painted white, rolled past, pulled by a fine pair of black horses. Lydia watched with wide eyes and a wider smile. The city hadn't disappointed her. Neither had the man beside her.

Jakob escorted Lydia from the telegraph office. "I promised your mother I'd let her know you're all right, and I figured Pa would want to know, too."

Lydia proudly smoothed the bright blue dress he'd bought her that morning, upon their arrival in Pittsburgh. Captivated by the sights and sounds surrounding her, she walked beside him with a spirited step, animated and talkative. Jakob had answered dozens of questions.

He paused at a corner and nodded toward the building where they'd stopped before. It was constructed of brick, with arched windows and white trim, and its doorway faced the intersection. Above the door, a camera—wooden, with black accordion pleats—hung from an iron rod. A sign read Simon Ulrich, Photographer; Tintypes, Ambrotypes, Daguerreotypes.

"Want to?" Jakob asked.

She glanced up into his face. "What?"

"Have a portrait done."

Their likenesses captured together forever? The thought pleased her immeasurably. She grabbed up his hand. "I'd love to!"

The photographer, a stout gray-haired gentleman with a neat mustache, smiled at the couple. He checked a watch on a gold chain and slid it back into the pocket of his brocade vest. "A wedding photograph, perhaps?"

Jakob smiled into his wife's eyes. "Yes."

They posed solemnly while the photographer hunkered beneath a black drape. One flash, a puff of smoke, and the sitting was over. Later they picked up their portrait. Having never seen a photograph of herself, Lydia stared in fascination.

She perched eternally on a chair, Jakob draped gracefully on its arm, their hands together on his knee. The floral bouquet the photographer had settled in her lap was silk, but appeared real in sepia tones. Her expression was placid, though slightly amused, and her skin was clear and white.

Jakob's face and hands photographed much darker than hers, and his hair was unusually neat. Studying his likeness, she silently thought what a shame it was not to see the vivid color of his eyes, a blue that always surprised her at first glance. The color was so much a part of him, the photograph seemed lifeless without it.

Jakob took her to supper at a distinctive restaurant and rented a carriage to show her the city by night. She snuggled against his side, full to bursting with the sights and experiences of the day. As exciting as the day had been, with so many of her dreams realized, she had discovered that nothing was as fulfilling as her life on the farm—life with Jakob. As his wife, all her needs and dreams were realized. She would never again doubt his honor or his sincerity.

They returned the carriage and walked to their hotel hand in hand. Lydia admired Jakob's tall form, his fair hair, shining in the moonlight. He went out of his way to please her and build their life together. If he hadn't come into her life, she would never have seen the city, ridden in a carriage, or met new people. No other man could make her feel the way Jakob did when he touched her, kissed her.

She had a life she enjoyed, a man she loved, good friends. Soon they'd have a home, and perhaps—dear God, please—a child.

It was enough.

* * *

The family welcomed her with open arms. Annette shed happy tears. Even Jessie seemed happy to see her, traipsing at Lydia's heels.

Anton took them aside and apologized. "I'm still not sure what's happened," he said with a shrug. "I know she lied. What scares me is that—" he sat on the sofa's edge and ran his thumbnail along the seam of his denims "—I'm not sure she knows she lied."

Jakob and Lydia glanced at one another then back to Anton. "What're you saying?" Jakob asked.

"I think she believes it. Either that, or she's a hell of an actress."

Lydia didn't see Peine until they sat down for supper. She swished into the kitchen in a vivid blue two-piece dress, hair and face flawless, the child she carried adding a lovely maternal glow. The Neubauers quieted, gazes touching uncertainly.

"What did you have for supper in Pittsburgh?" Annette asked, breaking the awkward silence.

"Roast beef," Jakob replied.

"Vegetables in a cream sauce, and little tarts," Lydia supplied, taking up the conversation and easing the others' discomfort. "I think I can make them."

"We missed you sorely, *Tochter*." Johann spoke his mind, and the others nodded. Daughter. Lydia's heart brimmed with the warmth her new family offered.

All but Peine. She diced a cooked carrot on Nikolaus's tray and ignored everyone.

Jakob's hand, near her knee, caught Lydia's attention. She reached down, and he gave her fingers a squeeze. "I plan to get the corner foundations laid before the cold weather," he said to those around the table. "If I have a little help, I may even get the fireplace built."

"Count on me," Anton offered. Franz and Johann nodded.

"We can stitch curtains and bedding this winter," Annette suggested.

An emotion almost like regret washed over Lydia. While having their own home would be wonderful, she knew she'd miss the warmth and congeniality of the extended family.

As if sensing her feelings, Jakob wrapped his arm around her shoulder and hugged her. She smiled up into his handsome face.

Later that evening, after the others had gone to bed, they lounged on the floor before the fireplace, watching the last log disintegrate into ashes.

"Next winter we'll be sitting in front of our own fireplace," Jakob said.

Wondering if they'd have a new family member by then, Lydia murmured, "Mm-hmm..."

"We'll build a roaring fire and lay naked."

Lydia laughed, but warmth beyond that which the fire created glowed inside her at the image.

He tucked a long strand of hair behind her ear and kissed the hollow under her jaw. "Funny how a fire pushed us together in the first place, isn't it? I wonder if we'd have ended up together if the bakery hadn't caught fire."

"I don't know." She drew a line along his lower lip with her finger. "I've thanked God for the fire many times. And thanked Him no one was hurt. You were very brave."

"Shucks, ma'am. T'weren't nothin'."

She laughed again and tipped her head to accept the kiss he offered.

Their shadows were barely outlined by the dwindling fire. Peine listened to their words with growing contempt, glowering at their huddled shapes. A serpentine hatred twisted and burgeoned inside her. Silently she stepped back against the hallway's papered wall, her hand automatically caressing her belly. *Damn Lydia!* She'd been a thorn in Peine's side since the first day she set eyes on her. That frowsy creature should've died in the fire! She should have stayed lost! Jakob should have been relieved, glad to have her gone and out of their hair!

But he was too nice. Her Jakob was too considerate and too sympathetic. As long as that woman was around, he'd feel responsible, and he'd continue to fulfill his duty. The only way to bring him peace was to remove the irritant. If Lydia was no longer a consideration...

The idea had merit. She liked it. She rolled it around and savored it. Peine's head lolled against the wall. The child inside her leapt. A definite sign of agreement. A wispy moment of lucidity brought a frown to her forehead. The baby. Jakob's baby? Anton's baby. She closed her eyes, and scenes of Jakob came—Jakob smiling at her, Jakob offering her kind words and attention, Jakob free to claim her as his own. The fog cleared from her mind. She remembered.

Jakob's baby. And hers. Not Lydia's.

Smiling, she tiptoed across the hall and up the stairs. She lifted the glass lamp from her bedside table and struck a match, staring at the tiny flame. Reverently she touched the flame to the wick and watched it flare into a searing, dancing solution. *Not long now, and you'll be free, Jakob darling. Not long at all.*

Opportunity didn't always knock. Sometimes a person had to get out and take the situation in hand. And Peine wanted Lydia out of the way. She wanted it badly. She had dreamed about it last night. When the men pulled away at the crack of dawn, Peine had been ready, and had set her plan in motion.

Annette was easily distracted. She always jumped at a chance to rock or change or play with Nikolaus. This morning Peine had feigned a backache and a throbbing headache, and, characteristically, Annette had scooped Nikolaus up and swept him upstairs.

Peine surveyed the barn. Everything was in place. Perfect. Waiting for Gerta. *Lydia,* she corrected. The leech. Nothing had worked so far. She'd wasted so much time trying to be nice, trying to find a kind way to dispose of her. Reese had tried to teach her to be nice. Well, old man, she'd tried. Nice didn't work with Lydia's type.

This was it. There was no time left. She couldn't take the emptiness any longer. The pious looks. The scathing comments. Those churchgoing, preachy types thought they could look down their noses at her again, thought she'd just take it and keep coming back for more. She'd thought she'd shown them all with Gerta, but they must've forgotten. Well, she wouldn't put up with their high-and-mighty attitudes. Not ever again.

And she was so tired these days. Tired of Anton's attitude, tired of Lydia's presence. Overweary of waiting for Jakob. She must do something to free him. Something permanent. Something that would eliminate the churchwoman. Something they wouldn't forget so easily this time. Now. Peine lifted her skirts and ran for the house.

This time, she would succeed—or die trying.

Lydia finished her first batch of soap, boiling down caustic soda and fat. She cut it into uniform pieces, pleased with her accomplishment. In the full pantry, she made space for the new supplies by rearranging jars and crocks. The room was cool and dim, dominated by the earthy smells of the potatoes and onions filling the barrels crowded together under hanging clusters of dried peppers, herbs and tulip bulbs. She paused a moment to rest, enjoying the smells, reveling in her newfound sense of belonging.

She'd been so lonely at the boarding house in Butler. The Neubauers had welcomed her back like the prodigal son in the parable. After three seasons, she at last felt like part of the family, and she looked forward to a long, cozy winter, and a new house in the spring.

"Lydia!" Peine shouted. "Come quickly! Jakob's been hurt!"

Instantly Lydia dropped the scrub bucket and ran into the kitchen, wiping reddened hands on her apron. "Where is he?"

"In the barn!"

Peine stood in the doorway, breathing hard.

"I thought the men were hauling stones for the house."

"They are, but Jakob came back for a wagon part. Hurry!"

Lydia had never seen Peine run. Even pregnant, the smaller woman sprinted ahead of her. A hundred scenes flashed through Lydia's mind as she imagined the accident that had befallen her husband. Had he been thrown from a horse? Had he cut himself? Had one of the machines fallen on him? Remembering the horror she'd experienced the day he drove the team into a nest of bees, she feared the worst and prayed for the best. Jessie loped beside Lydia, barking excitedly.

They reached the drive, and Lydia thought she caught a whiff of kerosene. Odd, she thought, and quickened her pace. Longer-legged and carrying less weight, she passed Peine on the upgrade. "Where?"

The smell of kerosene grew more prevalent inside the barn, and she hesitated in the doorway. Something wasn't right. Peine shoved her forward. "The tack room!"

They ran past full oat bins, their feet clattering down the center of the barn. In the tack room, Lydia's eyes adjusted to the semidarkness. "Jakob?"

No reply.

Apprehensive of the strange odor and the eerie smile on Peine's face, Lydia gazed around the room. Oiled harnesses hung neatly from nails and pegs; saddles and blankets rested on their wooden forms. A hot fire danced in the stove. A bale of hay, broken open, lay scattered across the floor. The heavy kerosene smell, almost overpowering, burned Lydia's nostrils. "There's no one here."

"Of course not, you stupid fool."

Heart hammering, Lydia pivoted.

Peine kicked the door shut and slid the bolt into place. Outside, Jessie barked furiously. Peine leveled a revolver at Lydia's breast.

"Peine?" Lydia asked slowly, as though speaking to a child—or a lunatic. "Where's Jakob?"

"Where he's supposed to be. Building our house. What a gullible idiot you are."

Lydia's gaze slid slowly from the barrel of the gun to her sister-in-law's wild eyes. "What are you doing?"

"What I must do . . . to free Jakob for me and the baby."

"You have a husband," Lydia reminded her in a calm tone.

A confused look suffused Peine's features. Instantly her expression changed, and she laughed. Sharply. Suddenly. Maniacally. "Husband? Anton? He placed an ad in the newspaper! He doesn't care about me."

"Yes, he does. He loves you," Lydia said soothingly.

"Shut up! Life isn't all sweet and lovely, you simpleminded fool! Everything isn't black-and-white. Anton doesn't give a damn about me. He never did. I gave him a son, something any woman could have bred. That's all he wanted. He won't care one way or the other if Jakob and I are together."

The conversation made no sense, and Lydia frantically scoured her brain for a reasonable response. "Then why did his heart break when you told him about the baby, if he doesn't care?"

"Pride. It hurt his stinking male pride to know his brother got his wife up a stump."

Mind-boggling realization sliced through Lydia's awareness with horrifying clarity. Anton was right. Peine believed her own web of lies. She stared at the other woman, and an unexpected calm settled over her. "You're upset. You haven't thought this through."

"Shut up!" Peine jerked the gun higher. "This is an accident. Don't make me shoot you." Pointing the gun at Lydia, she sidled toward the stove and picked up a stick, the end wrapped in strips of cloth. "The fire in the bakery should have stopped Jakob's visits to you. Jakob said the fire brought you together, and when I heard him I knew." An evil light flickered in her green eyes. "There's no more fitting way to end this, to separate you from my Jakob."

Peine had started the fire in the storeroom? Was that when all this had started? "Think about what you're doing, Peine."

"It's thought out." Peine waved the stick toward the open stove door. "If you'd stayed in the city, it wouldn't have come to this. But no! Jakob's sense of duty called, and he dragged you back."

Lydia knew the rag was soaked with kerosene. Undoubtedly the hay strewn on the floor had been saturated, too. The oily odor stung her eyes. She struggled to remain calm. "So, you're going to kill me?"

"No." Peine smiled, a terrible, vulturish smile that left Lydia chilled to the bone. "You're going to meet with an unfortunate accident."

She meant it. Lydia held her breath and called upon her heavenly Benefactor to help her through this situation, as He had every other since the beginning. "What about Anton? Will he have an 'accident,' too?"

"Only if he's as stupid as you are."

"Peine." Lydia fought to keep her tone calm, conversational. "Do you really think Jakob will turn to you if I die?"

"Yes!" she shouted. "He wants me! All of you have tried to keep us apart. You hate me, but Jakob loves me! I know he does. He's the only one who listens to me, the only one who's kind!" She poked the stick into the stove, then withdrew it. The flaming end crackled and spat above her head, and she stared at it in fascination. An eerie glee shone from her eyes.

Lydia glanced around the room. How could she stall Peine? How could she talk her out of this hideous plan? She'd lived twenty years preparing to meet her Savior, and she wasn't afraid to die. But icy fingers of dread gripped her with encompassing regret; she might not live out her earthly years with Jakob, might not—her heart thudded to a halt—might not have his baby. Determination steadied her soul.

"You know," she said. "This won't look like an accident. Not at all." She moved a fraction of an inch with each word, edging toward the door. "What will Nikolaus think when he knows his mother is a murderer?"

Peine's laugh burst out in an insane screech. "You may be naive, Lydia, but I'm not. You're not going to talk your way out of this."

"I'm only thinking of Nikky and . . . the baby."

Peine's eyes softened fractionally. "You've thought a lot about this baby, haven't you?"

"Yes," Lydia replied honestly, inching her way toward the door. "Yes, I have."

"You probably wish you were having Jakob's baby."

"As a matter of fact . . . I am."

Peine lowered the arm with the lit torch and stared.

"If you kill me, you'll kill Jakob's baby, too." She hoped the information would take a few precious seconds for Peine to absorb.

Peine's eyes glowed with a maniacal light. "You lie!"

"No. And Jakob will never forgive you for hurting his child."

"Jakob will never know."

The women stood equal distances from the door. Peine glared at Lydia and lowered the flaming stick to the hay-strewn floor with obvious enjoyment. The hay ignited in a breath-stealing *whoosh*. Snakelike flames sprang forward in a perfect line.

Lydia shot toward the exit, fumbling with the bolted lock. Panicky fingers worked the metal loose, and she yanked the door open. Heart hammering against her ribs, she ran from the tack room at full speed. Reaching the outside door, she paused with relief and drew her first deep breath in several minutes. She was safe!

Inside the barn, Peine shook with fury; determination roared in her ears. Lydia couldn't get away! She couldn't thwart the perfect plan—the perfect way to have Jakob for herself!

Graceful long-stemmed flames danced along the hay-strewn floor, a myriad of formless colors shimmering and reflecting their dazzling heat. The blaze hissed at her, crooked a sulfurous finger and spat hungry accusations. "It's not working," it mocked.

Not to worry. Peine stroked the gun barrel with an ardent caress. "For us, Jakob."

She stepped forward to take aim, then closer, so close her skirt brushed the famished, swelling flames.

Lydia hesitated outside the barn. She must alert the men. But if she took time to find them, the barn would burn to the ground! The storage bins brimmed full of oats and hay, nearly the entire year's harvest! She could send Annette and get water herself. Did the men have all the horses?

Behind her, a bloodcurdling scream rent the interior of the barn. Gooseflesh erupted on her neck and arms. She stopped, indecision contorting her plans. Blood pounded in her ears. How long would it take to find the men?

Peine shrieked again. Images of the burning bakery in Accord flashed before her eyes. She relived the terror of being trapped and choking for air, felt again the fire's consuming heat. She couldn't allow anyone to suffer such a fate. If she took time to get the men, would a rescue come too late?

Lydia spun on her heel and ran back into the barn. Fierce heat met her at the tack room doorway. Black smoke and enveloping flame transformed the room into a nightmare.

Peine screamed again, prodding Lydia. Pulling her apron up over her nose and mouth, she stepped into the room and peered through the smoke. A spot cleared, and she saw Peine flapping the flaming hem of her skirt. Lydia grabbed a horse blanket from a nearby saddle rack and beat the flames licking the other woman's skirts. Both women coughed, and tears streamed from Lydia's burning eyes. Determinedly she let her apron fall away from her nose and used both hands to wield the blanket.

Certain Peine's skirt was no longer aflame, Lydia turned. "Come on!"

"No!"

She pivoted and widened her eyes at the gun barrel leveled on her chest. "Peine . . ." she whispered. "No."

"Get back over there. You're not getting away this time." Peine fired a bullet into the rafters overhead. "Move."

Lydia jumped and scooted backward.

Dirt and splinters drifted down over Peine's shoulders. "See? *I* don't play around with empty guns."

The wall of leather harnesses smoldered, the acrid smell searing her lungs. Lydia considered her options. Stay put and surely burn to death, or make a run for it and take a bullet. Maybe Peine would miss. She steeled herself to run, but the intolerable smoke overcame her, and she bent at the waist in a painful spasm of coughing.

Overhead, wood splintered in an earsplitting crack as the weakened support beams buckled. A flaming rafter fell between the two women, blocking Lydia's view of Peine. Her heart wrenched painfully. The burning wood barred Lydia's escape through the only door.

Lydia choked and knelt, blinded.

"Mama! Mama!" Peine screamed, a hideous sound of agony. "Come back, Mama! Don't leave me here!"

Transported back to an April day when she'd been prepared to die, Lydia realized she wasn't resigned to such a fate this time. She pounded the floor with a fist and screamed.

The sound of wood splintering, rhythmically, repeatedly, combined with Jessie's incessant barking, floated through the flames. Fire filled Lydia's lungs. Each excruciating breath ripped through her throat and chest. She tried to cover her face and hold her breath. She fought for consciousness, but disorientation overcame her. She groped across the floor for an escape. Her fingers grasped blindly. Who, she wondered, was still screaming?

Jakob spotted the smoke before he saw the barn. Jessie had surprised him by showing up at the house site. The dog hadn't followed him farther than the pasture since she was a pup. Her persistent barking alerted the men, and they mounted and followed. Now Jakob spurred Gunter and leaned over his neck, alarm setting his nerves on edge.

Ahead, Jessie ran frantically through the open barn door. Jakob slid from the horse and hit the ground running.

"I heard a shot!" Annette called from the dooryard.

The interior of the barn billowed with dense, black smoke. A shrill scream had the hair on his neck standing on end. *Lydia!* The doorway to the tack room blazed, blocked by burning rafters. The stench of leather and kerosene gagged him. "Lydia!"

Lydia was trapped inside the burning room! Jakob ran back the other way, nearly colliding with his brothers. "Get water!"

Grabbing an ax from the wall, he sprinted outside and around the building. Planting both feet solidly, he raised the ax and swung. Again. And yet again. Smoke billowed through the hole he chopped in the barn wall. How long had she been in there? Had she been shot? Dear God, what if it was too late? His chest constricted, and he tightened his grip on the ax handle. No. It wasn't too late. He wouldn't let it be too late. He'd just found her. They had their whole life together ahead of them.

Determinedly he continued the assault on the wall until he broke into a sweat and the opening grew wide enough for him to climb through. "Lord, don't let her die. Lydia!"

Yipping shrilly, Jessie leapt through the hole ahead of him. Blindly Jakob followed her frantic barks until he stumbled over a soft form on the floor. "Lydia."

Eyes streaming, he picked up his wife and stepped out into the fresh air. Annette met him. At the blackened form in his arms, her eyes grew wide with horror. "Is she—?"

Jakob didn't stop his long strides. Lydia buckled inward in his arms, an agonizing cough racking her body.

"Oh, thank God." Annette blinked at Jakob, tears in her eyes. "Tell me what to do."

"Get water and rags. We'll wash her and see where she's hurt." He carried his wife free of the burning structure and laid her on the grass. She immediately rolled onto her side, a rough, racking cough curling her frame. Jakob ran his hands over her body, searching with dread for blood pouring from a bullet hole.

"You're all right, darlin'," he crooned, sweeping her hair back from her face and holding her shoulders while she hacked.

Lydia struggled to sit, trying to speak between hacking coughs. "P— Pe—"

"It's her lungs," Jakob declared quietly. "The fumes she inhaled."

Water forgotten, Annette touched his arm. "I'll stay with her, if you want to help with the barn."

He shook his head. "I can't."

Lydia's hand shot out, and she grasped his shirtfront. Jakob gaped down at her in surprise.

"Peine!" she managed to gasp. "She's—" She coughed until she gagged.

Jakob's startled gaze meshed with Annette's in silent horror. "Oh, my God!"

He jumped up, leaving his wife in Annette's care. "Anton! Franz!"

His brothers didn't pause in their futile struggle. They tossed bucketfuls of water through the opening Jakob had chopped in the side of the barn.

"Peine's in there!" Jakob shouted.

Anton dropped the empty bucket he held.

Franz laid a hand on Anton's shoulder. "It's too late."

Without thought, Anton lunged toward the opening, Jakob at his heels. Johann stepped in front of them, blocking their way. "You can't do any good. It's too late. Nobody could be alive in there."

"But the baby!" Anton broke past his father and dived for the small opening. Franz seized his leg, and Anton swung at him in a frantic attempt to dislodge him. Jakob grabbed Anton's other leg, and together the brothers dragged him from the blazing building. Anton fought like a madman.

Watching, Annette sobbed against her fingertips.

Johann gripped his son's jaw and spoke into his face. "Anton. It's too late. Don't risk yourself. Think o' Nikky."

Anton's rigid body went limp. He covered his face with his hands. "Maybe from the other side?"

Johann shook his head. "Other side's worse."

Helplessly the family watched the flames consume the side of their barn.

"C'mon," Franz said to his father. "We can still save the grain bins. We'll shovel dirt in from the other side."

Shakily Jakob ran back to Lydia. Annette left them and crossed the distance to where Anton's form slumped on the ground.

Lydia choked and coughed up black mucus. Frightened, Jakob remembered her telling him what the doctor in Accord had said last time. "*Herr Doktor* said I wouldn't have made it if you hadn't reached me when you did." What about this time? Had he been too late? Was she now hovering on the edge of death? Jakob blinked back the unfamiliar sting of tears and dropped his forehead on her shoulder.

Her lovely dark hair smelled of ash and burned wood. He couldn't bear the thought of spending the rest of his life without her. Not seeing her smile or hearing her laughter, not knowing her touch or having her love. She couldn't die! She couldn't! He loved her!

All along he'd foolishly plotted and planned his life just so. He'd thought he needed all his ducks in a row, hadn't he? Find a wife, bring her home, build a house . . . But a house was just rocks and wood and glass. A house would mean nothing without . . . Lydia. Nothing would have meaning without Lydia.

Jakob raised his head and ran his fingers along the delicate line of her jaw. Soot streaked her soft, pale skin. Her dark lashes were wet, and tears formed white rivulets down her cheeks. He'd wasted so much time!

"Darlin', please don't die. I love you." He ran a trembling finger across her lips. "Please, Lydia. I love you so much."

Instantly she turned her head, her gaze lifting to his. She could barely see him through her burning eyes. She opened her mouth to speak, to reassure him of her love, but she coughed instead.

"It's okay. Don't try to talk. Just know that I love you, all right?"

Lydia nodded, her breath coming easier, less painfully. She didn't know if the reason was the fresh air in her lungs or Jakob's unexpected declaration. Her sudden lightheartedness felt inappropriate, considering the fact that Peine was beyond any chance of rescue. The horrifying experience was cheerless, but irrepressible elation bubbled in her heart.

Jakob loved her.

He loved her! Tears streaming down her ash-streaked cheeks, Lydia flung herself into his arms. He loved her!

The four men quelled the fire. Jakob carried Lydia to their room.

"Did you find her?" Lydia couldn't help wondering.

"Yeah. Pa's building a box to bury her in." Jakob brought soap and water and helped her out of her clothing. Washed and dressed, she perched on the bed's edge.

"I came so close to losing you again." Jakob's voice rumbled from deep within his chest. He sat and wrapped his arms around her. She shared the tremor that rippled through his body. "I feel so..."

"What?"

"Responsible."

"Jakob."

"I'm the one who brought you here. I wanted to give you everything. Make up for takin' you away from your family. And I'm the reason she did this awful thing. Maybe if I'd paid more attention...if I hadn't been working and planning for that damned house!'' He raised his eyes, and she could see clear to his soul. ''You could've died!''

She couldn't bear his anguish. ''Jakob.''

Agonized blue eyes stared into hers.

''You think you've taken so much away from me?''

He shrugged.

''Anything I left behind has been replaced a thousand times over by what really matters. Jakob, you love me!'' She still marveled at the fact, and she knew she would forever! ''No one has ever loved me like this before. I belong. I don't have an empty place inside anymore.''

Lydia laid her palm along his jaw. ''That's all that matters. My *Mitgift* was only material things . . . things that can be replaced. I know now that my real birthright isn't my father's blessing or the wedding quilt and dishes. I had it in here all along.'' She placed her hand over her heart. ''The capacity to love and be loved.'' Tears filled her eyes. ''My grandmother tried to tell me.''

''Smart woman.''

''She liked you, didn't she?''

Jakob grinned. ''I love you, darlin'.''

''And I love you. Jakob, you've made all my dreams come true.''

''Not quite all.''

''All.''

Surprise lit his features. ''All?''

Her heart did a nervous allemande left, then right. She couldn't suppress a jubilant smile. ''We're going to have a baby.''

His dawning smile reassured her that she'd made him as happy as he made her. His blue eyes uncurled a warm response within her. His fervent kiss was heaven. And heaven was here on earth. . . .

Epilogue

Spring 1889

"Everything's almost ready. Lydia, you sit down and hold Clara while I get the rolls from the oven." Annette handed her the infant, and bustled across Lydia's kitchen. She'd become as comfortable there as in her own home.

Lydia smiled down into the healthy pink face of her blue-eyed niece.

Jakob set the last chair in place around their dining room table and pulled one up beside her. "I hope having dinner here hasn't been too much for you."

"I'm as healthy as a horse, Jakob."

Jakob bestowed a kiss on her lips. "For a while there, I thought you were going to be as big as one, too."

Franz laughed and seated himself on the other side of the table. "She'll lose it, Jake. It's only been a week. Look at Annie after a couple of months."

"Wanna eat!" Nikolaus stated from his chair at the table's corner.

Johann grinned and snitched his oldest grandson a slice of ham.

Anton, somewhat thinner and drawn, smiled, too. The winter had been difficult, but he was learning to adjust. Through the renewing season had come acceptance. Preparing the soil and again learning the sun's warmth had been a healing force.

With the family's love and help, he and Nikolaus would be all right.

From the bedroom off the kitchen came a healthy squall. At her baby's cry, Lydia's full breasts responded.

Anton gave Lydia a beseeching glance. "Can I get him?"

"Of course."

He returned with the flannel-wrapped infant tucked in the crook of his arm, looking much as Jakob did when he rocked his son each night.

Annette placed a basket of Lydia's warm rolls on the table and squeezed Anton's shoulder. He smiled up at her. "I'll pray."

Over Jakob and Lydia's table, the Neubauers' heads lowered, and they joined hands. "Father God," Anton began, "a lot has happened this past year. At times I didn't think you were even there."

Lydia's throat constricted, and she grasped Jakob's hand tightly. Tiny hiccups jerked against her breast, and she inhaled the clean, unique scent of baby. Warmth and love she could barely contain welled in her heart.

"Thank you for sparin' enough grain to see us through the winter," Anton continued. "Bless Jakob and Lydia's trip to Accord tomorrow, and thank You for the gradual softening of her father's heart. Watch over this family, especially Nikky and Clara, and this newest little fella, Seth. With Your help, we continue to take care of them. And love them. And someday... we'll all see You in heaven. Amen."

* * * * *

Harlequin® Historical

First there was **DESTINY'S PROMISE**...
A woman tries to escape from her past on a remote Georgia plantation, only to lose her heart to her employer's son.

And now **WINDS OF DESTINY**...
A determined young widow finds love with a half-breed Cherokee planter—though society and fate conspire to pull them apart.

Follow your heart deep into the Cherokee lands of Georgia in this exciting new series from Harlequin Historical author Laurel Pace.

1994 MISTLETOE MARRIAGES
HISTORICAL CHRISTMAS STORIES

With a twinkle of lights and a flurry of snowflakes, Harlequin Historicals presents *Mistletoe Marriages*, a collection of four of the most magical stories by your favorite historical authors. The perfect way to celebrate the season!

Brimming with romance and good cheer, these heartwarming stories will be available in November wherever Harlequin books are sold.

RENDEZVOUS by Elaine Barbieri
THE WOLF AND THE LAMB by Kathleen Eagle
CHRISTMAS IN THE VALLEY by Margaret Moore
KEEPING CHRISTMAS by Patricia Gardner Evans

Add a touch of romance to your holiday with *Mistletoe Marriages* Christmas Stories!

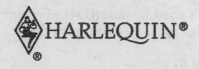

HARLEQUIN®

Georgina Devon

brings the past alive with

Untamed Heart

One of the most sensual Regencies ever published by Harlequin.

Lord Alaistair St. Simon has inadvertently caused the death of the young Baron Stone. Seeking to make amends, he offers his protection to the baron's sister, Liza. Unfortunately, Liza is not the grateful bride he was expecting.

St. Simon's good intentions set off a story of revenge, betrayal and consuming desire.

Don't miss it!

**Coming in October 1994,
wherever Harlequin books are sold.**

REG2